THE SHORT THE
LONG AND THE TALL

JEFFREY ARCHER

THE SHORT THE LONG AND THE TALL

Illustrated by
PAUL COX

ST. MARTIN'S PRESS
NEW YORK

First published in the United States by St. Martin's Press,
an imprint of St. Martin's Publishing Group

THE SHORT, THE LONG AND THE TALL. Copyright © 2020 by Jeffrey Archer.
Illustrations copyright © 2020 by Paul Cox. All rights reserved. Printed in China.
For information, address St. Martin's Publishing Group, 120 Broadway, New York, NY 10271.

www.stmartins.com

"Never Stop on the Motorway," "Cheap at Half the Price," and "One Man's Meat"
were first published 1994 in *Twelve Red Herrings*.

"Who Killed the Mayor?," "A Wasted Hour," "A Gentleman and a Scholar,"
"The Road to Damascus," and "A Good Toss to Lose" were first published 2017 in *Tell Tale*.
"Confession" was first published 2018 in the paperback edition of *Tell Tale*.

"It Can't Be October Already" was first published 2007 in *Cat O' Nine Tales*.

"Stuck on You," "The Queen's Birthday Telegram," and "Caste Off"
were first published 2010 in *And Thereby Hangs a Tale*.

"The Grass is Always Greener" and "Endgame"
were first published 2000 in *To Cut a Long Story Short*.

"Clean Sweep Ignatius," "Just Good Friends," and "Christina Rosenthal"
were first published 1988 in *A Twist in the Tale*.

"The First Miracle" and "Old Love"
were first published 1980 in *A Quiver Full of Arrows*.

The Library of Congress Cataloging-in-Publication Data is available upon request.

ISBN 978-1-250-06490-5 (hardcover)
ISBN 978-1-4668-7137-3 (ebook)

Our books may be purchased in bulk for promotional, educational, or business use.
Please contact your local bookseller or the Macmillan Corporate and Premium Sales Department at
1-800-221-7945, extension 5442, or by email at MacmillanSpecialMarkets@macmillan.com.

First published in Great Britain by Macmillan, an imprint of Pan Macmillan

First U.S. Edition: 2020

10 9 8 7 6 5 4 3 2 1

To Mary

Dear Reader,

I have always enjoyed writing short stories, and to celebrate my eightieth birthday I decided to ask my readers to select twenty from the ninety-two I have had published, for a new collection.

The resulting selection was fascinating, with almost everyone choosing the same seventeen tales, but there was such divergence in those selected for the final three that I had to step in and choose them myself.

I'm mad about art so I wanted the book to be illustrated, and was delighted when my first choice, the contemporary artist and distinguished illustrator Paul Cox, agreed to take up the challenge. Paul's work for *The Wind in the Willows* and Gerald Durrell's *My Family and Other Animals* perfectly matched how I wanted this book to look. The result of our collaboration is *The Short, the Long and the Tall*, which I hope you will enjoy.

Finally, I'd like to thank all those people who have inspired me over the years with their yarns, and do remember that while there may not be a book in every one of us, there is so often a damned good short story.

Jeffrey Archer

April 2020

Contents

Never Stop on the Motorway

DIANA HAD BEEN HOPING to get away by five, so she could be at the farm in time for dinner. She tried not to show her true feelings when at 4.37 her deputy, Phil Haskins, presented her with a complex twelve-page document that required the signature of a director before it could be sent out to the client. Haskins didn't hesitate to remind her that they had lost two similar contracts that week.

It was always the same on a Friday. The phones would go quiet in the middle of the afternoon and then, just as she thought she could slip away, an authorization would land on her desk. One glance at this particular document and Diana knew there would be no chance of escaping before six.

The demands of being a single parent as well as a director of a small but thriving City company meant there were few moments left in any day to relax, so when it came to the one weekend in four that James and Caroline spent with her ex-husband, Diana would try to leave the office a little earlier than usual to avoid getting snarled up in the weekend traffic.

She read through the first page slowly and made a couple of emendations, aware that any mistake made hastily on a Friday night could be regretted in the weeks to come. She glanced at the clock on her desk as she signed the final page of the document. It was just flicking over to 5.51.

Diana gathered up her bag and walked purposefully towards the door, dropping the contract on Phil's desk without bothering to suggest that he have a good weekend. She suspected that the paperwork had been on his desk since nine o'clock that morning, but that holding it until 4.37 was his only means of revenge now that she had been made head of department. Once she was safely in the lift, she pressed the button for the basement carpark, calculating that the delay would probably add an extra hour to her journey.

She stepped out of the lift, walked over to her Audi estate, unlocked the door and threw her bag onto the back seat. When she drove up onto the street the stream of twilight traffic was just about keeping pace with the pinstriped pedestrians who, like worker ants, were hurrying towards the nearest hole in the ground.

She flicked on the six o'clock news. The chimes of Big Ben rang out, before spokesmen from each of the three main political parties gave their views on the European election results. John Major was refusing to comment on his future. The Conservative Party's explanation for its poor showing was that only thirty-six per cent of the country had bothered to go to the polls. Diana felt guilty – she was among the sixty-four per cent who had failed to register their vote.

The newscaster moved on to say that the situation in Bosnia remained desperate, and that the UN was threatening dire consequences if Radovan Karadzic and the Serbs didn't come to an agreement with the other warring parties. Diana's mind began to drift – such a threat was hardly news any longer. She suspected that if she turned on the radio in a year's time they would probably be repeating it word for word.

As her car crawled round Russell Square, she began to think about the weekend ahead. It had been over a year since John had told her that he had met another woman and wanted a divorce. She still wondered why, after seven years of marriage, she hadn't been more shocked – or at least angry – at his betrayal. Since her appointment as a director, she had to admit they had spent less and less time together. And perhaps she had become anaesthetized by the fact that a third of the married couples in Britain were now divorced or separated. Her parents had been unable to hide their disappointment, but then they had been married for forty-two years.

The divorce had been amicable enough, as John, who earned less than she did – one of their problems, perhaps – had given in to most of her demands. She had kept the flat in Putney, the Audi estate and the children, to whom John was allowed access one weekend in four. He would have picked them up from school earlier that afternoon, and, as usual, he'd return them to the flat in Putney around seven on Sunday evening.

Diana would go to almost any lengths to avoid being left on her own in Putney when they weren't around, and although she regularly grumbled about being landed with the responsibility of bringing up two children without a father, she missed them desperately the moment they were out of sight.

She hadn't taken a lover and she didn't sleep around. None of the senior staff at the office had ever gone further than asking her out to lunch. Perhaps because only three of them were unmarried – and not without reason. The one person she might have

considered having a relationship with had made it abundantly clear that he only wanted to spend the night with her, not the days.

In any case, Diana had decided long ago that if she was to be taken seriously as the company's first woman director, an office affair, however casual or short-lived, could only end in tears. Men are so vain, she thought. A woman only had to make one mistake and she was immediately labelled as promiscuous. Then every other man on the premises either smirks behind your back, or treats your thigh as an extension of the arm on his chair.

Diana groaned as she came to a halt at yet another red light. In twenty minutes she hadn't covered more than a couple of miles. She opened the glove box on the passenger side and fumbled in the dark for a cassette. She found one and pressed it into the slot, hoping it would be Pavarotti, only to be greeted by the strident tones of Gloria Gaynor assuring her 'I will survive'. She smiled and thought about Daniel, as the light changed to green.

She and Daniel had read Economics at Bristol University in the early 1980s, friends but never lovers. Then Daniel met Rachael, who had come up a year after them, and from that moment he had never looked at another woman. They married the day he graduated, and after they returned from their honeymoon Daniel took over the management of his father's farm in Bedfordshire. Three children had followed in quick succession, and Diana had been proud when she was asked to be godmother to Sophie, the eldest. Daniel and Rachael had now been married for twelve years, and Diana felt confident that they wouldn't be disappointing *their* parents with any suggestion of a divorce. Although they were convinced she led an exciting and fulfilling life, Diana often envied their gentle and uncomplicated existence.

She was regularly asked to spend the weekend with them in the country, but for every two or three invitations Daniel issued, she only accepted one – not because she wouldn't have liked to join them more often, but because since her divorce she had no desire to take advantage of their hospitality.

Although she enjoyed her work, it had been a bloody week. Two contracts had fallen through, James had been dropped from the school football team, and Caroline had never stopped telling her that her father didn't mind her watching television when she ought to be doing her prep.

Another traffic light changed to red.

It took Diana nearly an hour to travel the seven miles out of the city, and when she reached the first dual carriageway, she glanced up at the A1 sign, more out of habit than to seek guidance, because she knew every yard of the road from her office to the farm. She tried to increase her speed, but it was quite impossible, as both lanes remained obstinately crowded.

'Damn.' She had forgotten to get them a present, even a decent bottle of claret. 'Damn,' she repeated: Daniel and Rachael always did the giving. She began to wonder if she could pick something up on the way, then remembered there was nothing but service stations between here and the farm. She couldn't turn up with yet another box of chocolates they'd never eat. When she reached the roundabout that led onto the A1, she managed to push the car over fifty for the

first time. She began to relax, allowing her mind to drift with the music.

There was no warning. Although she immediately slammed her foot on the brakes, it was already too late. There was a dull thump from the front bumper, and a slight shudder rocked the car.

A small dark creature had shot across her path, and despite her quick reactions, she hadn't been able to avoid hitting it. Diana swung onto the hard shoulder and screeched to a halt, wondering if the animal could possibly have survived. She reversed slowly back to the spot where she thought she had hit it as the traffic roared past her.

And then she saw it, lying on the grass verge – a cat that had crossed the road for the tenth time. She stepped out of the car, and walked towards the lifeless body. Suddenly Diana felt sick. She had two cats of her own, and she knew she would never be able to tell the children what she had done. She picked up the dead animal and laid it gently in the ditch by the roadside.

'I'm so sorry,' she said, feeling a little silly. She gave it one last look before walking back to her car. Ironically, she had chosen the Audi for its safety features.

She climbed back into the car and switched on the ignition to find Gloria Gaynor was still belting out her opinion of men. She turned her off, and tried to stop thinking about the cat as she waited for a gap in the traffic large enough to allow her to ease her way back into the slow lane. She eventually succeeded, but was still unable to erase the dead cat from her mind.

Diana had accelerated up to fifty again when she suddenly became aware of a pair of headlights shining through her rear windscreen. She put up her arm and waved in her rear-view mirror, but the lights

continued to dazzle her. She slowed down to allow the vehicle to pass, but the driver showed no interest in doing so. Diana began to wonder if there was something wrong with her car. Was one of her lights not working? Was the exhaust billowing smoke? Was . . .

She decided to speed up and put some distance between herself and the vehicle behind, but it remained within a few yards of her bumper. She tried to snatch a look at the driver in her rear-view mirror, but it was hard to see much in the harshness of the lights. As her eyes became more accustomed to the glare, she could make out the silhouette of a large black van bearing down on her, and what looked like a young man behind the wheel. He seemed to be waving at her.

Diana slowed down again as she approached the next roundabout, giving him every chance to overtake her on the outside lane, but once again he didn't take the opportunity, and just sat on her bumper, his headlights still undimmed. She waited for a small gap in the traffic coming from her right. When one appeared she slammed her foot on the accelerator, shot across the roundabout and sped on up the A1.

She was rid of him at last. She was just beginning to relax and to think about Sophie, who always waited up so that she could read to her, when suddenly those high-beam headlights were glaring through her rear windscreen and blinding her once again. If anything, they were even closer to her than before.

She slowed down, he slowed down. She accelerated,

who dared to remain in her path. She could only hope that the police might see her, wave her onto the hard shoulder and book her for speeding. A fine would be infinitely preferable to a crash with a young tearaway, she thought, as the Audi estate passed a hundred and ten for the first time in its life. But the black van couldn't be shaken off.

Without warning, she swerved back into the middle lane and took her foot off the accelerator, causing the van to draw level with her, which gave her a chance to look at the driver for the first time. He was wearing a black leather jacket and pointing menacingly at her. She shook her fist at him and accelerated away, but he simply swung across behind her like an Olympic runner determined not to allow his rival to break clear.

And then she remembered, and felt sick for a second time that night. 'Oh my God,' she shouted aloud in terror. In a flood, the details of the murder that had taken place on the same road a few months before came rushing back to her. A woman had been raped before having her throat cut with a knife with a serrated edge and dumped in a ditch. For weeks there had been signs posted on the A1 appealing to passing motorists to phone a certain number if they had any information that might assist the police with their enquiries. The signs had now disappeared, but the police were still searching for the killer. Diana began to tremble as she remembered their warning to all woman drivers: 'Never stop on the motorway'.

he accelerated. She tried to think what she could do next, and began waving frantically at passing motorists as they sped by, but they remained oblivious to her predicament. She tried to think of other ways she might alert someone, and suddenly recalled that when she had joined the board of the company they had suggested she have a car phone fitted. Diana had decided it could wait until the car went in for its next service, which should have been a fortnight ago.

She brushed her hand across her forehead and removed a film of perspiration, thought for a moment, then manoeuvred her car into the fast lane. The van swung across after her, and hovered so close to her bumper that she became fearful that if she so much as touched her brakes she might unwittingly cause an enormous pile-up.

Diana took the car up to ninety, but the van wouldn't be shaken off. She pushed her foot further down on the accelerator and touched a hundred, but it still remained less than a car's length behind.

She flicked her headlights onto high-beam, turned on her hazard lights and blasted her horn at anyone

A few seconds later she saw a road sign she knew well. She had reached it far sooner than she had anticipated. In three miles she would have to leave the motorway for the sliproad that led to the farm. She began to pray that if she took her usual turning, the black-jacketed man would continue on up the A1 and she would finally be rid of him.

Diana decided that the time had come for her to speed him on his way. She swung back into the fast lane and once again put her foot down on the accelerator. She reached a hundred miles per hour for the second time as she sped past the two-mile sign. Her body was now covered in sweat, and the speedometer touched a hundred and ten. She checked her rear-view mirror, but he was still right behind her. She would have to pick the exact moment if she was to execute her plan successfully. With a mile to go, she began to look to her left, so as to be sure her timing would be perfect. She no longer needed to check in her mirror to know that he would still be there.

The next signpost showed three diagonal white lines, warning her that she ought to be on the inside lane if she intended to leave the motorway at the next junction. She kept the car in the outside lane at a hundred miles per hour until she spotted a large enough gap. Two white lines appeared by the roadside: Diana knew she would have only one chance to make her escape. As she passed the sign with a single white line on it she suddenly swung across the road at ninety miles per hour, causing cars in the middle and inside lanes to throw on their brakes and blast out their angry opinions. But Diana didn't care what they thought of her, because she was now travelling down the sliproad to safety, and the black van was speeding on up the A1.

She laughed out loud with relief. To her right, she could see the steady flow of traffic on the motorway. But then her laugh turned to a scream as she saw the black van cut sharply across the motorway in front of a lorry, mount the grass verge and career onto the slip-road, swinging from side to side. It nearly drove over the edge and into a ditch, but somehow managed to steady itself, ending up a few yards behind her, its lights once again glaring through her rear windscreen.

When she reached the top of the sliproad, Diana turned left in the direction of the farm, frantically trying to work out what she should do next. The nearest town was about twelve miles away on the main road, and the farm was only seven, but five of those miles were down a winding, unlit country lane. She checked her petrol gauge. It was nearing empty, but there should still be enough in the tank for her to consider either option. There was less than a mile to go before she reached the turning, so she had only a minute in which to make up her mind.

With a hundred yards to go, she settled on the farm. Despite the unlit lane, she knew every twist and turn, and she felt confident that her pursuer wouldn't. Once she reached the farm she could be out of the car and inside the house long before he could catch her. In any case, once he saw the farmhouse, surely he would flee.

The minute was up. Diana touched the brakes and skidded into a country road illuminated only by the moon.

Diana banged the palms of her hands on the steering wheel. Had she made the wrong decision? She glanced up at her rear-view mirror. Had he given up? Of course he hadn't. The back of a Land Rover loomed up in front of her. Diana slowed down, waiting for a corner she knew well, where the road widened slightly. She held her breath, crashed into third gear, and overtook. Would a head-on collision be preferable to a cut throat? She rounded the bend and saw an empty road ahead of her. Once again she pressed her foot down, this time managing to put a clear seventy, perhaps even a hundred, yards between her and her pursuer, but this only offered her a few moments' respite. Before long the familiar headlights came bearing down on her once again.

With each bend Diana was able to gain a little time as the van continued to lurch from side to side, unfamiliar with the road, but she never managed a clear break of more than a few seconds. She checked the mileometer. From the turn-off on the main road to the farm it was just over five miles, and she must have covered about two by now. She began to watch each tenth of a mile clicking up, terrified at the thought of the van overtaking her and forcing her into the ditch. She stuck determinedly to the centre of the road.

Another mile passed, and still he clung on to her. Suddenly she saw a car coming towards her. She switched her headlights to full beam and pressed on the horn. The other car retaliated by mimicking her actions, which caused her to slow down and brush against the hedgerow as they shot past each other. She checked the mileometer once again. Only two miles to go.

Diana would slow down and then speed up at each familiar bend in the road, making sure the van was never given enough room to pull level with her. She tried to concentrate on what she should do once the farmhouse came into sight. She reckoned that the drive leading up to the house must be about half a mile long. It was full of potholes and bumps which Daniel had often explained he couldn't afford to have repaired. But at least it was only wide enough for one car.

The gate to the driveway was usually left open for her, though on the odd rare occasion Daniel had forgotten, and she'd had to get out of the car and open it for herself. She couldn't risk that tonight. If the gate was closed, she would have to travel on to the next town and stop outside the Crimson Kipper, which was always crowded at this time on a Friday night, or, if she could find it, on the steps of the local police station. She checked her petrol gauge again. It was now touching red. 'Oh my God,' she said, realizing she might not have enough petrol to reach the town.

She could only pray that Daniel had remembered to leave the gate open.

She swerved out of the next bend and speeded up, but once again she managed to gain only a few yards, and she knew that within seconds he would be back in place. He was. For the next few hundred yards they remained within feet of each other, and she felt certain he must run into the back of her. She didn't once dare to touch her brakes – if they crashed in that lane, far from any help, she would have no hope of getting away from him.

She checked her mileometer. A mile to go.

'The gate must be open. It must be open,' she prayed. As she swung round the next bend, she could make out the outline of the farmhouse in the distance. She almost screamed with relief when she saw that the lights were on in the downstairs rooms.

She shouted, 'Thank God!' then remembered the gate again, and changed her plea to 'Dear God, let it be open.' She would know what needed to be done as soon as she came round the last bend. 'Let it be open, just this once,' she pleaded. 'I'll never ask for anything again, ever.' She swung round the final bend only inches ahead of the black van. 'Please, please, please.' And then she saw the gate.

It was open.

Her clothes were now drenched in sweat. She slowed down, wrenched the gearbox into second, and threw the car between the gap and into the bumpy driveway, hitting the gatepost on her right-hand side as she careered on up towards the house. The van didn't hesitate to follow her, and was still only inches behind as she straightened up. Diana kept her hand pressed down on the horn as the car bounced and lurched over the mounds and potholes.

Flocks of startled crows flapped out of overhanging branches, screeching as they shot into the air. Diana began screaming, 'Daniel! Daniel!' Two hundred yards ahead of her, the porch light went on.

Her headlights were now shining onto the front of the house, and her hand was still pressed on the horn. With a hundred yards to go, she spotted Daniel coming out of the front door, but she didn't slow down, and neither did the van behind her. With fifty yards to go she began flashing her lights at Daniel. She could now make out the puzzled, anxious expression on his face.

With thirty yards to go she threw on her brakes. The heavy estate car skidded across the gravel in front of the house, coming to a halt in the flowerbed just below the kitchen window. She heard the screech of brakes behind her. The leather-jacketed man, unfamiliar with the terrain, had been unable to react quickly enough, and as soon as his wheels touched the gravelled forecourt he began to skid out of control. A second later the van came crashing into the back of her car, slamming it against the wall of the house and shattering the glass in the kitchen window.

Diana leapt out of the car, screaming, 'Daniel! Get a gun, get a gun!' She pointed back at the van. 'That bastard's been chasing me for the last twenty miles!'

The man jumped out of the van and began limping towards them. Diana ran into the house. Daniel followed and grabbed a shotgun, normally reserved for rabbits, that was leaning against the wall. He ran back outside to face the unwelcome visitor, who had come to a halt by the back of Diana's Audi.

Daniel raised the shotgun to his shoulder and stared straight at him. 'Don't move or I'll shoot,' he said calmly. And then he remembered the gun wasn't loaded. Diana ducked back out of the house, but remained several yards behind him.

'Not me! Not me!' shouted the leather-jacketed youth, as Rachael appeared in the doorway.

'What's going on?' she asked nervously.

'Ring for the police,' was all Daniel said, and his wife quickly disappeared back into the house.

Daniel advanced towards the terrified-looking young man, the gun aimed squarely at his chest.

'Not me! Not me!' he shouted again, pointing at the Audi. 'He's in the car!' He quickly turned to face Diana. 'I saw him get in when you were parked on the hard shoulder. What else could I have done? You just wouldn't pull over.'

Daniel advanced cautiously towards the rear door of the car and ordered the young man to open it slowly, while he kept the gun aimed at his chest.

The youth opened the door, and quickly took a pace backwards. The three of them stared down at a man crouched on the floor of the car. In his right hand he held a long-bladed knife with a serrated edge. Daniel swung the barrel of the gun down to point at him, but said nothing.

The sound of a police siren could just be heard in the distance.

Cheap at Half the Price

WOMEN ARE NATURALLY superior to men, and Mrs Consuela Rosenheim was no exception.

Victor Rosenheim, an American banker, was Consuela's third husband, and the gossip columns on both sides of the Atlantic were suggesting that, like a chain smoker, the former Colombian model was already searching for her next spouse before she had extracted the last gasp from the old one. Her first two husbands – one an Arab, the other a Jew (Consuela showed no racial prejudice when it came to signing marriage contracts) – had not quite left her in a position that would guarantee her financial security once her natural beauty had faded. But two more divorce settlements would sort that out. With this in mind, Consuela estimated that she only had another five years before the final vow must be taken.

The Rosenheims flew into London from their home in New York – or, to be more accurate, from their homes in New York. Consuela had travelled to the airport by chauffeur-driven car from their mansion in the Hamptons, while her husband had been taken from his Wall Street office in a second chauffeur-driven car. They met up in the Concorde lounge at JFK. When they had landed at Heathrow another limousine transported them to the Ritz, where they were escorted to their usual suite without any suggestion of having to sign forms or book in.

The purpose of their trip was twofold. Mr Rosenheim was hoping to take over a small merchant bank that had not benefited from the recession, while Mrs Rosenheim intended to occupy her time looking for a suitable birthday present – for herself. Despite considerable research I have been unable to discover exactly which birthday Consuela would officially be celebrating.

After a sleepless night induced by jetlag, Victor Rosenheim was whisked away to an early-morning meeting in the City, while Consuela remained in bed toying with her breakfast. She managed one piece of thin unbuttered toast and a stab at a boiled egg.

Once the breakfast tray had been removed, Consuela made a couple of phone calls to confirm luncheon dates for the two days she would be in London. She then disappeared into the bathroom.

Fifty minutes later she emerged from her suite dressed in a pink Olaganie suit with a dark blue collar, her fair hair bouncing on her shoulders. Few of the men she passed between the elevator and the revolving doors failed to turn their heads, so Consuela judged that the previous fifty minutes had not been wasted. She stepped out of the hotel and into the morning sun to begin her search for the birthday present.

Consuela began her quest in New Bond Street. As in the past, she had no intention of straying more than a few blocks north, south, east or west from that comforting landmark, while a chauffeur-driven car hovered a few yards behind her.

She spent some time in Asprey's considering the latest slimline watches, a gold statue of a tiger with jade eyes, and a Fabergé egg, before moving on to Cartier, where she dismissed a crested silver salver, a platinum watch and a Louis XIV long-case clock. From there she walked another few yards to Tiffany's, which, despite a determined salesman who showed her almost everything the shop had to offer, she still left empty-handed.

Consuela stood on the pavement and checked her watch. It was 12.52, and she had to accept that it had been a fruitless morning. She instructed her chauffeur to drive her to Harry's Bar, where she found Mrs Stavros Kleanthis waiting for her at their usual table. Consuela greeted her friend with a kiss on both cheeks, and took the seat opposite her.

Mrs Kleanthis, the wife of a not unknown ship-owner – the Greeks preferring one wife and several liaisons – had for the last few minutes been concentrating her attention on the menu to be sure that the restaurant served the few dishes that her latest diet would permit. Between them, the two women had read every book that had reached number one on the *New York Times* bestseller list which included the words 'youth', 'orgasm', 'slimming', 'fitness' or 'immortality' in its title.

'How's Victor?' asked Maria, once she and Consuela had ordered their meals.

Consuela paused to consider her response, and decided on the truth.

'Fast reaching his sell-by date,' she replied. 'And Stavros?'

'Well past his, I'm afraid,' said Maria. 'But as I have neither your looks nor your figure, not to mention the fact that I have three teenage children, I don't suppose I'll be returning to the market to select the latest brand.'

Consuela smiled as a salade niçoise was placed in front of her.

'So, what brings you to London – other than to have lunch with an old friend?' asked Maria.

'Victor has his eye on another bank,' replied Consuela, as if she were discussing a child who collected stamps. 'And I'm in search of a suitable birthday present.'

'And what are you expecting Victor to come up with this time?' asked Maria. 'A house in the country? A thoroughbred racehorse? Or perhaps your own Lear jet?'

'None of the above,' said Consuela, placing her fork by the half-finished salad. 'I need something that can't be bargained over at a future date, so my gift must be one that any court, in any state, will acknowledge is unquestionably mine.'

'Have you found anything appropriate yet?' asked Maria.

'Not yet,' admitted Consuela. 'Asprey's yielded nothing of interest, Cartier's cupboard was almost bare, and the only attractive thing in Tiffany's was the salesman, who was undoubtedly penniless. I shall have to continue my search this afternoon.'

The salad plates were deftly removed by a waiter whom Maria considered far too young and far too thin. Another waiter with the same problem poured them both a cup of fresh decaffeinated coffee. Consuela refused the proffered cream and sugar, though her companion was not quite so disciplined.

The two ladies grumbled on about the sacrifices they were having to make because of the recession until they were the only diners left in the room. At this point a fatter waiter presented them with the bill – an extraordinarily long ledger considering that neither of them had ordered a second course, or had requested more than Evian from the wine waiter.

On the pavement of South Audley Street they kissed again on both cheeks before going their separate ways, one to the east and the other to the west.

Consuela climbed into the back of her chauffeur-driven car in order to be returned to New Bond Street, a distance of no more than half a mile.

Once she was back on familiar territory, she began to work her way steadily down the other side of the street, stopping at Bentley's, where it appeared that they hadn't sold anything since last year, and moving rapidly on to Adler, who seemed to be suffering from much the same problem. She cursed the recession once again, and blamed it all on Bill Clinton, who Victor had assured her was the cause of most of the world's current problems.

Consuela was beginning to despair of finding anything worthwhile in Bond Street, and reluctantly began her journey back towards the Ritz, feeling she might even have to consider an expedition to Knightsbridge the following day, when she came to a sudden halt outside the House of Graff. Consuela could not recall the shop from her last visit to London some six months before, and as she knew Bond Street better than she had ever known any of her three husbands, she concluded that it must be a new establishment.

She gazed at the stunning gems in their magnificent settings, heavily protected behind the bulletproof windows. When she reached the third window her mouth opened wide, like a newborn chick demanding to be fed. From that moment she knew that no further excursions would be necessary, for there, hanging round a slender marble neck, was a peerless diamond and ruby necklace. She felt that she had seen the magnificent piece of jewellery somewhere before, but she quickly dismissed the

thought from her mind, and continued to study the exquisitely set rubies surrounded by perfectly cut diamonds, making up a necklace of unparalleled beauty. Without giving a moment's thought to how much the object might cost, Consuela walked slowly towards the thick glass door at the entrance to the shop, and pressed a discreet ivory button on the wall. The House of Graff obviously had no interest in passing trade.

The door was unlocked by a security officer who needed no more than a glance at Mrs Rosenheim to know that he should usher her quickly through to the inner portals, where a second door was opened and Consuela came face to face with a tall, imposing man in a long black coat and pinstriped trousers.

'Good afternoon, madam,' he said, bowing slightly. Consuela noticed that he surreptitiously admired her rings as he did so. 'Can I be of assistance?'

Although the room was full of treasures that might in normal circumstances have deserved hours of her attention, Consuela's mind was focused on only one object.

'Yes. I would like to study more closely the diamond and ruby necklace on display in the third window.'

'Certainly, madam,' the manager replied, pulling back a chair for his customer. He nodded almost imperceptibly to an assistant, who silently walked over to the window, unlocked a little door and extracted the necklace. The manager slipped behind the counter and pressed a concealed button. Four floors above, a slight burr sounded in the private office of Mr Laurence Graff, warning the proprietor that a customer had enquired after a particularly expensive item, and that he might wish to deal with them personally.

Laurence Graff glanced up at the television screen

on the wall to his left, which showed him what was taking place on the ground floor.

'Ah,' he said, once he saw the lady in the pink suit seated at the Louis XIV table. 'Mrs Consuela Rosenheim, if I'm not mistaken.' Just as the Speaker of the House of Commons can identify every one of its 650 members, so Laurence Graff recognized the 650 customers who might be able to afford the most extravagant of his treasures. He quickly stepped from behind his desk, walked out of his office and took the waiting lift to the ground floor.

Meanwhile, the manager had laid out a black velvet cloth on the table in front of Mrs Rosenheim, and the assistant placed the necklace delicately on top of it. Consuela stared down at the object of her desire, mesmerized.

'Good afternoon, Mrs Rosenheim,' said Laurence Graff as he stepped out of the lift and walked across the thick pile carpet towards his would-be customer. 'How nice to see you again.'

He had in truth only seen her once before – at a shoulder-to-shoulder cocktail party in Manhattan. But after that, he could have spotted her at a hundred paces on a moving escalator.

'Good afternoon, Mr . . .' Consuela hesitated, feeling unsure of herself for the first time that day.

'Laurence Graff,' he said, offering his hand. 'We met at Sotheby Parke Bernet last year – a charity function in aid of the Red Cross, if I remember correctly.'

'Of course,' said Mrs Rosenheim, unable to recall him, or the occasion.

Mr Graff bowed reverently towards the diamond and ruby necklace.

'The Kanemarra heirloom,' he purred, then paused, before taking the manager's place at the table. 'Fashioned in 1936 by Silvio di Larchi,' he continued. 'All the rubies were extracted from a single mine in Burma, over a period of twenty years. The diamonds

were purchased from De Beers by an Egyptian merchant who, after the necklace had been made up for him, offered the unique piece to King Farouk – for services rendered. When the monarch married Princess Farida he presented it to her on their wedding day, and she in return bore him four heirs, none of whom, alas, was destined to succeed to the throne.' Graff looked up from one object of beauty, and gazed on another.

'Since then it has passed through several hands before arriving at the House of Graff,' continued the proprietor. 'Its most recent owner was an actress, whose husband's oil wells unfortunately dried up.'

The flicker of a smile crossed the face of Consuela Rosenheim as she finally recalled where she had previously seen the necklace.

'Quite magnificent,' she said, giving it one final look. 'I will be back,' she added as she rose from her chair. Graff accompanied her to the door. Nine out of ten customers who make such a claim have no intention of returning, but he could always sense the tenth.

'May I ask the price?' Consuela asked indifferently as he held the door open for her.

'One million pounds, madam,' Graff replied, as casually as if she had enquired about the cost of a plastic keyring at a seaside gift shop.

Once she had reached the pavement, Consuela dismissed her chauffeur. Her mind was now working at a speed that would have impressed her husband. She slipped across the road, calling first at The White House, then Yves Saint Laurent, and finally at Chanel, emerging some two hours later with all the weapons she required for the battle that lay ahead. She did not arrive back at her suite at the Ritz until a few minutes before six.

Consuela was relieved to find that her husband had not yet returned from the bank. She used the time to take a long bath, and to contemplate how the trap should be set. Once she was dry and powdered, she dabbed a suggestion of a new scent on her neck, then slipped into some of her newly acquired clothes.

She was checking herself once again in the full-length mirror when Victor entered the room. He stopped on the spot, dropping his briefcase on the carpet. Consuela turned to face him.

'You look stunning,' he declared, with the same look of desire she had lavished on the Kanemarra heirloom a few hours before.

'Thank you, darling,' she replied. 'And how did your day go?'

'A triumph. The takeover has been agreed, and at half the price it would have cost me only a year ago.'

Consuela smiled. An unexpected bonus.

'Those of us who are still in possession of cash need have no fear of the recession,' Victor added with satisfaction.

Over a quiet supper in the Ritz's dining room, Victor described to his wife in great detail what had taken place at the bank that day. During the occasional break in this monologue Consuela indulged her husband by remarking 'How clever of you, Victor,' 'How amazing,' 'How you managed it I will never understand.' When he finally ordered a large brandy, lit a cigar and leaned back in his chair, she began to run her elegantly stockinged right foot gently along the inside of his thigh. For the first time that evening, Victor stopped thinking about the takeover.

As they left the dining room and strolled towards the lift, Victor placed an arm around his wife's slim waist. By the time the lift had reached the sixth floor he had already taken off his jacket, and his hand had slipped a few inches further down. Consuela giggled. Long before they had reached the door of their suite he had begun tugging off his tie.

When they entered the room, Consuela placed the 'Do Not Disturb' sign on the outside doorknob. For the next few minutes Victor was transfixed to the spot as he watched his slim wife slowly remove each garment she had purchased that afternoon. He quickly pulled off his own clothes, and wished once again that he had carried out his New Year's resolution.

Forty minutes later, Victor lay exhausted on the bed. After a few moments of sighing, he began to snore. Consuela pulled the sheet over their naked bodies, but her eyes remained wide open. She was already going over the next step in her plan.

Victor awoke the following morning to discover his wife's hand gently stroking the inside of his leg. He rolled over to face her, the memory of the previous night still vivid in his mind. They made love a second time, something they had not done for as long as he could recall.

It was not until he stepped out of the shower that Victor remembered it was his wife's birthday, and that he had promised to spend the morning with her selecting a gift. He only hoped that her eye had already settled on something she wanted, as he needed to spend most of the day closeted in the City with his lawyers, going over the offer document line by line.

'Happy birthday, darling,' he said as he padded back into the bedroom. 'By the way, did you have any luck finding a present?' he added as he scanned the front page of the *Financial Times*, which was already speculating on the possible takeover, describing it as a coup. A smile of satisfaction appeared on Victor's face for the second time that morning.

'Yes, my darling,' Consuela replied. 'I did come across one little bauble that I rather liked. I just hope it isn't too expensive.'

'And how much is this "little bauble"?' Victor asked. Consuela turned to face him. She was wearing only two garments, both of them black, and both of them remarkably skimpy.

Victor started to wonder if he still had the time, but then he remembered the lawyers, who had been up all night and would be waiting patiently for him at the bank.

'I didn't ask the price,' Consuela replied. 'You're so much cleverer than I am at that sort of thing,' she added, as she slipped into a navy silk blouse.

Victor glanced at his watch. 'How far away is it?' he asked.

'Just across the road, in Bond Street, my darling,' Consuela replied. 'I shouldn't have to delay you for too long.' She knew exactly what was going through her husband's mind.

'Good. Then let's go and look at this little bauble without delay,' he said as he did up the buttons on his shirt.

While Victor finished dressing, Consuela, with the help of the *Financial Times*, skilfully guided the conversation back to his triumph of the previous day. She listened once more to the details of the takeover as they left the hotel and strolled up Bond Street together arm in arm.

'Probably saved myself several million,' he told her yet again. Consuela smiled as she led him to the door of the House of Graff.

'Several million?' she gasped. 'How clever you are, Victor.'

The security guard quickly opened the door, and this time Consuela found that Mr Graff was already standing by the table waiting for her. He bowed low, then turned to Victor. 'May I offer my congratulations on your brilliant coup, Mr Rosenheim.' Victor smiled. 'How may I help you?'

'My husband would like to see the Kanemarra heirloom,' said Consuela, before Victor had a chance to reply.

'Of course, madam,' said the proprietor. He stepped behind the table and spread out the black velvet cloth. Once again the assistant removed the

tone, aware that he could not risk another superlative.

'I'll settle at half a million, no more,' came back the immediate reply.

'I am sorry to say, sir,' said Graff, 'that with this particular piece, there is no room for bargaining.'

'There's always room for bargaining, whatever one is selling,' said Victor. 'I repeat my offer. Half a million.'

'I fear that in this case, sir . . .'

'I feel confident that you'll see things my way, given time,' said Victor. 'But I don't have that much time to spare this morning, so I'll write out a cheque for half a million, and leave *you* to decide whether you wish to cash it or not.'

'I fear you are wasting your time, sir,' said Graff. 'I cannot let the Kanemarra heirloom go for less than one million.'

Victor took out a chequebook from his inside pocket, unscrewed the top of his fountain pen, and wrote out the words 'Five Hundred Thousand Pounds Only' below the name of the bank that bore his name. His wife took a discreet pace backwards.

Graff was about to repeat his previous comment, when he glanced up, and observed Mrs Rosenheim silently pleading with him to accept the cheque.

A look of curiosity came over his face as Consuela continued her urgent mime.

Victor tore out the cheque and left it on the table. 'I'll give you twenty-four hours to decide,' he said. 'We return to New York tomorrow morning – with or without the Kanemarra heirloom. It's your decision.'

Graff left the cheque on the table as he accompanied Mr and Mrs Rosenheim to the front door and bowed them out onto Bond Street.

'You were brilliant, my darling,' said Consuela as the chauffeur opened the car door for his master.

magnificent necklace from its stand in the third window, and carefully laid it out on the centre of the velvet cloth to show the jewels to their best advantage. Mr Graff was about to embark on the piece's history, when Victor simply said, 'How much is it?'

Mr Graff raised his head. 'This is no ordinary piece of jewellery. I feel . . .'

'How much?' repeated Victor.

'Its provenance alone warrants . . .'

'How much?'

'The sheer beauty, not to mention the craftsmanship involved . . .'

'How much?' asked Victor, his voice now rising.

'. . . the word unique would not be inappropriate.'

'You may be right, but I still need to know how much it's going to cost me,' said Victor, who was beginning to sound exasperated.

'One million pounds, sir,' Graff said in an even

'The bank,' Rosenheim instructed as he fell into the back seat. 'You'll have your little bauble, Consuela. He'll cash the cheque before the twenty-four hours are up, of that I'm sure.' The chauffeur closed the back door, and the window purred down as Victor added with a smile, 'Happy birthday, darling.'

Consuela returned his smile, and blew him a kiss as the car pulled out into the traffic and edged its way towards Piccadilly. The morning had not turned out quite as she had planned, because she felt unable to agree with her husband's judgement – but then, she still had twenty-four hours to play with.

Consuela returned to the suite at the Ritz, undressed, took a shower, opened another bottle of perfume, and slowly began to change into the second outfit she had purchased the previous day. Before she left the room she turned to the commodities section of the *Financial Times*, and checked the price of green coffee.

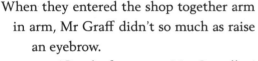

She emerged from the Arlington Street entrance of the Ritz wearing a double-breasted navy blue Yves Saint Laurent suit and a wide-brimmed red and white hat. Ignoring her chauffeur, she hailed a taxi, instructing the driver to take her to a small, discreet hotel in Knightsbridge. Fifteen minutes later she entered the foyer with her head bowed, and after giving the name of her host to the manager, was accompanied to a suite on the fourth floor. Her luncheon companion stood as she entered the room, walked forward, kissed her on both cheeks and wished her a happy birthday.

After an intimate lunch, and an even more intimate hour spent in the adjoining room, Consuela's companion listened to her request and, having first checked his watch, agreed to accompany her to Mayfair. He didn't mention to her that he would have to be back in his office by four o'clock to take an important call from South America. Since the downfall of the Brazilian president, coffee prices had gone through the roof.

As the car travelled down Brompton Road, Consuela's companion telephoned to check the latest spot price of green coffee in New York (only her skill in bed had managed to stop him from calling earlier). He was pleased to learn that it was up another two cents, but not as pleased as she was. Eleven minutes later, the car deposited them outside the House of Graff.

When they entered the shop together arm in arm, Mr Graff didn't so much as raise an eyebrow.

'Good afternoon, Mr Carvalho,' he said. 'I do hope that your estates yielded an abundant crop this year.'

Mr Carvalho smiled and replied, 'I cannot complain.'

'And how may I assist you?' enquired the proprietor.

'We would like to see the diamond necklace in the third window,' said Consuela, without a moment's hesitation.

'Of course, madam,' said Graff, as if he were addressing a complete stranger.

Once again the black velvet cloth was laid out on the table, and once again the assistant placed the Kanemarra heirloom in its centre.

This time Mr Graff was allowed to relate its history, before Carvalho politely enquired after the price.

'One million pounds,' said Graff.

After a moment's hesitation, Carvalho said, 'I'm willing to pay half a million.'

'This is no ordinary piece of jewellery,' replied the proprietor. 'I feel . . .'

'Possibly not, but half a million is my best offer,' said Carvalho.

'The sheer beauty, not to mention the craftsmanship involved . . .'

'Nevertheless, I am not willing to go above half a million.'

'. . . the word unique would not be inappropriate.'

'Half a million, and no more,' insisted Carvalho.

'I am sorry to say, sir,' said Graff, 'that with this particular piece there is no room for bargaining.'

'There's always room for bargaining, whatever one is selling,' the coffee grower insisted.

'I fear that is not true in this case, sir. You see . . .'

'I suspect you will come to your senses in time,' said Carvalho. 'But, regrettably, I do not have any time to spare this afternoon. I will write out a cheque for half a million pounds, and leave *you* to decide whether you wish to cash it.'

Carvalho took a chequebook from his inside pocket, unscrewed the top of his fountain pen, and wrote out the words 'Five Hundred Thousand Pounds Only'. Consuela looked silently on.

Carvalho tore out the cheque, and left it on the counter.

'I'll give you twenty-four hours to decide. I leave for Chicago on the early evening flight tomorrow. If the cheque has not been presented by the time I reach my office . . .'

Graff bowed his head slightly, and left the cheque on the table. He accompanied them to the door, and bowed again when they stepped out onto the pavement.

'You were brilliant, my darling,' said Consuela as the chauffeur opened the car door for his employer.

'The Exchange,' said Carvalho. Turning back to face his mistress, he added, 'You'll have your necklace before the day is out, of that I'm certain, my darling.'

Consuela smiled and waved as the car disappeared in the direction of Piccadilly, and on this occasion she felt able to agree with her lover's judgement. Once the car had turned the corner, she slipped back into the House of Graff.

The proprietor smiled, and handed over the smartly wrapped gift. He bowed low and simply said, 'Happy birthday, Mrs Rosenheim.'

Who Killed the Mayor?

CORTOGLIA IS A delightfully picturesque town in the heart of Campania. It rests high on a hill, forty miles north of Naples, with commanding views towards Monte Taburno to the east, and Vesuvius to the south. It is described in *Fodor's Italy* quite simply as 'heaven on earth'.

The population of the town is 1,463, and hasn't varied greatly for over a century. The town's income is derived from three main sources: wine, olive oil and truffles. The Cortoglia White, aromatic with a vibrant acidity, is one of the most sought-after wines on earth and, because its production is limited, is sold out long before it's bottled. And as for the olive oil, the only reason you never see a bottle on the shelves of your local supermarket is because many of the leading Michelin-starred restaurants won't consider allowing any other brand on their premises.

The bonus, which allows the locals to enjoy a standard of living envied by their neighbours, is their truffles. Restaurateurs travel from all four corners of the globe in search of the Cortoglia truffle, which is then only offered to their most discerning customers.

It is true that some people have been known to leave Cortoglia and seek their fortunes further afield, but the more sensible among them return fairly quickly. But then, life expectancy in the medieval hill town is eighty-six years for men and ninety-one for women, eight years above the national average.

In the centre of the main square is a statue of Garibaldi, now more famous for biscuits than battles, and the town boasts only half a dozen shops and a restaurant. The council wouldn't sanction any more for fear it might attract tourists. There is no train service, and a bus appears in the town once a week for those foolish enough to wish to travel to Naples. A few of the residents own cars, but have little use for them.

The town is run by the Consiglio Comunale, made up of six elders. The most junior member, whose lineage only goes back three generations, is not considered by all to be a local. The mayor, Salvatore Farinelli, his son Lorenzo Farinelli, chairman (ex officio), Mario Pellegrino, the manager of the olive oil company, Paolo Carrafini, the owner of the winery, and Pietro De Rosa, the truffle master, are all automatically members of the council, while the one remaining place comes up for election every five years. As no one had stood against Umberto Cattaneo, the butcher, for the past fifteen years, the voters had almost forgotten how to conduct an election.

The Polizia Locale had consisted of a single officer, Luca Gentile, whose authority derived from the city of Naples, and Luca tried not to disturb them unnecessarily. This story concerns the one occasion when it was necessary.

•

No one in the village could be certain where Dino Lombardi had come from but, like a black cloud, he appeared overnight, and was clearly more interested in thunderstorms than showers. Lombardi must have been around one metre ninety-three, with the build of a heavyweight boxer who didn't expect his bouts to last for more than a couple of rounds.

He began his reign of terror with the weaker inhabitants of the town, the shopkeepers, the local tradesmen and the restaurateur, whom he persuaded needed protection, even if they couldn't be sure from whom, as there hadn't been a serious crime in Cortoglia in living memory. Even the Germans hadn't bothered to climb that particular hill.

To be fair, Constable Gentile was due to retire in a few months' time, at the age of sixty-five, and the council hadn't got round to finding his replacement. But a further problem arose when the mayor, Salvatore Farinelli, died at the age of 102, and an election had to be held to replace him.

It was assumed that his son Lorenzo would succeed him. Mario Pellegrino would then become chairman of the council, and everyone else would move up a place, with the one vacancy being filled by Gian Lucio Altana, the local restaurateur. That was until Lombardi turned up at the town hall, and entered his name on the list for mayor. Of course, no one doubted Lorenzo Farinelli would win by a landslide, so it came as something of a surprise when the town clerk, on crutches, his left leg in plaster, announced from the steps of the Palazzo dei Municipio that Lombardi had polled 511 votes, to Farinelli's 486. On hearing the result, there was a gasp of disbelief from the crowd, not least because no one knew anyone who had voted for Lombardi.

Lombardi immediately took over the town hall, occupied the mayor's residence, and dismissed the council. He'd only been in office for a few days when the citizens were informed he would be imposing a

Within a year, heaven on earth had been turned into hell on earth, with the mayor quite happy to be cast in the role of Beelzebub. So, frankly, it didn't come as a surprise to anyone when Lombardi was murdered.

Constable Gentile told the chairman of the council that as murder was out of his league, he would have to inform the authorities in Naples. He admitted in his report that there were 1,462 suspects, and he had absolutely no idea who had committed the crime.

Naples, a city that knows a thing or two about murder, sent one of its brightest young detectives to investigate the crime, arrest the culprit and bring them back to the city to stand trial.

Antonio Rossetti, who at the tender age of thirty-two had recently been promoted to lieutenant, was assigned to the case, although he considered it an inconvenience that would take him out of the front line – but surely not for long. He was already aware of Lombardi's past criminal record; extortion, bribery and corruption were but a few of his crimes, so the citizens of Cortoglia would be among many who wouldn't mourn him. He had assured the chief of police that he would wrap up the case as quickly as possible, and return to Naples so he could deal with some real criminals.

sales tax on all three of the town's main companies, which was later extended to the shopkeepers and restaurateur. And if that wasn't enough, he began to demand a kickback from the buyers as well as the sellers.

However, it didn't help that Luca Gentile had disappeared even before Lieutenant Rossetti had set foot in Cortoglia. Some suggested Gentile was suffering from the strain of the whole affair, as the last murder in the town had been in 1846, when his great-great-great-grandfather had been the town's constable. But where had he disappeared to, and why, because Gentile was the only other person who knew how the mayor had been killed.

Rossetti was appalled to discover Lombardi had been cremated, and his ashes scattered on the far side of Mount Taburno within hours of his death, such was the locals' hatred of the man.

'So you, Gentile and the coroner are the only people who know how the murder was committed,' said the chief as he handed over the results of the autopsy to his lieutenant.

'And the murderer,' Rossetti reminded him.

Lieutenant Antonio Rossetti arrived in Cortoglia later that morning, to be told that the council had decreed he should reside in the mayor's home until the murderer had been apprehended.

'After all,' the chairman said, 'let's get this over with so the young man can return to Naples as quickly as possible and leave us in peace.'

Antonio set up office in the local police station, which consisted of one small room, one unoccupied cell and a lavatory. He took the relevant case files out of his bag and placed them on the desk. He looked at the large, empty board on the wall and pinned a photograph of Lombardi in the centre.

He then decided to leave his office and roam around the town, in the hope that someone might approach him, wanting to supply information. But even though he walked slowly, and smiled a lot, people crossed the road when they saw him as if he had some contagious disease. He was clearly not looked upon as the Good Samaritan.

After a fruitless morning, Antonio returned to his office and made a list of those people who had most to gain from Lombardi's death and came to the reluctant conclusion that he would have to start with the members of the Consiglio Comunale. He wrote Wine, Olive Oil and Truffles on his notepad and took the photographs of the five councillors from the case file, and pinned them around Lombardi's photograph. Rossetti decided to start with Truffles. He called at Signor De Rosa's office to make an appointment with the councillor at his shop later that afternoon.

'Would you care for a glass of wine, Lieutenant?' said De Rosa, before the policeman had even sat down. 'The Cortoglia White is favoured by connoisseurs and 1947 was considered a vintage year.'

'No, thank you, sir. Not while I'm on duty.'

'Quite right,' said De Rosa. 'But forgive me if I do, as it may be my last for some time.' Rossetti looked surprised but didn't comment. De Rosa took a sip. 'So how can I help you?'

The policeman opened his notepad, and looked down at his prepared questions. 'As your family have lived in Cortoglia for over two hundred years—'

'Over three hundred years,' corrected the truffle master with a smile.

'I was rather hoping you might be able to shed some light on who killed Dino Lombardi?' continued Antonio.

De Rosa emptied his glass with a large gulp before saying, 'I most certainly can. You need look no further, Lieutenant, because I killed Lombardi.'

Antonio was taken by surprise but delighted to have a confession on his first day. He was already thinking about returning to Naples in triumph, and getting back to locking up some serious criminals.

'Are you willing to accompany me to the station

and sign a written statement to that effect, Signor De Rosa?'

De Rosa nodded. 'Whenever it suits you.'

'You do realize, Signor De Rosa, that if you confess to the murder, I will have no choice but to arrest you, and take you to Naples, where you will stand trial, and could spend the rest of your life in the prison at Poggioreale?'

'I have thought of little else since the day I murdered the bastard. But I can't complain, I've had a good life.'

'Why did you kill Lombardi?' asked Antonio, who accepted that motive invariably accounted for any crime.

De Rosa filled his glass a second time. 'Dino Lombardi was an evil and ruthless man, Lieutenant, who preyed on everyone he came into contact with.' He paused and took a sip of his wine, before adding, 'He made their lives unbearable, mine included.'

'What do you mean by evil and ruthless, signor?'

'He intimidated the shopkeepers and the local tradesmen, and even brought Gian Lucio, our local restaurateur, to his knees.'

Antonio kept on writing. 'How did he manage that?'

'He demanded protection money, even though he never made it clear who he was protecting us from as there hasn't been a serious crime in Cortoglia in living memory. And when he became mayor – a mystery in itself – he introduced a sales tax on all of our goods. If he had been allowed to continue for much longer, he would have put us all out of business. Last year my little company made a loss for the first time in three hundred years. So I took it upon myself to rid my fellow citizens of the fiend.' He put down his wine glass and smiled. 'I hear the council are planning to build a statue of me in the town square.'

'I only have one more question,' the detective said, looking up from his notebook. 'How did you kill Lombardi?'

'I stabbed him with my truffle knife,' said De Rosa without hesitation. 'It seemed appropriate at the time.'

'How many times did you stab him?'

'Six or seven,' he said, picking up a knife from his desk and giving a demonstration.

Antonio stopped writing and closed his notebook. 'I feel sure you know, Signor De Rosa, that it's a serious crime to waste police time.'

'Of course I do, Lieutenant,' said De Rosa, 'but now I have confessed, you can arrest me, drag me off to Naples and throw me in jail.'

'Which I would be only too happy to do, signor,' said Antonio, 'if only Lombardi had been stabbed.'

The truffle master shrugged his shoulders. 'But how can you possibly know how he died when he has been cremated?'

'Because I have read the autopsy report,' said Antonio, 'so I know exactly how he was killed. What I don't know is who murdered him, but it certainly wasn't you.'

'Does it really matter?' said De Rosa. 'Just tell me how Lombardi was killed and I'll confess to the crime.'

This was the first time Antonio had ever known someone admit to a crime they hadn't committed.

'I'm going to leave, signor, before you get yourself into even more trouble.'

The truffle master looked disappointed.

Antonio closed his notepad, stood up, walked out

of De Rosa's shop and back into the square without another word.

He tried not to laugh as he passed a pen full of the most contented pigs he'd ever seen, almost as if they knew they would never be slaughtered. He was on his way back to the police station when he spotted a pharmacy on the other side of the square, and remembered he needed a bar of soap and some toothpaste. A little bell above the door rang as he stepped inside. He stood by the counter for a few moments, before a young woman came through from the dispensary and said, 'Good morning, Signor Rossetti, how can I help you?'

Hardened criminals from the back streets of Naples couldn't silence Antonio Rossetti, but a chemist from Cortoglia managed it with one sentence. She waited patiently for her customer to respond.

'I need a bar of soap,' he eventually managed.

'You'll find a good selection behind you on the third shelf down, Lieutenant.'

'Is it that obvious that I'm a policeman?' said Antonio.

'When you're the only person in town that nobody knows, everyone knows you,' she said.

Antonio selected a bar of soap but ignored the toothpaste, because he wanted an excuse to return as

soon as possible. He placed the soap on the counter and tried not to stare at her.

'Will there be anything else, signor?'

'No, thank you.' Antonio picked up the bar of soap and headed for the door.

'Were you considering paying or don't the police in Naples bother with anything quite so mundane?' she asked, suppressing a smile.

'I'm so sorry,' said Antonio, quickly placing a note on the counter.

'Do call again if there is anything else I can help you with,' she said, passing him a small bag and his change.

'There is just one thing. You don't, by any chance, happen to know who killed the mayor?'

'I thought Signor De Rosa had already confessed to murdering Lombardi? I assumed by now you would have arrested him and locked him up.'

Antonio frowned, left the shop without another word and made his way back to the police station. He sat at his desk and began to write a report on his abortive meeting with De Rosa, but found it hard to concentrate. Once he'd completed it, he returned to the photographs on the board and put a large black cross through De Rosa.

Antonio decided he would have to pay a visit to Mario Pellegrino, the owner of the olive oil shop, next, but this time he wouldn't call to warn him.

Rossetti left the police station just after breakfast the following morning, and set out for the olive oil shop in the square, pleased he would have to pass the pharmacy on his way. He slowed down as he approached the shop and glanced through the window. She was standing by the door, turning the closed sign to open, and looked up as he passed by. They exchanged a glance before he hurried on.

When Antonio arrived at the olive oil shop, Mario Pellegrino was waiting for him at the door.

'Good morning, Lieutenant,' he said, 'have you come to purchase a bottle of the finest olive oil on earth or is this a police raid?'

'I'm sorry I didn't call and make an appointment, Signor Pellegrino, but—' Antonio said as he followed him into the shop.

'You were hoping to take me by surprise,' said Pellegrino, 'but I have to tell you, Lieutenant, I am not at all surprised.'

'You were expecting me?' said Antonio as he stood beside the counter and took out his notepad and pen.

'Yes, everyone knows you've been sent from Naples to investigate the death of Lombardi, and I assumed I would be among the first people you would want to question.'

'But why you in particular, signor?'

'It's no secret that I detested the man. So if you were going to arrest me, the last thing you'd do is to call up and make an appointment, because that would give me enough time to escape.'

Antonio put down his pen. 'But why would you want to escape, Signor Pellegrino?'

'Because everyone knows I killed Lombardi, and I realized that it wouldn't take too long for a smart young detective like you to work out who the murderer was.'

'But why would you want to kill the mayor?' asked Antonio.

'He was ruining my business with his protection racket and added taxes. And if that wasn't enough, he was demanding kickbacks from my buyers, some of whom began to avoid the journey to Cortoglia as they feared they might be next. Another year and I would have had nothing to leave the children. I'm only thankful that my son Roberto is ready to take over the business while I'm locked up in prison.' Pellegrino stood up and stretched his arms across the counter as if expecting to be handcuffed.

'Before I arrest you, Signor Pellegrino,' said the

policeman, 'I will need to know how you killed the mayor.'

Pellegrino didn't hesitate. 'I strangled the damn man,' he said.

'With what?'

This time he did hesitate. 'Does it matter?'

'No, not really—' said Antonio.

'Good, then let's get on with it,' Pellegrino said, once again stretching his arms across the counter.

'Just one minor problem,' Antonio continued. 'I'm afraid Lombardi wasn't strangled by you, or anyone else for that matter.'

'But as he was cremated, how can you be so sure?'

'Because, unlike you, I've studied the police report, and can assure you, Signor Pellegrino, that wasn't the way that Lombardi died.'

'What a pity. But as I would have liked to have strangled the man, can't you just charge me with attempted murder, and that will solve all our problems?'

'Except for the problem that the culprit will still be on the loose,' said Antonio. 'So if you'd be kind enough to advise your friends that I intend to catch the real murderer and put him behind bars, I'd be very grateful,' he added, as he slammed his notebook closed.

As Antonio turned to leave, he spotted a photograph behind the counter. Pellegrino smiled. 'My daughter's wedding,' he announced with pride. 'She married the son of my dear friend, Signor De Rosa. Oil and water may not mix, Lieutenant, but olive oil and truffles certainly do.' He laughed at a joke Antonio presumed he'd made many times before.

'And the chief bridesmaid?' said Antonio, pointing to a young woman who was standing behind the bride.

'Francesca Farinelli, the mayor's daughter. Lorenzo

and I had assumed she would marry my second son, Bruno, but it was not to be.'

'Why not?' said Antonio. 'Wasn't there enough olive oil left over?'

'More than enough. But modern Italian women seem to have minds of their own. I blame her father. He should never have let her go to university. It's not natural.'

Antonio would have laughed, but he suspected the old man meant it.

'I wonder if I might ask you for a small favour,' Pellegrino said, holding up a large bottle of olive oil.

'If it's in my power, signor, I'd be only too happy to do so.'

'I just wondered if you could let me know how the mayor was killed.'

The policeman ignored the offering and quickly left the shop.

Rossetti was on his way back to the police station to write up another abortive report but hesitated when he reached the pharmacy. He entered and found Francesca standing behind the counter, chatting to a customer.

'That should ease the pain, signora, but make sure that you only take one pill a day before going to bed. And if it doesn't get any better, come back and see me,' she said. Francesca turned to face Rossetti. 'Is it my turn to be arrested, Lieutenant?'

'No, something far simpler than that. I've run out of toothpaste.'

'You know, we do have customers who buy soap, toothpaste and razor blades all at the same time, or is this nothing more than subtle police tactics to wear the suspect down and make her admit she killed the mayor?'

Antonio laughed.

'However,' Francesca continued, 'if your plan was

simply to ask me out for a drink after I get off work this evening, I might just say yes.'

'Was it that obvious?' Antonio asked.

'Why don't we meet at Lucio's around six?'

'I'll look forward to it,' said Antonio as he turned to leave.

'Don't forget your toothpaste, Lieutenant.'

When Antonio turned up at the police station, there was a large, burly man wearing a long white coat and a blue-and-white striped apron waiting for him outside the front door.

'Good morning, Inspector. My name is Umberto Cattaneo.'

'Lieutenant, Signor Cattaneo,' corrected Antonio.

'I feel confident, Lieutenant, that promotion will not be far away when you hear what I have to tell you.'

'Please don't tell me you killed the mayor?'

'Certainly not,' said the butcher as he lowered his voice. 'However, I can tell you who did kill Lombardi.'

At last, an informer, thought Antonio. He unlocked the door to the station and led Cattaneo through to his little office.

'But before I let you know who the murderer is,' continued Cattaneo as he sat down, 'I need to be sure that it won't be traced back to me.'

'You have my word on that,' said Antonio, opening his notepad. 'That's assuming we won't need you to act as a witness when the case comes to trial.'

'You won't need a witness,' said Cattaneo, 'because I can tell you where the gun is buried.'

Antonio snapped his notepad shut, and let out a deep sigh.

'But I haven't even told you who the murderer is,' Cattaneo protested.

'You needn't bother, Signor Cattaneo, because Lombardi wasn't shot.'

'But Gian Lucio told me he'd shot him. He even showed me the weapon,' insisted Cattaneo.

'Before I lock you both up for a couple of days, if for no other reason than to stop any more of you wasting my time, may I ask why you are so willing to get your friend arrested for a crime I can assure you he didn't commit?'

'Gian Lucio Altana is my oldest and dearest friend,' protested the butcher.

'Then why accuse him of murder?'

'Because I lost the toss,' said Cattaneo.

'You lost the toss?'

'Yes, we agreed that whoever won would give himself up and admit that he'd killed the mayor.'

'Then why hasn't he given himself up?' said Antonio, unable to hide his frustration.

'Signor De Rosa advised us against that. Said there had been far too many confessions already, and he felt Gian Lucio would have a better chance of being arrested if you thought I was an informer.'

'Just out of interest, Signor Cattaneo,' said Antonio, 'if you had won the toss, dare I ask how you would have killed the mayor?'

'I would have shot him as well, but unfortunately we only have one gun between us, so I had to bury the weapon in his garden, where you can still find it.'

'Again, just so that I understand his motive, may I ask why Gian Lucio was so willing to be charged with a murder that he didn't commit?'

'Oh, that's easy to explain, Lieutenant. Lombardi used to eat at Gian Lucio's restaurant three times a day and he never once paid the bill.'

'That's hardly a good enough reason to kill someone.'

'It is when you lose all your regular customers because none of them want to eat in the same restaurant as the mayor.'

'But that doesn't explain why you wanted to kill him.'

'Gian Lucio is my best customer, and he could no longer afford my finest cuts, so it wouldn't have been much longer before we were both out of business. By the way, Lieutenant, was Lombardi electrocuted by any chance?'

'Get out of here, Signor Cattaneo, before I get myself arrested for murder.'

Not a totally wasted morning, considered Antonio, because he was now confident only he, Constable Gentile and the murderer had any idea how Lombardi had been killed. But where was Gentile?

Antonio arrived at Lucio's just before 6 p.m., looking forward to seeing Francesca. He sat at an outside table and placed a bunch of lilies on the chair next to him, smiling when Gian Lucio joined him.

'Can I get you a drink, Lieutenant?'

'No, thank you. I'll wait until my guest arrives. And Gian Lucio,' Antonio said as the restaurateur turned to leave, 'just to let you know your friend Signor Cattaneo failed to get you arrested for murder this morning.'

'I know, but then I did win the toss,' sighed Gian Lucio.

'My bet is that both of you know who killed Lombardi.'

'Can I get you a glass of wine while you're waiting, Lieutenant?' Gian Lucio said, quickly changing the subject. 'Francesca prefers the Cortoglia White.'

'Then why don't you make it two?'

Gian Lucio left quickly.

Antonio continued to look across the square to the pharmacy until he spotted Francesca locking up. He watched her crossing the square and immediately realized it was the first time he'd seen her not wearing a long white coat. She was dressed in a red silk blouse, a black skirt and a pair of high-heeled shoes that certainly hadn't been bought in Cortoglia. He tried not to stare at her. What else was different? Of course, she'd let her hair down. He hadn't thought it possible that she could be even more beautiful.

'As you're a highly trained detective,' Francesca said when she sat down next to him, 'you will know that my name is Francesca, while I'm not sure if you are Antonio or Toni?'

'My mother calls me Antonio, but my friends call me Toni.'

'Do your family also come from Naples?'

'Yes,' said Antonio. 'My parents are both school-teachers. My father is the headmaster of the Michelangelo Illioneo School, where my mother teaches history, but no one is in any doubt who runs the place.'

Francesca laughed. 'Any brothers or sisters?'

'Just one brother, Darius. He's a lawyer. So once I've locked any criminals up, he puts on a long black gown and defends them. That way we keep it all in the family.'

Francesca laughed again. 'Did you always want to be a policeman?' she asked, as Gian Lucio handed them both a glass of wine.

'From the age of six when someone stole my sweets. But to be fair, if you're brought up in Naples, you have to decide at an early age which side of the law you're going to be on. Did you always want to be a pharmacist?'

'I first worked in the shop at the age of twelve,' she said, looking across the square, 'and with the exception of four years at Milan University studying chemistry, it's been my second home. So when the owner retired, I took over.'

'How did your father feel about that?'

'He was too busy fight-ing the mayoral election

at the time, and I do mean fighting, to have even noticed.'

'Which everyone assumed your father would win.'

'By a landslide. So it came as something of a surprise when the town clerk announced that Lombardi had won.'

'But I haven't come across anyone who voted for Lombardi,' said Antonio.

'In that election, it didn't matter how you voted, Toni, only who was counting the votes.'

'But your father became mayor soon after Lombardi was murdered?'

'No one even stood against him the second time, so I hope you'll attend his inauguration on Saturday?'

'I wouldn't miss it,' said Antonio, raising his glass. 'That's assuming I haven't arrested Lombardi's murderer before then.'

'How many people admitted to killing the mayor today?'

'Two. Pellegrino and the florist, Signor Burgoni.'

'So how did he bump off Lombardi?' Francesca asked.

'Claimed he ran him down in his Ferrari, and then reversed over him to make sure he was dead. Right here in the town square.'

'Sounds pretty convincing to me, so why didn't you arrest him?'

'Because he doesn't own a Fiat, let alone a Ferrari, and what's more, doesn't even have a driving licence,' said Antonio, as he handed Francesca the lilies. 'So he'll be able to continue selling his flowers.'

Francesca laughed, just as Gian Lucio appeared and suggested another glass of wine.

'No, no, Gian Lucio,' said Francesca, 'I must get home. There's so much I have to do before Saturday.'

'When your father will take up his rightful position as mayor of Cortoglia. But I do hope that we'll see you both before then,' said Gian Lucio as he offered a slight bow.

'If I'm given a second chance,' said Antonio as Francesca stood up, and they began to walk across the square towards the pharmacy. Francesca explained that she lived in an apartment above the shop.

'Where are you staying?' said Francesca.

'They've put me in Lombardi's old home while I'm here. I've never lived in such luxury, and I'm trying not to get used to it as it won't be long before I have to return to my little flat in Naples.'

'Not if you don't catch the killer,' she teased.

'Nice idea, but my chief's becoming restless. He's made it clear he expects me back at my desk within a fortnight, with or without the murderer.'

When they reached Francesca's door, she took out a key, but before she could put it in the lock Antonio bent down and kissed her.

'I look forward to seeing you tomorrow, Toni.'

Antonio looked puzzled until Francesca added, 'I have a feeling that it can't be too long before you'll need another bar of soap. By the way, Toni, some of our customers buy them in boxes of three, even six.'

Francesca opened the door and disappeared inside. Antonio walked across to the other side of the square to find several of the locals were grinning.

The following day started badly for Antonio. He was studying the pinboard, now covered in photographs, several with crosses through them. His thoughts were interrupted by Riccardo Forte, the local postman, who marched in and even before delivering the morning mail said, 'I can't bear the strain any longer, Lieutenant. I've decided to give myself up and admit that it was me who murdered the mayor.'

'I was just making a cup of coffee, Riccardo, would you like one?'

'Not before you arrest me and beat me up.'

'Later perhaps, but first a few questions.'

'Of course.'

'Black or white?'

'Black, no sugar.'

Toni poured a cup of coffee and handed it to the postman. 'How did you kill the mayor, Riccardo?' he asked, no longer wasting any time with preliminaries.

'I drowned him,' said the postman.

'In the sea?' suggested Antonio, raising an eyebrow.

'No, in his bath. I took him by surprise.'

'It must have come as quite a surprise,' said Antonio, opening his notebook. 'But before I charge you, Riccardo, I still have one or two more questions.'

'I'll admit to anything,' he said.

'I'm sure you will, but first, how old are you?'

'Sixty-three.'

'And your height?'

'One metre sixty-two.'

'And your weight?'

'Around seventy-six kilos.'

'And you want me to believe, Riccardo, that you overpowered a man who was almost two metres tall and weighed around a hundred kilos. A man who some suggested never took a bath. Tell me, Riccardo, was Lombardi asleep at the time?'

'No,' said the postman, 'but he was drunk.'

'Ah, that would explain it,' said Antonio. 'Although, frankly, if he'd passed out before you attempted to drown him, it would still have been a close-run thing.' The postman tried to look offended. 'In any case, there's something else you've overlooked.'

'What's that?'

'Lombardi couldn't have been drowned in a bath, because there's only a shower in the house.'

'In the sea?' said the postman hopefully.

'Not an option. Not least because eleven other younger men have already confessed to drowning him in the sea.' Antonio closed his notebook. 'But a good try, Riccardo. More importantly, have I got any letters this morning?'

'Yes, three,' said the postman, putting the opened envelopes on the table. 'One from your mother, who wonders if you will be back in time for lunch on Sunday. The second is from the chief of police in Naples who wants to know why you haven't arrested anyone yet, and a third from your brother.'

'And what does he want?' Antonio asked, ignoring the fact that the postman had illegally tampered with the mail.

'Could you let him know as soon as you have arrested

someone, and if they've got any money, would you remember to recommend him?'

'Are there any secrets in this town?'

'Just one,' said the postman.

Dinner with Francesca at Lucio's restaurant was about as public as an execution. If Antonio had even thought about holding her hand, it would have been front-page news in the *Cortoglia Gazzetta*.

'Don't you ever get bored living in a small town?' he asked her after a waiter had whisked away their plates.

'Never, I have the best of both worlds,' she replied. 'I can read the same books as you, watch the same television programmes, eat the same food and even enjoy the same wine but at half the price. And if I want to go to the opera, visit an art gallery or buy some new clothes, I can always spend the day in Naples and be back in Cortoglia before the sun sets. And perhaps you haven't noticed, Toni, the magnificent rolling hills or how fresh the air is, and when people pass you in the street they smile and know your name.'

'But the bustle, the excitement, the variety of everyday life?'

'The traffic, the pollution, the graffiti, not to mention the manners of some of your fellow Neapolitans who consider women should only be seen in the kitchen or the bedroom, and then not necessarily the same woman.'

Antonio leant across the table and took her hand. 'I couldn't tempt you to come back to Naples with me?'

'For the day, yes,' said Francesca. 'But then I'd want us to be back in Cortoglia by nightfall.'

'Then you'll have to go on murdering some more of the locals.'

'Certainly not. One will be quite enough for the next hundred years. So who's the latest person who tried to convince you they disposed of Lombardi?'

'Paolo Carrafini.'

'Whose wine we are both enjoying,' said Francesca, raising her glass.

'And will continue to do so,' said Antonio, 'as Signor Carrafini's attempt to prove he murdered the mayor turned out to be the least convincing so far.'

'What was wrong with Lombardi falling through a trap door into the wine cellar and breaking his neck?'

'Nothing wrong with the idea,' said Antonio, 'it's just a pity Signor Carrafini would have had to lift up the trap door before he could push Lombardi through. You should tell any other potential murderers that they must be prepared for something to go wrong even when they're innocent.'

'So who's next on your list?'

'I'm afraid it's your father's turn and he's the last person I want to arrest. Although when it comes to motive, he's an obvious candidate.'

'Why?'

'Because we know Lombardi removed him as mayor and within days of the murder, your father was back in the town hall.'

'Along with his friends,' Francesca reminded him.

'Who we now know are all innocent, so I can't wait to find out how your father killed Lombardi.'

Francesca leant across the table and touched his

cheek. 'Don't worry, my father isn't going to admit to the murder.'

'All the more reason to believe he did it.'

'Except in his case he has a cast-iron alibi. He was in Florence at the time, attending a local government conference.'

'That's a relief, assuming there are witnesses.'

'Over a hundred.'

'More than enough. But if it wasn't your father who killed Lombardi, I'm fast running out of suspects. Although there still remains the mystery of the missing policeman, because Luca Gentile hasn't been seen in Cortoglia since the day Lombardi was murdered, which is suspicious in and of itself.'

'Luca isn't capable of murder,' said Francesca. 'Although I suspect he knows who did it, which is why he won't be returning to Cortoglia and resuming his former duties until you're safely back in Naples.'

'Then I've still got a few more days left to surprise you all,' said Antonio.

'I think you'll find there are at least three more potential murderers who can't wait to give themselves up.'

'Surely they must be running out of ideas by now?'

'I think you'll enjoy tomorrow's, which is a great improvement on trap doors, truffle knives or being shot.'

'Tell them not to bother tomorrow,' said Antonio. 'I'm taking the day off to watch your father being inaugurated as mayor. Why don't I get the bill?'

'There won't be a bill, Toni, however long you decide to stay,' said Francesca. 'Gian Lucio is telling everyone that although he confessed to shooting Lombardi, even producing the gun, you still refused to lock him up.'

'Because he wasn't guilty,' protested an exasperated Antonio, 'and if we hadn't been having dinner here tonight, I would have locked him up for the possession of a firearm.'

'But it wasn't even his.'

'Ah, but he won the toss,' said Antonio.

'Won the toss?'

'At last I have found something you don't know about,' he said as he stood up to leave. Antonio took her hand as they crossed the square to Francesca's home.

When she opened the door this time Antonio followed her inside.

The Naples chief of police called Antonio a few days later, and asked if he was making any progress.

'I can't pretend I am, chief,' admitted Antonio. 'To date,' he said, opening a thick file, 'forty-four people have confessed to killing the mayor, and I'm fairly sure none of them are guilty. And worse, I think they all know who did murder Lombardi.'

'Someone will crack,' said the chief. 'They always do.'

'This isn't Naples, chief,' Antonio heard himself saying.

'So who's the latest one to confess?'

'Not one, but eleven. The local football team claim they pushed Lombardi over a cliff and he drowned in the sea.'

'And what makes you so sure they didn't?'

'I interviewed all eleven of them. The nearest coastline is over forty miles away, and they couldn't even agree on which cliff they pushed him over, where they pulled him out of the water, or how they managed to get him back to Cortoglia and tuck him up in bed. And in any case, I'm not convinced that lot could have murdered Lombardi between them.'

'What makes you say that?'

'They haven't won a football match in the past fifteen years and, don't forget, this was an away game. Frankly, I think it's more likely Lombardi would have pushed all eleven of them over a cliff before they laid a hand on him.'

'All the more reason for you to come back,' said the chief. 'Lombardi's clearly not going to be missed by anyone in Cortoglia, because I've just received a confidential report from the Guardia di Finanza to let me know even the Mafia expelled him. They felt he was too violent. So if you haven't discovered who murdered him by the end of next week, I want you back in Naples where real criminals are still roaming the streets.'

Antonio wasn't given a chance to respond.

Everyone took the day off, Antonio included, to celebrate the installation of the new mayor. Lorenzo Farinelli had been elected unopposed, which didn't come as a surprise to anyone, and the council of six remained in place. Dancing and drinking in the town square went on until the early hours, right outside Antonio's bedroom window, and that wasn't the only reason he couldn't get to sleep.

The next morning he called his mother to tell her he'd met the woman he was going to marry, and she would be captivated, and not just by her beauty.

'I can't wait to meet her,' said his mother. 'Why don't you bring her to Naples for the weekend?'

'Why don't you and Papa come to Cortoglia?'

During the next few days, the number of citizens who confessed to killing Lombardi rose from forty-four to fifty-one, and when the chief called again from Naples to tell him to wrap up the case, Antonio had to admit that the locals had defeated him, and he accepted that perhaps the time had come to head back to the real world.

Indeed, Antonio might have done so if the new mayor hadn't phoned and asked to see him on a private matter.

As the young detective walked across the square to the town hall, he assumed that the number of murderers in the town was about to rise from fifty-one to fifty-two, as Farinelli was now the only person on the council who hadn't confessed to murdering Lombardi, and Antonio had recently discovered he hadn't been at a conference in Florence on the day of the murder. But he did know who had been.

'Those in favour?' said the mayor, looking around the council chamber that he and his fellow members of the Consiglio Comunale had recaptured.

The five other members of the council – Pellegrino, De Rosa, Carrafini, Cattaneo and Altana – all raised their hands.

'And are we also agreed on the sum of money we should offer him?'

The five hands were raised once again, without a murmur of dissent.

'But do you think it will be enough?' asked Pellegrino, as there was a knock on the door.

'I suspect we're about to find out,' said the mayor as Antonio entered the room, surprised to find the whole council awaiting him. Farinelli nodded towards the empty seat at the other end of the table.

Once Antonio had poured himself a glass of water and sat back, the mayor said, 'We've just finished our first meeting of the new council, and wondered if you would bring us up to date on how your investigation is progressing.'

'Although I don't have sufficient proof, Mr Mayor, I'm fairly sure I now know who killed Lombardi.' His eyes remained fixed on the person seated at the other end of the table. 'However, despite my suspicions, I've been instructed by my chief to close the case and return to Naples.'

Antonio couldn't have missed the collective sigh of relief from those seated around the table.

'I am sure your chief has made a wise decision,' said the mayor. 'However, I confess,' he paused as Antonio continued to stare at him, 'that wasn't the reason we wanted to see you. As you probably know, Lieutenant, Luca Gentile has recently been in touch to let us know that he will not be returning to Cortoglia for personal reasons, and the Consiglio voted unanimously to offer you the position of chief of police.'

'But the town has only ever had one policeman.'

'Yes,' said De Rosa, 'but we all also felt with so many murderers on the loose, you ought to have a deputy.'

'But there's barely enough space for one officer in the police station. There's only one desk and there isn't even a lock on the cell door.'

'True, but then we've never needed one in the past,' said Pellegrino. 'However, the council have agreed we should build a new police station, worthy of your status.'

'But—'

'We'd also be happy for you to go on living in your present accommodation,' Cattaneo interjected.

'That's incredibly generous, but I still feel—'

'And we'd pay you the same amount as the chief of police in Naples,' Farinelli said, hoping to close the deal.

'That's more than generous—' began Antonio.

'However,' the mayor continued, 'although we didn't put it to a vote, there is one thing we all felt strongly about. If you were able to marry a local girl . . .'

Several guests, including Antonio's parents and brother, arrived from Naples on the morning of Antonio Rossetti and Francesca Farinelli's wedding.

However, Antonio assured the mayor they would all be leaving the next day.

The whole town turned out to witness the vows of eternal love sworn by the couple, including several locals who hadn't been invited. When il Signor and la Signora Rossetti left the wedding celebrations to set off for Venice, Antonio suspected the festivities would still be going on when they returned home in a fortnight's time.

The newly-weds spent their honeymoon in Venice, eating too much spaghetti alle vongole, and drinking too much wine, while still finding a way of not putting on too much weight.

On the final night Antonio sat up in bed and watched his wife undress. When she slipped under the covers to join him, he took her in his arms.

'It's been the most wonderful fortnight, my darling,' Francesca said. 'So many memories to share with everyone when we get back home.'

'Including your feeble effort to climb St Mark's, while pretending you weren't out of breath when you finally reached the top.'

'That hardly compares to your pathetic attempt to manoeuvre a gondola under the Bridge of Sighs, despite the gondolier pointing out that it was the widest stretch of water on the canal.'

'Don't tell anyone!'

'I have photographs,' Francesca teased.

'But I confess the highlight was this evening's candlelit dinner at Harry's Bar overlooking the Rialto.'

'Memorable,' sighed Francesca as she kissed him, 'but if Gian Lucio was to open a restaurant in Venice, they'd have a genuine rival.'

'If you'd only come to Naples, Francesca, I would introduce you to one or two restaurants you might enjoy just as much.'

'Perhaps I'll come for lunch one day. Although

I confess I'm looking forward to getting back to Cortoglia.'

'Me too,' admitted Toni. 'And I wouldn't be surprised to find they're all still in the market square celebrating.'

'Let's just hope no one's murdered my father.'

'Not least because I still haven't solved the mystery of who killed the last mayor. Come to think of it, you're about the only person who didn't confess to murdering Lombardi.'

'I was going to when you first visited the pharmacy. But you seemed more interested in trying to pick me up.'

Toni laughed. 'Then all I need to know, my darling, is how you killed Lombardi?'

'A spoonful of cyanide dropped into his coffee after dinner, just before he went to bed. A slow and painful death, but no more than he deserved.'

Antonio sat bolt upright and stared at his wife.

'And I don't have to remind you, my darling,' continued Francesca, 'that in Italy, a man cannot give evidence against his wife.'

It Can't Be October Already

PATRICK O'FLYNN stood in front of H. Samuel, the jeweller's, holding a brick in his right hand. He was staring intently at the window. He smiled, raised his arm and hurled the brick at the glass pane. The window shattered like a spider's web, but remained firmly in place. An alarm was immediately set off, which in the still of a clear, cold October night could be heard half a mile away. More important to Pat, the alarm was directly connected to the local police station.

Pat didn't move as he continued to stare at his handiwork. He only had to wait ninety seconds before he heard the sound of a siren in the distance. He bent down and retrieved the brick from the pavement, as the whining noise grew louder and louder. When the police car came to a screeching halt by the kerbside, Pat raised the brick above his head and leant back, like an Olympic javelin thrower intent on a gold medal. Two policemen leapt out of the car. The older one ignored Pat, who remained poised, arm above his head with the brick in his hand, and walked across to the window to check the damage. Although the pane was shattered, it was still firmly in place. In any case, an iron security grille had descended behind the window, something Pat knew full well would happen. But when the sergeant returned to the station, he would still have to phone the manager, get him out of bed and ask him to come down to the shop and turn off the alarm.

The sergeant turned round to find Pat still standing with the brick high above his head.

'OK, Pat, hand it over and get in,' said the sergeant, as he held open the back door of the police car.

Pat smiled, passed the brick to the fresh-faced constable and said, 'You'll need this as evidence.'

The young constable was speechless.

'Thank you, Sergeant,' said Pat as he climbed into the back of the car, and, smiling at the young constable, who took his place behind the wheel, asked, 'Have I ever told you about the time I tried to get a job on a building site in Liverpool?'

'Many times,' interjected the sergeant, as he took his place next to Pat and pulled the back door closed.

'No handcuffs?' queried Pat.

'I don't want to be handcuffed to you,' said the sergeant, 'I want to be rid of you. Why don't you just go back to Ireland?'

'An altogether inferior class of prison,' Pat explained, 'and in any case, they don't treat me with the same degree of respect as you do, Sergeant,' he added, as the car moved away from the kerb and headed back towards the police station.

'Can you tell me your name?' Pat asked, leaning forward to address the young constable.

'Constable Cooper.'

'Are you by any chance related to Chief Inspector Cooper?'

'He's my father.'

'A gentleman,' said Pat. 'We've had many a cup of tea and biscuits together. I hope he's in fine fettle.'

'He's just retired,' said Constable Cooper.

'I'm sorry to hear that,' said Pat. 'Will you tell him that Pat O'Flynn asked after him? And please send him, and your dear mother, my best wishes.'

'Stop taking the piss, Pat,' said the sergeant. 'The boy's only been out of Peel House for a few weeks,' he added, as the car came to a halt outside the police station. The sergeant climbed out of the back and held the door open for Pat.

'Thank you, Sergeant,' said Pat, as if he was addressing the doorman at the Ritz. The constable grinned as the sergeant accompanied Pat up the stairs and into the police station.

'Ah, and a very good evening to you, Mr Baker,' said Pat when he saw who it was standing behind the desk.

'Oh, Christ,' said the duty sergeant. 'It can't be October already.'

'I'm afraid so, Sergeant,' said Pat. 'I was wondering if my usual cell is available. I'll only be staying overnight, you understand.'

'I'm afraid not,' said the desk sergeant, 'it's already occupied by a real criminal. You'll have to be satisfied with cell number two.'

'But I've always had cell number one in the past,' protested Pat.

The desk sergeant looked up and raised an eyebrow.

'No, I'm to blame,' admitted Pat. 'I should have asked my secretary to call and book in advance. Do you need to take an imprint of my credit card?'

'No, I have all your details on file,' the desk sergeant assured him.

'How about fingerprints?'

'Unless you've found a way of removing your old

ones, Pat, I don't think we need another set. But I suppose you'd better sign the charge sheet.'

Pat took the proffered biro and signed on the bottom line with a flourish.

'Take him down to cell number two, Constable.'

'Thank you, Sergeant,' said Pat as he was led away. He stopped, turned around and said, 'I wonder, Sergeant, if you could give me a wake-up call around seven, a cup of tea, Earl Grey preferably, and a copy of the *Irish Times*.'

'Piss off, Pat,' said the desk sergeant, as the constable tried to stifle a laugh.

'Which reminds me,' said Pat, 'have I told you about the time I tried to get a job on a building site in Liverpool, and the foreman—'

'Get him out of my sight, Constable, if you don't want to spend the rest of the month on traffic duty.'

The constable grabbed Pat by the elbow and hurried him downstairs.

'No need to come with me,' said Pat. 'I can find my own way.' This time the constable did laugh as he placed a key in the lock of cell number two. The young policeman unlocked the cell and pulled open the heavy door, allowing Pat to stroll in.

'Thank you, Constable Cooper,' said Pat. 'I look forward to seeing you in the morning.'

'I'll be off duty,' said Constable Cooper.

'Then I'll see you this time next year,' said Pat without explanation, 'and don't forget to pass on my best wishes to your father,' he added as the four-inch-thick iron door was slammed shut.

Pat studied the cell for a few moments: a steel washbasin, a bog and a bed, one sheet, one blanket and one pillow. Pat was reassured by the fact that nothing had changed since last year. He fell on the horsehair mattress, placed his head on the rock-hard pillow and slept all night – for the first time in weeks.

Pat was woken from a deep sleep at seven the following morning, when the cell-door flap was flicked open and two black eyes stared in.

'Good morning, Pat,' said a friendly voice.

'Good morning, Wesley,' said Pat, not even opening his eyes. 'And how are you?'

'I'm well,' replied Wesley, 'but sorry to see you back.' He paused. 'I suppose it must be October.'

'It certainly is,' said Pat, climbing off the bed, 'and it's important that I look my best for this morning's show trial.'

'Anything you need in particular?'

'A cup of tea would be most acceptable, but what I really require is a razor, a bar of soap, a toothbrush and some toothpaste. I don't have to remind you, Wesley, that a defendant is entitled to this simple request before he makes an appearance in court.'

'I'll see you get them,' said Wesley, 'and would you like to read my copy of the *Sun*?'

'That's kind of you, Wesley, but if the chief superintendent has finished with yesterday's *Times*, I'd prefer that.' A West Indian chuckle was followed by the closing of the shutter on the cell door.

Pat didn't have to wait long before he heard a key turn in the lock. The heavy door was pulled open to reveal the smiling face of Wesley Pickett, a tray in one hand, which he placed on the end of the bed.

'Thank you, Wesley,' said Pat as he stared down at the bowl of cornflakes, small carton of skimmed milk, two slices of burnt toast and a boiled egg. 'I do hope Molly remembered,' added

Pat, 'that I like my eggs lightly boiled, for two and a half minutes.'

'Molly left last year,' said Wesley. 'I think you'll find the egg was boiled last night by the desk sergeant.'

'You can't get the staff nowadays,' said Pat. 'I blame it on the Irish, myself. They're no longer committed to domestic service,' he added as he tapped the top of his egg with a plastic spoon. 'Wesley, have I told you about the time I tried to get a labouring job on a building site in Liverpool, and the foreman, a bloody Englishman—' Pat looked up and sighed as he heard the door slam and the key turn in the lock. 'I suppose I must have told him the story before,' he muttered to himself.

After Pat had finished breakfast, he cleaned his teeth with a toothbrush and a tube of toothpaste that were even smaller than the ones they'd supplied on his only experience of an Aer Lingus flight to Dublin. Next, he turned on the hot tap in the tiny steel wash-

basin. The slow trickle of water took some time to turn from cold to lukewarm. He rubbed the mean piece of soap between his fingers until he'd whipped up enough cream to produce a lather, which he then smeared all over his stubbled face. Next he picked up the plastic Bic razor, and began the slow process of removing a four-day-old stubble. He finally dabbed his face with a rough green hand towel, not much larger than a flannel.

Pat sat on the end of the bed and, while he waited, read Wesley's *Sun* from cover to cover in four minutes. Only an article by their political editor Trevor Kavanagh – he must surely be an Irishman, thought Pat – was worthy of his attention. Pat's thoughts were interrupted when the heavy metal door was pulled open once again.

'Let's be 'avin you, Pat,' said Sergeant Webster. 'You're first on this morning.'

Pat accompanied the officer back up the stairs, and when he saw the desk sergeant, asked, 'Could I have my valuables back, Mr Baker? You'll find them in the safe.'

'Like what?' said the desk sergeant, looking up.

'My pearl cufflinks, the Cartier Tank watch and a silver-topped cane engraved with my family crest.'

'I flogged 'em all off last night, Pat,' said the desk sergeant.

'Probably for the best,' remarked Pat. 'I won't be needing them where I'm going,' he added, before following Sergeant Webster out of the front door and onto the pavement.

'Jump in the front,' said the sergeant, as he climbed behind the wheel of a panda car.

'But I'm entitled to two officers to escort me to court,' insisted Pat. 'It's a Home Office regulation.'

'It may well be a Home Office regulation,' the ser-geant replied, 'but we're short-staffed this morning, two off sick, and one away on a training course.'

'But what if I tried to escape?'

'A blessed release,' said Sergeant Webster, as he pulled away from the kerb, 'because that would save us all a lot of trouble.'

'And what would you do if I decided to punch you?'

'I'd punch you back,' said an exasperated sergeant.

'That's not very friendly,' suggested Pat.

'Sorry, Pat,' said the sergeant. 'It's just that I promised my wife that I'd be off duty by ten this morning, so we could go shopping.' He paused. 'So she won't be best pleased with me – or you for that matter.'

'I apologize, Sergeant Webster,' said Pat. 'Next October I'll try to find out which shift you're on, so I can be sure to avoid it. Perhaps you'd pass on my apologies to Mrs Webster.'

The sergeant would have laughed, if it had been anyone else, but he knew Pat meant it.

'Any idea who I'll be up in front of this morning?' asked Pat as the car came to a halt at a set of traffic lights.

'Thursday,' said the sergeant, as the lights turned green and he pushed the gear lever back into first. 'It must be Perkins.'

'Councillor Arnold Perkins OBE, oh good,' said Pat. 'He's got a very short fuse. So if he doesn't give me a long enough sentence, I'll just have to light it,' he added as the car swung into the private carpark at the back of Marylebone Road Magistrates' Court. A court officer was heading towards the police car just as Pat stepped out.

'Good morning, Mr Adams,' said Pat.

'When I looked at the list of defendants this morning, Pat, and saw your name,' said Mr Adams, 'I assumed it must be that time of the year when you make your annual appearance. Follow me, Pat, and let's get this over with as quickly as possible.'

Pat accompanied Mr Adams through the back door of the courthouse and on down the long corridor to a holding cell.

'Thank you, Mr Adams,' said Pat as he took a seat on a thin wooden bench that was cemented to a wall along one side of the large oblong room. 'If you'd be kind enough to just leave me for a few moments,' Pat added, 'so that I can compose myself before the curtain goes up.'

Mr Adams smiled, and turned to leave.

'By the way,' said Pat, as Mr Adams touched the handle of the door, 'did I tell you about the time I tried to get a labouring job on a building site in Liverpool, but the foreman, a bloody Englishman, had the nerve to ask me—'

'Sorry, Pat, some of us have got a job to do, and in any case, you told me that story last October.' He paused. 'And, come to think of it, the October before.'

Pat sat silently on the bench and, as he had nothing else to read, considered the graffiti on the wall. *Perkins is a prat.* He felt able to agree with that sentiment. *Man U are the champions.* Someone had crossed out *Man U* and replaced it with *Chelsea.* Pat wondered if he should cross out Chelsea, and write in Cork, whom neither team had ever defeated. As there was no clock on the wall, Pat couldn't be sure how much time had passed before Mr Adams finally returned to escort him up to the courtroom. Adams was now dressed in a long black gown, looking like Pat's old headmaster.

'Follow me,' Mr Adams intoned solemnly.

Pat remained unusually silent as they proceeded down the yellow brick road, as the old lags call the last few yards before you climb the steps and enter the back door of the court. Pat ended up standing in the dock, with a bailiff by his side.

Pat stared up at the bench and looked at the three magistrates who made up this morning's panel. Something was wrong. He had been expecting to see Mr Perkins, who had been bald this time last year, almost Pickwickian. Now, suddenly, he seemed to have sprouted a head of fair hair. On his right was Councillor Steadman, a liberal, who was much too lenient for Pat's liking. On the chairman's left sat a middle-aged lady whom Pat had never seen before; her thin lips and piggy eyes gave Pat a little confidence that the liberal could be outvoted two to one, especially if he played his cards right. Miss Piggy looked as if she would have happily supported capital punishment for shoplifters.

Sergeant Webster stepped into the witness box and took the oath.

'What can you tell us about this case, Sergeant?' Mr Perkins asked, once the oath had been administered.

'May I refer to my notes, your honour?' asked Sergeant Webster, turning to face the chairman of the panel. Mr Perkins nodded, and the sergeant turned over the cover of his notepad.

'I apprehended the defendant at two o'clock this morning, after he had thrown a brick at the window of H. Samuel, the jeweller's, on Mason Street.'

'Did you see him throw the brick, Sergeant?'

'No, I did not,' admitted Webster, 'but he was standing on the pavement with the brick in his hand when I apprehended him.'

'And had he managed to gain entry?' asked Perkins.

'No, sir,' said the sergeant, 'but he was about to throw the brick again when I arrested him.'

'The same brick?'

'I think so.'

'And had he done any damage?'

'He had shattered the glass, but a security grille prevented him from removing anything.'

'How valuable were the goods in the window?' asked Mr Perkins.

'There were no goods in the window,' replied the

sergeant, 'because the manager always locks them up in the safe, before going home at night.'

Mr Perkins looked puzzled and, glancing down at the charge sheet, said, 'I see you have charged O'Flynn with attempting to break and enter.'

'That is correct, sir,' said Sergeant Webster, returning his notebook to a back pocket of his trousers.

Mr Perkins turned his attention to Pat. 'I note that you have entered a plea of guilty on the charge sheet, O'Flynn.'

'Yes, m'lord.'

'Then I'll have to sentence you to three months, unless you can offer some explanation.' He paused and looked down at Pat over the top of his half-moon spectacles. 'Do you wish to make a statement?' he asked.

'Three months is not enough, m'lord.'

'I am not a lord,' said Mr Perkins firmly.

'Oh, aren't you?' said Pat. 'It's just that I thought as you were wearing a wig, which you didn't have this time last year, you must be a lord.'

'Watch your tongue,' said Mr Perkins, 'or I may have to consider putting your sentence up to six months.'

'That's more like it, m'lord,' said Pat.

'If that's more like it,' said Mr Perkins, barely able to control his temper, 'then I sentence you to six months. Take the prisoner down.'

'Thank you, m'lord,' said Pat, and added under his breath, 'see you this time next year.'

The bailiff hustled Pat out of the dock and quickly down the stairs to the basement.

'Nice one, Pat,' he said before locking him back up in a holding cell.

Pat remained in the holding cell while he waited for all the necessary forms to be filled in. Several hours passed before the cell door was finally opened

and he was escorted out of the courthouse to his waiting transport; not on this occasion a panda car driven by Sergeant Webster, but a long blue-and-white van with a dozen tiny cubicles inside, known as the sweat box.

'Where are they taking me this time?' Pat asked a not very communicative officer whom he'd never seen before.

'You'll find out when you get there, Paddy,' was all he got in reply.

'Have I ever told you about the time I tried to get a job on a building site in Liverpool?'

'No,' replied the officer, 'and I don't want to 'ear—'

'—and the foreman, a bloody Englishman, had the nerve to ask me if I knew the difference between a—' Pat was shoved up the steps of the van and pushed into a little cubicle that resembled a lavatory on a plane. He fell onto the plastic seat as the door was slammed behind him.

Pat stared out of the tiny square window, and when the vehicle turned south onto Baker Street, realized it had to be Belmarsh. Pat sighed. At least they've got a half-decent library, he thought, and I may even be able to get back my old job in the kitchen.

When the Black Maria pulled up outside the prison gates, his guess was confirmed. A large green board attached to the prison gate announced BELMARSH, and some wag had replaced BEL with HELL. The van proceeded through one set of double-barred gates, and then another, before finally coming to a halt in a barren yard.

Twelve prisoners were herded out of the van and marched up the steps to an induction area, where they waited in line. Pat smiled when he reached the front of the queue and saw who was behind the desk, checking them all in.

'And how are we this fine pleasant evening, Mr Jenkins?' Pat asked.

The Senior Officer looked up from behind his desk and said, 'It can't be October already.'

'It most certainly is, Mr Jenkins,' Pat confirmed, 'and may I offer my commiserations on your recent loss.'

'My recent loss,' repeated Mr Jenkins. 'What are you talking about, Pat?'

'Those fifteen Welshmen who appeared in Dublin earlier this year, passing themselves off as a rugby team.'

'Don't push your luck, Pat.'

'Would I, Mr Jenkins, when I was hoping that you would allocate me my old cell?'

The SO ran his finger down the list of available cells. ''Fraid not, Pat,' he said with an exaggerated sigh, 'it's

already double-booked. But I've got just the person for you to spend your first night with,' he added, before turning to the night officer. 'Why don't you escort O'Flynn to cell one nineteen.'

The night officer looked uncertain, but after a further look from Mr Jenkins, all he said was, 'Follow me, Pat.'

'So who has Mr Jenkins selected to be my pad mate on this occasion?' enquired Pat, as the night officer accompanied him down the long, grey-brick corridor before coming to a halt at the first set of double-barred gates. 'Is it to be Jack the Ripper, or Michael Jackson?'

'You'll find out soon enough,' responded the night officer as the second of the barred gates slid open.

'Have I ever told you,' asked Pat, as they walked out on to the ground floor of B block, 'about the time I tried to get a job on a building site in Liverpool, and the foreman, a bloody Englishman, had the nerve to ask me if I knew the difference between a joist and a girder?'

Pat waited for the officer to respond, as they came to a halt outside cell number 119. He placed a large key in the lock.

'No, Pat, you haven't,' the night officer said as he pulled open the heavy door. 'So what is the difference between a joist and a girder?' he demanded.

Pat was about to reply, but when he looked into the cell was momentarily silenced.

'Good evening, m'lord,' said Pat, for the second time that day. The night officer didn't wait for a reply. He slammed the door closed, and turned the key in the lock.

Pat spent the rest of the evening telling me, in graphic detail, all that had taken place since two o'clock that morning. When he had finally come to the end of his tale, I simply asked, 'Why October?'

'Once the clocks go back,' said Pat, 'I prefer to be inside, where I'm guaranteed three meals a day and a cell with central heating. Sleeping rough is all very well in the summer, but it's not so clever during an English winter.'

'But what would you have done if Mr Perkins had sentenced you to a year?' I asked.

'I'd have been on my best behaviour from day one,' said Pat, 'and they would have released me in six months. They have a real problem with overcrowding at the moment,' he explained.

'But if Mr Perkins had stuck to his original sentence of just three months, you would have been released in January, mid-winter.'

'Not a hope,' said Pat. 'Just before I was due to be let out, I would have been found with a bottle of Guinness in my cell. A misdemeanour for which the

governor is obliged to automatically add a further three months to your sentence, and that would have taken me comfortably through to April.'

I laughed. 'And is that how you intend to spend the rest of your life?' I asked.

'I don't think that far ahead,' admitted Pat. 'Six months is quite enough to be going on with,' he added, as he climbed on to the top bunk and switched off the light.

'Goodnight, Pat,' I said, as I rested my head on the pillow.

'Have I ever told you about the time I tried to get a job on a building site in Liverpool?' asked Pat, just as I was falling asleep.

'No, you haven't,' I replied.

'Well, the foreman, a bloody Englishman, no offence intended –' I smiled – 'had the nerve to ask me if I knew the difference between a joist and a girder.'

'And do you?' I asked.

'I most certainly do. Joyce wrote *Ulysses*, and Goethe wrote *Faust*.'

~

Patrick O'Flynn died of hypothermia on 23 November 2005, while sleeping under the arches on Victoria Embankment in central London.

His body was discovered by a young constable, just a hundred yards away from the Savoy Hotel.

Stuck on You

JEREMY LOOKED ACROSS the table at Arabella and still couldn't believe she had agreed to be his wife. He was the luckiest man in the world.

She was giving him the shy smile that had so entranced him the first time they met, when a waiter appeared by his side. 'I'll have an espresso,' said Jeremy, 'and my fiancée' – it still sounded strange to him – 'will have a mint tea.'

'Very good, sir.'

Jeremy tried to stop himself looking around the room full of 'at home' people who knew exactly where they were and what was expected of them, whereas he had never visited the Ritz before. It became clear from the waves and blown kisses from customers who flitted in and out of the morning room that Arabella knew everyone, from the maître d' to several of 'the set', as she often referred to them. Jeremy sat back and tried to relax.

They'd first met at Ascot. Arabella was inside the royal enclosure looking out, while Jeremy was on the outside, looking in; that was how he'd assumed it would always be, until she gave him that beguiling smile as she strolled out of the enclosure and whispered as she passed him, 'Put your shirt on Trumpeter.' She then disappeared off in the direction of the private boxes.

Jeremy took her advice, and placed twenty pounds on Trumpeter – double his usual wager – before returning to the stands to see the horse romp home at 5–1. He hurried back to the royal enclosure to thank her, at the same time hoping she might give him another tip for the next race, but she was nowhere to be seen. He was disappointed, but still placed fifty pounds of his winnings on a horse the *Daily Express* tipster fancied. It turned out to be a nag that would be described in tomorrow's paper as an 'also-ran'.

Jeremy returned to the royal enclosure for a third time in the hope of seeing her again. He searched the paddock full of elegant men dressed in morning suits with little enclosure badges hanging from their lapels, all looking exactly like each other. They were accompanied by wives and girlfriends adorned in designer dresses and outrageous hats, desperately trying not to look like anyone else. Then he spotted her, standing next to a tall, aristocratic-looking man who was bending down and listening intently to a jockey dressed in red-and-yellow hooped silks. She didn't appear to be interested in their conversation and began to look around. Her eyes settled on Jeremy and he received that same friendly smile once again. She whispered something to the tall man, then walked across the enclosure to join him at the railing.

'I hope you took my advice,' she said.

'Sure did,' said Jeremy. 'But how could you be so confident?'

'It's my father's horse.'

'Should I back your father's horse in the next race?'

'Certainly not. You should never bet on anything unless you're sure it's a certainty. I hope you won enough to take me to dinner tonight?'

If Jeremy didn't reply immediately, it was only because he couldn't believe he'd heard her correctly. He eventually stammered out, 'Where would you like to go?'

'The Ivy, eight o'clock. By the way, my name's Arabella Warwick.' Without another word she turned on her heel and went back to join her set.

Jeremy was surprised Arabella had given him a second look, let alone suggested they should dine together that evening. He expected that nothing would come of it, but as she'd already paid for dinner, he had nothing to lose.

Arabella arrived a few minutes after the appointed hour, and when she entered the restaurant, several pairs of male eyes followed her progress as she made her way to Jeremy's table. He had been told they were fully booked until he mentioned her name. Jeremy rose from his place long before she joined him. She took the seat opposite him as a waiter appeared by her side.

'The usual, madam?'

She nodded, but didn't take her eyes off Jeremy.

By the time her Bellini had arrived, Jeremy had begun to relax a little. She listened intently to everything he had to say, laughed at his jokes, and even seemed to be interested in his work at the bank. Well, he had slightly exaggerated his position and the size of the deals he was working on.

After dinner, which was a little more expensive than he'd anticipated, he drove her back to her home in Pavilion Road, and was surprised when she invited him in for coffee, and even more surprised when they ended up in bed.

Jeremy had never slept with a woman on a first date before. He could only assume that it was what 'the set' did, and when he left the next morning, he certainly didn't expect ever to hear from her again. But she called that afternoon and invited him over for supper at her place. From that moment, they hardly spent a day apart during the next month.

What pleased Jeremy most was that Arabella didn't seem to mind that he couldn't afford to take her to her usual haunts, and appeared quite happy to share a Chinese or Indian meal when they went out for dinner, often insisting that they split the bill. But he didn't believe it could last, until one night she said, 'You do realize I'm in love with you, don't you, Jeremy?'

Jeremy had never expressed his true feelings for Arabella. He'd assumed their relationship was nothing more than what her set would describe as a fling. Not that she'd ever introduced him to anyone from her set. When he fell on one knee and proposed to her on the dance floor at Annabel's, he couldn't believe it when she said yes.

'I'll buy a ring tomorrow,' he said, trying not to think about the parlous state of his bank account, which had turned a deeper shade of red since he'd met Arabella.

'Why bother to buy one, when you can steal the best there is?' she said.

Jeremy burst out laughing, but it quickly became clear Arabella wasn't joking. That was the moment he should have walked away, but he realized he couldn't if it meant losing her. He knew he wanted to spend the rest of his life with this beautiful and intoxicating woman, and if stealing a ring was what it took, it seemed a small price to pay.

'What type shall I steal?' he asked, still not altogether sure that she was serious.

'The expensive type,' she replied. 'In fact, I've already chosen the one I want.' She passed him a De Beers catalogue. 'Page forty-three,' she said. 'It's called the Kandice Diamond.'

'But have you worked out how I'm going to steal it?' asked Jeremy, studying a photograph of the faultless yellow diamond.

'Oh, that's the easy part, darling,' she said. 'All you'll have to do is follow my instructions.'

Jeremy didn't say a word until she'd finished outlining her plan.

That's how he had ended up in the Ritz that morning, wearing his only tailored suit, a pair of Links cufflinks, a Cartier Tank watch and an old Etonian tie, all of which belonged to Arabella's father.

'I'll have to return everything by tonight,' she said, 'otherwise Pa might miss them and start asking questions.'

'Of course,' said Jeremy, who was enjoying becoming acquainted with the trappings of the rich, even if it was only a fleeting acquaintance.

The waiter returned, carrying a silver tray. Neither of them spoke as he placed a cup of mint tea in front of Arabella and a pot of coffee on Jeremy's side of the table.

'Will there be anything else, sir?'

'No, thank you,' said Jeremy with an assurance he'd acquired during the past month.

'Do you think you're ready?' asked Arabella, her knee brushing against the inside of his leg while she once again gave him the smile that had so captivated him at Ascot.

out another word, walked out of the morning room, across the corridor, through the swing doors and out on to Piccadilly. He placed a stick of chewing gum in his mouth, hoping it would help him to relax. Normally Arabella would have disapproved, but on this occasion she had recommended it. He stood nervously on the pavement and waited for a gap to appear in the traffic, then nipped across the road, coming to a halt outside De Beers, the largest diamond merchant in the world. This was his last chance to walk away. He knew he should take it, but just the thought of her made it impossible.

He rang the doorbell, which made him aware that his palms were sweating. Arabella had warned him that you couldn't just stroll into De Beers as if it was a supermarket, and that if they didn't like the look of you, they would not even open the door. That was why he had been measured for his first hand-tailored suit and acquired a new silk shirt, and was wearing Arabella's father's watch, cufflinks and old Etonian tie. 'The tie will ensure that the door is opened immediately,' Arabella had told him, 'and once they spot the watch and the

'I'm ready,' said Jeremy, trying to sound convincing.

'Good. I'll wait here until you return, darling.' That same smile. 'You know how much this means to me.'

Jeremy nodded, rose from his place and, with-

cufflinks, you'll be invited into the private salon, because by then they'll be convinced you're one of the rare people who can afford their wares.'

Arabella turned out to be correct, because when the doorman appeared, he took one look at Jeremy and immediately unlocked the door.

'Good morning, sir. How may I help you?'

'I was hoping to buy an engagement ring.'

'Of course, sir. Please step inside.'

Jeremy followed him down a long corridor, glancing at photographs on the walls that depicted the history of the company since its foundation in 1888. Once they had reached the end of the corridor, the doorman melted away, to be replaced by a tall, middle-aged man wearing a well-cut dark suit, a white silk shirt and a black tie.

'Good morning, sir,' he said, giving a slight bow. 'My name is Crombie,' he added, before ushering Jeremy into his private lair. Jeremy walked into a small, well-lit room. In the centre was an oval table covered in a black velvet cloth, with comfortable-looking leather chairs on either side. The assistant waited until Jeremy had sat down before he took the seat opposite him.

'Would you care for some coffee, sir?' Crombie enquired solicitously.

'No, thank you,' said Jeremy, who had no desire to hold up proceedings any longer than necessary, for fear he might lose his nerve.

'And how may I help you today, sir?' Crombie asked, as if Jeremy were a regular customer.

'I've just become engaged . . .'

'Many congratulations, sir.'

'Thank you,' said Jeremy, beginning to feel a little more relaxed. 'I'm looking for a ring, something a bit special,' he added, still sticking to the script.

'You've certainly come to the right place, sir,' said Crombie, and pressed a button under the table.

The door opened immediately, and a man in an identical dark suit, white shirt and dark tie entered the room.

'The gentleman would like to see some engagement rings, Partridge.'

'Yes, of course, Mr Crombie,' replied the porter, and disappeared as quickly as he had arrived.

'Good weather for this time of year,' said Crombie as he waited for the porter to reappear.

'Not bad,' said Jeremy.

'No doubt you'll be going to Wimbledon, sir.'

'Yes, we've got tickets for the women's semi-finals,' said Jeremy, feeling rather pleased with himself, remembering that he'd strayed off script.

A moment later, the door opened and the porter reappeared carrying a large oak box which he placed reverentially in the centre of the table, before leaving without uttering a word. Crombie waited until the door had closed before selecting a small key from a chain that hung from the waistband of his trousers, unlocking the box and opening the lid slowly to reveal three rows of assorted gems that took Jeremy's breath away. Definitely not the sort of thing he was used to seeing in the window of his local H. Samuel.

It was a few moments before he fully recovered, and then he remembered Arabella telling him he would be presented with a wide choice of stones so the salesman could estimate his price range without having to ask him directly.

Jeremy studied the box's contents intently, and after some thought selected a ring from the bottom row with three perfectly cut small emeralds set proud on a gold band.

'Quite beautiful,' said Jeremy as he studied the stones more carefully. 'What is the price of this ring?'

'One hundred and twenty-four thousand, sir,' said Crombie, as if the amount was of little consequence.

Jeremy placed the ring back in the box, and turned his attention to the row above. This time he selected a ring with a circle of sapphires on a white-gold band.

He removed it from the box and pretended to study it more closely before asking the price.

'Two hundred and sixty-nine thousand pounds,' replied the same unctuous voice, accompanied by a smile that suggested the customer was heading in the right direction.

Jeremy replaced the ring and turned his attention to a large single diamond that lodged alone in the top row, leaving no doubt of its superiority. He removed it and, as with the others, studied it closely. 'And this magnificent stone,' he said, raising an eyebrow. 'Can you tell me a little about its provenance?'

'I can indeed, sir,' said Crombie. 'It's a flawless, eighteen-point-four carat cushion-cut yellow diamond that was recently extracted from our Rhodes mine. It has been certified by the Gemmological Institute of America as a Fancy Intense Yellow, and was cut from the original stone by one of our master craftsmen in Amsterdam. The stone has been set on a platinum band. I can assure sir that it is quite unique, and therefore worthy of a unique lady.'

Jeremy had a feeling that Mr Crombie might just have delivered that line before. 'No doubt there's a quite unique price to go with it.' He handed the ring to Crombie, who placed it back in the box.

'Eight hundred and fifty-four thousand pounds,' he said in a hushed voice.

'Do you have a loupe?' asked Jeremy. 'I'd like to study the stone more closely.' Arabella had taught him the word diamond merchants use when referring to a small magnifying glass, assuring him that it would make him sound as if he regularly frequented such establishments.

'Yes, of course, sir,' said Crombie, pulling open a drawer on his side of the table and extracting a small tortoiseshell loupe. When he looked back up, there was no sign of the Kandice Diamond, just a gaping space in the top row of the box.

'Do you still have the ring?' he asked, trying not to sound concerned.

'No,' said Jeremy. 'I handed it back to you a moment ago.'

Without another word, the assistant snapped the box closed and pressed the button below his side of the table. This time he didn't indulge in any small talk while he waited. A moment later, two burly, flat-nosed men who looked as if they'd be more at home in a boxing ring than De Beers entered the room. One remained by the door while the other stood a few inches behind Jeremy.

'Perhaps you'd be kind enough to return the ring,' said Crombie in a firm, flat, unemotional voice.

'I've never been so insulted,' said Jeremy, trying to sound insulted.

'I'm going to say this only once, sir. If you return the ring, we will not press charges, but if you do not—'

'And I'm going to say this only once,' said Jeremy, rising from his seat. 'The last time I saw the ring was when I handed it back to you.'

Jeremy turned to leave, but the man behind him placed a hand firmly on his shoulder and pushed him back down into the chair. Arabella had promised him there would be no rough stuff as long as he cooperated and did exactly what they told him. Jeremy remained seated, not moving a muscle. Crombie rose from his place and said, 'Please follow me.'

One of the heavyweights opened the door and led Jeremy out of the room, while the other remained a pace behind him. At the end of the corridor they stopped outside a door marked 'Private'. The first guard opened the door and they entered another room which once again contained only one table, but this time it wasn't covered in a velvet cloth. Behind it sat a man who looked as if he'd been waiting for them. He didn't invite Jeremy to sit, as there wasn't another chair in the room.

'My name is Granger,' the man said without expression. 'I've been the head of security at De Beers for the past fourteen years, having previously served as a detective inspector with the Metropolitan Police. I can tell you there's nothing I haven't seen, and no story I haven't heard before. So do not imagine even

for one moment that you're going to get away with this, young man.'

How quickly the fawning *sir* had been replaced by the demeaning *young man*, thought Jeremy.

Granger paused to allow the full weight of his words to sink in. 'First, I am obliged to ask if you are willing to assist me with my enquiries, or whether you would prefer us to call in the police, in which case you will be entitled to have a solicitor present.'

'I have nothing to hide,' said Jeremy haughtily, 'so naturally I'm happy to cooperate.' Back on script.

'In that case,' said Granger, 'perhaps you'd be kind enough to take off your shoes, jacket and trousers.'

Jeremy kicked off his loafers, which Granger picked up and placed on the table. He then removed his jacket and handed it to Granger as if he was his valet. After taking off his trousers he stood there, trying to look appalled at the treatment he was being subjected to.

Granger spent some considerable time pulling out every pocket of Jeremy's suit, then checking the lining and the seams.

Having failed to come up with anything other than a handkerchief – there was no wallet, no credit card, nothing that could identify the suspect, which made him even more suspicious – Granger placed the suit back on the table. 'Your tie?' he said, still sounding calm.

Jeremy undid the knot, pulled off the old Etonian tie and put it on the table. Granger ran the palm of his right hand across the blue stripes, but again, nothing. 'Your shirt.' Jeremy undid the buttons slowly, then handed his shirt over. He stood there shivering in just his pants and socks.

As Granger checked the shirt, for the first time the hint of a smile appeared on his lined face when he touched the collar. He pulled out two silver Tif-

fany collar stiffeners. Nice touch, Arabella, thought Jeremy as Granger placed them on the table, unable to mask his disappointment. He handed the shirt back to Jeremy, who replaced the collar stiffeners before putting his shirt and tie back on.

'Your underpants, please.'

Jeremy pulled down his pants and passed them across. Another inspection which he knew would reveal nothing. Granger handed them back and waited for him to pull them up before saying, 'And finally your socks.'

Jeremy pulled off his socks and laid them out on the table. Granger was now looking a little less sure of himself, but he still checked them carefully before turning his attention to Jeremy's loafers. He spent some time tapping, pushing and even trying to pull them apart, but there was nothing to be found. To Jeremy's surprise, he once again asked him to remove his shirt and tie. When he'd done so, Granger came

around from behind the table and stood directly in front of him. He raised both his hands, and for a moment Jeremy thought the man was going to hit him. Instead, he pressed his fingers into Jeremy's scalp and ruffled his hair the way his father used to do when he was a child, but all he ended up with was greasy nails and a few stray hairs for his trouble.

'Raise your arms,' he barked. Jeremy held his arms high in the air, but Granger found nothing under his armpits. He then stood behind Jeremy. 'Raise one leg,' he ordered. Jeremy raised his right leg. There was nothing taped underneath the heel, and nothing between the toes. 'The other leg,' said Granger, but he ended up with the same result. He walked round to face him once again. 'Open your mouth.' Jeremy opened wide as if he was in the dentist's chair. Granger shone a pen-torch around his cavities, but didn't find so much as a gold tooth. He could not hide his discomfort as he asked Jeremy to accompany him to the room next door.

'May I put my clothes back on?'

'No, you may not,' came back the immediate reply.

Jeremy followed him into the next room, feeling apprehensive about what torture they had in store for him. A man in a long white coat stood waiting next to what looked like a sun bed. 'Would you be kind enough to lie down so that I can take an X-ray?' he asked.

'Happily,' said Jeremy, and climbed on to the

machine. Moments later there was a click and the two men studied the results on a screen. Jeremy knew it would reveal nothing. Swallowing the Kandice Diamond had never been part of their plan.

'Thank you,' said the man in the white coat courteously, and Granger added reluctantly, 'You can get dressed now.'

Once Jeremy had his new school tie on, he followed Granger back into the interrogation room, where Crombie and the two guards were waiting for them.

'I'd like to leave now,' Jeremy said firmly.

Granger nodded, clearly unwilling to let him go, but he no longer had any excuse to hold him. Jeremy turned to face Crombie, looked him straight in the eye and said, 'You'll be hearing from my solicitor.' He thought he saw him grimace. Arabella's script had been flawless.

The two flat-nosed guards escorted him off the premises, looking disappointed that he hadn't tried to escape. As Jeremy stepped back out on to the crowded Piccadilly pavement, he took a deep breath and waited for his heartbeat to return to something like normal before crossing the road. He then strolled confidently back into the Ritz and took his seat opposite Arabella.

'Your coffee's gone cold, darling,' she said, as if he'd just been to the loo. 'Perhaps you should order another.'

'Same again,' said Jeremy when the waiter appeared by his side.

'Any problems?' whispered Arabella once the waiter was out of earshot.

'No,' said Jeremy, suddenly feeling guilty, but at the same time exhilarated. 'It all went to plan.'

'Good,' said Arabella. 'So now it's my turn.' She rose from her seat and said, 'Better give me the watch and the cufflinks. I'll need to put them back in Daddy's room before we meet up this evening.'

Jeremy reluctantly unstrapped the watch, took out the cufflinks and handed them to Arabella. 'What about the tie?' he whispered.

'Better not take it off in the Ritz,' she said. She leaned over and kissed him gently on the lips. 'I'll come to your place around eight, and you can give it back to me then.' She gave him that smile one last time before walking out of the morning room.

A few moments later, Arabella was standing outside De Beers. The door was opened immediately: the Van Cleef & Arpels necklace, the Balenciaga bag and the Chanel watch all suggested that this lady was not in the habit of being kept waiting.

'I want to look at some engagement rings,' she said shyly before stepping inside.

'Of course, madam,' said the doorman, and led her down the corridor.

During the next hour, Arabella carried out almost the same routine as Jeremy, and after much prevarication she told Mr Crombie, 'It's hopeless, quite hopeless. I'll have to bring Archie in. After all, he's the one who's going to foot the bill.'

'Of course, madam.'

'I'm joining him for lunch at Le Caprice,' she added, 'so we'll pop back this afternoon.'

'We'll look forward to seeing you both then,' said the sales associate as he closed the jewel box.

'Thank you, Mr Crombie,' said Arabella as she rose to leave.

Arabella was escorted to the front door by the sales associate without any suggestion that she should take her clothes off. Once she was back on Piccadilly, she hailed a taxi and gave the driver an address in Lowndes Square. She checked her watch, confident that she would be back at the flat long before her father, who would never find out that his watch and cufflinks had been borrowed for a few hours, and who certainly wouldn't miss one of his old school ties.

As she sat in the back of the taxi, Arabella admired

'Goodnight, sir,' said Doris, opening the door to the viewing room so she could continue to vacuum. This was where the customers selected the finest gems on earth, Mr Crombie had once told her, so it had to be spotless. She turned off the machine, removed the black velvet cloth from the table and began to polish the surface; first the top, then the rim. That's when she felt it.

Doris bent down to take a closer look. She stared in disbelief at the large piece of chewing gum stuck under the rim of the table. She began to scrape it off, not stopping until there wasn't the slightest trace of it left, then dropped it into the rubbish bag attached to her cleaning cart before placing the velvet cloth back on the table.

'Such a disgusting habit,' she muttered as she closed the viewing-room door and continued to vacuum the carpet in the corridor.

the flawless yellow diamond. Jeremy had carried out her instructions to the letter. She would of course have to explain to her friends why she'd broken off the engagement. Frankly, he just wasn't one of our set, never really fitted in. But she had to admit she would quite miss him. She'd grown rather fond of Jeremy, and he was very enthusiastic between the sheets. And to think that all he'd get out of it was a pair of silver collar stiffeners and an old Etonian tie. Arabella hoped he still had enough money to cover the bill at the Ritz.

She dismissed Jeremy from her thoughts and turned her attention to the man she'd chosen to join her at Wimbledon, whom she had already lined up to assist her in obtaining a matching pair of earrings.

When Mr Crombie left De Beers that night, he was still trying to work out how the man had managed it. After all, he'd had no more than a few seconds while his head was bowed.

'Goodnight, Doris,' he said as he passed a cleaner who was vacuuming in the corridor.

The Grass is Always Greener

BILL WOKE with a start. It was always the same following a long sleep-in over the weekend. Once the sun had risen on Monday morning they would expect him to move on. He had slept under the archway of Critchley's Bank for more years than most of the staff had worked in the building.

Bill would turn up every evening at around seven o'clock to claim his spot. Not that anyone else would have dared to occupy his pitch after all these years. Over the past decade he had seen them come and go, some with hearts of gold, some silver and some bronze. Most of the bronze ones were only interested in the other kind of gold. He had sussed out which was which, and not just by the way they treated him.

He glanced up at the clock above the door: ten to six. Young Kevin would appear through that door at any moment and ask if he would be kind enough to move on. Good lad, Kevin – often slipped him a bob or two, which must have been a sacrifice, what with another baby on the way. He certainly wouldn't have been treated with the same consideration by most of the posher ones who came in later.

Bill allowed himself a moment to dream. He would have liked to have Kevin's job, dressed in that heavy, warm coat and peaked hat. He would still have been on the street, but with a real job and regular pay. Some people had all the luck. All Kevin had to do was say, 'Good morning, sir. Hope you had a pleasant weekend.' Didn't even have to hold the door open since they'd made it automatic.

But Bill wasn't complaining. It hadn't been too bad a weekend. It didn't rain, and nowadays the police never tried to move him on – not since he'd spotted that IRA man parking his van outside the bank all those years ago. That was his army training.

He'd managed to get hold of a copy of Friday's *Financial Times* and Saturday's *Daily Mail*. The *Financial Times* reminded him that he should have invested in Internet companies and kept out of clothes manufacturers, because their stocks were dropping rapidly following the slowdown in High Street sales. He was probably the only person attached to the bank who read the *Financial Times* from cover to cover, and certainly the only one who then used it as a blanket.

He'd picked up the *Mail* from the bin at the back of the building – amazing what some of those yuppies dropped in that bin. He'd had everything from a Rolex watch to a packet of condoms. Not that he had any use for either. There were quite enough clocks in the City without needing another one, and as for the condoms – not much point in those since he'd left the army. He had sold the watch and given the condoms to Vince, who worked the Bank of America pitch. Vince was always bragging about his latest conquests, which seemed a little unlikely given his circumstances. Bill had decided to call his bluff and give him the condoms as a Christmas present.

The lights were being switched on all over the building, and when Bill glanced through the plate-glass window he spotted Kevin putting on his coat. Time to gather up his belongings and move on: he didn't want to get Kevin into any trouble, on account of the fact he hoped the lad would soon be getting the promotion he deserved.

Bill rolled up his sleeping bag – a present from the Chairman, who hadn't waited until Christmas to give it to him. No, that wasn't Sir William's style. A born gentleman, with an eye for the ladies – and who could blame him? Bill had seen one or two of them go up in the lift late at night, and he doubted if they were seeking advice on their PEPs. Perhaps he should have given *him* the packet of condoms.

He folded up his two blankets – one he'd bought with some of the money from the watch sale, the other he'd inherited when Irish died. He missed Irish. Half a loaf of bread from the back of the City Club, after he'd advised the manager to get out of clothes manufacturers and into the Internet, but he'd just laughed. He shoved his few possessions into his QC's bag – another dustbin job, this time from the back of the Old Bailey.

Finally, like all good City men, he must check his cash position – always important to be liquid when there are more sellers than buyers. He fumbled around in his pocket, the one without a hole, and pulled out a pound, two 10p pieces and a penny. Thanks to government taxes, he wouldn't be able to afford any fags today, let alone his usual pint. Unless of course Maisie was behind the bar at The Reaper. He would have liked to reap her, he thought, even though he was old enough to be her father.

Clocks all over the city were beginning to chime six. He tied up the laces of his Reebok trainers – another yuppie reject: the yuppies all wore Nikes now. One last glance as Kevin stepped out onto the pavement. By the time Bill returned at seven that evening – more reliable than any security guard – Kevin would be back home in Peckham with his pregnant wife Lucy. Lucky man.

Kevin watched as Bill shuffled away, disappearing among the early-morning workers. He was good like that, Bill. He would never embarrass Kevin, or want to be the cause of him losing his job. Then he spotted the penny underneath the arch. He picked it up and smiled. He would replace it with a pound coin that evening. After all, wasn't that what banks were meant to do with your money?

Kevin returned to the front door just as the cleaners were leaving. They arrived at three in the morning, and had to be off the premises by six. After four years he knew all of their names, and they always gave him a smile.

Kevin had to be out on the pavement by six o'clock on the dot, shoes polished, clean white shirt, the bank's crested tie and the regulation brass-buttoned long blue coat – heavy in winter, light in summer. Banks are sticklers for rules and regulations. He was expected to salute all board members as they entered the building, but he had added one or two others he'd heard might soon be joining the board.

Between six and seven the yuppies would arrive with, 'Hi, Kev. Bet I make a million today.' From seven to eight, at a slightly slower pace, came the middle management, already having lost their edge after dealing with the problems of young children, school fees, new car or new wife: 'Good morning,' not bothering to make eye contact. From eight to nine, the dignified pace of senior management, having parked their cars in reserved spaces in the carpark.

Although they went to football matches on a Saturday like the rest of us, thought Kevin, they had seats in the directors' box. Most of them realized by now that they weren't going to make the board, and had settled for an easier life. Among the last to arrive would be the bank's Chief Executive, Phillip Alexander, sitting in the back of a chauffeur-driven Jaguar, reading the *Financial Times*. Kevin was expected to run out onto the pavement and open the car door for Mr Alexander, who would then march straight past him without so much as a glance, let alone a thank-you.

Finally, Sir William Selwyn, the bank's Chairman, would be dropped off in his Rolls-Royce, having been driven up from somewhere in Surrey. Sir William always found time to have a word with him. 'Good morning, Kevin. How's the wife?'

'Well, thank you, sir.'

'Let me know when the baby's due.'

Kevin grinned as the yuppies began to appear, the automatic door sliding open as they dashed through. No more having to pull open heavy doors since they'd installed that contraption. He was surprised they bothered to keep him on the payroll – at least, that

was the opinion of Mike Haskins, his immediate superior.

Kevin glanced around at Haskins, who was standing behind the reception desk. Lucky Mike. Inside in the warmth, regular cups of tea, the odd perk, not to mention a rise in salary. That was the job Kevin was after, the next step up the bank's ladder. He'd earned it. And he already had ideas for making reception run more efficiently. He turned back the moment Haskins looked up, reminding himself that his boss only had five months, two weeks and four days to go before he was due to retire. Then Kevin would take over his job – as long as they didn't bypass him and offer the position to Haskins's son.

Ronnie Haskins had been appearing at the bank pretty regularly since he'd lost his job at the brewery. He made himself useful, carrying parcels, delivering letters, hailing taxis and even getting sandwiches from the local Pret A Manger for those who wouldn't or couldn't risk leaving their desks.

Kevin wasn't stupid – he knew exactly what Haskins's game was. He intended to make sure Ronnie got the job that was Kevin's by right, while Kevin remained out on the pavement. It wasn't fair. He had served the bank conscientiously, never once missing a day's work, standing out there in all weathers.

'Good morning, Kevin,' said Chris Parnell, almost running past him. He had an anxious look on his face. He should have my problems, thought Kevin, glancing round to see Haskins stirring his first cup of tea of the morning.

'That's Chris Parnell,' Haskins told Ronnie, before sipping his tea. 'Late again – he'll blame it on British Rail, always does. I should have been given his job years ago, and I would have been, if like him I'd been a Sergeant in the Pay Corps, and not a Corporal in the Greenjackets. But management didn't seem to appreciate what I had to offer.'

Ronnie made no comment, but then, he had heard his father express this opinion every workday morning for the past six weeks.

'I once invited him to my regimental reunion, but he said he was too busy. Bloody snob. Watch him, though, because he'll have a say in who gets my job.'

'Good morning, Mr Parker,' said Haskins, handing the next arrival a copy of the *Guardian*.

'Tells you a lot about a man, what paper he reads,' Haskins said to Ronnie as Roger Parker disappeared into the lift. 'Now, you take young Kevin out there. He reads the *Sun*, and that's all you need to know about him. Which is another reason I wouldn't be surprised if he doesn't get the promotion he's after.' He winked at his son. 'I, on the other hand, read the *Express* – always have done, always will do.

'Good morning, Mr Tudor-Jones,' said Haskins, as he passed a copy of the *Telegraph* to the bank's Chief Administrator. He didn't speak again until the lift doors had closed.

'Important time for Mr Tudor-Jones,' Haskins informed his son. 'If he doesn't get promoted to the board this year, my bet is he'll be marking time until he retires. I sometimes look at these jokers and think I could do their jobs. After all, it wasn't my fault my old man was a brickie, and I didn't get the chance to go to the local grammar school. Otherwise I might have ended up on the sixth or seventh floor, with a desk of my own and a secretary.

'Good morning, Mr Alexander,' said Haskins as the bank's Chief Executive walked past him without acknowledging his salutation.

'Don't have to hand him a paper. Miss Franklyn, his secretary, picks the lot up for him long before he arrives. Now he wants to be Chairman. If he gets the job, there'll be a lot of changes round here, that's for sure.' He looked across at his son. 'You been booking in all those names, the way I taught you?'

'Sure have, Dad. Mr Parnell, 7.47; Mr Parker, 8.09; Mr Tudor-Jones, 8.11; Mr Alexander, 8.23.'

'Well done, son. You're learning fast.' He poured himself another cup of tea, and took a sip. Too hot, so

he went on talking. 'Our next job is to deal with the mail – which, like Mr Parnell, is late. So, I suggest . . .' Haskins quickly hid his cup of tea below the counter and ran across the foyer. He jabbed the 'up' button, and prayed that one of the lifts would return to the ground floor before the Chairman entered the building. The doors slid open with seconds to spare.

'Good morning, Sir William. I hope you had a pleasant weekend.'

'Yes, thank you, Haskins,' said the Chairman, as the doors closed. Haskins blocked the way so that no one could join Sir William in the lift, and he would have an uninterrupted journey to the fourteenth floor.

Haskins ambled back to the reception desk to find his son sorting out the morning mail. 'The Chairman once told me that the lift takes thirty-eight seconds to reach the top floor, and he'd worked out that he'd spend a week of his life in there, so he always read the *Times* leader on the way up and the notes for his next meeting on the way down. If he spends a week trapped in there, I reckon I must spend half my life,' he added, as he picked up his tea and took a sip. It was cold. 'Once you've sorted out the post, you can take it up to Mr Parnell. It's his job to distribute it, not mine. He's got a cushy enough number as it is, so there's no reason why I should do his work for him.'

Ronnie picked up the basket full of mail and headed for the lift. He stepped out on the second floor, walked over to Mr Parnell's desk and placed the basket in front of him.

Chris Parnell looked up, and watched as the lad disappeared back out of the door. He stared at the pile of letters. As always, no attempt had been made to sort them out. He must have a word with Haskins. It wasn't as if the man was run off his feet, and now he wanted his boy to take his place. Not if *he* had anything to do with it.

Didn't Haskins understand that his job carried real responsibility? He had to make sure the office ticked like a Swiss clock. Letters on the correct desks before nine, check for any absentees by ten, deal with any machinery breakdowns within moments of being notified of them, arrange and organize all staff meetings, by which time the second post would have arrived. Frankly, the whole place would come to a halt if he ever took a day off. You only had to look at the mess he always came back to whenever he returned from his summer holiday.

He stared at the letter on the top of the pile. It was addressed to 'Mr Roger Parker'. 'Rog', to him. He should have been given Rog's job as Head of Personnel years ago – he could have done it in his sleep, as his wife Janice never stopped reminding him: 'He's no more than a jumped-up office clerk. Just because he was at the same school as the Chief Cashier.' It wasn't fair.

Janice had wanted to invite Roger and his wife round to dinner, but Chris had been against the idea from the start.

'Why not?' she had demanded. 'After all, you both support Chelsea. Is it because you're afraid he'll turn you down, the stuck-up snob?'

To be fair to Janice, it had crossed Chris's mind to invite Roger out for a drink, but not to dinner at their home in Romford. He couldn't explain to her that when Roger went to Stamford Bridge he didn't sit at the Shed end with the lads, but in the members' seats.

Once the letters had been sorted out, Chris placed them in different trays according to their departments. His two assistants could cover the first ten floors, but he would never allow them anywhere near the top four. Only *he* got into the Chairman and Chief Executive's offices.

Janice never stopped reminding him to keep his eyes open whenever he was on the executive floors.

'You can never tell what opportunities might arise, what openings could present themselves.' He laughed to himself, thinking about Gloria in Filing, and the openings she offered. The things that girl could do behind a filing cabinet. That was one thing he didn't need his wife to find out about.

He picked up the trays for the top four floors, and headed towards the lift. When he reached the eleventh floor, he gave a gentle knock on the door before entering Roger's office. The Head of Personnel glanced up from a letter he'd been reading, a pre-occupied look on his face.

'Good result for Chelsea on Saturday, Rog, even if it was only against West Ham,' Chris said as he placed a pile of letters in his superior's in-tray. He didn't get any response, so he left hurriedly.

Roger looked up as Chris scurried away. He felt guilty that he hadn't chatted to him about the Chelsea match, but he didn't want to explain why he had missed a home game for the first time that season. He should be so lucky as only to have Chelsea on his mind.

He turned his attention back to the letter he had been reading. It was a bill for £1,600, the first month's fee for his mother's nursing home.

Roger had reluctantly accepted that she was no longer well enough to remain with them in Croydon, but he hadn't been expecting a bill that would work out at almost £20,000 a year. Of course he hoped she'd be around for another twenty years, but with Adam and Sarah still at school, and Hazel not wanting to go back to work, he needed a further rise in salary, at a time when all the talk was of cutbacks and redundancies.

It had been a disastrous weekend. On Saturday he had begun to read the McKinsey report, outlining what the bank would have to do if it was to continue as a leading financial institution into the twenty-first century.

The report had suggested that at least seventy employees would have to participate in a downsizing programme – a euphemism for 'You're sacked.' And who would be given the unenviable task of explaining to those seventy individuals the precise meaning of the word 'downsizing'? The last time Roger had had to sack someone, he hadn't slept for days. He had felt so depressed by the time he put the report down that he just couldn't face the Chelsea match.

He realized he would have to make an appointment to see Godfrey Tudor-Jones, the bank's Chief Administrator, although he knew that Tudor-Jones would brush him off with, 'Not my department, old boy, people problems. And you're the Head of Personnel, Roger, so I guess it's up to you.' It wasn't as if he'd been able to strike up a personal relationship with the man, which he could now fall back on. He had tried hard enough over the years, but the Chief Administrator had made it all too clear that he didn't mix business with pleasure – unless, of course, you were a board member.

'Why don't you invite him to a home game at Chelsea?' suggested Hazel. 'After all, you paid enough for those two season tickets.'

'I don't think he's into football,' Roger had told her. 'More a rugby man, would be my guess.'

'Then invite him to your club for dinner.'

He didn't bother to explain to Hazel that Godfrey was a member of the Carlton Club, and he didn't imagine he would feel at ease at a meeting of the Fabian Society.

The final blow had come on Saturday evening, when the headmaster of Adam's school had phoned to say he needed to see him urgently, about a matter that couldn't be discussed over the phone. He had driven there on the Sunday morning, apprehensive about what it could possibly be that couldn't be dis-

cussed over the phone. He knew that Adam needed to buckle down and work a lot harder if he was to have a chance of being offered a place at any university, but the headmaster told him that his son had been caught smoking marijuana, and that the school rules on that particular subject couldn't be clearer – immediate expulsion and a full report to the local police the following day. When he heard the news, Roger felt as if he were back in his own headmaster's study.

Father and son had hardly exchanged a word on the journey home. When Hazel had been told why Adam had come back in the middle of term she had broken down in tears, and proved inconsolable. She feared it would all come out in the *Croydon Advertiser*, and they would have to move. Roger certainly couldn't afford a move at the moment, but he didn't think this was the right time to explain to Hazel the meaning of negative equity.

On the train up to London that morning, Roger couldn't help thinking that none of this would have arisen if he had landed the Chief Administrator's job. For months there had been talk of Godfrey joining the board, and when he eventually did, Roger would be the obvious candidate to take his place. But he needed the extra cash right now, what with his mother in a nursing home and having to find a sixth-form college that would take Adam. He and Hazel would have to forget celebrating their twentieth wedding anniversary in Venice.

As he sat at his desk, he thought about the consequences of his colleagues finding out about Adam. He wouldn't lose his job, of course, but he needn't bother concerning himself with any further promotion. He could hear the snide whispers in the washroom that were meant to be overheard.

'Well, he's always been a bit of a lefty, you know. So, frankly, are you surprised?' He would have liked to explain to them that just because you read the *Guardian*, it doesn't automatically follow that you go on Ban the Bomb marches, experiment with free love and smoke marijuana at weekends.

He returned to the first page of the McKinsey report, and realized he would have to make an early appointment to see the Chief Administrator. He knew it would be no more than going through the motions, but at least he would have done his duty by his colleagues.

He dialled an internal number, and Godfrey Tudor-Jones's secretary picked up the phone.

'The Chief Administrator's office,' said Pamela, sounding as if she had a cold.

'It's Roger. I need to see Godfrey fairly urgently. It's about the McKinsey report.'

'He has appointments most of the day,' said Pamela, 'but I could fit you in at 4.15 for fifteen minutes.'

'Then I'll be with you at 4.15.'

Pamela replaced the phone and made a note in her boss's diary.

'Who was that?' asked Godfrey.

'Roger Parker. He says he has a problem and needs to see you urgently. I fitted him in at 4.15.'

He doesn't know what a problem is, thought Godfrey, continuing to sift through his letters to see if any had 'Confidential' written on them. None had, so he crossed the room and handed them all back to Pamela.

She took them without a word passing between them. Nothing had been the same since that weekend in Manchester. He should never have broken the golden rule about sleeping with your secretary. If it hadn't rained for three days, or if he'd been able to get a ticket for the United match, or if her skirt hadn't been quite so short, it might never have happened. If, if, if. And it wasn't as if the earth had moved, or he'd had it more than once. What a wonderful start to the week to be told she was pregnant.

As if he didn't have enough problems at the moment, the bank was having a poor year, so his bonus was likely to be about half what he'd budgeted for. Worse, he had already spent the money long before it had been credited to his account.

He looked up at Pamela. All she'd said after her initial outburst was that she hadn't made up her mind whether or not to have the baby. That was all he needed right now, what with two sons at Tonbridge and a daughter who couldn't make up her mind if she wanted a piano or a pony, and didn't understand why she couldn't have both, not to mention a wife who had become a shopaholic. He couldn't remember when his bank balance had last been in credit. He looked up at Pamela again, as she left his office. A private abortion wouldn't come cheap either, but it would be a damn sight cheaper than the alternative.

It would all have been so different if he had taken over as Chief Executive. He'd been on the shortlist, and at least three members of the board had made it clear that they supported his application. But the board in its wisdom had offered the position to an outsider. He had reached the last three, and for the first time he understood what it must feel like to win an Olympic silver medal when you're the clear favourite. Damn it, he was just as well qualified for the job as Phillip Alexander, and he had the added advantage of having worked for the bank for the past twelve years. There had been hints of a place on the board as compensation, but that would bite the dust the moment they found out about Pamela.

And what was the first recommendation Alexander had put before the board? That the bank should invest heavily in Russia, with the cataclysmic result that seventy people would now be losing their jobs and everyone's bonus was having to be readjusted. What made it worse was that Alexander was now trying to shift the blame for his decision onto the Chairman.

Once again, Godfrey's thoughts returned to Pamela. Perhaps he should take her out to lunch and try to convince her that an abortion would be the wisest course of action. He was about to pick up the phone and suggest the idea to her when it rang.

It was Pamela. 'Miss Franklyn just called. Could you pop up and see Mr Alexander in his office?' This was a ploy Alexander used regularly, to ensure you never forgot his position. Half the time, whatever needed to be discussed could easily have been dealt with over the phone. The man had a bloody power-complex.

On the way up to Alexander's office, Godfrey remembered that his wife had wanted to invite him to dinner, so she could meet the man who had robbed her of a new car.

'He won't want to come,' Godfrey had tried to explain. 'You see, he's a very private person.'

'No harm in asking,' she had insisted. But Godfrey had turned out to be right: '*Phillip Alexander thanks Mrs Tudor-Jones for her kind invitation to dinner, but regrets that due to…*'

Godfrey tried to concentrate on why Alexander wanted to see him. He couldn't possibly know about

Pamela – not that it was any of his business in the first place. Especially if the rumours about his own sexual preferences were to be believed. Had he been made aware that Godfrey was well in excess of the bank's overdraft limit? Or was he going to try to drag him onside over the Russian fiasco? Godfrey could feel the palms of his hands sweating as he knocked on the door.

'Come in,' said a deep voice.

Godfrey entered to be greeted by the Chief Executive's secretary, Miss Franklyn, who had joined him from Morgans. She didn't speak, just nodded in the direction of her boss's office.

He knocked for a second time, and when he heard 'Come,' he entered the Chief Executive's office. Alexander looked up from his desk.

'Have you read the McKinsey report?' he asked. No 'Good morning, Godfrey.' No 'Did you have a pleasant weekend?' Just 'Have you read the McKinsey report?'

'Yes, I have,' replied Godfrey, who hadn't done much more than speed-read through it, checking the paragraph headings and then studying in more detail the sections that would directly affect him. On top of everything else, he didn't need to be one of those who were about to be made redundant.

'The bottom line is that we can make savings of three million a year. It will mean having to sack up to seventy of the staff, and halving most of the bonuses. I need you to give me a written assessment on how we go about it, which departments can afford to shed staff, and which personnel we would risk losing if we halved their bonuses. Can you have that ready for me in time for tomorrow's board meeting?'

The bastard's about to pass the buck again, thought Godfrey. And he doesn't seem to care if he passes it up or down, as long as he survives. Wants to present the board with a *fait accompli*, on the back of my recommendations. No way.

'Have you got anything on at the moment that might be described as priority?'

'No, nothing that can't wait,' Godfrey replied. He didn't think he'd mention his problem with Pamela, or the fact that his wife would be livid if he failed to turn up for the school play that evening, in which their younger son was playing an angel. Frankly, it wouldn't have mattered if he were playing Jesus. Godfrey would still have to be up all night preparing his report for the board.

'Good. I suggest we meet up again at ten o'clock tomorrow morning, so you can brief me on how we should go about implementing the report.' Alexander lowered his head and returned his attention to the papers on his desk – a sign that the meeting was over.

Phillip Alexander looked up once he heard the door close. Lucky man, he thought, not to have any real problems. He was up to his eyes in them. The most important thing now was to make sure he continued to distance himself from the Chairman's disastrous decision to invest so heavily in Russia. He had backed the move at a board meeting the previous year, and the Chairman had made sure that his support had been minuted. But the moment he found out what was happening over at the Bank of America and Barclays, he had put an immediate stop on the bank's second instalment – as he continually reminded the board.

Since that day Phillip had flooded the building

with memos, warning every department to be sure it covered its own positions, and urging them all to retrieve whatever money they could. He kept the memos flowing on a daily basis, with the result that by now almost everyone, including several members of the board, was convinced that he had been sceptical about the decision from the outset.

The spin he'd put on events to one or two board members who were not that close to Sir William was that he hadn't felt he could go against the Chairman's wishes when he'd only been in the Chief Executive's job for a few weeks, and that had been his reason for not opposing Sir William's recommendation for a £500 million loan to the Nordsky Bank in St Petersburg. The situation could still be turned to his advantage, because if the Chairman was forced to resign, the board might feel an internal appointment would be the best course of action, given the circumstances. After all, when they had appointed Phillip as Chief Executive, the Deputy Chairman, Maurice Kington, had made it clear that he doubted if Sir William would serve his full term – and that was before the Russian débâcle. About a month later, Kington had resigned; it was well known in the City that he only resigned when he could see trouble on the horizon, as he had no intention of giving up any of his thirty or so other directorships.

When the *Financial Times* published an unfavourable article about Sir William, it covered itself by opening with the words: *'No one will deny that Sir William Selwyn's record as Chairman of Critchley's Bank has been steady, even at times impressive. But recently there have been some unfortunate errors, which appear to have emanated from the Chairman's office.'* Alexander had briefed the journalist with chapter and verse of those 'unfortunate errors'.

Some members of the board were now whispering 'Sooner rather than later.' But Alexander still had one or two problems of his own to sort out.

Another call last week, and demands for a further payment. The damn man seemed to know just how much he could ask for each time. Heaven knows, public opinion was no longer so hostile towards homosexuals. But with a rent boy it was still different – somehow the press could make it sound far worse than a heterosexual man paying a prostitute. And how the hell was he to know the boy was under age at the time? In any case, the law had changed since then – not that the tabloids would allow that to influence them.

And then there was the problem of who should become Deputy Chairman now that Maurice Kington had resigned. Securing the right replacement would be crucial for him, because that person would be presiding when the board came to appoint the next Chairman. Phillip had already made a pact with Michael Butterfield, who he knew would support his cause, and had begun dropping hints in the ears of other board members about Butterfield's qualifications for the job: 'We need someone who voted against the Russian loan . . . Someone who wasn't appointed by Sir William . . . Someone with an independent mind . . . Someone who . . .'

He knew the message was getting through, because one or two directors had already dropped into his office and suggested that Butterfield was the obvious candidate for the job. Phillip was happy to fall in with their sage opinion.

And now it had all come to a head, because a decision would have to be made at tomorrow's board meeting. If Butterfield was appointed Deputy Chairman, everything else would fall neatly into place.

The phone on his desk rang. He picked it up and shouted, 'I said no calls, Alison.'

'It's Julian Burr again, Mr Alexander.'

'Put him through,' said Alexander quietly.

'Good morning, Phil. Just thought I'd call in and wish you all the best for tomorrow's board meeting.'

'How the hell did you know about that?'

'Oh, Phil, surely you must realize that not everyone at the bank is heterosexual.' The voice paused. 'And one of them in particular doesn't love you any more.'

'What do you want, Julian?'

'For you to be Chairman, of course.'

'What do you want?' repeated Alexander, his voice rising with every word.

'I thought a little break in the sun while you're moving up a floor. Nice, Monte Carlo, perhaps a week or two in St Tropez.'

'And how much do you imagine that would cost?' Alexander asked.

'Oh, I would have thought ten thousand would comfortably cover my expenses.'

'Far too comfortably,' said Alexander.

'I don't think so,' said Julian. 'Try not to forget that I know exactly how much you're worth, and that's without the rise in salary you can expect once you become Chairman. Let's face it, Phil, it's far less than the *News of the World* would be willing to offer me for an exclusive. I can see the headline now: "Rent Boy's Night with Chairman of Family Bank".'

'That's criminal,' said Alexander.

'No. As I was under age at the time, I think you'll find it's you who's the criminal.'

'You can go too far, you know,' said Alexander.

'Not while you have ambitions to go even further,' said Julian, with a laugh.

'I'll need a few days.'

'I can't wait that long – I want to catch the early flight to Nice tomorrow. Be sure that the money has been transferred to my account before you go into the board meeting at eleven, there's a good chap. Don't forget it was you who taught me about electronic transfers.'

The phone went dead, then rang again immediately.

'Who is it this time?' snapped Alexander.

'The Chairman's on line two.'

'Put him through.'

'Phillip, I need the latest figures on the Russian loans, along with your assessment of the McKinsey report.'

'I'll have an update on the Russian position on your desk within the hour. As for the McKinsey report, I'm broadly in agreement with its recommendations, but I've asked Godfrey Tudor-Jones to let me have a written opinion on how we should go about implementing it. I intend to present his report at tomorrow's board meeting. I hope that's satisfactory, Chairman?'

'I doubt it. I have a feeling that by tomorrow it will be too late,' the Chairman said without explanation, before replacing the phone.

Sir William knew it didn't help that the latest Russian losses had exceeded £500 million. And now the McKinsey report had arrived on every director's desk, recommending that seventy jobs, perhaps even more, should be shed in order to make a saving of around £3 million a year. When would management consultants begin to understand that human beings were involved, not just numbers on a balance sheet – among them seventy loyal members of staff, some of whom had served the bank for more than twenty years?

There wasn't a mention of the Russian loan in the McKinsey report, because it wasn't part of their brief; but the timing couldn't have been worse. And in banking, timing is everything.

Phillip Alexander's words to the board were indelibly fixed in Sir William's memory: 'We mustn't allow our rivals to take advantage of such a one-off windfall. If Critchley's is to remain a player on the international stage, we have to move quickly while there's still a profit to be made.' The short-term gains could be enormous, Alexander had assured the board – whereas in truth the opposite had turned out to be the case. And within moments of things falling apart, the little shit had begun digging himself out of the Russian hole, while dropping his Chairman right into it. He'd been on holiday at the time, and Alexander had phoned him at his hotel in Marrakech to tell him that he had everything under control, and there was no need for him to rush home. When he did eventually return, he found that Alexander had already filled in the hole, leaving him at the bottom of it.

After reading the article in the *Financial Times*, Sir William knew his days as Chairman were numbered. The resignation of Maurice Kington had been the final blow, from which he knew he couldn't hope to recover. He had tried to talk him out of it, but there was only one person's future Kington was ever interested in.

The Chairman stared down at his handwritten letter of resignation, a copy of which would be sent to every member of the board that evening.

His loyal secretary Claire had reminded him that he was fifty-seven, and had often talked of retiring at sixty to make way for a younger man. It was ironic when he considered who that younger man might be.

True, he was fifty-seven. But the last Chairman hadn't retired until he was seventy, and that was what the board and the shareholders would remember. It would be forgotten that he had taken over an ailing bank from an ailing Chairman, and increased its profits year on year for the past decade. Even if you included the Russian disaster, they were still well ahead of the game.

Those hints from the Prime Minister that he was being considered for a peerage would quickly be forgotten. The dozen or so directorships that are nothing more than routine for the retiring Chairman of a major bank would suddenly evaporate, along with the invitations to Buck House, the Guildhall and the centre court at Wimbledon – the one official outing his wife always enjoyed.

He had told Katherine over dinner the night before that he was going to resign. She had put down her knife and fork, folded her napkin and said, 'Thank God for that. Now it won't be necessary to go on with this sham of a marriage any longer. I shall wait for a decent interval, of course, before I file for divorce.' She had risen from her place and left the room without uttering another word.

Until then, he'd had no idea that Katherine felt so strongly. He'd assumed she was aware that there had been other women, although none of his affairs had been all that serious. He thought they had reached an understanding, an accommodation. After all, so many married couples of their age did. After dinner he had travelled up to London and spent the night at his club.

He unscrewed the top of his fountain pen and signed the twelve letters. He had left them on his desk all day, in the hope that before the close of business some miracle would occur which would make it possible for him to shred them. But in truth he knew that was never likely.

When he finally took the letters through to his secretary, she had already typed the recipients' names on the twelve envelopes. He smiled at Claire, the best secretary he'd ever had.

'Goodbye, Claire,' he said, giving her a kiss on the cheek.

'Goodbye, Sir William,' she replied, biting her lip.

He returned to his office, picked up his empty

briefcase and a copy of *The Times*. Tomorrow he would be the lead story in the Business Section – he wasn't quite well enough known to make the front page. He looked around the Chairman's office once again before leaving it for the last time. He closed the door quietly behind him and walked slowly down the corridor to the lift. He pressed the button and waited. The doors opened and he stepped inside, grateful that the lift was empty, and that it didn't stop on its journey to the ground floor.

He walked out into the foyer and glanced towards the reception desk. Haskins would have gone home long ago. As the plate-glass door slid open he thought about Kevin sitting at home in Peckham with his pregnant wife. He would have liked to have wished him luck for the job on the reception desk. At least that wouldn't be affected by the McKinsey report.

As he stepped out onto the pavement, something caught his eye. He turned to see an old tramp settling down for the night in the far corner underneath the arch.

Bill touched his forehead in a mock salute. 'Good evening, Chairman,' he said with a grin.

'Good evening, Bill,' Sir William replied, smiling back at him.

If only they could change places, Sir William thought, as he turned and walked towards his waiting car.

The Queen's Birthday Telegram

Her Majesty the Queen sends her congratulations to Albert Webber on the occasion of his 100th birthday, and wishes him many more years of good health and happiness.

ALBERT WAS still smiling after he'd read the message for the twentieth time.

'You'll be next, ducks,' he said as he passed the royal missive across to his wife. Betty only had to read the telegram once for a broad smile to appear on her face too.

The festivities had begun a week earlier, culminating in a celebration party at the town hall. Albert's photograph had appeared on the front page of the *Somerset Gazette* that morning, and he had been interviewed on *BBC Points West*, his wife seated proudly by his side.

His Worship the Mayor of Street, Councillor Ted Harding, and the leader of the local council, Councillor Brocklebank, were waiting on the town hall steps to greet the centenarian. Albert was escorted to the mayor's parlour, where he was introduced to Mr David Heathcote-Amory, the local Member of Parliament, as well as the local MEP, although when asked later he couldn't remember her name.

At 3.27 p.m., the precise minute Albert had been born in 1907, the old man, surrounded by his five children, eleven grandchildren and nineteen great-grandchildren, thrust a silver-handled knife into a three-tier cake. This simple act was greeted by another burst of applause, followed by cries of *speech, speech, speech!*

Albert had prepared a few words, but as quiet fell in the room, they went straight out of his head.

'Say something,' said Betty, giving her husband a gentle nudge in the ribs.

He blinked, looked around at the expectant crowd, paused and said, 'Thank you very much.'

Once the assembled gathering realized that was all he was going to say, someone began to sing 'Happy Birthday', and within moments everyone was joining in. Albert managed to blow out seven of the hundred candles before the younger members of the family came to his rescue, which was greeted by even more laughter and clapping.

Once the applause had died down, the mayor rose to his feet, tugged at the lapels of his black and gold braided gown and cleared his throat, before delivering a far longer speech.

'My fellow citizens,' he began, 'we are gathered together today to celebrate the birthday, the one hundredth birthday, of Albert Webber, a much-loved member of our community. Albert was born in Street on the fifteenth of April 1907. He married his wife Betty at Holy Trinity Church in 1931, and spent his working life at C. and J. Clark's, our local shoe factory. In fact,' he continued, 'Albert has spent his entire life in Street, with the notable exception of four years when he served as a private soldier in the Somerset Light Infantry. When the

After several more photographs had been taken, Albert was ushered through to a large reception room where over a hundred invited guests were waiting to greet him. As he entered the room he was welcomed by a spontaneous burst of applause, and people he'd never met before began shaking hands with him.

war ended in 1945, Albert was discharged from the army and returned to Street to take up his old job as a leather cutter at Clark's. At the age of sixty, he retired as Deputy Floor Manager. But you can't get rid of Albert that easily, because he then took on part-time work as a night watchman, a responsibility he carried out until his seventieth birthday.'

The mayor waited for the laughter to fade before he continued. 'From his early days, Albert has always been a loyal supporter of Street Football Club, rarely missing a Cobblers' home game, and indeed the club has recently made him an honorary life member. Albert also played darts for the Crown and Anchor, and was a member of that team when they were runners-up in the town's pub championship.

'I'm sure you will all agree,' concluded the mayor, 'that Albert has led a colourful and interesting life, which we all hope will continue for many years to come, not least because in three years' time we will be celebrating the same landmark for his dear wife Betty. It's hard to believe, looking at her,' said the mayor, turning towards Mrs Webber, 'that in 2010 she will also be one hundred.'

'Hear, hear,' said several voices, and Betty shyly bowed her head as Albert leaned across and took her hand.

After several other dignitaries had said a few words, and many more had had their photograph taken with Albert, the mayor accompanied his two guests out of the town hall to a waiting Rolls-Royce, and instructed the chauffeur to drive Mr and Mrs Webber home.

Albert and Betty sat in the back of the car holding hands. Neither of them had ever been in a Rolls-Royce before, and certainly not in one driven by a chauffeur.

By the time the car drew up outside their council house in Marne Terrace, they were both so exhausted and so full of salmon sandwiches and birthday cake that it wasn't long before they retired to bed.

The last thing Albert murmured before turning out his bedside light was, 'Well, it will be your turn next, ducks, and I'm determined to live another three years so we can celebrate your hundredth together.'

'I don't want all that fuss made over me when my time comes,' she said. But Albert had already fallen asleep.

Not a lot happened in Albert and Betty Webber's life during the next three years: a few minor ailments, but nothing life-threatening, and the birth of their first great-great-grandchild, Jude.

When the historic day approached for the second Webber to celebrate a hundredth birthday, Albert had become so frail that Betty insisted the party be held at their home and only include the family. Albert reluctantly agreed, and didn't tell his wife how much he'd been looking forward to returning to the town hall and once again being driven home in the mayor's Rolls-Royce.

The new mayor was equally disappointed, as he'd anticipated that the occasion would guarantee his photograph appearing on the front page of the local paper.

When the great day dawned, Betty received over a hundred cards, letters and messages from well-wishers, but to Albert's profound dismay, there was no telegram from the Queen. He assumed the Post Office was to blame and that it would surely be delivered the following day. It wasn't.

'Don't fuss, Albert,' Betty insisted. 'Her Majesty is a very busy lady and she must have far more important things on her mind.'

But Albert did fuss, and when no telegram arrived the next day, or the following week, he felt a pang of disappointment for his wife who seemed to be taking the whole affair in such good spirit. However, after another week, and still no sign of a telegram, Albert decided the time had come to take the matter into his own hands.

Every Thursday morning, Eileen, their youngest daughter, aged seventy-three, would come to pick up Betty and drive her into town to go shopping. In reality this usually turned out to be just window shopping, as Betty couldn't believe the prices the shops had the nerve to charge. She could remember when a loaf of bread cost a penny, and a pound a week was a working wage.

That Thursday Albert waited for them to leave the house, then he stood by the window until the car had disappeared around the corner. Once they were out of sight, he shuffled off to his little den, where he sat by the phone, going over the exact words he would say if he was put through.

After a little while, and once he felt he was word perfect, he looked up at the framed telegram on the wall above him. It gave him enough confidence to pick up the phone and dial a six-digit number.

'Directory Enquiries. What number do you require?'

'Buckingham Palace,' said Albert, hoping his voice sounded authoritative.

There was a slight hesitation, but the operator finally said, 'One moment please.'

Albert waited patiently, although he quite expected to be told that the number was either unlisted or ex-directory. A moment later the operator was back on the line and read out the number.

'Can you please repeat that?' asked a surprised Albert as he took the top off his biro. 'Zero two zero, seven seven six six, seven three zero zero. 'Thank you,' he said, before putting the phone down. Several minutes passed before he gathered enough courage to pick it up again. Albert dialled the number with a shaky hand. He listened to the familiar ringing tone and was just about to put the phone back down when a woman's voice said, 'Buckingham Palace, how may I help you?'

'I'd like to speak to someone about a one hundredth birthday,' said Albert, repeating the exact words he had memorized.

'Who shall I say is calling?'

'Mr Albert Webber.'

'Hold the line please, Mr Webber.'

This was Albert's last chance of escape, but before he could put the phone down, another voice came on the line.

'Humphrey Cranshaw speaking.'

The last time Albert had heard a voice like that was when he was serving in

the army. 'Good morning, sir,' he said nervously. 'I was hoping you might be able to help me.'

'I certainly will if I can, Mr Webber,' replied the courtier.

'Three years ago I celebrated my hundredth birthday,' said Albert, returning to his well-rehearsed script.

'Many congratulations,' said Cranshaw.

'Thank you, sir,' said Albert, 'but that isn't the reason why I'm calling. You see, on that occasion Her Majesty the Queen was kind enough to send me a telegram, which is now framed on the wall in front of me, and which I will treasure for the rest of my life.'

'How kind of you to say so, Mr Webber.'

'But I wondered,' said Albert, gaining in confidence, 'if Her Majesty still sends telegrams when people reach their hundredth birthday?'

'She most certainly does,' replied Cranshaw. 'I know that it gives Her Majesty great pleasure to continue the tradition, despite the fact that so many more people now attain that magnificent milestone.'

'Oh, that is most gratifying to hear, Mr Cranshaw,' said Albert, 'because my dear wife celebrated her hundredth birthday some two weeks ago, but sadly has not yet received a telegram from the Queen.'

'I am sorry to hear that, Mr Webber,' said the courtier. 'It must be an administrative oversight on our part. Please allow me to check. What is your wife's full name?'

'Elizabeth Violet Webber, née Braithwaite,' said Albert with pride.

'Just give me a moment, Mr Webber,' said Cranshaw, 'while I check our records.'

This time Albert had to wait a little longer before Mr Cranshaw came back on the line. 'I am sorry to have kept you waiting, Mr Webber, but you'll be pleased to learn that we have traced your wife's telegram.'

'Oh, I'm so glad,' said Albert. 'May I ask when she can expect to receive it?'

There was a moment's hesitation before the courtier said, 'Her Majesty sent a telegram to your wife to congratulate her on reaching her hundredth birthday some five years ago.'

Albert heard a car door slam, and moments later a key turned in the lock. He quickly put the phone down, and smiled.

Clean Sweep Ignatius

EW SHOWED MUCH INTEREST when Ignatius Agarbi was appointed Nigeria's Minister of Finance. After all, the cynics pointed out, he was the seventeenth person to hold the office in seventeen years.

In Ignatius's first major policy statement to Parliament he promised to end graft and corruption in public life and warned the electorate that no one holding an official position could feel safe unless he led a blameless life. He ended his maiden speech with the words, 'I intend to clear out Nigeria's Augean stables.'

Such was the impact of the minister's speech that it failed to get a mention in the Lagos *Daily Times*. Perhaps the editor considered that, since the paper had covered the speeches of the previous sixteen ministers *in extenso*, his readers might feel they had heard it all before.

Ignatius, however, was not to be disheartened by the lack of confidence shown in him, and set about his new task with vigour and determination. Within days of his appointment he had caused a minor official at the Ministry of Trade to be jailed for falsifying documents relating to the import of grain. The next to feel the bristles of Ignatius's new broom was a leading Lebanese financier, who was deported without trial for breach of the exchange control regulations. A month later came an event which even Ignatius considered a personal coup: the arrest of the Inspector General of Police for accepting bribes – a perk the citizens of Lagos had in the past considered went with the job. When four months later the Police Chief was sentenced to eighteen months in jail, the new Finance Minister finally made the front page of the Lagos *Daily Times*. A leader on the centre page dubbed him 'Clean Sweep Ignatius', the new broom every guilty man feared. Ignatius's reputation as Mr Clean continued to grow as arrest followed arrest and unfounded rumours began circulating in the capital that even General Otobi, the Head of State, was under investigation by his own Finance Minister.

Ignatius alone now checked, vetted and authorized all foreign contracts worth over one hundred million dollars. And although every decision he made was meticulously scrutinized by his enemies, not a breath of scandal ever became associated with his name.

When Ignatius began his second year of office as Minister of Finance even the cynics began to acknowledge his achievements. It was about this time that General Otobi felt confident enough to call Ignatius in for an unscheduled consultation.

The Head of State welcomed the Minister to Dodan Barracks and ushered him to a comfortable chair in his study overlooking the parade ground.

'Ignatius, I have just finished going over the latest budget report and I am alarmed by your conclusion that the Exchequer is still losing millions of dollars each year in bribes paid to go-betweens by foreign companies. Have you any idea into whose pockets this money is falling? That's what I want to know.'

Ignatius sat bolt upright, his eyes never leaving the Head of State.

'I suspect a great percentage of the money is ending up in private Swiss bank accounts but I am at present unable to prove it.'

'Then I will give you whatever added authority you require to do so,' said General Otobi. 'You can use any means you consider necessary to ferret out these villains. Start by investigating every member of my Cabinet, past and present. And show no fear or favour in your endeavours, no matter what their rank or connections.'

'For such a task to have any chance of success I would need a special letter of authority signed by you, General . . .'

'Then it will be on your desk by six o'clock this evening,' said the Head of State.

'And the rank of Ambassador Plenipotentiary whenever I travel abroad.'

'Granted.'

'Thank you,' said Ignatius, rising from his chair on the assumption that the audience was over.

'You may also need this,' said the General as they walked towards the door. The Head of State handed Ignatius a small automatic pistol. 'Because I suspect by now that you have almost as many enemies as I.'

Ignatius took the pistol from the soldier awkwardly, put it in his pocket and mumbled his thanks.

Without another word passing between the two men, Ignatius left his leader and was driven back to his Ministry.

Without the knowledge of the Governor of the Central Bank of Nigeria, and unhindered by any senior civil servants, Ignatius enthusiastically set about his new task. He researched alone at night, and by day discussed his findings with no one. Three months later he was ready to pounce.

The Minister selected the month of August to make an unscheduled visit abroad, as it was the time when most Nigerians went on holiday, and his absence would therefore not be worthy of comment.

He asked his Permanent Secretary to book him, his wife and their two children on a flight to Orlando, and to be certain that the tickets were charged to his personal account.

On their arrival in Florida, the family checked into the local Marriott Hotel. Ignatius then informed his wife, without warning or explanation, that he would be spending a few days in New York on business before rejoining them for the rest of the holiday. The following morning he left his family to the mysteries of Disney World while he took a flight to New York. It was a short taxi ride from LaGuardia to Kennedy, where, after a change of clothes and the purchase of a return tourist ticket for cash, he boarded a Swissair flight for Geneva unobserved.

Once he had arrived, Ignatius booked into an inconspicuous hotel, retired to bed and slept soundly for eight hours. Over breakfast the following morning he studied the list of banks he had so carefully drawn up after completing his research in Nigeria: each name was written out boldly in his own hand. Ignatius decided to start with Gerber et Cie, whose building, he observed from the hotel bedroom, took

up half the Avenue de Parchine. He checked the telephone number with the concierge before placing a call. The chairman agreed to see him at twelve o'clock.

Carrying only a battered briefcase, Ignatius arrived at the bank a few minutes before the appointed hour – an unusual occurrence for a Nigerian, thought the young man dressed in a smart grey suit, white shirt and grey silk tie, who was waiting in the marble hall to greet him. He bowed to the Minister, introducing himself as the chairman's personal assistant, and explained that he would accompany Ignatius to the chairman's office. The young executive led the Minister to a waiting lift and neither man uttered another word until they had reached the eleventh floor. A gentle tap on the chairman's door elicited '*Entrez*,' which the young man obeyed.

'The Nigerian Minister of Finance, sir.'

The chairman rose from behind his desk and stepped forward to greet his guest. Ignatius could not help noticing that he too wore a grey suit, white shirt and grey silk tie.

'Good morning, Minister,' the chairman said. 'Won't you have a seat?' He ushered Ignatius towards a low glass table surrounded by comfortable chairs on the far side of the room. 'I have ordered coffee for both of us if that is acceptable.'

Ignatius nodded, placed the battered briefcase on the floor by the side of his chair and stared out of the large plate-glass window. He made some small-talk about the splendid view of the magnificent fountain while a girl served all three men with coffee.

Once the young woman had left the room Ignatius got down to business.

'My Head of State has requested that I visit your bank with a rather unusual request,' he began. Not a flicker of surprise appeared on the face of the chairman or his young assistant. 'He has honoured me with the task of discovering which Nigerian citizens hold numbered accounts with your bank.'

On learning this piece of information only the chairman's lips moved. 'I am not at liberty to disclose –'

'Allow me to put my case,' said the Minister, raising a white palm. 'First, let me assure you that I come with the absolute authority of my government.'

Without another word, Ignatius extracted an envelope from his inside pocket with a flourish. He handed it to the chairman, who removed the letter inside and read it slowly.

Once he had finished reading, the banker cleared his throat. 'This document, I fear, sir, carries no validity in my country.' He replaced it in the envelope and handed it back to Ignatius. 'I am, of course,' continued the chairman, 'not for one moment doubting that you have the full backing of your Head of State, both as a Minister and an Ambassador, but that does not change the bank's rule of confidentiality in such matters. There are no circumstances in which we would release the names of any of our account holders without their authority. I'm sorry to be of so little help, but those are, and will always remain, the bank rules.' The chairman rose to his feet, as he considered the meeting was now at an end; but he had not bargained for Clean Sweep Ignatius.

'My Head of State,' said Ignatius, softening his tone perceptibly, 'has authorized me to approach your bank to act as the intermediary for all future transactions between my country and Switzerland.'

'We are flattered by your confidence in us, Minister,' replied the chairman, who remained standing. 'However, I feel sure that you will understand that it cannot alter our attitude to our customers' confidentiality.'

Ignatius remained unperturbed.

'Then I am sorry to inform you, Mr Gerber, that our Ambassador in Geneva will be instructed to make an official communiqué to the Swiss Foreign Office about the lack of co-operation your bank has shown concerning requests for information about our nationals.' He waited for his words to sink in. 'You could avoid such embarrassment, of course, by simply letting me know the names of my countrymen who hold accounts with Gerber et Cie and the amounts involved. I can assure you we would not reveal the source of our information.'

'You are most welcome to lodge such a communiqué, sir, and I feel sure that our Minister will explain to your Ambassador in the most courteous of diplomatic language that the Foreign Ministry does not have the authority under Swiss law to demand such disclosures.'

'If that is the case, I shall instruct my own Ministry of Trade to halt all future dealings in Nigeria with any Swiss nationals until these names are revealed.'

'That is your privilege, Minister,' replied the chairman, unmoved.

'And we may also have to reconsider every contract currently being negotiated by your countrymen in Nigeria. And in addition I shall personally see to it that no penalty clauses are honoured.'

'Would you not consider such action a little precipitate?'

'Let me assure you, Mr Gerber, that I would not lose one moment of sleep over such a decision,' said Ignatius. 'Even if my efforts to discover those names were to bring your country to its knees I would not be moved.'

'So be it, Minister,' replied the chairman. 'However, it still does not alter the policy or the attitude of this bank to confidentiality.'

'If that remains the case, sir, this very day I shall give instructions to our Ambassador to close our Embassy in Geneva and I shall declare your Ambassador in Lagos *persona non grata*.'

For the first time the chairman raised his eyebrows.

'Furthermore,' continued Ignatius, 'I will hold a conference in London which will leave the world's press in no doubt of my Head of State's displeasure with the conduct of this bank. After such publicity I feel confident you will find that many of your customers would prefer to close their accounts, while others who have in the past considered you a safe haven may find it necessary to look elsewhere.'

The Minister waited but still the chairman did not respond.

'Then you leave me no choice,' said Ignatius, rising from his seat.

The chairman stretched out his arm, assuming that at last the Minister was leaving, only to watch with horror as Ignatius placed a hand in his jacket pocket and removed a small pistol. The two Swiss bankers froze as the Nigerian Minister of Finance stepped forward and pressed the muzzle against the chairman's temple.

'I need those names, Mr Gerber, and by now you must realize I will stop at nothing. If you don't supply

them immediately I'm going to blow your brains out. Do you understand?'

The chairman gave a slight nod, beads of sweat appearing on his forehead. 'And he will be next,' said Ignatius, gesturing towards the young assistant, who stood speechless and paralysed a few paces away.

'Get me the names of every Nigerian who holds an account in this bank,' Ignatius said quietly, looking towards the young man, 'or I'll blow your chairman's brains all over his soft pile carpet. Immediately, do you hear me?' he added sharply.

The young man looked towards the chairman, who was now trembling but said quite clearly, '*Non, Pierre, jamais.*'

'*D'accord,*' replied the assistant in a whisper.

'You can't say I didn't give you every chance.' Ignatius pulled back the hammer. The sweat was now pouring down the chairman's face and the young man had to turn his eyes away as he waited in terror for the pistol shot.

'Excellent,' said Ignatius, as he removed the gun from the chairman's head and returned to his seat. Both bankers were still trembling and quite unable to speak.

The Minister picked up the battered briefcase by the side of his chair and placed it on the glass table in front of him. He pressed back the clasps and the lid flicked up.

The two bankers stared down at the neatly packed rows of hundred-dollar bills. Every inch of the briefcase had been taken up. The chairman quickly estimated that it probably amounted to around five million dollars.

'I wonder, sir,' said Ignatius, 'how I go about opening an account with your bank?

The First Miracle

TOMORROW IT WOULD BE 1 AD, but nobody had told him.

If anyone had, he wouldn't have understood because he thought that it was the forty-third year in the reign of the Emperor, and in any case, he had other things on his mind. His mother was still cross with him and he had to admit that he'd been naughty that day, even by the standards of a normal thirteen-year-old. He hadn't meant to drop the pitcher when she had sent him to the well for water. He tried to explain to his mother that it wasn't his fault that he had tripped over a stone; and that at least was true. What he hadn't told her was that he was chasing a stray dog at the time. And then there was that pomegranate; how was he meant to know that it was the last one, and that his father had taken a liking to them? The boy was now dreading his father's return and the possibility that he might be given another thrashing. He could still remember the last one when he hadn't been able to sit down for two days without feeling the pain, and the thin red scars didn't completely disappear for over three weeks.

He sat on the window ledge in a shaded corner of his room trying to think of some way he could redeem himself in his mother's eyes, now that she had thrown him out of the kitchen. Go outside and play, she had insisted, after he had spilt some cooking oil on his tunic. But that wasn't much fun as he was only allowed to play by himself. His father had forbidden him to mix with the local boys. How he hated this country; if only he were back home with his friends, there would be so much to do. Still, only another three weeks and he could . . . The door swung open and his mother came into the room. She was dressed in the thin black garments so favoured by locals: they kept her cool, she had explained to the boy's father. He had grunted his disapproval so she always changed back into imperial dress before he returned in the evening.

'Ah, there you are,' she said, addressing the crouched figure of her son.

'Yes, Mother.'

'Daydreaming as usual. Well, wake up because I need you to go into the village and fetch some food for me.'

'Yes, Mother, I'll go at once,' the boy said as he jumped off the window ledge.

'Well, at least wait until you've heard what I want.'

'Sorry, Mother.'

'Now listen, and listen carefully.' She started counting on her fingers as she spoke. 'I need a chicken, some raisins, figs, dates and . . . ah yes, two pomegranates.'

The boy's face reddened at the mention of the pomegranates and he stared down at the stone floor, hoping she might have forgotten. His mother put her hand into the leather purse that hung from her waist and removed two small coins, but before she handed them over she made her son repeat the instructions.

'One chicken, raisins, figs, dates, and two pomegranates,' he recited, as he might the modern poet, Virgil.

'And be sure to see they give you the correct change,' she added. 'Never forget the locals are all thieves.'

'Yes, Mother . . .' For a moment the boy hesitated.

'If you remember everything and bring back the right amount of money, I might forget to tell your father about the broken pitcher and the pomegranate.'

The boy smiled, pocketed the two small silver coins in his tunic, and ran out of the house into the compound. The guard who stood on duty at the gate removed the great wedge of wood which allowed the massive door to swing open. The boy jumped through the hole in the gate and grinned back at the guard.

'Been in more trouble again today?' the guard shouted after him.

'No, not this time,' the boy replied. 'I'm about to be saved.'

He waved farewell to the guard and started to walk briskly towards the village while humming a tune that reminded him of home. He kept to the centre of the dusty winding path that the locals had the nerve to call a road. He seemed to spend half his time removing little stones from his sandals. If his father had been posted here for any length of time he would have made some changes; then they would have had a real road, straight and wide enough to take a chariot. But not before his mother had sorted out the serving girls. Not one of them knew how to lay a table or even prepare food so that it was at least clean. For the first time in his life he had seen his mother in a kitchen, and he felt sure it would be the last, as they would all be returning home now that his father was coming to the end of his assignment.

The evening sun shone down on him as he walked; it was a very large red sun, the same red as his father's tunic. The heat it gave out made him sweat and long for something to drink. Perhaps there would be enough money left over to buy himself a pomegranate. He couldn't wait to take one home and show his friends how large they were in this barbaric land. Marcus, his best friend, would undoubtedly have seen one as big because his father had commanded a whole army in these parts, but the rest of the class would still be impressed.

The village to which his mother had sent him was only two miles from the compound and the dusty path ran alongside a hill overlooking a large valley. The road was already crowded with travellers who would be seeking shelter in the village. All of them had come down from the hills at the express orders of his father, whose authority had been vested in him by the Emperor himself. Once he was sixteen, he too would serve the Emperor. His friend Marcus wanted to be a soldier and conquer the rest of the world. But he was more interested in the law and teaching his country's customs to the heathens in strange lands.

Marcus had said, 'I'll conquer them and then you can govern them.'

A sensible division between brains and brawn, he had told his friend, who didn't seem impressed and had ducked him in the nearest bath.

The boy quickened his pace as he knew he had to be back in the compound before the sun disappeared behind the hills. His father had told him many times that he must always be locked safely inside before sunset. He was aware that his father was not a popular man with the locals, and he had warned his son that he would always be safe while it was light as no one would dare to harm him while others could watch what was going on, but once it was dark anything could happen. One thing he knew for certain: when he grew up he wasn't going to be a tax collector or work in the census office.

When he reached the village he found the narrow twisting lanes that ran between the little white houses swarming with people who had come from all the neighbouring lands to obey his father's order and be registered for the census, in order that they might be taxed. The boy dismissed the plebs from his mind. (It was Marcus who had taught him to refer to all foreigners as plebs.) When he entered the market place he also dismissed Marcus from his mind and began to concentrate on the supplies his mother wanted. He mustn't make any mistakes this time or he would undoubtedly end up with that thrashing from his father. He ran nimbly between the stalls, checking the food carefully. Some of the local people stared at the fair-skinned boy with the curly brown hair and the straight, firm nose. He displayed no imperfections or disease like the majority of them. Others turned their eyes away from him; after all, he had come from the land of the natural rulers. These thoughts did not pass through his mind. All the boy noticed was that their native skins were parched and lined from too much sun. He knew that too much sun was bad for

you: it made you old before your time, his tutor had warned him.

At the end stall, the boy watched an old woman haggling over an unusually plump live chicken and as he marched towards her she ran away in fright, leaving the fowl behind her. He stared at the stallkeeper and refused to bargain with the peasant. It was beneath his dignity. He pointed to the chicken and gave the man one denarius. The man bit the round silver coin and looked at the head of Augustus Caesar, ruler of half the world. (When his tutor had told him, during a history lesson, about the Emperor's achievements, he remembered thinking, I hope Caesar doesn't conquer the whole world before I have a chance to join in.) The stallkeeper was still staring at the silver coin.

'Come on, come on, I haven't got all day,' said the boy, sounding like his father.

The local did not reply because he couldn't understand what the boy was saying. All he knew for certain was that it would be unwise for him to annoy the invader. The stallkeeper held the chicken firmly by the neck and taking a knife from his belt cut its head off in one movement and passed the dead fowl over to the boy. He then handed back some of his local coins, which had stamped on them the image of a man the boy's father described as 'that useless Herod'. The boy kept his hand held out, palm open, and the local placed bronze talents into it until he had no more. The boy left him talentless and moved to another stall, this time pointing to bags containing raisins, figs and dates. The new stallkeeper made a measure of each for which he received five of the useless Herod coins. The man was about to protest about the barter but the boy stared at him fixedly in the eyes, the way he had seen his father do so often. The stallkeeper backed away and only bowed his head.

Now, what else did his mother want? He racked his brains. A chicken, raisins, dates, figs and . . . of course, two pomegranates. He searched among the fresh-fruit stalls and picked out three pomegranates, and breaking one open, began to eat it, spitting out the pips on the ground in front of him. He paid the stallkeeper with the two remaining bronze talents, feeling pleased that he had carried out his mother's wishes while still being able to return home with one of the silver denarii. Even his father would be impressed by that. He finished the pomegranate and, with his arms laden, headed slowly out of the market back towards the compound, trying to avoid the stray dogs that continually got under his feet. They barked and sometimes snapped at his ankles: they did not know who he was.

When the boy reached the edge of the village he noticed the sun was already disappearing behind the highest hill, so he quickened his pace, remembering his father's words about being home before dusk. As he walked down the stony path, those still on the way towards the village kept a respectful distance, leaving him a clear vision as far as the eye could see, which wasn't all that far as he was carrying so much in his arms. But one sight he did notice a little way ahead of him was a man with a beard – a dirty, lazy habit, his father had told him – wearing the ragged dress that signified that he was of the tribe of Jacob, tugging a reluctant donkey which in turn was carrying a very fat woman. The woman was, as their custom demanded, covered from head to toe in black. The boy was about to order them out of his path when the man left the donkey on the side of the road and went into a house which, from its sign, claimed to be an inn.

Such a building in his own land would never

have passed the scrutiny of the local councillors as a place fit for paying travellers to dwell in. But the boy realized that this particular week to find even a mat to lay one's head on might be considered a luxury. He watched the bearded man reappear through the door with a forlorn look on his tired face. There was clearly no room at the inn.

The boy could have told him that before he went in, and wondered what the man would do next, as it was the last dwelling house on the road. Not that he was really interested; they could both sleep in the hills for all he cared. It was about all they looked fit for. The man with the beard was telling the woman something and pointing behind the inn, and without another word he led the donkey off in the direction he had been indicating. The boy wondered what could possibly be at the back of the inn and, his curiosity roused, followed them. As he came to the corner of the building, he saw the man was coaxing the donkey through an open door of what looked like a barn. The boy followed the strange trio and watched them through the crack left by the open door. The barn was covered in dirty straw and full of chickens, sheep and oxen, and smelled to the boy like the sewers they built in the side streets back home. He began to feel sick. The man was clearing away some of the worst of the straw from the centre of the barn, trying to make a clean patch for them to rest on – a near hopeless task, thought the boy. When the man had done as best he could he lifted the fat woman down from the donkey and placed her gently in the straw. Then he left her and went over to a trough on the other side of the barn where one of the oxen was drinking. He cupped his fingers together, put them in the trough and, filling his hands with water, returned to the fat woman.

The boy was beginning to get bored and was about to leave when the woman leaned forward to drink from the man's hands. The shawl fell from her head and he saw her face for the first time.

95

He stood transfixed, staring at her. He had never seen anything more beautiful. Unlike the common members of her tribe, the woman's skin was translucent in quality, and her eyes shone, but what most struck the boy was her manner and presence. Never had he felt so much in awe, even remembering his one visit to the Senate House to hear a declamation from Augustus Caesar.

For a moment he remained mesmerized, but then he knew what he must do. He walked through the open door towards the woman, fell on his knees before her and offered the chicken. She smiled and he gave her the pomegranates and she smiled again. He then dropped the rest of the food in front of her, but she remained silent. The man with the beard was returning with more water, and when he saw the young foreigner he fell on his knees spilling the water onto the straw and then covered his face. The boy stayed on his knees for some time before he rose, and walked slowly towards the barn door. When he reached the opening, he turned back and stared once more into the face of the beautiful woman. She still did not speak.

The young Roman hesitated only for a second, and then bowed his head.

It was already dusk when he ran back out on to the winding path to resume his journey home, but he was not afraid. Rather he felt he had done something good and therefore no harm could come to him. He looked up into the sky and saw directly above him the first star, shining so brightly in the east that he wondered why he could see no others. His father had told him that different stars were visible in different lands, so he dismissed the puzzle from his mind, replacing it with the anxiety of not being home before dark. The road in front of him was now empty so he was able to walk quickly towards the compound, and was not all that far from safety when he first heard the singing and shouting. He turned quickly to see where the

danger was coming from, staring up into the hills above him. To begin with, he couldn't make sense of what he saw. Then his eyes focused in disbelief on one particular field in which the shepherds were leaping up and down, singing, shouting and clapping their hands. The boy noticed that all the sheep were safely penned in a corner of the field for the night, so they had nothing to fear. He had been told by Marcus that sometimes the shepherds in this land would make a lot of noise at night because they believed it kept away the evil spirits. How could anyone be that stupid, the boy wondered, when there was a flash of lightning across the sky and the field was suddenly ablaze with light. The shepherds fell to their knees, silent, staring up into the sky for several minutes as though they were listening intently to something. Then all was darkness again.

The boy started running towards the compound as fast as his legs could carry him; he wanted to be inside and hear the safety of the great gate close behind him and watch the centurion put the wooden wedge firmly back in its place. He would have run all the way had he not seen something in front of him that brought him to a sudden halt. His father had taught him never to show any fear when facing danger. The boy caught his breath in case it would make them think that he was frightened. He was frightened, but he marched proudly on, determined he would never be forced off the road. When they did meet face to face, he was amazed.

Before him stood three camels and astride the beasts three men, who stared down at him. The first was clad in gold and with one arm protected something hidden beneath his cloak. By his side hung a large sword, its sheath covered in all manner of rare stones, some of which the boy could not even name. The second was dressed in white and held a silver casket to his breast, while the third wore red and carried a large wooden box. The man robed in gold

put up his hand and addressed the boy in a strange tongue which he had never heard uttered before, even by his tutor. The second man tried Hebrew but to no avail and the third yet another tongue without eliciting any response from the boy.

The boy folded his arms across his chest and told them who he was, where he was going, and asked where they might be bound. He hoped his piping voice did not reveal his fear. The one robed in gold replied first and questioned the boy in his own tongue.

'Where is he that is born King of the Jews? For we have seen his star in the east, and are come to worship him.'

'King Herod lives beyond the . . .'

'We speak not of King Herod,' said the second man, 'for he is but a king of men as we are.'

'We speak,' said the third, 'of the King of Kings and are come to offer him gifts of gold, frankincense and myrrh.'

'I know nothing of the King of Kings,' said the boy, now gaining in confidence. 'I recognize only Augustus Caesar, Emperor of the known world.'

The man robed in gold shook his head and, pointing to the sky, enquired of the boy: 'You observe that bright star in the east. What is the name of the village on which it shines?'

The boy looked up at the star, and indeed the village below was clearer to the eye than it had been in sunlight.

'But that's only Bethlehem,' said the boy, laughing. 'You will find no King of Kings there.'

'Even there we shall find him,' said the second king, 'for did not Herod's chief priest tell us:

And thou Bethlehem, in the land of Judah,

Art not least among the princes of Judah,

For out of thee shall come a Governor

That shall rule my people Israel.'

'It cannot be,' said the boy, now almost shouting at them. 'Augustus Caesar rules Israel and all the known world.'

But the three robed men did not heed his words and left him to ride on towards Bethlehem.

Mystified, the boy set out on the last part of his journey home. Although the sky had become pitch black, whenever he turned his eyes towards Bethlehem the village was still clearly visible in the brilliant starlight. Once again he started running towards the compound, relieved to see its outline rising up in front of him. When he reached the great wooden gate, he banged loudly and repeatedly until a centurion, sword drawn, holding a flaming torch, came out to find out who it was that disturbed his watch. When he saw the boy, he frowned.

'Your father is very angry. He returned at sunset and is about to send out a search party for you.'

The boy darted past the centurion and ran all the way to his family's quarters, where he found his father addressing a sergeant of the guard. His mother was standing by his side, weeping.

The father turned when he saw his son and shouted: 'Where have you been?'

'To Bethlehem.'

'Yes, I know that, but whatever possessed you to return so late? Have I not told you countless times never to be out of the compound after dark? Come to my study at once.'

The boy looked helplessly towards his mother, who was still crying, but not out of relief, and turned to follow his father into the study. The guard sergeant winked at him as he passed by but the boy knew nothing could save him now. His father strode ahead of him into the study and sat on a leather stool by his table. His mother followed and stood silently by the door.

'Now tell me exactly where you have been and why you took so long to return, and be sure to tell me the truth.'

The boy stood in front of his father and told him everything that had come to pass. He started with how he had gone to the village and taken great care in choosing the food and in so doing had saved half the money his mother had given him. How on the way back he had seen a fat lady on a donkey unable to find a place at the inn and then he explained why he had given her the food. He went on to describe how the shepherds had shouted and beat their breasts until there was a great light in the sky at which they had all fallen silent on their knees, and then finally how he had met the three robed men who were searching for the King of Kings.

The father grew angry at his son's words.

'What a story you tell,' he shouted. 'Do tell me more. Did you find this King of Kings?'

'No, Sir. I did not,' he replied, as he watched his father rise and start pacing around the room.

'Perhaps there is a more simple explanation as to why your face and fingers are stained red with pomegranate juice,' he suggested.

'No, Father. I did buy an extra pomegranate but even after I had bought all the food, I still managed to save one silver denarius.'

The boy handed the coin over to his mother believing it would confirm his story. But the sight of the piece of silver only made his father more angry. He stopped pacing and stared down into the eyes of his son.

'You have spent the other denarius on yourself and now you have nothing to show for it?'

'That's not true, Father, I . . .'

'Then I will allow you one more chance to tell me the truth,' said his father as he sat back down. 'Fail me, boy, and I shall give you a thrashing that you will never forget for the rest of your life.'

'I have already told you the truth, Father.'

'Listen to me carefully, my son. We were born Romans, born to rule the world because our laws and customs are tried and trusted and have always been based firmly on absolute honesty. Romans never lie; it remains our strength and the weakness of our enemies. That is why we rule while others are ruled and as long as that is so the Roman Empire will never fall. Do you understand what I am saying, my boy?'

'Yes, Father, I understand.'

'Then you'll also understand why it is imperative to tell the truth.'

'But I have not lied, Father.'

'Then there is no hope for you,' said the man angrily. 'And you leave me only one way to deal with this matter.'

The boy's mother wanted to come to her son's aid, but knew any protest would be useless. The father rose from his chair and removed the leather belt from around his waist and folded it double, leaving the heavy brass studs on the outside. He then ordered his son to touch his toes. The young boy obeyed without hesitation and the father raised the leather strap above his head and brought it down on the child with all his strength. The boy never flinched or murmured, while his mother turned away from the sight, and wept. After the father had administered the twelfth stroke he ordered his son to go to his room. The boy left without a word and his mother followed and watched him climb the stairs. She then hurried away to the kitchen and gathered together some olive oil and ointments which she hoped would soothe the pain of her son's wounds. She carried the little jars up to his room, where she found him already in bed. She went over to his side and pulled the sheet back. He turned on to his chest while she prepared the oils. Then she removed his night tunic gently for fear of adding to his pain. Having done so, she stared down at his body in disbelief.

The boy's skin was unmarked.

She ran her fingers gently over her son's unblemished body and found it to be as smooth as if he had just bathed. She turned him over, but there was not a mark on him anywhere. Quickly she covered him with the sheet.

'Say nothing of this to your father, and remove the memory of it from your mind forever, because the very telling of it will only make him more angry.'

'Yes, Mother.'

The mother leaned over and blew out the candle by the side of the bed, gathered up the unused oils and tiptoed to the door. At the threshold, she turned in the dim light to look back at her son and said:

'Now I know you were telling the truth, Pontius.'

Caste Off

THE DRIVER of the open-top red Porsche touched his brakes, slipped the gear lever into neutral and brought the car to a halt at the lights before checking his watch. He was running a few minutes late for his lunch appointment. As he waited for the light to turn green, he noticed several men admiring his car, while the women smiled at him.

Jamwal gently touched the accelerator. The engine purred like a tiger and the smiles became even broader. Far more men than usual seemed to be looking in his direction. As the light turned green, he heard an engine revving up to his left. He glanced across to see a Ferrari accelerate away before dodging in and out of the morning traffic. He put his foot down and chased after the man who had dared to steal his thunder.

The Ferrari screeched to a halt at the next set of lights, only just avoiding a cow that was sitting in the middle of the road like a traffic bollard. Jamwal drew up by the side of his challenger, and couldn't believe his eyes. The young woman seated behind the wheel didn't give him so much as a glance, although he couldn't take his eyes off her.

When the light turned green, she accelerated away and left him standing again. Jamwal threw the gear lever into first and chased after her, searching for even the hint of a gap in the traffic that might allow him to overtake her. For the next minute, he kept one hand on the steering wheel and the other on the horn as he swerved from lane to lane, narrowly missing bicycles, rickshaws, taxis, buses and trucks that had no intention of moving aside for him. She matched him yard for yard, and he only just managed to catch her up by the time she came to a reluctant halt at the next traffic lights.

Jamwal drew up by her side and took a closer look. She was wearing an elegant cream silk dress that, like her car, could only have been designed by an Italian, although his mother certainly wouldn't have approved of the way the hemline rose high enough for him to admire her shapely legs. His eyes returned to her face as she once again accelerated away, leaving him in her slipstream. When he caught up with her at the next intersection, she turned and graced him with a smile that lit up her whole face.

When the lights changed this time, Jamwal was ready to pounce, and they took off together, matching each other cyclist for cyclist, cow for cow, rickshaw for rickshaw, until they both had to throw on their brakes and screech to a halt when a traffic cop held up an insistent arm.

When the policeman waved them on, Jamwal took off like a greyhound out of the slips and shot into the lead for the first time. But his smile of triumph turned to a frown when he glanced in his rear-view mirror to see her slowing down and driving into the entrance of the Taj Mahal Hotel. He cursed, threw on his brakes and executed a U-turn that resulted in a cacophony of horns, shaking fists and crude expletives as he tried not to lose sight of her.

He glided up to the front of the hotel, where he watched as she stepped out of her car and handed the keys to a valet. Jamwal leapt out of his Porsche without bothering to open the door, threw his keys to the valet, ran up the steps and followed her into the hotel. As he entered the lobby, she was disappearing into a lift. He waited to see which floor she would get out on. First stop was the mezzanine: fashionable shops, a hair salon and a French bistro. Would it be minutes or hours before she reappeared? Jamwal walked over to the reception desk. 'Did you see that girl?' he asked the clerk.

'I think every man in the lobby saw her, sahib.'

Jamwal grinned. 'Do you know who she is?'

'Yes, sir, she is Miss Chowdhury.'

'The daughter of Shyam Chowdhury?'

'I believe so.'

Jamwal smiled again. A few phone calls and he would know everything he needed to about Shyam Chowdhury's daughter. By the time they next met, he would already be in first gear. The only thing that surprised him was that he hadn't come across her before. He picked up the guest phone and dialled a local number.

'Hi, Sunita. I've been held up at the office, someone needed to see me urgently. Let's try and catch up this evening. Yes, of course I remembered,' he said, keeping a watchful eye on the bank of lifts. 'Yes, yes. We're having dinner tonight. I'll be with you around eight,' he promised.

The lift door opened and she stepped out carrying a Ferragamo bag. 'Got to rush,' he said. 'Can't keep my next appointment waiting.' He put the phone down, just as she walked past him, and quickly caught up with her.

'I didn't want to bother you . . .' he began.

She turned and smiled sweetly, but did not stop walking. 'It's no bother, but I'm not looking for a chauffeur at the moment.'

'How about a boyfriend?' he said, not missing a beat.

'Thank you but no. I don't think you could handle the pace.'

'Well, why don't we try and find out over dinner tonight?'

'How kind of you to ask,' she said, still not slackening her pace, 'but I already have a dinner date tonight.'

'Then how about tomorrow?'

'Not tomorrow, and tomorrow, and tomorrow.'

'Creeps in this petty pace from day to day,' he quoted back at her.

'Sorry,' she said, as an attendant opened the door for her, 'but I don't have a day free before the last syllable of recorded time.'

'How about a coffee?' said Jamwal. 'I'm free right now.'

'I feel sure you are,' she said, finally coming to a halt and looking at him more closely. 'You've clearly forgotten, Jamwal, what happened the last time we met.'

'The last time we met?' said Jamwal, unusually lost for words.

'Yes. You tied my pigtails together.'

'That bad?'

'Worse. You tied them round a lamp post.'

'Is there no end to my infamy?'

'No, there isn't, because not satisfied with tying me up, you then left me.'

'I don't remember that. Are you sure it was me?' he added, refusing to give up.

'I can assure you, Jamwal, it's not something I'd be likely to forget.'

'I'm flattered that you still remember my name.'

'And I'm equally touched,' she said, giving him the same sweet smile, 'that you clearly don't remember mine.'

'But how long ago was that?' he protested as she stepped into her car.

'Certainly long enough for you to have forgotten me.'

'But perhaps I've changed since—'

'You know, Jamwal,' she said as she switched on the ignition, 'I was beginning to wonder if you could possibly have grown up after all these years.' Jamwal looked hopeful. 'And had you bothered to open the car door for me, I might have been persuaded. But you are so clearly the same arrogant, self-satisfied child who imagines every girl is available, simply because you're the son of a maharaja.' She put the car into first gear and accelerated away.

Jamwal stood and watched as she eased her Ferrari into the afternoon traffic. What he couldn't see was how often she checked in her rear-view mirror to make sure he didn't move until she was out of sight.

Jamwal drove slowly back to his office on Bay Street. Within an hour he'd found out all he needed to know about Nisha Chowdhury. His secretary had carried out similar tasks for him on several occasions in the past. Nisha was the daughter of Shyam Chowdhury, one of the nation's leading industrialists. She had been educated in Paris, before going on to Stanford University to study fashion design. She would graduate in the summer and was hoping to join one of the leading couture houses when she returned to Delhi.

Such gaps as Jamwal's secretary hadn't been able to fill in, the gossip columns supplied. Nisha was currently to be seen on the arm of a well-known racing driver, which answered two more of his questions. She had also been offered several modelling assignments in the past, and even a part in a Bollywood film, but had turned them all down as she was determined to complete her course at Stanford.

Jamwal had already accepted that Nisha Chowdhury was going to be more of a challenge than some of the girls he'd been dating recently. Sunita Desai, who he was meant to be having lunch with, was the latest in a long line of escorts who had already survived far longer than he'd expected, but that would rapidly change now that he'd identified her successor.

Jamwal wasn't all that concerned who he slept with. He didn't care what race, colour or creed his girlfriends were. Such matters were of little importance once the light was switched off. The only thing he would not consider was sleeping with a girl from his own Rajput caste, for fear that she might think there was a chance, however slim, of ending up as his wife. That decision would ultimately be made by his parents, and the one thing they would insist on was that Jamwal married a virgin.

As for those who had ideas above their station, Jamwal had a well-prepared exit line when he felt the time had come to move on: 'You do realize that there's absolutely no possibility of us having a long-term relationship, because you simply wouldn't be acceptable to my parents.'

This line was delivered with devastating effect, often when he was dressing to leave in the morning. Nine out of ten girls never spoke to him again. One in ten remained in his phone book, with an asterisk by their names which indicated 'available at any time'.

Jamwal intended to continue this very satisfactory way of life until his parents decided the time had come for him to settle down with the bride they had chosen for him. He would then start a family, which must include at least two boys, so he could fulfil the traditional requirement of siring an heir and a spare.

As Jamwal was only months away from his thirtieth birthday, he suspected his mother had already drawn up a list of families whose daughters would be interviewed to see if they would make suitable brides for the second son of a maharaja.

Once a shortlist had been agreed upon, Jamwal would be introduced to the candidates, and if his parents were not of one mind, he might even be allowed to offer an opinion. If by chance one of the contenders was endowed with intelligence or beauty, that would be considered a bonus, but not one of real significance. As for love, that could always follow some time later, and if it didn't, Jamwal could return to his old way of life, albeit a little more discreetly. He had never fallen in love, and he assumed he never would.

Jamwal picked up the phone on his desk, dialled a number he didn't need to look up, and ordered a bunch of red roses to be sent to Nisha the following morning – hello flowers; and a bunch of lilies to be sent to Sunita at the same time – farewell flowers.

Jamwal arrived a few minutes late for his date with Sunita that evening, something no one complains about in Delhi, where the traffic has a mind of its own.

The door was opened by a servant even before Jamwal had reached the top step, and as he walked into the house, Sunita came out of the drawing room to greet him.

'What a beautiful dress,' said Jamwal, who had taken it off several times.

'Thank you,' said Sunita as he kissed her on both cheeks. 'A couple of friends are joining us for dinner,' she continued as they linked arms and began walking towards the drawing room. 'I think you'll find them amusing.'

'I was sorry to have to cancel our lunch date at the last moment,' he said, 'but I became embroiled in a take-over bid.'

'And were you successful?'

'I'm still working on it,' Jamwal replied as they entered the drawing room together.

She turned to face him, and the second impression was just as devastating as the first.

'Do you know my old school friend, Nisha Chowdhury?' asked Sunita.

'We bumped into each other quite recently,' said Jamwal, 'but were not properly introduced.' He tried not to stare into her eyes as they shook hands.

'And Sanjay Promit.'

'Only by reputation,' said Jamwal, turning to the other guest. 'But of course I'm a great admirer.'

Sunita handed Jamwal a glass of champagne, but didn't let go of his arm.

'Where are we dining?' Nisha asked.

'I've booked a table at the Silk Orchid,' said Sunita. 'So I hope you all like Thai food.'

Jamwal could never remember the details of their first date, as Nisha so often described it, except that

during dinner he couldn't take his eyes off her. The moment the band struck up, he asked her if she would like to dance. To the undisguised annoyance of both their partners, they didn't return to the table again until the band took a break. When the evening came to an end, Jamwal and Nisha reluctantly parted.

As Jamwal drove Sunita home, neither of them spoke. There was nothing to say. When she stepped out of the car, she didn't bother to kiss him goodbye. All she said was, 'You're a shit, Jamwal,' which meant that at least he could cancel the farewell flowers.

The following morning Jamwal sent a handwritten note with Nisha's red roses, inviting her to lunch. Every time the phone on his desk rang, he picked it up hoping to hear her voice saying, 'Thank you for the beautiful flowers, where shall we meet for lunch?' But it was never Nisha on the end of the line.

At twelve o'clock he decided to call her at home, just to make sure the flowers had been delivered.

'Oh, yes,' said the houseman who answered the phone, 'but Miss Chowdhury was already on her way to the airport by the time they arrived, so I'm afraid she never saw them.'

'The airport?' said Jamwal.

'She took the early morning flight to San Francisco. Miss Chowdhury begins her final term at Stanford on Monday,' the houseman explained.

Jamwal thanked him, put the phone down and pressed a button on his intercom. 'Get me on the next plane to San Francisco,' he said to his secretary. He then called home and asked his manservant to pack a suitcase, as he would be going away.

'For how long, sahib?'

'I've no idea,' Jamwal replied.

Jamwal had visited San Francisco many times over the years, but had never been to Stanford. After Oxford he had completed his education on the Eastern seaboard, finishing up at Harvard Business School.

Although the gossip columns regularly described Jamwal Rameshwar Singh as a millionaire playboy, the implied suggestion was far from the mark. Jamwal was indeed a prince, the second son of a maharaja, but the family wealth had been steadily eroding over the years, which was the reason the palace had become the Palace Hotel. And when he had left Harvard to return to Delhi, the only extra baggage he carried with him was the Parker Medal for Mathematics, along with a citation recording the fact that he had been in the top ten students of his year, which now hung proudly on the wall of the guest toilet. However, Jamwal did nothing to dispel the gossip columnists' raffish image of him, as it helped to attract exactly the type of girl he liked to spend his evenings with, and often the rest of the night.

On returning to his homeland, Jamwal had applied for a position as a management trainee with the Raj Group, where he was quickly identified as a rising star. Despite rumours to the contrary, he was often the first to arrive in the office in the morning, and he could still be found at his desk long after most of his colleagues had returned home.

But once he had left the office, Jamwal entered another world, to which he devoted the same energy and enthusiasm that he applied to his work.

The phone on his desk rang. 'There's a car waiting for you at the front door, sir.'

Jamwal had rarely been known to cross the dance floor for a woman, let alone an ocean.

When the 747 touched down at San Francisco International Airport at five forty-five the following morning, Jamwal took the first available cab and headed for the Palo Alto Hotel.

Some discreet enquiries at the concierge's desk, accompanied by a ten-dollar bill, produced the information he required. After a quick shower, shave and change of clothes, another cab drove him across to the university campus.

When the smartly dressed young man wearing a Harvard tie walked into the registrar's office and asked where he might find Miss Nisha Chowdhury, the woman behind the counter smiled and directed him to the north block, room forty-three.

As Jamwal strolled across the campus, few students were to be seen, other than early morning joggers or those returning from very late-night parties. It brought back memories of Harvard.

When he reached the north block, he made no attempt to enter the building, fearing he might find her with another man. He took a seat on a bench facing the front door and waited. He checked his watch every few minutes, and began to wonder if she had already gone to breakfast. A dozen thoughts flashed through his mind while he waited. What would he do if she appeared on Sanjay Promit's arm? He'd slink back to Delhi on the next flight, lick his wounds and move on to the next girl. But what if she was away for the weekend and didn't plan to return until Monday morning, when term began? He had several pressing appointments on Monday, none of whom would be impressed to learn that Jamwal was on the other side of the world chasing a girl he'd only met twice – well, three times if you counted the pigtail incident.

When she came through the swing doors, he immediately knew

why he'd circled half the globe to sit on a wooden bench at eight o'clock in the morning.

Nisha walked straight past him. She wasn't ignoring Jamwal this time, but simply hadn't registered who it was sitting on the bench. Even when he rose to greet her, she didn't immediately recognize him, perhaps because he was the last person on earth she expected to see. Suddenly her whole face lit up, and it seemed only natural that he should take her in his arms.

'What brings you to Stanford, Jamwal?' she asked once he'd released her.

'You,' he replied simply.

'But why—' she began.

'I'm just trying to make up for tying you to a lamp post.'

'I could still be there for all you cared,' she said, grinning. 'So tell me, Jamwal, have you already had breakfast with another woman?'

'I wouldn't be here if there was another woman,' he said.

'I was only teasing,' she said softly, surprised that he had risen so easily to her bait. Not at all his reputation. She took his hand as they walked across the lawn together.

Jamwal could always recall exactly how they had spent the rest of that day. They ate breakfast in the refectory with five hundred chattering students; walked hand-in-hand around the lake – several times; lunched at Benny's diner in a corner booth, and only left when they became aware that they were the last customers. They talked about going to the theatre, a film, perhaps a concert, and even checked what was playing at the Globe, but in the end they just walked and talked.

When he took Nisha back to the north block just after midnight, he kissed her for the first time, but made no attempt to cross the threshold. The gossip columnists had got that wrong as well; at least that was something his mother would approve of. His final words before they parted were, 'You do realize that we're going to spend the rest of our lives together?'

Jamwal couldn't sleep on the long flight back to Delhi as he thought about how he would break the news to his parents that he had fallen in love. Within moments of landing, he was on the phone to Nisha to let her know what he'd decided to do.

'I'm going to fly up to Jaipur during the week and tell my parents that I've found the woman I want to spend the rest of my life with, and ask for their blessing.'

'No, my darling,' she pleaded. 'I don't think it would be wise to do that while I'm stuck here on the other side of the world. Perhaps we should wait until I return.'

'Does that mean you're having second thoughts?' he asked in a subdued voice.

'No, I'm not,' she replied calmly, 'but I also have to think about how I break the news to *my* parents, and I'd prefer not to do it over the phone. After all, my father may be just as opposed to the marriage as yours.'

Jamwal reluctantly agreed that they should do nothing until Nisha had graduated and returned to Delhi. He thought about visiting his brother in Chennai and asking him to act as an intermediary, but just as quickly dismissed the idea, only too aware that in time he would have to face up to his father. He would have discussed the problem with his sister Shilpa, but however much she might have wanted to keep his secret, within days she would have shared it with their mother.

In the end Jamwal didn't even tell his closest friends why he boarded a flight to San Francisco every Friday afternoon, and why his phone bill had recently tripled.

As each week went by, he became more certain that he'd found the only woman he would ever love. He also accepted that he couldn't put off telling his parents for much longer.

Every Saturday morning Nisha would be standing by the arrivals gate at San Francisco International airport waiting for him to appear. On Sunday evening, he would be among the last passengers to have their passports checked before boarding the overnight flight to Delhi.

When Nisha walked up on to the stage to be awarded her degree by the President of Stanford, two proud parents were sitting in the fifth row warmly applauding their daughter.

A young man was standing at the back of the hall, applauding just as enthusiastically. But when Nisha stepped down from the stage to join her parents for the reception, Jamwal decided the time had come to slip away. When he arrived back at his hotel, the concierge handed him a message:

Jamwal,

Why don't you join us for dinner at the Bel Air?

Shyam Chowdhury

It became clear to Jamwal within moments of meeting Nisha's parents that they had known about the relationship for some time, and they left him in no doubt that they were delighted to have a double cause for celebration: their daughter's graduation from Stanford, and meeting the man there she'd fallen in love with.

The dinner lasted long into the night, and Jamwal found it easy to relax in the company of Nisha's parents. He only wished . . .

'A toast to my daughter on her graduation day,' said Shyam Chowdhury, raising his glass.

'Daddy, you've already proposed that toast at least six times,' said Nisha.

'Is that right?' he said, raising his glass a seventh time. 'Then let's toast Jamwal's graduation day.'

'I'm afraid that was several years ago, sir,' said Jamwal.

Nisha's father laughed, and turning to his prospective son-in-law, said, 'If you plan to marry my daughter, young man, then the time has come for me to ask you about your future.'

'That may well depend, sir, on whether my father decides to cut me off, or simply sacrifice me to the gods,' he replied. Nobody laughed.

'You have to remember, Jamwal,' said Nisha's father, placing his glass back on the table, 'that you are the son of a maharaja, a Rajput, whereas Nisha is the daughter of a—'

'I don't give a damn about that,' said Jamwal.

'I feel sure you don't,' said Shyam Chowdhury. 'But I have no doubt that your father does, and that he always will. He is a proud man, steeped in the Hindi

tradition. So if you decide to go ahead and marry my daughter against his wishes, you must be prepared to face the consequences.'

'I appreciate what you are saying, sir,' said Jamwal, now calmer. 'I love my parents, and will always respect their traditions. But I have made my choice and I will stand by it.'

'It is not only you who will have to stand by it, Jamwal,' said Mr Chowdhury. 'If you decide to defy the wishes of your father, Nisha will have to spend the rest of her life proving that she is worthy of you.'

'Your daughter has nothing to prove to me, sir,' said Jamwal.

'It isn't you I am worried about.'

Nisha returned to Delhi a few days later and moved back into her parents' home in Chanakyapuri. Jamwal wanted them to be married as soon as possible, but Nisha was more cautious, only because she wanted him to be certain before he took such an irrevocable step.

Jamwal had never been more certain about anything in his life. He worked harder than ever by day, buoyed up by the knowledge that he would be spending the evening with the woman he adored. He no longer had any desire to visit the flesh-pots of the young. The fashionable clubs and fast cars had been replaced by visits to the theatre and cinema, followed by quiet dinners in restaurants that cared more about their cuisine than about which Bollywood star was sitting next to which model at which table. Each night after he'd driven her home he always left her with the same words: 'How much longer do I have to wait before you will agree to be my wife?'

Nisha was about to tell him that she could see no reason why they should wait any longer, when the decision was taken out of her hands.

•

One evening, just as Jamwal had finished work and was leaving to join Nisha for dinner, the phone on his desk rang.

'Jamwal, it's your mother. I'm so glad to catch you.' He could feel his heart beating faster as he anticipated her next sentence. 'I was hoping you might be able to come up to Jaipur for the weekend. There's a young lady your father and I are keen for you to meet.'

After he had put the phone down, Jamwal didn't call Nisha. He knew that he would have to explain to her face to face why there had been a change of plan. Jamwal drove slowly over to her home in Chanakyapuri, relieved that her parents were away for the weekend visiting relatives in Hyderabad.

When Nisha opened the front door, she only had to look into his eyes to realize what must have happened. She was about to speak, when he said, 'I'll be flying up to Jaipur this weekend to visit my parents, but before I leave, there's something I have to ask you.'

Nisha had prepared herself for this moment, and if they were to part, as she had always feared they might, she was determined not to break down in front of him. That could come later, but not until he'd left. She dug her fingernails into the palms of her hands – something she'd always done as a child when she didn't want her parents to realize she was trembling – before looking up at the man she loved.

'I want you to try to understand why I'm flying to Jaipur,' he said. Nisha dug her nails deeper into the palms of her hands, but it was Jamwal who was trembling. 'Before I see my father, I need to know if you still want to be my wife, because if you do not, I have nothing to live for.'

•

'Jamwal, welcome home,' said his mother as she greeted her son with a kiss. 'I'm so glad you were able to join us for the weekend.'

'It's wonderful to be back,' said Jamwal, giving her a warm hug.

'Now, there's no time to waste,' she said as they walked into the hall. 'You must go and change for dinner. Your father and I have something very important to discuss with you before our guests arrive.'

Jamwal remained at the bottom of the sweeping marble staircase while a servant took his bags up to his room. 'And I have something very important to discuss with you,' he said quietly.

'Nothing that can't wait, I'm sure,' said his mother, smiling up at her son, 'because among our guests tonight is someone who I know is very much looking forward to meeting you.'

How Jamwal wished it was he who was saying those same words because he was about to introduce his mother to Nisha. But he doubted if petals would ever be strewn at the entrance of this home to welcome his bride on their wedding day.

'Mother, what I have to tell you can't wait,' he said. 'It's something that has to be discussed before we sit down for dinner.' His mother was about to respond when Jamwal's father came out of his study, a broad smile on his face.

'How are you, my boy?' he asked, shaking hands with his son as if he'd just returned from prep school.

'I'm well, thank you, Father,' Jamwal replied, giving him a traditional bow, 'as I hope you are.'

'Never better. And I hear great things about your progress at work. Most impressive.'

'Thank you, Father.'

'No doubt your mother has already warned you that we have a little surprise for you this evening.'

'And I have one for you, Father,' he said quietly.

'Another promotion in the pipeline?'

'No, Father. Something far more important than that.'

'That sounds ominous, my boy. Shall we retire to my study for a few moments while your mother changes for dinner?'

'I would like Mother to be present when I tell you my news.'

The Maharaja looked apprehensive, but stood aside to allow his wife and son to enter the study. Both men remained standing until the Maharani had taken her seat.

Once the Maharani had sat down, Jamwal turned to his mother and said in a gentle voice, 'Mother, I have fallen in love with the most wonderful young woman, and I want you to know that I have asked her to be my wife.'

The Maharani bowed her head.

Jamwal turned to face his father, who was gripping the arms of his chair, ashen-faced, but before Jamwal could continue, the Maharaja said, 'I have never concerned myself with the way you conduct your life in Delhi, even when those activities have been reported in the gutter press. Heaven knows, I was young myself once. But I have always assumed that you were aware of your duties to this family, and that in time would marry a young woman not only from your own background, but who also met with the approval of your mother and myself.'

'Nisha and I are from the same background, Father, so let's be frank, it's not her background we're discussing, but my caste.'

'No,' said his father, 'what we are discussing is your responsibility to the family that raised you, and

bestowed on you all the privileges you have taken for granted since the day you were born.'

'Father,' said Jamwal quietly, 'I didn't fall in love simply to annoy you. What has happened between Nisha and me is something rare and beautiful, and a cause for celebration, not anger. That is why I returned home in the hope of receiving your blessing.'

'You will never have my blessing,' said his father. 'And if you are foolish enough to go ahead with this unacceptable union, you will not be welcome in this house again.'

Jamwal looked towards his mother, but her head remained bowed and she didn't speak.

'Father,' Jamwal said, turning back to face him, 'won't you even meet Nisha before you make your decision?'

'Not only will I never meet this young woman, but also no member of this family will ever be permitted to come into contact with her. Your grandmother must go to her grave unaware of this misalliance, and your brother, who married wisely, will now become not only my successor, but also my sole heir, while your sister will enjoy all the privileges that were once to be bestowed on you.'

'If it was a lack of wisdom that caused me to fall in love, Father, so be it, because the woman I have asked to be my wife and the mother of my children is a beautiful, intelligent and remarkable human being, with whom I intend to spend the rest of my life.'

'But she is not a Rajput,' said his father defiantly.

'That was not her choice,' replied Jamwal, 'as it was not mine.'

'It is clear to me,' said his father, 'that there is no point in continuing with this conversation. You have obviously made up your mind, and chosen to bring dishonour on this house and humiliation to the family we have invited to share our name.'

'And if I were not to marry Nisha, having given her my word, Father, I would bring dishonour on the woman I love and humiliation to the family whose name she bears.'

The Maharaja rose slowly from his chair and glowered defiantly at his youngest child. Jamwal had never seen such anger in those eyes. He stood to face his wrath, but his father didn't speak for some time, as if he needed to measure his words.

'As it appears to me that you are determined to marry this young woman against the wishes of your family, and that nothing I can say will prevent this inappropriate and distasteful union, I now tell you, in the presence of your mother, that you are no longer my son.'

Nisha had been standing by the barrier for over an hour before Jamwal's plane was due to land, painfully aware that as he was returning on the same day, it could not be good news. She did not want him to see that she'd been crying. While he was away she had resolved that if his father demanded he must choose between her and his family, she would release him from any obligation he felt to her.

When Jamwal strode into the arrivals hall, he looked grim-faced but resolute. He took Nisha firmly by the hand and, without saying a word, led her out on to the concourse, clearly unwilling to tell her what had happened in front of strangers. She feared the worst, but said nothing.

At the taxi rank, Jamwal opened the door for Nisha before climbing in beside her.

'Where to, sahib?' asked the driver cheerfully.

'The District Court,' Jamwal said without emotion.

'Why are we going to the District Court?' asked Nisha.

'To get married,' Jamwal replied.

•

Nisha's mother and father held a more formal ceremony on the lawn of their home in Chanakyapuri a few days later to celebrate their daughter's marriage. The festivities had gone on for several days, and culminated in a large party that was attended by over a thousand guests, although not a single member of Jamwal's family attended the ceremony.

After completing the seven pheras of the sacred flame, the final confirmation of their wedding vows, the newly married couple strolled around the grounds, speaking to as many of their guests as possible.

'So where are you spending your honeymoon, dare I ask?' said Noel Kumar.

'We're flying to Goa, to spend a few days at the Raj,' said Jamwal.

'I can't think of a more beautiful place to spend your first few days as man and wife,' said Noel.

'A wedding gift from your uncle,' said Nisha. 'So generous of him.'

'Just be sure you have him back in time for the board meeting on Monday week, young lady, because one of the items under discussion is a new project that I know the chairman wants Jamwal to mastermind.'

'Any clues?' asked Jamwal.

'Certainly not,' said Noel. 'You just go away and enjoy your honeymoon. Nothing's so important that it can't wait until you're back.'

'And if we hang around here any longer,' said Nisha, taking her husband by the hand, 'we might miss our plane.'

A large crowd gathered by the entrance to the house and threw marigold petals in their path and waved as the couple were driven away.

When Mr and Mrs Rameshwar Singh drove on to the airport's private runway forty minutes later, the company's Gulfstream jet awaited them, door open, steps down.

'I do wish someone from your family had attended the wedding,' said Nisha as she fastened her seat belt. 'I was hoping that perhaps your brother or sister might have turned up unannounced.'

'If either of them had,' said Jamwal, 'they would have suffered the same fate as me.' Nisha felt the first moment of sadness that day.

Two and a half hours later the plane touched down at Goa's Dabolim airport, where another car was waiting to whisk them off to their hotel. They had planned to have a quiet supper in the hotel dining room, but that was before they were shown around the bridal suite, where they immediately started undressing each other. The bellboy left hurriedly and placed a 'Do not disturb' sign on the door. In fact, they missed dinner, and breakfast, only surfacing in time for lunch the following day.

'Let's have a swim before breakfast,' said Jamwal as he placed his feet on the thick carpet.

'I think you mean lunch, my darling,' said Nisha as she slipped out of bed and disappeared into the bathroom.

Jamwal pulled on a pair of swimming trunks and sat on the end of the bed waiting for Nisha to return. She emerged from the bathroom a few minutes later wearing a turquoise swimsuit that made Jamwal think about skipping lunch.

'Come on, Jamwal, it's a perfect day,' Nisha said as she drew the curtains and opened the French windows that led on to a freshly cut lawn surrounded by a luxuriant tropical garden of deep red frangipani, orange dahlias and fragrant hibiscus.

They were walking hand in hand towards the beach when Jamwal spotted the large swimming pool at the far end of the lawn. 'Did I ever tell you, my darling, that when I was at school I won a gold medal for diving?'

'No, you didn't,' Nisha replied. 'It must have been

some other woman you were showing off to,' she added with a grin.

'You'll live to regret those words,' he said, releasing her hand and beginning to run towards the pool. When he reached the edge of the pool he took off and leapt high into the air before executing a perfect dive, entering the water so smoothly he hardly left a ripple on the surface.

Nisha ran towards the pool laughing. 'Not bad,' she called out. 'I bet the other girl was impressed.'

She stood at the edge of the pool for a moment before falling to her knees and peering down into the shallow water. When she saw the blood slowly rising to the surface, she screamed.

I have a passion, almost an obsession, about not being late, and it's always severely tested whenever I visit India. And however much I cajoled, remonstrated with and simply shouted at my poor driver, I was still several minutes late that night for a dinner being held in my honour.

I ran into the dining room of the Raj and apologized profusely to my host, who wasn't at all put out, although the rest of the party were already seated. He introduced me to some old friends, some recent acquaintances and a couple I'd never met before.

What followed was one of those evenings you just don't want to end: that rare combination of good food, vintage wine and sparkling conversation which was emphasized by the fact that we were the last people to leave the dining room, long after midnight.

One of the guests I hadn't met before was seated opposite me. He was a handsome man, with the type of build that left you in no doubt he must have been a fine athlete in his youth. His conversation was witty and well informed, and he had an opinion on most things, from Sachin Tendulkar (who was certain to be the first cricketer to reach fifty test centuries) to Rahul Gandhi (undoubtedly a future prime minister, if that's the road he chooses to travel down). His wife, who was sitting on my right, possessed that rare middle-aged beauty that the callow young can only look forward to, and rarely achieve.

I decided to flirt with her outrageously in the hope of getting a rise out of her self-possessed husband, but he simply flicked me away as if I were some irritating fly that had interrupted his afternoon snooze. I gave up the losing battle and began a serious conversation with his wife instead.

I discovered that Mrs Rameshwar Singh worked for one of India's leading fashion houses. She told me how much she always enjoyed visiting England whenever she could get away. It was not always easy to drag her husband from his work, she explained, adding, 'He's still quite a handful.'

'Do you have any children?' I asked.

'Sadly not,' she replied wistfully.

'And what does your husband do?' I asked, quickly changing the subject.

'Jamwal is on the board of the Raj Group. He's headed up their hotel operation for the past fifteen years.'

'I've stayed at six Raj hotels in the last nine days,' I told her, 'and I've rarely come across their equal.'

'Oh, do tell him that,' she whispered. 'He'll be so touched, especially as the two of you have spent most of the evening trying to prove how macho you are.' Both of us put nicely in our place, I felt.

When the evening finally came to an end, everyone stood except the man seated opposite me. Nisha moved swiftly round to the other side of the table to join her husband, and it was not until that moment that I realized Jamwal was in a wheelchair.

I watched sympathetically as she wheeled him slowly out of the room. No one who saw the way she touched his shoulder and gave him a smile the rest of us had not been graced with, could have had any doubt of their affection for each other.

He teased her unmercifully. 'You never stopped flirting with the damn author all evening, you hussy,' he said, loud enough to be sure that I could hear.

'So he did get a rise out of you after all, my darling,' she responded.

I laughed, and whispered to my host, 'Such an interesting couple. How did they ever get together?'

He smiled. 'She claims that he tied her to a lamp post and then left her.'

'And what's his version?' I asked.

'That they first met at a traffic light in Delhi . . . and she left him.'

And thereby hangs a tale.

A Wasted Hour

KELLEY ALWAYS thumbed a ride back to college, but never told her parents. She knew they wouldn't approve.

Her father would drive her to the station on the first day of term, when she would hang around on the platform until she was certain he was on his way back home. She would then walk the couple of miles to the freeway.

There were two good reasons why Kelley preferred to thumb a ride back to Stanford rather than take a bus or train. Twelve round trips a year meant she could save over a hundred dollars, which her father could ill afford after being laid off by the water company. In any case he and Ma had already made quite enough sacrifices to ensure she could attend college, without causing them any further expense.

But Kelley's second reason for preferring to thumb rides was that when she graduated she wanted to be a writer, and during the past three years she'd met some fascinating people on the short journey from Salinas to Palo Alto, who were often willing to share their experiences with a stranger they were unlikely to meet again.

One fellow had worked as a messenger on Wall Street during the Depression, while another had won the Silver Star at Monte Cassino, but her favourite was the man who'd spent a day fishing with President Roosevelt.

Kelley also had golden rules about who she wouldn't accept a ride from. Truck drivers were top of the list as they only ever had one thing on their mind. The next were vehicles with two or three young men on board. In fact she avoided most drivers under the age of sixty, especially those behind the wheel of a sports car.

The first car to slow down had two young fellows in it, and if that wasn't warning enough, the empty beer cans on the back seat certainly were. They looked disappointed when she firmly shook her head,

and after a few raucous catcalls continued on their way.

The next vehicle to pull over was a truck, but she didn't even look up at the driver, just continued walking. He eventually drove off, honking his horn in disgust.

The third was a pick-up truck, with a couple in the front who looked promising, until she saw a German shepherd lounging across the back seat that looked as if he hadn't been fed in a while. Kelley politely told them she was allergic to dogs – well, except for Daisy, her cocker spaniel back home, whom she adored.

And then she spotted a pre-war Studebaker slowly ambling along towards her. Kelley faced the oncoming car, smiled, and raised her thumb. The car slowed, and pulled off the road. She walked quickly up to the passenger door to see an elderly gentleman leaning across and winding down the window.

'Where are you headed, young lady?' he asked.

'Stanford, sir,' she replied.

'I'll be driving past the front gates, so jump in.'

Kelley didn't hesitate, because he met all of her most stringent requirements: over sixty, wearing a wedding ring, well-spoken and polite. When she got in, Kelley sank back into the leather seat, her only worry being whether either the car or the old man would make it.

While he looked to his left and concentrated on getting back onto the road, she took a closer look at him. He had mousy grey hair, a sallow, lined complexion, like well-worn leather, and the only thing she didn't like was the cigarette dangling from the corner of his mouth. He wore an open-neck checked shirt, and a corduroy jacket with leather patches on the elbows.

Her supervisor had told her on numerous occasions that if she wanted to be a writer she would have to get some experience of life, especially other people's lives, and although her driver didn't look an obvious candidate to expand her horizons, there was only one way she was going to find out.

'Thanks for stopping,' she said. 'My name's Kelley.'

'John,' he replied, taking one hand off the wheel to shake hands with her. The rough hands of a farm labourer, was her first thought. 'What are you majoring in, Kelley?' he asked.

'Modern American literature.'

'There hasn't been much of that lately,' he suggested. 'But then times are a changin'. When I was at Stanford, there were no women on the campus, even at night.'

Kelley was surprised that John had been to Stanford. 'What degree did you take, sir?'

'John,' he insisted. 'It's bad enough being old, without being reminded of the fact by a young woman.' She laughed. 'I studied English literature, like you. Mark Twain, Herman Melville, James Thurber, Longfellow, but I'm afraid I flunked out. Never took my degree, which I still bitterly regret.'

Kelley gave him another look and wondered if the car would ever move out of third gear. She was just about to ask why he flunked out, when he said, 'And who are now considered to be the modern giants of American literature, dare I ask?'

'Hemingway, Steinbeck, Bellow and Faulkner,' she replied.

'Do you have a favourite?' he asked, his eyes never leaving the road ahead.

'Yes I do. I read *The Grapes of Wrath* when I was twelve years old, and I consider it to be one of the great novels of the twentieth century. "*And the little screaming fact that sounds through all history: repression works only to strengthen and knit the repressed.*"'

'I'm impressed,' he said. 'Although my favourite will always be *Of Mice and Men*.'

'"*Guy don't need no sense to be a nice fella,*"' said Kelley. '"*Seems to me sometimes it jus' works the other way around. Take a real smart guy and he ain't hardly ever a nice fella.*"'

'I don't think you'll be flunking your exams,' said John with a chuckle, which gave Kelley the opportunity to begin her interrogation.

'So what did you do after you left Stanford?'

'My father wanted me to work on his farm back in Monterey, which I managed for a couple of years, but it just wasn't me, so I rebelled and got a job as a tour guide at Lake Tahoe.'

'That must have been fun.'

'Sure was. Lots of dames, but the pay was lousy. So my friend Ed and I decided to travel up and down the California coast collecting biological specimens, but that didn't turn out to be very lucrative either.'

'Did you try and look for something more permanent after that?' asked Kelley.

'No, can't pretend I did. Well, at least not until war broke out, when I got a job as a war correspondent on the *Herald Tribune*.'

'Wow, that must have been exciting,' said Kelley. 'Right there among the action, and then reporting everything you'd seen to the folks back home.'

'That was the problem. I got too close to the action and ended up with a whole barrel of shotgun up my backside, and had to be shipped back to the States. So I lost my job at the *Trib*, along with my first wife.'

'Your first wife?'

'Did I forget to mention Carol?' he said. 'She lasted thirteen years before she was replaced by Gwyn, who only managed five. But to do her justice, which is quite difficult, she gave me two great sons.'

'So what happened once you'd fully recovered from your wounds?'

'I began working with some of the immigrants who were flooding into California after the war. I'm from German stock myself, so I knew what they were going through, and felt a lot of sympathy for them.'

'Is that what you've been doing ever since?'

'No, no. When Johnson decided to invade Vietnam, the *Trib* offered me my old job back. Seems they couldn't find too many people who considered being shipped off to 'Nam a good career move.'

Kelley laughed. 'But at least this time you survived.'

'Well, I would have done if the CIA hadn't asked me to work for them at the same time.'

'Am I allowed to ask what you did for them?' she said, looking more closely at the old man.

'Wrote one version of what was going on in 'Nam for the *Trib*, while letting the CIA know what was really happening. But then I had an advantage over my colleagues that only the CIA knew about.'

Kelley would have asked how come, but John answered her question before she could speak.

'Both my sons, John Jr and Thomas, were serving in the front line, so I was getting information my fellow hacks weren't.'

'The *Trib* must have loved that.'

'I'm afraid not,' said John. 'The editor sacked me the minute he found out I was workin' for the CIA. Said I'd forfeited my journalistic integrity and gone native, not to mention the fact I was being paid by two masters.'

Kelley was spellbound.

'And to be fair,' he continued, 'I couldn't disagree with them. And in any case, I was gettin' more and more disillusioned by what was happening in 'Nam, and even began to question whether we still occupied the moral high ground.'

'So what did you do when you got back home this time?' asked Kelley, who was beginning to consider the trip was every bit as exciting as the journey she'd experienced with the fellow who'd spent a day fishing with President Roosevelt.

'When I got home,' John continued, 'I discovered my second wife had shacked up with some other fella. Can't say I blame her. Not that I was single for too long, because soon after I married Elaine. I can

only tell you one thing I know for sure, Kelley, three wives is more than enough for any man.'

'So what did you do next?' asked Kelley, aware it wouldn't be too long before they reached the university campus.

'Elaine and I went down South, where I wrote about the Civil Rights movement for any rag that was willing to print my views. But unfortunately I got myself into trouble again when I locked horns with J. Edgar Hoover and refused to cooperate with the FBI, and tell them what I'd found out following my meetings with Martin Luther King Jr and Ralph Abernathy. In fact Hoover got so angry, he tried to label me a communist. But this time he couldn't make it stick, so he amused himself by having the IRS audit me every year.'

'You met Martin Luther King Jr and Ralph Abernathy?'

'Sure did. And John Kennedy come to that, God rest his soul.'

On hearing that he'd actually met JFK, Kelley suddenly had so many more questions she wanted to ask, but she could now see the university's Hoover Tower becoming larger by the minute.

'What an amazing life you've led,' said Kelley, who was disappointed the journey was coming to an end.

'I fear I may have made it sound more exciting than it really was,' said John. 'But then an old man's reminiscences cannot always be relied on. So, Kelley, what are you going to do with your life?'

'I want to be a writer,' she told him. 'My dream is that in fifty years' time, students studying modern

American literature at Stanford will include the name of Kelley Ragland.'

'Nothing wrong with that,' said John. 'But if you'll allow an old man to give you a piece of advice, don't be in too much of a hurry to write the Great American Novel. Get as much experience of the world and people as you can before you sit down and put pen to paper,' he added as he brought the car to a stuttering halt outside the college gates. 'I can promise you, Kelley, you won't regret it.'

'Thank you for the lift, John,' said Kelley, as she got out of the car. She walked quickly round to the driver's side to say goodbye to the old man as he wound down the window. 'It's been fascinating to hear all about your life.'

'I enjoyed talking to you too,' said John, 'and can only hope I live long enough to read your first novel, especially as you were kind enough to say how much you'd enjoyed my work, which, if I remember, you first read when you were only twelve years old.'

Just Good Friends

I WOKE UP before him feeling slightly randy but I knew there was nothing I could do about it.

I blinked and my eyes immediately accustomed themselves to the half light. I raised my head and gazed at the large expanse of motionless white flesh lying next to me. If only he took as much exercise as I did he wouldn't have that spare tyre, I thought unsympathetically.

Roger stirred restlessly and even turned over to face me, but I knew he would not be fully awake until the alarm on his side of the bed started ringing. I pondered for a moment whether I could go back to sleep again or should get up and find myself some breakfast before he woke. In the end I settled for just lying still on my side day-dreaming, but making sure I didn't disturb him. When he did eventually open his eyes I planned to pretend I was still asleep – that way he would end up getting breakfast for me. I began to go over the things that needed to be done after he had left for the office. As long as I was at home ready to greet him when he returned from work, he didn't seem to mind what I got up to during the day.

A gentle rumble emanated from his side of the bed. Roger's snoring never disturbed me. My affection for him was unbounded, and I only wished I could find the words to let him know. In truth, he was the first man I had really appreciated. As I gazed at his unshaven face I was reminded that it hadn't been his looks which had attracted me in the pub that night.

I had first come across Roger in the Cat and Whistle, a public house situated on the corner of Mafeking Road. You might say it was our local. He used to come in around eight, order a pint of mild and take it to a small table in the corner of the room just beyond the dartboard.

Mostly he would sit alone, watching the darts being thrown towards double top but more often settling in one or five, if they managed to land on the board at all. He never played

the game himself, and I often wondered, from my vantage point behind the bar, if he were fearful of relinquishing his favourite seat or just had no interest in the sport.

Then things suddenly changed for Roger – for the better, was no doubt how he saw it – when one evening in early spring a blonde named Madeleine, wearing an imitation fur coat and drinking double gin and its, perched on the stool beside him. I had never seen her in the pub before but she was obviously known locally, and loose bar talk led me to

believe it couldn't last. You see, word was about that she was looking for someone whose horizons stretched beyond the Cat and Whistle.

In fact the affair – if that's what it ever came to – lasted for only twenty days. I know because I counted every one of them. Then one night voices were raised and heads turned as she left the small stool just as suddenly as she had come. His tired eyes watched her walk to a vacant place at the corner of the bar, but he didn't show any surprise at her departure and made no attempt to pursue her.

Her exit was my cue to enter. I almost leapt from behind the bar and, moving as quickly as dignity allowed, was seconds later sitting on the vacant stool beside him. He didn't comment and certainly made no attempt to offer me a drink, but the one glance he shot in my direction did not suggest he found me an unacceptable replacement. I looked around to see if anyone else had plans to usurp my position. The men standing round the dart-board didn't seem to care.

Treble seventeen, twelve and a five kept them more than occupied. I glanced towards the bar to check if the boss had noticed my absence, but he was busy taking orders. I saw Madeleine was already sipping a glass of champagne from the pub's only bottle, purchased by a stranger whose stylish double-breasted blazer and striped bow tie convinced me she wouldn't be bothering with Roger any longer. She looked well set for at least another twenty days.

I looked up at Roger – I had known his name for some time, although I had never addressed him as such and I couldn't be sure that he was aware of mine. I began to flutter my eyelashes in a rather exaggerated way. I felt a little stupid but at least it elicited a gentle smile. He leaned over and touched my cheek, his hands surprisingly gentle. Neither of us felt the need to speak. We were both lonely and it seemed unnecessary to explain why. We sat in silence, he occasionally sipping his beer, I from time to time rearranging my legs, while a few feet from us the darts pursued their undetermined course.

When the publican cried, 'Last orders,' Roger downed the remains of his beer while the dart players completed what had to be their final game.

No one commented when we left together and I was surprised that Roger made no protest as I accompanied him back to his little semi-detached. I already knew exactly where he lived because I had seen him on several occasions standing at the bus queue in Dobson Street in a silent line of reluctant morning passengers. Once I even positioned myself on a nearby wall in order to study his features more carefully. It was an anonymous, almost commonplace face but he had the warmest eyes and the kindest smile I had observed in any man.

My only anxiety was that he didn't seem aware of my existence, just constantly preoccupied, his eyes each evening and his thoughts each morning only for Madeleine. How I envied that girl. She had everything I wanted – except a decent fur coat, the only thing my mother had left me. In truth, I have no right to be catty about Madeleine, as her past couldn't have been more murky than mine.

All that had taken place well over a year ago and, to prove my total devotion to Roger, I have never entered the Cat and Whistle since. He seemed to have forgotten Madeleine because he never once spoke of her in front of me. An unusual man, he didn't question me about any of my past relationships either.

Perhaps he should have. I would have liked him to know the truth about my life before we'd met,

I wanted was a warm home, regular food and perhaps in time a family of my own. He ensured that one of my wishes was fulfilled, because a few weeks after he left me I ended up with twins, two girls. Derek never set eyes on them: he had returned to sea even before I could tell him I was pregnant. He hadn't needed to promise me the earth; he was so good-looking he must have known I would have been his just for a night on the tiles.

I tried to bring up the girls decently, but the authorities caught up with me this time and I lost them both.

I wonder where they are now? God knows. I only hope they've ended up in a good home. At least they inherited Derek's irresistible looks, which can only help them through life. It's just one more thing Roger will never know about. His unquestioning trust only makes me feel more guilty, and now I never seem able to find a way of letting him know the truth.

though it all seems irrelevant now. You see, I had been the youngest in a family of four so I always came last in line. I had never known my father, and I arrived home one night to discover that my mother had run off with another man. Tracy, one of my sisters, warned me not to expect her back. She turned out to be right, for I have never seen my mother since that day. It's awful to have to admit, if only to oneself, that one's mother is a tramp.

Now an orphan, I began to drift, often trying to stay one step ahead of the law – not so easy when you haven't always got somewhere to put your head down. I can't even recall how I ended up with Derek – if that was his real name. Derek, whose dark sensual looks would have attracted any susceptible female, told me that he had been on a merchant steamer for the past three years. When he made love to me I was ready to believe anything. I explained to him that all

After Derek had gone back to sea I was on my own for almost a year before getting part-time work at the Cat and Whistle. The publican was so mean that he wouldn't have even provided food and drink for me, if I hadn't kept to my part of the bargain.

Roger used to come in about once, perhaps twice a week before he met the blonde with the shabby fur coat.

After that it was every night until she upped and left him.

I knew he was perfect for me the first time I heard him order a pint of mild. A pint of mild – I can't think of a better description of Roger. In those early days the barmaids used to flirt openly with him, but he didn't show any interest. Until Madeleine latched on to him I wasn't even sure that it was women he preferred. Perhaps in the end it was my androgynous looks that appealed to him.

I think I must have been the only one in that pub who was looking for something more permanent.

And so Roger allowed me to spend the night with him. I remember that he slipped into the bathroom to undress while I rested on what I assumed would be my side of the bed. Since that night he has never once asked me to leave, let alone tried to kick me out. It's an easy-going relationship. I've never known him raise his voice or scold me unfairly. Forgive the cliché, but for once I have fallen on my feet.

Brr. Brr. Brr. That damned alarm. I wished I could have buried it. The noise would go on and on until at last Roger decided to stir himself. I once tried to stretch across him and put a stop to its infernal ringing, only ending up knocking the contraption on to the floor, which annoyed him even more than the ringing. Never again, I concluded. Eventually a long arm emerged from under the blanket and a palm dropped on to the top of the clock and the awful din subsided. I'm a light sleeper – the slightest movement stirs me. If only he had asked me I could have woken him far more gently each morning. After all, my

methods are every bit as reliable as any man-made contraption.

Half awake, Roger gave me a brief cuddle before kneading my back, always guaranteed to elicit a smile. Then he yawned, stretched and declared as he did every morning, 'Must hurry along or I'll be late for the office.' I suppose some females would have been annoyed by the predictability of our morning routine – but not this lady. It was all part of a life that made me feel secure in the belief that at last I had found something worthwhile.

Roger managed to get his feet into the wrong slippers – always a fifty-fifty chance – before lumbering towards the bathroom. He emerged fifteen minutes later, as he always did, looking only slightly better than he had when he entered. I've learned to live with what some would have called his foibles, while he has

learned to accept my mania for cleanliness and a need to feel secure.

'Get up, lazy-bones,' he remonstrated but then only smiled when I re-settled myself, refusing to leave the warm hollow that had been left by his body.

'I suppose you expect me to get your breakfast before I go to work?' he added as he made his way downstairs. I didn't bother to reply. I knew that in a few moments' time he would be opening the front door, picking up the morning newspaper, any mail, and our regular pint of milk. Reliable as ever, he would put on the kettle, then head for the pantry, fill a bowl with my favourite breakfast food and add my portion of the milk, leaving himself just enough for two cups of coffee.

I could anticipate almost to the second when breakfast would be ready. First I would hear the kettle boil, a few moments later the milk would be poured, then finally there would be the sound of a chair being pulled up. That was the signal I needed to confirm it was time for me to join him.

I stretched my legs slowly, noticing my nails needed some attention. I had already decided against a proper wash until after he had left for the office. I could hear the sound of the chair being scraped along the kitchen lino. I felt so happy that I literally jumped off the bed before making my way towards the open door. A few seconds later I was downstairs. Although he had already taken his first mouthful of cornflakes he stopped eating the moment he saw me.

'Good of you to join me,' he said, a grin spreading over his face.

I padded over towards him and looked up expectantly. He bent down and pushed my bowl towards me. I began to lap up the milk happily, my tail swishing from side to side.

It's a myth that we only swish our tails when we're angry.

Christina Rosenthal

THE RABBI KNEW he couldn't hope to begin on his sermon until he'd read the letter. He had been sitting at his desk in front of a blank sheet of paper for over an hour and still couldn't come up with a first sentence. Lately he had been unable to concentrate on a task he had carried out every Friday evening for the last thirty years. They must have realized by now that he was no longer up to it. He took the letter out of the envelope and slowly unfolded the pages. Then he pushed his half-moon spectacles up the bridge of his nose and started to read.

My dear Father,

'Jew boy! Jew boy! Jew boy!' were the first words I ever heard her say as I ran past her on the first lap of the race. She was standing behind the railing at the beginning of the home straight, hands cupped around her lips to be sure I couldn't miss the chant. She must have come from another school because I didn't recognize her, but it only took a fleeting glance to see that it was Greg Reynolds who was standing by her side.

After five years of having to tolerate his snide comments and bullying at school all I wanted to retaliate with was, 'Nazi, Nazi, Nazi,' but you had always taught me to rise above such provocation.

I tried to put them both out of my mind as I moved into the second lap. I had dreamed for years of winning the mile in the West Mount High School championships, and I was determined not to let them do anything to stop me.

As I came into the back straight a second time I took a more careful look at her. She was standing amid a cluster of friends who were wearing the scarves of Marianapolis Convent. She must have been about sixteen, and as slim as a willow. I wonder if you would have chastised me had I only shouted, 'No breasts, no breasts, no breasts,' in the hope it might at least provoke the boy standing next to her into a fight. Then I would have been able to tell you truthfully that he had thrown the first punch but the moment you had learned that it was Greg Reynolds you would have realized how little provocation I needed.

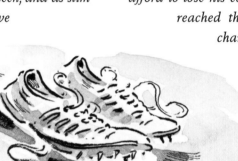

As I reached the back straight I once again prepared myself for the chants. Chanting at track meetings had become fashionable in the late 1950s when 'Zat-o-pek, Zat-o-pek, Zat-o-pek' had been roared in adulation across running stadiums around the world for the great Czech champion. Not for me was there to be the shout of 'Ros-en-thal, Ros-en-thal, Ros-en-thal' as I came into earshot.

'Jew boy! Jew boy! Jew boy!' she said, sounding like a gramophone record that had got stuck. Her friend Greg, who would nowadays be described as a preppie, began laughing. I knew he had put her up to it, and how I would like to have removed that smug grin from his face. I reached the half-mile mark in two minutes seventeen seconds, comfortably inside the pace necessary to break

the school record, and I felt that was the best way to put the taunting girl and that fascist Reynolds in their place. I couldn't help thinking at the time how unfair it all was. I was a real Canadian, born and bred in this country, while she was just an immigrant. After all, you, Father, had escaped from Hamburg in 1937 and started with nothing. Her parents did not land on these shores until 1949, by which time you were a respected figure in the community.

I gritted my teeth and tried to concentrate. Zatopek had written in his autobiography that no runner can afford to lose his concentration during a race. When I reached the penultimate bend the inevitable chanting began again, but this time it only made me speed up and even more determined to break that record. Once I was back in the safety of the home straight I could hear some of my friends roaring, 'Come on, Benjamin, you can do it,' and the timekeeper called out, 'Three twenty-three, three twenty-four, three twenty-five' as I passed the bell to begin the last lap.

I knew that the record — four thirty-two — was now well within my grasp and all those dark nights of winter training suddenly seemed worthwhile. As I reached the back straight I took the lead, and even felt that I could face the girl again. I summoned up my strength for one last effort. A quick glance over my shoulder confirmed I was already yards in front of any of my rivals, so it was only me against the clock. Then I heard the chanting, but this time it was even louder than before, 'Jew boy! Jew boy! Jew boy!' It was louder because the two of them were now working in unison, and just as I came round the bend Reynolds raised his arm in a flagrant Nazi salute.

If I had only carried on for another twenty yards I would have reached the safety of the home straight and the cheers of my friends, the cup and the record. But they

sure Greg wasn't going to get up, I walked slowly back on to the track as the last of the runners were coming round the final bend.

'Last again, Jew boy,' I heard her shout as I jogged down the home straight, so far behind the others that they didn't even bother to record my time.

How often since have you quoted me those words: 'Still have I borne it with a patient shrug, for sufferance is the badge of all our tribe'. Of course you were right, but I was only seventeen then, and even after I had learned the truth about Christina's father I still couldn't understand how anyone who had come from a defeated Germany, a Germany condemned by the rest of the world for its treatment of the Jews, could still behave in such a manner. And in those days I really believed her family were Nazis, but I remember you patiently explaining to me that her father had been an admiral in the German navy, and had won an Iron Cross for sinking Allied ships. Do you remember me asking how could you tolerate such a man, let alone allow him to settle down in our country?

You went on to assure me that Admiral von Braumer, who came from an old Roman Catholic family and probably despised the Nazis as much as we did, had acquitted himself honourably as an officer and a gentleman throughout his life as a German sailor. But I still couldn't accept your attitude, or didn't want to.

It didn't help, Father, that you always saw the other man's point of view, and even though Mother had died

had made me so angry that I could no longer control myself.

I shot off the track and ran across the grass over the long-jump pit and straight towards them. At least my crazy decision stopped their chanting because Reynolds lowered his arm and just stood there staring pathetically at me from behind the small railing that surrounded the outer perimeter of the track. I leaped right over it and landed in front of my adversary. With all the energy I had saved for the final straight I took an almighty swing at him. My fist landed an inch below his left eye and he buckled and fell to the ground by her side. Quickly she knelt down and, staring up, gave me a look of such hatred that no words could have matched it. Once I was

prematurely because of those bastards you could still find it in you to forgive.

If you had been born a Christian, you would have been a saint.

The rabbi put the letter down and rubbed his tired eyes before he turned over another page written in that fine script that he had taught his only son so many years before. Benjamin had always learned quickly, everything from the Hebrew scriptures to a complicated algebraic equation. The old man had even begun to hope the boy might become a rabbi.

Do you remember my asking you that evening why people couldn't understand that the world had changed? Didn't the girl realize that she was no better than we were? I shall never forget your reply. She is, you said, far better than us, if the only way you can prove your superiority is to punch her friend in the face.

I returned to my room angered by your weakness. It was to be many years before I understood your strength.

When I wasn't pounding round that track I rarely had time for anything other than working for a scholarship to McGill, so it came as a surprise that her path crossed mine again so soon.

It must have been about a week later that I saw her at the local swimming pool. She was standing at the deep end, just under the diving board, when I came in. Her long fair hair was dancing on her shoulders, her bright eyes eagerly taking in everything going on around her. Greg was by her side. I was pleased to notice a deep purple patch remained under his left eye for all to see. I also remember chuckling to myself because she really did have the flattest chest I had ever seen on a sixteen-year-old girl, though I have to confess she had fantastic legs. Perhaps she's a freak, I thought. I turned to go in to the changing room – a split second before I hit

the water. When I came up for breath there was no sign of who had pushed me in, just a group of grinning but innocent faces. I didn't need a law degree to work out who it must have been, but as you constantly reminded me, Father, without evidence there is no proof . . . I wouldn't have minded that much about being pushed into the pool if I hadn't been wearing my best suit – in truth, my only suit with long trousers, the one I wore on days I was going to the synagogue.

I climbed out of the water but didn't waste any time looking round for him. I knew Greg would be a long way off by then. I walked home through the back streets, avoiding taking the bus in case someone saw me and told you what a state I was in. As soon as I got home I crept past your study and on upstairs to my room, changing before you had the chance to discover what had taken place.

Old Isaac Cohen gave me a disapproving look when I turned up at the synagogue an hour later wearing a blazer and jeans.

I took the suit to the cleaners the next morning. It cost me three weeks' pocket money to be sure that you were never aware of what had happened at the swimming pool that day.

The rabbi picked up the picture of his seventeen-year-old son in that synagogue suit. He well remembered Benjamin turning up to his service in a blazer and jeans and Isaac Cohen's outspoken reprimand. The rabbi was thankful that Mr Atkins, the swimming instructor, had phoned to warn him of what had taken place that afternoon so at least he didn't add to Mr Cohen's harsh words. He continued gazing at the photograph for a long time before he returned to the letter.

The next occasion I saw Christina – by now I had found out her name – was at the end-of-term dance held in the school gymnasium. I thought I looked pretty cool in my neatly pressed suit until I saw Greg standing by her side in a smart new dinner jacket. I remember wondering at the time if I would ever be able to afford a dinner jacket.

Greg had been offered a place at McGill and was announcing the fact to everyone who cared to listen, which made me all the more determined to win a scholarship there the following year.

I stared at Christina. She was wearing a long red dress that completely covered those beautiful legs. A thin gold belt emphasized her tiny waist and the only jewellery she wore was a simple gold necklace. I knew if I waited a moment longer I wouldn't have the courage to go through with it. I clenched my fists, walked over to where they were sitting, and as you had always taught me, Father, bowed slightly before I asked, 'May I have the pleasure of this dance?'

She stared into my eyes. I swear if she had told me to go

out and kill a thousand men before I dared ask her again I would have done it.

She didn't even speak, but Greg leaned over her shoulder and said, 'Why don't you go and find yourself a nice Jewish girl?' I thought I saw her scowl at his remark, but I only blushed like someone who's been caught with their hands in the cookie jar. I didn't dance with anyone that night. I walked straight out of the gymnasium and ran home.

I was convinced then that I hated her.

That last week of term I broke the school record for the mile. You were there to watch me but, thank heavens, she wasn't. That was the holiday we drove over to Ottawa to spend our summer vacation with Aunt Rebecca. I was told by a school friend that Christina had spent hers in Vancouver with a German family. At least Greg had not gone with her, the friend assured me.

You went on reminding me of the importance of a good education, but you didn't need to, because every time I saw Greg it made me more determined to win that scholarship.

I worked even harder in the summer of '65 when you explained that, for a Canadian, a place at McGill was like going to Harvard or Oxford and would clear a path for the rest of my days.

For the first time in my life running took second place.

Although I didn't see much of Christina that term she was often in my mind. A classmate told me that she and Greg were no longer seeing each other, but could give me no reason for this sudden change of heart. At the time I had a so-called girlfriend who always sat on the other side of the synagogue – Naomi Goldblatz, you remember her – but it was she who dated me.

As my exams drew nearer, I was grateful that you always found time to go over my essays and tests after I had finished them. What you couldn't know was that I inevitably returned to my own room to do them a third time. Often I would fall asleep at my desk. When I woke I would turn over the page and read on.

Even you, Father, who have not an ounce of vanity in you, found it hard to disguise from your congregation the pride you took in my eight straight 'A's' and the award of a top scholarship to McGill. I wondered if Christina was aware of it. She must have been. My name was painted up on the Honours Board in fresh gold leaf the following week, so someone would have told her.

It must have been three months later when I was in my first term at McGill that I saw her next. Do you remember taking me to St Joan at the Centaur Theatre? There she was, seated a few rows in front of us with her parents and a sophomore called Bob Richards. The admiral and his wife looked straitlaced and very stern but not unsympathetic. In the interval I watched her laughing and joking with them: she had obviously enjoyed herself. I hardly saw St Joan, and although I couldn't take my eyes off Christina she never once noticed me. I just wanted to be on the stage playing the Dauphin so she would have to look up at me.

When the curtain came down she and Bob Richards left her parents and headed for the exit. I followed the two of them out of the foyer and into the car park, and watched them get into a Thunderbird. A Thunderbird! I remember thinking I might one day be able to afford a dinner jacket, but never a Thunderbird.

From that moment she was in my thoughts whenever I trained, wherever I worked and even when I slept. I found out everything I could about Bob Richards and discovered that he was liked by all who knew him.

For the first time in my life I hated being a Jew.

When I next saw Christina I dreaded what might happen. It was the start of the mile against the University of Vancouver and as a freshman I had been lucky to be selected for McGill. When I came out on to the track to warm up I saw her sitting in the third row of the stand alongside Richards. They were holding hands.

I was last off when the starter's gun fired but as we went into the back straight moved up into fifth position. It was the largest crowd I had ever run in front of, and when I reached the home straight I waited for the chant 'Jew boy! Jew boy! Jew boy!' but nothing happened. I wondered if she had failed to notice that I was in the race. But she had noticed because as I came round the bend I could hear her voice clearly. 'Come on, Benjamin, you've got to win!' she shouted.

I wanted to look back to make sure it was Christina who had called those words; it would be another quarter of a mile before I could pass her again. By the time I did so I had moved up into third place, and I could hear her clearly: 'Come on, Benjamin, you can do it!'

I immediately took the lead because all I wanted to do was get back to her. I charged on without thought of who was behind me, and by the time I passed her the third time I was several yards ahead of the field. 'You're going to win!' she shouted as I ran on to reach the bell in three minutes eight seconds, eleven seconds faster than I had ever done before. I remember thinking that they ought to put something in those training manuals about love being worth two to three seconds a lap.

I watched her all the way down the back straight and when I came into the final bend for the last time the crowd rose to their feet. I turned to search for her. She was jumping up and down shouting, 'Look out! Look out!' which I didn't understand until I was overtaken on the inside by the Vancouver Number One string who the coach had warned me was renowned for his strong finish. I staggered over the line a few yards behind him in second place but went on running until I was safely inside the changing room. I sat alone by my locker. Four minutes seventeen, someone told me: six seconds faster than I had ever run before. It didn't help. I stood in the shower for a long time, trying to work out what could possibly have changed her attitude.

When I walked back on to the track only the ground staff were still around. I took one last look at the finishing line before I strolled over to the Forsyth Library. I felt unable to face the usual team get-together, so I tried to settle down to write an essay on the property rights of married women.

The library was almost empty that Saturday evening and I was well into my third page when I heard a voice say, 'I hope I'm not interrupting you but you didn't come to Joe's.' I looked up to see Christina standing on the other side of the table. Father, I didn't know what to say. I just stared up at the beautiful creature in her fashionable blue mini-skirt and tight-fitting sweater that emphasized the most perfect breasts, and said nothing.

'I was the one who shouted "Jew boy" when you were still at High School. I've felt ashamed about it ever since. I wanted to apologize to you on the night of the prom dance but couldn't summon up the courage with Greg standing there.' I nodded my understanding – couldn't think of any words that seemed appropriate. 'I never spoke to him again,' she said. 'But I don't suppose you even remember Greg.'

I just smiled. 'Care for coffee?' I asked, trying to sound as if I wouldn't mind if she replied, 'I'm sorry, I must get back to Bob.'

'I'd like that very much,' she said.

I took her to the library coffee shop, which was about all I could afford at the time. She never bothered to explain what had happened to Bob Richards, and I never asked.

Christina seemed to know so much about me that I felt embarrassed. She asked me to forgive her for what she had shouted on the track that day two years before. She made no excuses, placed the blame on no one else, just asked to be forgiven.

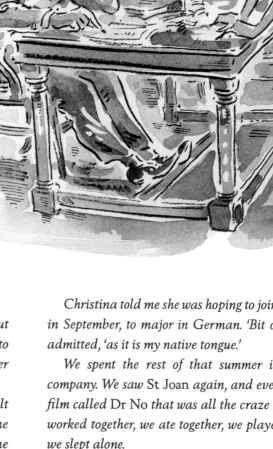

Christina told me she was hoping to join me at McGill in September, to major in German. 'Bit of a cheek,' she admitted, 'as it is my native tongue.'

We spent the rest of that summer in each other's company. We saw St Joan again, and even queued for a film called Dr No that was all the craze at the time. We worked together, we ate together, we played together, but we slept alone.

I said little about Christina to you at the time, but I'd bet you knew already how much I loved her; I could never hide anything from you. And after all your teaching of forgiveness and understanding you could hardly disapprove.

The rabbi paused. His heart ached because he knew so much of what was still to come although he could not have foretold what would happen in the end. He had never thought he would live to regret his Orthodox upbringing but when Mrs Goldblatz first told him about Christina he had been unable to mask his disapproval. It will pass, given time, he told her. So much for wisdom.

Whenever I went to Christina's home I was always treated with courtesy but her family were unable to hide their disapproval. They uttered words they didn't believe in an attempt to show that they were not anti-Semitic, and whenever I brought up the subject with Christina she told me I was over-reacting. We both knew I wasn't. They quite simply thought I was unworthy of their daughter. They were right, but it had nothing to do with my being Jewish.

I shall never forget the first time we made love. It was the day that Christina learned she had won a place at McGill.

We had gone to my room at three o'clock to change for a game of tennis. I took her in my arms for what I thought would be a brief moment and we didn't part until the next morning. Nothing had been planned. But how could it have been, when it was the first time for both of us?

I told her I would marry her – don't all men the first time? – only I meant it.

Then a few weeks later she missed her period. I begged her not to panic, and we both waited for another month because she was fearful of going to see any doctor in Montreal.

If I had told you everything then, Father, perhaps my life would have taken a different course. But I didn't, and have only myself to blame.

I began to plan for a marriage that neither Christina's

family nor you could possibly have found acceptable, but we didn't care. Love knows no parents, and certainly no religion. When she missed her second period I agreed Christina should tell her mother. I asked her if she would like me to be with her at the time, but she simply shook her head, and explained that she felt she had to face them on her own.

'I'll wait here until you return,' I promised.

She smiled. 'I'll be back even before you've had the time to change your mind about marrying me.'

I sat in my room at McGill all that afternoon reading and pacing – mostly pacing – but she never came back, and I didn't go in search of her until it was dark. I crept round to her home, all the while trying to convince myself there must be some simple explanation as to why she hadn't returned.

When I reached her road I could see a light on in her bedroom but nowhere else in the house so I thought she must be alone. I marched through the gate and up to the front porch, knocked on the door and waited.

Her father answered the door.

'What do you want?' he asked, his eyes never leaving me for a moment.

'I love your daughter,' I told him, 'and I want to marry her.'

'She will never marry a Jew,' he said simply and closed the door. I remember that he didn't slam it; he just closed it, which made it somehow even worse.

I stood outside in the road staring up at her room for over an hour until the light went out. Then I walked home. I recall there was a light drizzle that night and few people were on the streets. I tried to work out what I should do next, although the situation seemed hopeless to me. I went to bed that night hoping for a miracle. I had forgotten that miracles are for Christians, not Jews.

By the next morning I had worked out a plan. I phoned Christina's home at eight and nearly put the phone down when I heard the voice at the other end.

'Mrs von Braumer,' she said.

'Is Christina there?' I asked in a whisper.

'No, she's not,' came back the controlled impersonal reply.

'When are you expecting her back?' I asked.

'Not for some time,' she said, and then the phone went dead.

'Not for some time' turned out to be over a year. I wrote, telephoned, asked friends from school and university but could never find out where they had taken her.

Then one day, unannounced, she returned to Montreal accompanied by a husband and my child. I learned the bitter details from that font of all knowledge, Naomi Goldblatz, who had already seen all three of them.

I received a short note from Christina about a week later begging me not to make any attempt to contact her.

I had just begun my last year at McGill and like some eighteenth-century gentleman I honoured her wish to the letter and turned all my energies to the final exams. She still continued to preoccupy my thoughts and I considered myself lucky at the end of the year to be offered a place at Harvard Law School.

I left Montreal for Boston on September 12th, 1968.

You must have wondered why I never came home once during those three years. I knew of your disapproval. Thanks to Mrs Goldblatz everyone was aware who the father of Christina's child was and I felt an enforced absence might make life a little easier for you.

The rabbi paused as he remembered Mrs Goldblatz letting him know what she had considered was 'only her duty'.

'You're an interfering old busybody,' he had told her. By the following Saturday she had moved to another synagogue and let everyone in the town know why.

He was more angry with himself than with Benjamin. He should have visited Harvard to let his son know that his love for him had not changed. So much for his powers of forgiveness.

He took up the letter once again.

Throughout those years at law school I had plenty of friends of both sexes, but Christina was rarely out of my mind for more than a few hours at a time. I wrote over forty letters to her while I was in Boston, but didn't post one of them. I even phoned, but it was never her voice that answered. If it had been, I'm not even sure I would have said anything. I just wanted to hear her.

Were you ever curious about the women in my life? I had affairs with bright girls from Radcliffe who were reading law, history or science, and once with a shop assistant who never read anything. Can you imagine, in the very act of making love, always thinking of another woman? I seemed to be doing my work on autopilot, and even my passion for running became reduced to an hour's jogging a day.

Long before the end of my last year, leading law firms in New York, Chicago and Toronto were turning up to interview us. The Harvard tom-toms can be relied on to beat across the world, but even I was surprised by a visit from the senior partner of Graham Douglas & Wilkins of Toronto. It's not a firm known for its Jewish partners, but I liked the idea of their letterhead one day reading 'Graham Douglas Wilkins & Rosenthal'. Even her father would surely have been impressed by that.

At least if I lived and worked in Toronto, I convinced myself, it would be far enough away for me to forget her, and perhaps with luck find someone else I could feel that way about.

Graham Douglas & Wilkins found me a spacious apartment overlooking the park and started me off at a handsome salary. In return I worked all the hours God – whoever's God – made. If I thought they had pushed me at McGill or Harvard, Father, it turned out to be no more than a dry run for the real world. I didn't complain. The work was exciting, and the rewards beyond my expectation. Only now that I could afford a Thunderbird I didn't want one.

New girlfriends came, and went as soon as they talked of marriage. The Jewish ones usually raised the subject within a week, the Gentiles, I found, waited a little longer. I even began living with one of them, Rebecca Wertz, but that too ended – on a Thursday.

I was driving to the office that morning – it must have been a little after eight, which was late for me – when I saw Christina on the other side of the busy highway, a barrier separating us. She was standing at a bus stop holding the hand of a little boy, who must have been about five – my son.

The heavy morning traffic allowed me a little longer to stare in disbelief. I found that I wanted to look at them both at once. She wore a long lightweight coat that showed she had not lost her figure. Her face was serene and only reminded me why she was rarely out of my thoughts. Her son – our son – was wrapped up in an oversize duffle coat and his head was covered by a baseball hat that informed me that he supported the Toronto Dolphins. Sadly, it really stopped me seeing what he looked like. You can't be in Toronto, I remember thinking, you're meant to be in Montreal. I watched them both in my side-mirror as they climbed on to a bus. That particular Thursday I must have been an appalling counsellor to every client who sought my advice.

For the next week I passed by that bus stop every morning within minutes of the time I had seen them standing there but never saw them again. I began to wonder if I had imagined the whole scene. Then I spotted Christina again when I was returning across the city, having visited a client. She was on her own and I braked hard as I watched her entering a shop on Bloor Street. This time I double-parked the car and walked quickly across the road feeling like a sleazy private detective who spends his life peeping through keyholes.

What I saw took me by surprise – not to find her in a beautiful dress shop, but to discover it was where she worked.

The moment I saw that she was serving a customer I hurried back to my car. Once I had reached my office I asked my secretary if she knew of a shop called 'Willing's'.

My secretary laughed. 'You must pronounce it the German way, the W becomes a V,' she explained, 'thus Villing's'. If you were married you would know that it's the most expensive dress shop in town,' she added.

'Do you know anything else about the place?' I asked, trying to sound casual.

'Not a lot,' she said. 'Only that it is owned by a wealthy German lady called Mrs Klaus Willing whom they often write about in the women's magazines.'

I didn't need to ask my secretary any more questions and I won't trouble you, Father, with my detective work. But, armed with those snippets of information, it didn't take me long to discover where Christina lived, that her

husband was an overseas director with BMW, and that they only had the one child.

The old rabbi breathed deeply as he glanced up at the clock on his desk, more out of habit than any desire to know the time. He paused for a moment before returning to the letter. He had been so proud of his lawyer son then; why hadn't he made the first step towards a reconciliation? How he would have liked to have seen his grandson.

My ultimate decision did not require an acute legal mind, just a little common sense – although a lawyer who advises himself undoubtedly has a fool for a client. Contact, I decided, had to be direct and a letter was the only method I felt Christina would find acceptable.

I wrote a simple message that Monday morning, then rewrote it several times before I telephoned 'Fleet Deliveries' and asked them to hand it to her in person at the shop. When the young man left with the letter I wanted to follow him, just to be certain he had given it to the right person. I can still repeat it word for word.

> *Dear Christina,*
>
> *You must know I live and work in Toronto. Can we meet? I will wait for you in the lounge of the Royal York Hotel every evening between six and seven this week. If you don't come be assured I will never trouble you again.*
> *Benjamin*

I arrived that evening nearly thirty minutes early. I remember taking a seat in a large impersonal lounge just off the main hall and ordering coffee.

'Will anyone be joining you, sir?' the waiter asked.

'I can't be sure,' I told him. No one did join me, but I still hung around until seven forty.

By Thursday the waiter had stopped asking if anyone would be joining me as I sat alone and allowed yet another cup of coffee to grow cold. Every few minutes I

checked my watch. Each time a woman with blonde hair entered the lounge my heart leaped but it was never the woman I hoped for.

It was just before seven on Friday that I finally saw Christina standing in the doorway. She wore a smart blue suit buttoned up almost to the neck and a white blouse that made her look as if she were on her way to a business conference. Her long fair hair was pulled back behind her ears to give an impression of severity, but however hard she tried she could not be other than beautiful. I stood and raised my arm. She walked quickly over and took the seat beside me. We didn't kiss or shake hands and for some time didn't even speak.

'Thank you for coming,' I said.

'I shouldn't have, it was foolish.'

Some time passed before either of us spoke again.

'Can I pour you a coffee?' I asked.

'Yes, thank you.'

'Black?'

'Yes.'

'You haven't changed.'

How banal it all would have sounded to anyone eaves-dropping.

She sipped her coffee.

I should have taken her in my arms right then but I had no way of knowing that that was what she wanted. For several minutes we talked of inconsequential matters, always avoiding each other's eyes, until I suddenly said, 'Do you realize that I still love you?'

Tears filled her eyes as she replied, 'Of course I do. And I still feel the same about you now as I did the day we parted. And don't forget I have to see you every day, through Nicholas.'

She leaned forward and spoke almost in a whisper. She told me about the meeting with her parents that had taken place more than five years before as if we had not been parted in between. Her father had shown no anger when he learned she was pregnant but the family still left for Vancouver the following morning. There they had stayed with the Willings, a family also from Munich, who were old friends of the von Braumers. Their son, Klaus, had always been besotted with Christina and didn't care about her being pregnant, or even the fact she felt nothing for him. He was confident that, given time, it would all work out for the best.

It didn't, because it couldn't. Christina had always known it would never work, however hard Klaus tried. They even left Montreal in an attempt to make a go of it. Klaus bought her the shop in Toronto and every luxury that money could afford, but it made no difference. Their marriage was an obvious sham. Yet they could not bring themselves to distress their families further with a divorce so they had led separate lives from the beginning.

As soon as Christina finished her story I touched her cheek and she took my hand and kissed it. From that moment on we saw each other every spare moment that could be stolen, day or night. It was the happiest year of my life, and I was unable to hide from anyone how I felt.

Our affair – for that's how the gossips were describing it – inevitably became public. However discreet we tried to be, Toronto, I quickly discovered, is a very small place, full of people who took pleasure in informing those whom we also loved that we had been seen together regularly, even leaving my home in the early hours.

Then quite suddenly we were left with no choice in the matter: Christina told me she was pregnant again. Only this time it held no fears for either of us.

Once she had told Klaus the settlement went through

as quickly as the best divorce lawyer at Graham Douglas & Wilkins could negotiate. We were married only a few days after the final papers were signed. We both regretted that Christina's parents felt unable to attend the wedding but I couldn't understand why you didn't come.

The rabbi still could not believe his own intolerance and short-sightedness. The demands on an Orthodox Jew should be waived if it meant losing one's only child. He had searched the Talmud in vain for any passage that would allow him to break his lifelong vows. In vain.

The only sad part of the divorce settlement was that Klaus was given custody of our child. He also demanded, in exchange for a quick divorce, that I not be allowed to see Nicholas before his twenty-first birthday, and that he should not be told that I was his real father. At the time it seemed a hard price to pay, even for such happiness. We both knew that we had been left with no choice but to accept his terms.

I used to wonder how each day could be so much better than the last. If I was apart from Christina for more than a few hours I always missed her. If the firm sent me out of town on business for a night I would phone her two, three, perhaps four times, and if it was for more than a night then she came with me. I remember you once describing your love for my mother and wondering at the time if I could ever hope to achieve such happiness.

We began to make plans for the birth of our child. William, if it was a boy – her choice; Deborah, if it was a girl – mine. I painted the spare room pink, assuming I had already won.

Christina had to stop me buying too many baby clothes, but I warned her that it didn't matter as we were going to have a dozen more children. Jews, I reminded her, believed in dynasties.

She attended her exercise classes regularly, dieted carefully, rested sensibly. I told her she was doing far more than was required of a mother, even of my daughter. I asked if I could be present when our child was born and her gynaecologist seemed reluctant at first, but then agreed. By the time the ninth month came the hospital must have thought from the amount of fuss I was making they were preparing for the birth of a royal prince.

I drove Christina into Women's College Hospital on the way to work last Tuesday. Although I went on to the office I found it impossible to concentrate. The hospital rang in the afternoon to say they thought the child would be born early that evening: obviously Deborah did not wish to disrupt the working hours of Graham Douglas & Wilkins. However, I still arrived at the hospital far too early. I sat on the end of Christina's bed until her contractions started coming every minute and then to my surprise they asked me to leave. They needed to rupture her membranes, a nurse explained. I asked her to remind the midwife that I wanted to be present to witness the birth.

I went out into the corridor and began pacing up and down, the way expectant fathers do in B-movies. Christina's gynaecologist arrived about half an hour later and gave me a huge smile. I noticed a cigar in his top pocket, obviously reserved for expectant fathers. 'It's about to happen,' was all he said.

A second doctor whom I had never seen before arrived a few minutes later and went quickly into her room. He only gave me a nod. I felt like a man in the dock waiting to hear the jury's verdict.

It must have been at least another fifteen minutes before I saw the unit being rushed down the corridor by a team of three young interns. They didn't even give me so much as a second glance as they disappeared into Christina's room.

I heard the screams that suddenly gave way to the plaintive cry of a new-born child. I thanked my God and hers. When the doctor came out of her room I remember noticing that the cigar had disappeared.

'It's a girl,' he said quietly. I was overjoyed. 'No need to repaint the bedroom immediately' flashed through my mind.

'Can I see Christina now?' I asked.

He took me by the arm and led me across the corridor and into his office.

'Would you like to sit down?' he asked. 'I'm afraid I have some sad news.'

'Is she all right?'

'I am sorry, so very sorry, to tell you that your wife is dead.'

At first I didn't believe him, I refused to believe him. Why? Why? I wanted to scream.

'We did warn her,' he added.

'Warn her? Warn her of what?'

'That her blood pressure might not stand up to it a second time.'

Christina had never told me what the doctor went on to explain – that the birth of our first child had been complicated, and that the doctors had advised her against becoming pregnant again.

'Why hadn't she told me?' I demanded. Then I realized why. She had risked everything for me – foolish, selfish, thoughtless me – and I had ended up killing the one person I loved.

They allowed me to hold Deborah in my arms for just a moment before they put her into an incubator and told me it would be another twenty-four hours before she came off the danger list.

You will never know how much it meant to me, Father, that you came to the hospital so quickly. Christina's parents arrived later that evening. They were magnificent. He begged for my forgiveness – begged for my forgiveness. It could never have happened, he kept repeating, if he hadn't been so stupid and prejudiced.

His wife took my hand and asked if she might be allowed to see Deborah from time to time. Of course I agreed. They left just before midnight. I sat, walked, slept in that corridor for the next twenty-four hours until they told me that my daughter was off the danger list. She would have to remain in the hospital for a few more days, they explained, but she was now managing to suck milk from a bottle.

Christina's father kindly took over the funeral arrangements.

You must have wondered why I didn't appear and I owe you an explanation. I thought I would just drop into the hospital on my way to the funeral so that I could spend a few moments with Deborah. I had already transferred my love.

The doctor couldn't get the words out. It took a brave man to tell me that her heart had stopped beating a few minutes before my arrival. Even the senior surgeon was in tears. When I left the hospital the corridors were empty.

I want you to know, Father, that I love you with all my heart, but I have no desire to spend the rest of my life without Christina or Deborah.

I only ask to be buried beside my wife and daughter and to be remembered as their husband and father. That way unthinking people might learn from our love. And when you finish this letter, remember only that I had such total happiness when I was with her that death holds no fears for me.

Your son,
Benjamin.

The old rabbi placed the letter down on the table in front of him. He had read it every day for the last ten years.

A Gentleman and a Scholar

WHEN SHE ENTERED the lecture theatre for the last time, the entire faculty rose and cheered. She progressed up the steps and onto the stage, feigning to be unaffected by their warm reception. She waited for her students to resume their places before she began to deliver her final lecture.

She held her emotions in check as she looked up at the assembled audience for the first time. A lecture theatre that held three hundred and was rarely full was now so packed with professors, lecturers and scholars she had taught over the past four decades, that some of them had spilled out onto the steps at the sides, while others stood hugger-mugger at the back.

Many had travelled from across the nation to sit at her feet and acknowledge the curtain coming down on an illustrious career. But as she stood and looked at them, Professor Burbage couldn't help recalling it hadn't always been that way.

•

Margaret Alice Burbage had studied English literature at Radcliffe before sailing across the ocean to spend a couple of years at the other Cambridge, where she completed a PhD on Shakespeare's early sonnets.

Dr Burbage was offered the chance to remain in Cambridge as a teaching fellow at Girton, but declined as she wished to return to her native land, and like a disciple spreading the Gospel, preach about the Bard of Stratford-upon-Avon to her fellow countrymen.

Although vast areas of America had become emancipated, there still remained a small group of universities who were not quite ready to believe a woman could teach a man – anything. Among the worst examples of these heathens were Yale and Princeton, who did not allow women to darken their doors until 1969.

In 1970, when Dr Burbage applied for the position of assistant professor at Yale, she told her mother after being interviewed by the all-male panel that she had no hope of being offered the post, and indeed, she expected to return to Amersham, where she would happily teach English at the local girls' school where she had been educated. But to everyone's surprise, other than that of the interviewing panel, she was offered the position, albeit at two-thirds of the salary of her male colleagues.

Questions were whispered in the cloisters as to where she would go to the lavatory, who would cover for her when she was having her period, and even who would sit next to her in the dining room.

Several former alumni made their feelings clear to the president of Yale, and some even moved their offspring to other universities lest they be contaminated, while another more active group were already plotting her downfall.

When Dr Burbage had entered the same theatre some forty-two years before to deliver her first lecture, the troops were lined up and ready for battle. As she walked onto that same stage, she was greeted by an eerie silence. She looked up at the 109 students, who were ranged in the amphitheatre around her like lions who'd spotted a stray Christian.

Dr Burbage opened her notebook and began her lecture.

'Gentlemen,' she said, as there weren't any other ladies in the room, 'my name is Margaret Burbage, and I shall be giving twelve lectures this term, covering the canon of William Shakespeare.'

'But did he even write the plays?' said a voice who didn't attempt to make himself known.

She looked around the tiered benches, but wasn't able to identify which of the students had addressed her.

'There's no conclusive proof that anyone else wrote the plays,' she said, abandoning her prepared notes, 'and indeed—'

'What about Marlowe?' another voice demanded.

'Christopher Marlowe was unquestionably one of the leading playwrights of the day, but in 1593 he was killed in a bar-room brawl, so—'

'What does that prove?' Yet another voice.

'That he couldn't have written *Richard II*, *Romeo and Juliet*, *Hamlet* or *Twelfth Night*, all of which were penned after Marlowe's death.'

'Some say Marlowe wasn't killed, but to escape the law, went to live in France, where he wrote the plays, sent them back to England, and allowed his friend Shakespeare to take the credit.'

'For those who indulge in conspiracy theories, that rates alongside believing the moon landings were set up in a TV studio somewhere in Nebraska.'

'The same doesn't apply to the Earl of Oxford.' Another voice.

'Edward de Vere, the seventeenth Earl of Oxford, was unquestionably a well-educated and accomplished scholar, but unfortunately he died in 1604, so he couldn't have written *Othello*, *Macbeth*, *Coriolanus* or *King Lear*, arguably Shakespeare's greatest work.'

'Unless Oxford wrote them before his death.' The same voice.

'There can't be many playwrights who, having written nine masterpieces, then leave them to languish in their bottom drawer and forget to mention them to anyone, including the producers and theatre owners of the day, one of whom, Edward Parsons, we know paid Shakespeare six pounds for *Hamlet*, because the British Museum has the receipt to prove it.'

'Henry James, Mark Twain and Sigmund Freud wouldn't agree with you.' Another voice.

'Neither would Orson Welles, Charlie Chaplin or Marilyn Monroe,' said Dr Burbage, 'and perhaps more interesting, they were unable to agree with one another.'

One young man had the grace to laugh.

'Can Francis Bacon be dismissed quite so easily? After all, he was born before Shakespeare, and died after him, so at least the dates fit.'

'Which is about the only thing that does,' said Dr Burbage. 'However, I acknowledge without question that Bacon was a true Renaissance man. What we would today call a polymath. A talented writer, an able lawyer, and a brilliant philosopher, who ended up as Lord Chancellor of England during the reign of King James I. But the one thing Bacon doesn't seem to have managed during his busy career was to write a play, let alone thirty-seven.'

'Then how do you explain that Shakespeare left school at fourteen, was not well versed in Latin, and somehow managed to write *Hamlet* without visiting Denmark, not to mention half a dozen plays set in Italy, having never set foot outside of England?'

'Only five of Shakespeare's plays are set in Italy,' she said, landing her first blow. 'And scholars also accept that neither Marlowe nor Oxford, or even Bacon, ever visited Denmark.' Which seemed to send her recalcitrant pupils into retreat, allowing her to add, 'However, the distinguished satirist, Jonathan Swift, who was born a mere fifty years after Shakespeare's death, put it so much better than I could:

'When a true genius appears in the world, you may know him by this sign, that the dunces are all in confederacy against him.'

As that seemed to silence them, Dr Burbage felt she had won the first skirmish, but suspected the battalions were reforming before they launched an all-out attack.

'How important is it to have a good knowledge of the text?' asked someone who at least had the courtesy to raise a hand so she could identify him.

'Most important,' said Dr Burbage, 'but not as important as being able to interpret the meaning of the words, so you have a better understanding of the text.'

Assuming the battle was over, she returned to her lecture notes. 'During this semester, I shall require you all to read one of the history plays, a comedy and a tragedy, and at least ten sonnets. Although you may make your own selection, I shall expect you, by the end of term, to be able to quote at length from the plays and sonnets you have chosen.'

'If we were to, between us, select every play and every sonnet, could you also quote at length from the entire canon?' The first voice again.

Dr Burbage looked down at the names on the seating plan in front of her and identified Mr Robert Lowell, whose grandfather had been a former president of Yale.

'I consider myself familiar with most of Shake-speare's work, but like you, Mr Lowell, I am still learning,' she said, hoping this would keep him in his place.

Lowell immediately stood, clearly the leader of the rebels. 'Then perhaps you would allow me to test that claim, Dr Burbage.' And before she could tell the young man to sit down and stop showing off, he added, 'Shall we begin with something easy?

> *'Our revels now are ended. These our actors,*
> *As I foretold you, were all spirits and*
> *Are melted into air, into thin air.*
> *And, like the baseless fabric of this vision,*
> *The cloud-capp'd towers, the gorgeous palaces,*
> *The solemn temples, the great globe itself—'*

Dr Burbage was impressed that he didn't once look down at the text, so she obliged him and took up where he had left off.

> *'Yea, all which it inherit, shall dissolve,*
> *And, like this insubstantial pageant faded,*
> *Leave not a rack behind. We are such stuff*
> *As dreams are made on, and our little life*
> *Is rounded with a sleep.'*

One or two of the students nodded when she added, '*The Tempest*, act four, scene one.' But Lowell was right, he'd begun with something easy. Their leader sat down to allow a lieutenant to take his place, who looked equally well prepared.

> *'Give every man thy ear, but few thy voice;*
> *Take each man's censure, but reserve thy judgement.*

Costly thy habit as thy purse can buy,
But not express'd in fancy; rich, not gaudy;
For the apparel oft proclaims the man,'
the lieutenant recited, his eyes never leaving her, but she didn't flinch.

'*And they in France of the best rank and station*
Are most select and generous, chief in that.
Neither a borrower nor a lender be;
For loan oft loses both itself and friend,
And borrowing dulls the edge of husbandry.
This above all: to thine own self be true,
And it must follow, as the night the day,
Thou canst not then be false to any man.
Hamlet, act one, scene three.'

It was now clear to her that several among their dwindling ranks were not only following the text word for word in open books, but then turning a few pages clearly aware where the next volley would come from, and although another foot soldier had been shot down, someone quite happily rose to take his place. But this one looked as if he'd have been more at home on a football field, and read directly from the text.

'*There shall be in England seven half-penny loaves sold for a penny: the three-hooped pot shall have ten hoops and I will make it felony to drink small beer. All the realm shall be in common; and in Cheapside shall my palfrey go to grass.'*

Dr Burbage had to concentrate as it had been some time since she'd read *Henry VI*. She hesitated for a moment while everyone's eyes remained fixed on her. A flicker of triumph appeared on Mr Lowell's face.

'*And when I am king, as king I will be, there shall be no money: all shall eat and drink on my score; and I will apparel them all in one livery, that they may agree like brothers, and worship me their lord.*

Henry VI, Part Two—' She couldn't remember the act or scene, so to cover herself immediately said, 'But can you tell me the next line?'

A blank look appeared on the young man's face, and he clearly wanted to sit down.

'"*The first thing we do*",' said Dr Burbage, '"*let's kill all the lawyers.*"'

This was greeted with laughter and a smattering of applause, as the questioner sank back in his place. But they hadn't given up yet, because another foot soldier quickly took his place.

'*Now is the winter of our discontent—*'

'Too easy, move on,' she said, as another soldier bit the dust to allow the next brave soul to advance over his fallen comrades. But one look at this particular young man, and Dr Burbage knew she was in trouble. He was clearly at home on the battlefield, his bayonet fixed, and ready for the charge. He spoke softly, without once referring to the text.

'*Take but degree away, untune that sting,*
And, hark, what discord follows! Each thing meets . . .'

She couldn't remember the play the lines were from, and she certainly wasn't able to complete the verse, but he'd made a mistake which just might rescue her.

'Wrong word,' she said firmly. 'Not sting, but string. Next?' she added, confident that no one would doubt she could have delivered the next four lines. She would have to look up the scene once she was back in the safety of her room.

Dr Burbage stared defiantly down at a broken army in retreat, but still their commanding officer refused to surrender. Lowell stood among the fallen, undaunted, unbowed, but she suspected he only had one bullet left in his barrel.

'*The painful warrior famoused for fight,*
After a thousand victories once foil'd—'
She smiled, and said:

'*—Is from the book of honour razed quite,*
And all the rest forgot for which he toil'd.

Can you tell me the number of the sonnet, Mr Lowell?'

Lowell just stood there, like a man facing the firing squad, as his fallen comrades looked on in despair. But in her moment of triumph, Margaret Alice Burbage allowed her pride to get the better of her.

'"*I would challenge you to a battle of wits,*" Mr Lowell, "*but I see you are unarmed.*"'

The students burst out laughing, and she felt ashamed.

Professor Burbage looked down at her class.

'If I may be allowed to leave you with a single thought,' she said. 'It has been my life's mission to introduce fertile and receptive minds to the greatest poet and playwright that ever lived in the tide of times. However, I have come to realize in old age that Will was also the greatest storyteller of them all, and in this, my final lecture, I shall attempt to make my case.

'If we had all been visiting London in 1595, when I would have been a whore or a lady-in-waiting – often the same thing . . .'
Professor Burbage had to wait for the laughter to die down before she could continue, 'I would have taken you to the Globe Theatre on Cheapside to see the Lord Chamberlain's Men, and for a penny, we could have stood among a thousand groundlings to watch my great

ancestor Richard Burbage give you his Romeo. Of course we would have marvelled at the poetry, been entranced by the verse, but I would suggest that it would have been the tale that would have had you on the edge of your seats as we all waited to find out what was going to happen to our hero and his Juliet. What modern playwright would dare to poison the heroine, only to bring her back to life to find her lover, thinking she was dead, has taken his own life, and she, no longer wanting to live, stabs herself? Of course, we are all familiar with the story of Romeo

and Juliet, but if there are those among you who have not read all thirty-seven plays, or seen them performed, you now have a unique opportunity to find out if I'm right. However, I wouldn't bother with *The Two Noble Kinsmen*, as I'm not altogether convinced Shakespeare wrote it.'

She looked at her enthralled audience, and waited only for a moment before she broke the spell.

'On a higher note, I would also suggest that if Shakespeare were alive today, Hollywood would insist on a happy ending to *Romeo and Juliet*, with the two star-crossed lovers standing on the prow of Drake's *Golden Hind* staring out into the sunset.'

It was some time before the laughter and applause died down, and she was able to continue.

'And as for the politically correct, what would the *New York Times* have made of a fourteen-year-old boy having sex with a thirteen-year-old girl on Broadway?'

While the professor waited for the applause to die down, she turned the last page of her notes.

'And so, ladies and gentlemen, despite this being my final lecture, you will not escape without attempting the Burbage witch test to discover who among you is a genuine scholar.' An exaggerated groan went up around the room, which she ignored. 'I shall now read a couplet from one of Shakespeare's plays, in the hope that one of the brighter ones among you will give me the next three lines.' She looked up and smiled at her audience, to be met with apprehensive looks.

'*For time is like a fashionable host*
That slightly shakes his parting guest by the hand.'

A silence followed, and Professor Burbage allowed herself a moment to enjoy the thought that she had defeated young and old alike in her final lecture, until a tall, distinguished-looking gentleman rose slowly from his place near the back of the auditorium.

Although she hadn't seen him for over forty years, Margaret knew exactly who he was. Now gaunt of face, with grey hair, and a severed arm from war to remind her that he wasn't someone who retreated in the face of the enemy.

'*And with his arms outstretch'd, as he would fly,*
Grasps in the comer: the welcome ever smiles,
And farewell goes out sighing,'
he offered in a voice she could never forget.

'Which play?' she demanded.

'*Troilus and Cressida*,' he said confidently.

'Correct. But for your bonus, which act and which scene?'

He hesitated for a moment before saying, 'Act three, scene two.'

It was the right act but the wrong scene, but Professor Burbage simply smiled and said, 'You're quite right, Mr Lowell.'

The Road to Damascus

D O YOU, LIKE ME, sometimes wonder what happened to your school contemporaries when they left and went out into the real world, particularly those in the year above you, whose names you could never forget? While those who followed in the forms below, you would rarely remember.

Take Nick Atkins, for example, who was captain of cricket. I assumed he would captain Yorkshire and England, but in fact after a couple of outings for the county Second XI, he ended up as a regional manager for the Halifax Building Society. And then there was Stuart Baggaley, who told everyone he was going to be the Member of Parliament for Leeds Central, and twenty years later reached the dizzy heights of chairman of Ways and Means on the Huddersfield District Council. And last, and certainly least, was Derek Mott, who trained to be an actuary, and when I last heard, was running an amusement arcade in Blackpool.

However, it was clear to me even then that one boy was certain to fulfil his ambition, not least because his destiny had been decided while he was still in the womb. After all, Mark Bairstow was the son of Sir Ernest Bairstow, the chairman of Bairstow & Son, the biggest iron foundry in Yorkshire, and therefore in the world.

The Short, the Long and the Tall

I never got to know Bairstow while we were at school: not only because he was in the year above me, but because he was literally in a different class. While most boys walked, cycled or took the bus to school, Bairstow arrived each morning in a chauffeur-driven limousine. His father couldn't spare the time to drive his son to school, it was explained, because he was already at the foundry, and his mother couldn't drive.

I really didn't mind the fact that his school uniform was so much smarter than mine, and that his shoes were handmade escaped me altogether. However, I was aware that he was taller and better-looking than me, and clearly brighter, because he was offered a place at Gonville and Caius College, Cambridge (pronounced Keys – something else I didn't know at the time), to read modern languages.

I actually spoke to Bairstow for the first time when I entered the lower sixth, and he had been appointed school captain, but then only because I was a library monitor and had to report to him once a month. And indeed, if we hadn't gone on holiday together – well, I shouldn't exaggerate . . .

Fred Costello, the senior history master, was organizing one of his annual school excursions to the Continent, as it was known before it became the Common Market, or the EEC, and as I was studying history and hoping to go to university, my parents thought it might be wise for me to sign up for the trip to Germany.

When we all clambered on board the train at Leeds Central to set out on the journey, I was surprised to see Mark Bairstow was among our party. Well, not quite, because he sat in a first-class carriage with Clive Dangerfield, who was also going up to Cambridge, so we didn't see them again until we all pitched up at our little hotel in Berlin. I shared a room with my best friend Ben Levy, while Bairstow and Dangerfield occupied a suite on the top floor.

The Road to Damascus

There were fifteen of us in the party, and I spent most of my time with Ben who, like me, supported Leeds United, Yorkshire and England, in that order. It was our first trip abroad and therefore one we weren't likely to forget.

Mr Costello was an enlightened schoolmaster who had served as a lieutenant in the Second World War and seen action at El Alamein, but believed passionately that Britain should join the Common Market, if for no other reason than it would ensure there wouldn't be a third world war.

My abiding memory of Berlin was not the Opera House, or even the Brandenburg Gate, but a concrete monstrosity that stretched like a poisonous snake across the centre of a once united city.

'I want you to imagine,' said Mr Costello, as we stared up at the Wall, 'a twelve-foot barrier being built from the Mersey to the Humber, and you never being able to visit any of your family or friends who live on the other side.'

The thought had never crossed my mind.

After a few days in Berlin, we boarded a charabanc for Dresden, but never once left the coach as we stared out of the windows in disbelief to see what was left of that once historic city. It made me feel that perhaps at times the British had also behaved like barbarians. I was pleased when the coach turned round and headed back to Berlin.

The following day was a schoolboy's dream. After driving to Regensburg, we spent the morning on a coal barge trudging sedately up the Danube, billowing black smoke as we made our way to Passau. After lunch, we took a train to Munich, where we spent three days in a youth hostel with young women actually sleeping in dorms on the floor below us. The next morning we explored the capital of Bavaria, and there wasn't much sign that this had once been the birthplace of the Nazi party. I much admired the Residenz, the vast palace of the Wittelsbachs, where Mark Bairstow looked so relaxed he might have been visiting an old friend at home.

In the evening, we went to the Cuvilliés-Theater to see *La Bohème*, my

first introduction to opera, which was to become a lifelong passion. It would be years before I appreciated how much I owed to Mr Costello, a teacher whose lessons stretched far beyond the classroom.

The following day, we visited the Alte Pinakothek, and I can't pretend I was able to fully appreciate Dürer or Cranach, as I couldn't take my eyes off a group of girls who were being shown around the gallery by the same guide. One in particular caught my attention.

My extra-curricular activities in Bavaria included my first experience of beer, frankfurters, attending the opera, and being kissed goodnight by a girl, although I don't think she was overwhelmed. I just wished we'd had another week as she was clearly in the class above me.

On our final day, Mr Costello brought us all back down to earth when we boarded a bus that didn't announce its destination on the front. We must have travelled some fourteen miles north of Munich before we reached a small town called Dachau. Of course, I knew my closest friend was Jewish, but I

only thought of him as a classmate, and we never quarrelled about anything except who should open the batting for Yorkshire. And when Ben once told me that his grandmother kept a packed suitcase by the front door, I had no idea what he was talking about.

When the bus came to a halt outside the entrance of the concentration camp, we all got off in an uneasy silence and stared up at the uninviting rusty gates. I didn't want to go in, but as everyone else trooped after Mr Costello, I meekly followed. Our first stop was at a vast black wall, where a thousand names had been chiselled into the marble to remind us who had been there only a few years before, and not during a holiday excursion with a tour guide. I saw Ben weeping quietly as he stared at the thirty-seven Levys, three of whom hadn't lived as long as he had. I looked across to see Mark Bairstow looking thoughtful, but apparently unmoved, while the rest of the group remained unusually silent.

The Road to Damascus

The young German guide then took us through the huts that had remained untouched since their occupants were liberated by the Americans. Row upon row of four-tiered bunks, with inch-thick mattresses and no pillows. At one end of the hut, a half-filled bucket of water that had been the lavatory for the fifty-six occupants, emptied once a day. But worse was to come, because Mr Costello had no intention of sparing us.

We climbed back on the bus and took the journey to Hartheim, where our young guide led us into a large soulless building, where we entered a cold eerie room where time had stood still. He pointed to the holes in the ceiling where, he explained, the gas was released into the chamber, but only after the prisoners had been stripped and the doors locked. I felt sick, and didn't have the courage to enter the final room to view the vast ovens that our guard told us had been built in 1933 soon after Hitler had come into power, and where the bodies of his innocent victims were finally turned into dust.

When Ben eventually emerged, he fell to his knees and was violently sick. I thought of his grandmother, and for the first time understood the 'packed suitcase'. I rushed across to join my friend, surprised to find Mark Bairstow already kneeling beside him with an arm around his shoulders, trying to comfort a boy he'd never spoken to before.

I was delighted to follow Mark Bairstow as school captain, even if I couldn't hope to emulate his style and panache. I worked diligently during my final year and, with the conscientious help of Mr Costello, was offered a place at Manchester University to read history. I accepted the offer, even though for a Yorkshireman to cross the Pennines into Lancashire in order to further his education was tantamount to high treason.

By the time I graduated, I didn't need Mr Costello to tell me the profession I was best suited for. And if this tale had been about a schoolmaster, and the years of fulfilment he gained from being a teacher . . . but it isn't.

•   •

I was teaching at a grammar school in Norfolk when my wife became pregnant, and I had to explain to her why she would have to travel up to Yorkshire to give birth to our son; otherwise the lad couldn't play for the county. Not that she had any interest in the game of cricket. It turned out to be a girl, so the subject was never mentioned again. However, I took advantage of being back in Leeds to look up my old friend Ben Levy, now a local solicitor, to suggest we spend a day at Headingley and watch the Roses Match.

Being Yorkshiremen, we were in our seats long before the first ball was bowled, and by the morning break the county were at 77 for two. 'A spot of lunch?' I suggested as I rose from my place in the Hutton stand and glanced up at the President's box to see a face I could have sworn I recognized, despite the passing of time. But he was wearing a dog collar and purple shirt, which threw me for a moment.

I touched Ben on the elbow and, pointing to the box, said, 'Is that who I think it is?'

'Yes, it's Mark Bairstow, the new Bishop of Ripon. Still loves his cricket.'

'But I always assumed he was destined to be the next chairman of Bairstow's, the finest iron forgers in the county.'

'And therefore the world,' laughed Ben. 'But when he went up to Cambridge, he changed courses in his first term and read theology. So no one was surprised he ended up as a bishop.'

Like Mr Costello, I too organized an annual trip to Europe, and after excursions to Rome, Paris and Madrid, I felt the time had come to return to Berlin and see how much the German capital had changed, since the Wall had finally come down.

I found the city was transformed. Only one small graffiti-covered section of the Wall still stood firmly in place, an ugly monument to remind the next generation what their parents and grandparents had endured, which they were now studying as history.

Dresden turned out to be a modern city of steel and glass, and you would have had to search Munich to believe the Germans had ever been involved in a war. And when we visited the Cuvilliés-Theater, two of the boys showed the same excitement that I had felt when I saw my first opera.

When the final day came, I considered, like Mr Costello, it was my duty to visit Dachau, as anti-Semitism was once again rearing its ugly head in my country. I was just as apprehensive as I had been the first time, although I tried not to let the boys and girls know how I felt. When the bus came to a halt outside the main entrance, I silently led the children through the even rustier gates and into the camp, and as far as I could see nothing had changed. My young wards spent some time staring at the names on the memorial wall, and when I saw the thirty-seven Levys, I thought of Ben. The huts remained untouched, and I could see the look of disbelief in the children's eyes when they saw the water bucket at the end of the room. They would never complain again about their cramped dormitories.

Our guide then took us into the museum, where we studied the photographs of prisoners whose black-and-white striped pyjamas hung on their skeletal frames, and of the bodies of lifeless men and

women being dragged from the gas chambers to the ovens. There was even a photograph of Himmler to remind us who had carried out Hitler's orders.

I felt sorry for our German guide, not much older than myself, whose sad eyes suggested that the Nazi era couldn't be that easily cast aside, although like myself, he would have been born after the war.

And then the final stage of the tour, which I had been dreading. I still felt sick when I entered the gas chamber, but at least this time I had the courage to follow my wards into the building where the ovens were situated. I stared at the temperature gauges and switches on the wall and bowed my head. When I raised it again, my eyes settled on the large oven door, and I understood for the first time the journey one young man had taken before he became the Bishop of Ripon.

BAIRSTOW & SON
IRON FORGERS
FOUNDED 1866

Old Love

SOME PEOPLE, it is said, fall in love at first sight, but that was not what happened to William Hatchard and Philippa Jameson. They hated each other from the moment they met. This mutual loathing commenced at the first tutorial of their freshmen terms. Both had come up in the early thirties with major scholarships to read English language and literature, William to Merton, Philippa to Somerville. Each had been reliably assured by their schoolteachers that they would be the star pupil of their year.

Their tutor, Simon Jakes of New College, was both bemused and amused by the ferocious competition that so quickly developed between his two brightest pupils, and he used their enmity skilfully to bring out the best in both of them without ever allowing either to indulge in outright abuse. Philippa, an attractive, slim red-head with a rather high-pitched voice, was the same height as William so she conducted as many of her arguments as possible standing in newly acquired high-heeled shoes, while William, whose deep voice had an air of authority, would always try to expound his opinions from a sitting position. The more

163

intense their rivalry became the harder the one tried to outdo the other. By the end of their first year they were far ahead of their contemporaries while remaining neck and neck with each other. Simon Jakes told the Merton Professor of Anglo-Saxon Studies that he had never had a brighter pair up in the same year and that it wouldn't be long before they were holding their own with him.

During the long vacation both worked to a gruelling timetable, always imagining the other would be doing a little more. They stripped bare Blake, Wordsworth, Coleridge, Shelley, Byron, and only went to bed with Keats. When they returned for the second year, they found that absence had made the heart grow even more hostile; and when they were both awarded alpha plus for their essays on *Beowulf*, it didn't help. Simon Jakes remarked at New College high table one night that if Philippa Jameson had been born a boy some of his tutorials would undoubtedly have ended in blows.

'Why don't you separate them?' asked the Dean, sleepily.

'What, and double my work-load?' said Jakes. 'They teach each other most of the time: I merely act as referee.'

Occasionally the adversaries would seek his adjudication as to who was ahead of whom, and so confident was each of being the favoured pupil that one would always ask in the other's hearing. Jakes was far too canny to be drawn; instead he would remind them that the examiners would be the final arbiters. So they began their own subterfuge by referring to each other, just in earshot, as 'that silly woman', and 'that arrogant man'. By the end of their second year they were almost unable to remain in the same room together.

In the long vacation William took a passing interest in Al Jolson and a girl called Ruby while Philippa flirted with the Charleston and a young naval lieu-

tenant from Dartmouth. But when term started in earnest these interludes were never admitted and soon forgotten.

At the beginning of their third year they both, on Simon Jakes' advice, entered for the Charles Oldham Shakespeare prize along with every other student in the year who was considered likely to gain a First. The Charles Oldham was awarded for an essay on a set aspect of Shakespeare's work, and Philippa and William both realized that this would be the only time in their academic lives that they would be tested against each other in closed competition. Surreptitiously, they worked their separate ways through the entire Shakespearian canon, from *Henry VI* to *Henry VIII*, and kept Jakes well over his appointed tutorial hours, demanding more and more refined discussion of more and more obscure points.

The chosen theme for the prize essay that year was 'Satire in Shakespeare'. *Troilus and Cressida* clearly called for the most attention but both found there were nuances in virtually every one of the bard's thirty-seven plays. 'Not to mention a gross of sonnets,' wrote Philippa home to her father in a rare moment of self-doubt. As the year drew to a close it became obvious to all concerned that either William or Philippa had to win the prize while the other would undoubtedly come second. Nevertheless no one was willing to venture an opinion as to who the victor would be. The New College porter, an expert in these matters, opening his usual book for the Charles Oldham, made them both evens, ten to one the rest of the field.

Before the prize essay submission date was due, they both had to sit their final degree examinations. Philippa and William confronted the examination papers every morning and afternoon for two weeks with an appetite that bordered on the vulgar. It came as no surprise to anyone that they both achieved first class degrees in the final honours school. Rumour spread around the university that the two rivals had been awarded alphas in every one of their nine papers.

'I would be willing to believe that is the case,' Philippa told William. 'But I feel I must point out to you that there is a considerable difference between an alpha plus and an alpha minus.'

'I couldn't agree with you *more*,' said William. 'And when you discover who has won the Charles Oldham, you will know who was awarded *less*.'

With only three weeks left before the prize essay had to be handed in they both worked twelve hours a day, falling asleep over open text books, dreaming that the other was still beavering away. When the appointed hour came they met in the marble-floored entrance hall of the Examination Schools, sombre in subfusc.

'Good morning, William, I do hope your efforts will manage to secure a place in the first six.'

'Thank you, Philippa. If they don't I shall look for the names C. S. Lewis, Nichol Smith, Nevill Coghill, Edmund Blunden, R. W. Chambers and H. W. Garrard ahead of me. There's certainly no one else in the field to worry about.'

'I am only pleased,' said Philippa, as if she had not heard his reply, 'that you were not seated next to me when I wrote my essay, thus ensuring for the first time in three years that you weren't able to crib from my notes.'

'The only item I have ever cribbed from you, Philippa, was the Oxford to London timetable, and that I discovered

later to be out-of-date, which was in keeping with the rest of your efforts.'

They both handed in their twenty-five-thousand-word essays to the collector's office in the Examination Schools and left without a further word, returning to their respective colleges impatiently to await the result.

William tried to relax the weekend after submitting his essay, and for the first time in three years he played some tennis, against a girl from St Anne's, failing to win a game, let alone a set. He nearly sank when he went swimming, and actually did so when

punting. He was only relieved that Philippa had not been witness to any of his feeble physical efforts.

On Monday night after a resplendent dinner with the Master of Merton, he decided to take a walk along the banks of the Cherwell to clear his head before going to bed. The May evening was still light as he made his way down through the narrow confines of Merton Wall, across the meadows to the banks of the Cherwell. As he strolled along the winding path, he thought he spied his rival ahead of him under a tree reading. He considered turning back but decided she might already have spotted him, so he kept on walking.

He had not seen Philippa for three days although she had rarely been out of his thoughts: once he had won the Charles Oldham, the silly woman would have to climb down from that high horse of hers. He smiled at the thought and decided to walk nonchalantly past her. As he drew nearer, he lifted his eyes from the path in front of him to steal a quick glance in her direction, and could feel himself reddening in anticipation of her inevitable well-timed insult. Nothing happened so he looked more carefully, only to discover on closer inspection that she was not reading: her head was bowed in her hands and she appeared to be sobbing quietly. He slowed his progress to observe, not the formidable rival who had for three years dogged his every step, but a forlorn and lonely creature who looked somewhat helpless.

William's first reaction was to think that the winner of the prize essay competition had been leaked to her and that he had indeed achieved his victory. On reflection, he realized that could not be the case: the examiners would only have received the essays that morning and as all the assessors read each submission the results could not possibly be forth-

coming until at least the end of the week. Philippa did not look up when he reached her side – he was even unsure whether she was aware of his presence. As he stopped to gaze at his adversary William could not help noticing how her long red hair curled just as it touched the shoulder. He sat down beside her but still she did not stir.

'What's the matter?' he asked. 'Is there anything I can do?'

She raised her head, revealing a face flushed from crying.

'No, nothing William, except leave me alone. You deprive me of solitude without affording me company.'

William was pleased that he immediately recognized the little literary allusion. 'What's the matter, Madame de Sévigné?' he asked, more out of curiosity than concern, torn between sympathy and catching her with her guard down.

It seemed a long time before she replied.

'My father died this morning,' she said finally, as if speaking to herself.

It struck William as strange that after three years of seeing Philippa almost every day he knew nothing about her home life.

'And your mother?' he said.

'She died when I was three. I don't even remember her. My father is—' She paused. 'Was a parish priest and brought me up, sacrificing everything he had to get me to Oxford, even the family silver. I wanted so much to win the Charles Oldham for him.'

William put his arm tentatively on Philippa's shoulder.

'Don't be absurd. When you win the prize, they'll pronounce you the star pupil of the decade. After all, you will have had to beat me to achieve the distinction.'

'Come on then, you silly woman,' he said. 'I'll walk you back to your college.'

'Last time you called me "silly woman" you meant it.'

William found it natural that they should hold hands as they walked along the river bank. Neither spoke until they reached Somerville.

'What time shall I pick you up?' he asked, not letting go of her hand.

'I didn't know you had a car.'

'My father presented me with an old MG when I was awarded a First. I have been longing to find some excuse to show the damn thing off to you. It has a press button start, you know.'

'Obviously he didn't want to risk waiting to give you the car on the Charles Oldham results.' William laughed more heartily than the little dig merited.

'Sorry,' she said. 'Put it down to habit. I shall look forward to seeing if you drive as appallingly as you write, in which case the journey may never come to any conclusion. I'll be ready for you at ten.'

On the journey down to Hampshire, Philippa talked about her father's work as a parish priest and enquired after William's family. They stopped for lunch at a pub in Winchester. Rabbit stew and mashed potatoes.

'The first meal we've had together,' said William.

No sardonic reply came flying back; Philippa simply smiled.

After lunch they travelled on to the village of Brockenhurst. William brought his car to an uncertain

She tried to laugh. 'Of course I wanted to beat you, William, but only for my father.'

'How did he die?'

'Cancer, only he never let me know. He asked me not to go home before the summer term as he felt the break might interfere with my finals and the Charles Oldham. While all the time he must have been keeping me away because he knew if I saw the state he was in that would have been the end of my completing any serious work.'

'Where do you live?' asked William, again surprised that he did not know.

'Brockenhurst. In Hampshire. I'm going back there tomorrow morning. The funeral's on Wednesday.'

'May I take you?' asked William.

Philippa looked up and was aware of a softness in her adversary's eyes that she had not seen before. 'That would be kind, William.'

halt on the gravel outside the vicarage. An elderly maid, dressed in black, answered the door, surprised to see Miss Philippa with a man. Philippa introduced Annie to William and asked her to make up the spare room.

'I'm so glad you've found yourself such a nice young man,' remarked Annie later. 'Have you known him long?'

Philippa smiled. 'No, we met for the first time yesterday.'

Philippa cooked William dinner, which they ate by a fire he had made up in the front room. Although hardly a word passed between them for three hours, neither was bored. Philippa began to notice the way William's untidy fair hair fell over his forehead and thought how distinguished he would look in old age.

The next morning, she walked into the church on William's arm and stood bravely through the funeral. When the service was over William took her back to the vicarage, crowded with the many friends the parson had made.

'You mustn't think ill of us,' said Mr Crump, the vicar's warden, to Philippa. 'You were everything to your father and we were all under strict instructions not to let you know about his illness in case it should interfere with the Charles Oldham. That is the name of the prize, isn't it?'

'Yes,' said Philippa. 'But that all seems so unimportant now.'

'She will win the prize in her father's memory,' said William.

Philippa turned and looked at him, realizing for the first time that he actually wanted her to win the Charles Oldham.

They stayed that night at the vicarage and drove back to Oxford on the Thursday. On the Friday morning at ten o'clock William returned to Philippa's college and asked the porter if he could speak to Miss Jameson.

'Would you be kind enough to wait in the Horsebox, sir,' said the porter as he showed William into a little room at the back of the lodge and then scurried off to find Miss Jameson. They returned together a few minutes later.

'What on earth are you doing here?'

'Come to take you to Stratford.'

'But I haven't even had time to unpack the things I brought back from Brockenhurst.'

'Just do as you are told for once; I'll give you fifteen minutes.'

'Of course,' she said. 'Who am I to disobey the next winner of the Charles Oldham? I shall even allow you to come up to my room for one minute and help me unpack.'

The porter's eyebrows nudged the edge of his cap but he remained silent, in deference to Miss Jameson's recent bereavement. Again it surprised William to think that he had never been to Philippa's room during their three years. He had climbed the walls of all the women's colleges to be with a variety of girls of varying stupidity but never with Philippa. He sat down on the end of the bed.

'Not there, you thoughtless creature. The maid has only just made it. Men are all the same, you never sit in chairs.'

'I shall one day,' said William. 'The chair of English Language and Literature.'

'Not as long as I'm at this university, you won't,' she said, as she disappeared into the bathroom.

'Good intentions are one thing but talent is quite another,' he shouted at her retreating back, privately pleased that her competitive streak seemed to he returning.

Fifteen minutes later she came out of the bathroom in a yellow flowered dress with a neat white collar and matching cuffs. William thought she might even be wearing a touch of make-up.

'It will do our reputations no good to be seen together,' she said.

'I've thought about that,' said William. 'If asked, I shall say you're my charity.'

'Your charity?'

'Yes, this year I'm supporting distressed orphans.'

Philippa signed out of college until midnight and the two scholars travelled down to Stratford, stopping off at Broadway for lunch. In the afternoon they rowed on the River Avon. William warned Philippa of his last disastrous outing in a punt. She admitted that she had already heard of the exhibition he had made of himself, but they arrived safely back at the shore: perhaps because Philippa took over the rowing. They went to see John Gielgud playing Romeo and dined at the Dirty Duck. Philippa was even quite rude to William during the meal.

They started their journey home just after eleven and Philippa fell into a half sleep as they could hardly hear each other above the noise of the car engine. It must have been about twenty-five miles outside of Oxford that the MG came to a halt.

'I thought,' said William, 'that when the petrol gauge showed empty there was at least another gallon left in the tank.'

'You're obviously wrong, and not for the first time, and because of such foresight you'll have to walk to the nearest garage all by yourself – you needn't imagine that I'm going to keep you company. I intend to stay put, right here in the warmth.'

'But there isn't a garage between here and Oxford,' protested William.

'Then you'll have to carry me. I am far too fragile to walk.'

'I wouldn't be able to manage fifty yards after that sumptuous dinner and all that wine.'

'It is no small mystery to me, William, how you could have managed a first-class honours degree in English when you can't even read a petrol gauge.'

'There's only one thing for it,' said William. 'We'll have to wait for the first bus in the morning.'

Philippa clambered into the back seat and did not speak to him again before falling asleep. William donned his hat, scarf and gloves, crossed his arms for warmth, and touched the tangled red mane of Philippa's hair as she slept. He then took off his coat and placed it so that it covered her.

Philippa woke first, a little after six, and groaned as she tried

to stretch her aching limbs. She then shook William awake to ask him why his father hadn't been considerate enough to buy him a car with a comfortable back seat.

'But this is the niftiest thing going,' said William, gingerly kneading his neck muscles before putting his coat back on.

'But it isn't going, and won't without petrol,' she replied, getting out of the car to stretch her legs.

'But I only let it run out for one reason,' said William, following her to the front of the car.

Philippa waited for a feeble punch line and was not disappointed.

'My father told me if I spent the night with a barmaid then I should simply order an extra pint of beer, but if I spent the night with the vicar's daughter, I would have to marry her.'

Philippa laughed. William, tired, unshaven, and encumbered by his heavy coat, struggled to get down on one knee.

'What are you doing, William?'

'What do you think I'm doing, you silly woman? I am going to ask you to marry me.'

'An invitation I am happy to decline, William. If I accepted such a proposal I might end up spending the rest of my life stranded on the road between Oxford and Stratford.'

'Will you marry me if I win the Charles Oldham?'

'As there is absolutely no fear of that happening I can safely say, yes. Now do get off your knee, William, before someone mistakes you for a straying stork.'

The first bus arrived at five past seven that Saturday morning and took Philippa and William back to Oxford. Philippa went to her rooms for a long hot bath while William filled a petrol can and returned to his deserted MG. Having completed the task, he drove straight to Somerville and once again asked if he could see Miss Jameson. She came down a few minutes later.

'What, you again?' she said. 'Am I not in enough trouble already?'

'Why so?'

'Because I was out after midnight, unaccompanied.'

'You were accompanied.'

'Yes, and that's what's worrying them.'

'Did you tell them we spent the night together?'

'No, I did not. I don't mind our contemporaries thinking I'm promiscuous, but I have strong objections to their believing that I have no taste. Now kindly go away, as I am contemplating the horror of your winning the Charles Oldham and my having to spend the rest of my life with you.'

'You know I'm bound to win, so why don't you come live with me now?'

'I realize that it has become fashionable to sleep with just anyone nowadays, William, but if this is to be my last weekend of freedom I intend to savour it, especially as I may have to consider committing suicide.'

'I love you.'

'For the last time, William, go away. And if you haven't won the Charles Oldham don't ever show your face in Somerville again.'

William left, desperate to know the result of the prize essay competition. Had he realized how much Philippa wanted him to win he might have slept that night.

On Monday morning they both arrived early in the Examination Schools and stood waiting impatiently without speaking to each other, jostled by the other undergraduates of their year who had also been entered for the prize. On the stroke of ten the chairman of the examiners, in full academic dress, walking at tortoise-like pace, arrived in the great hall and with a considerable pretence at indifference pinned a notice to the board. All the undergraduates who had entered for the prize rushed forward except for William and Philippa, who stood alone, aware that it was now too late to influence a result they were both dreading.

A girl shot out from the mêlée around the notice board and ran over to Philippa.

'Well done, Phil. You've won.'

Tears came to Philippa's eyes as she turned towards William.

'May I add my congratulations,' he said quickly, 'you obviously deserved the prize.'

'I wanted to say something to you on Saturday.'

'You did, you said if I lost I must never show my face in Somerville again.'

'No, I wanted to say: I do love nothing in the world so well as you; is not that strange?'

He looked at her silently for a long moment. It was impossible to improve upon Beatrice's reply.

'As strange as the thing I know not,' he said softly.

A college friend slapped him on the shoulder, took his hand and shook it vigorously. *Proxime accessit* was obviously impressive in some people's eyes, if not in William's.

'Well done, William.'

'Second place is not worthy of praise,' said William disdainfully.

'But you won, Billy boy.'

Philippa and William stared at each other.

'What do you mean?' said William.

'Exactly what I said. You've won the Charles Oldham.'

Philippa and William ran to the board and studied the notice.

CHARLES OLDHAM
MEMORIAL PRIZE

The examiners felt unable on this occasion to award the prize to one person and have therefore decided that it should be shared by

They gazed at the notice board in silence for some moments. Finally, Philippa bit her lip and said in a small voice:

'Well, you didn't do too badly, considering the competition. I'm prepared to honour my undertaking but by this light I take thee for pity.'

William needed no prompting. 'I would not deny you, but by this good day I yield upon great persuasion, for I was told you were in a consumption.'

And to the delight of their peers and the amazement of the retreating don, they embraced under the notice board.

Rumour had it that from that moment on they were never apart for more than a few hours.

The marriage took place a month later in Philippa's family church at Brockenhurst. 'Well, when you

think about it,' said William's room-mate, 'who else could she have married?' The contentious couple started their honeymoon in Athens arguing about the relative significance of Doric and Ionic architecture, of which neither knew any more than they had covertly conned from a half-crown tourist guide. They sailed on to Istanbul, where William prostrated himself at the front of every mosque he could find while Philippa stood on her own at the back fuming at the Turks' treatment of women.

'The Turks are a shrewd race,' declared William, 'so quick to appreciate real worth.'

'Then why don't you embrace the Muslim religion, William, and I need only be in your presence once a year.'

'The misfortune of birth, a misplaced loyalty and the signing of an unfortunate contract dictate that I spend the rest of my life with you.'

Back at Oxford, with junior research fellowships at their respective colleges, they settled down to serious creative work. William embarked upon a massive study of word usage in Marlowe and, in his spare moments, taught himself statistics to assist his findings. Philippa chose as her subject the influence of the Reformation on seventeenth-century English writers and was soon drawn beyond literature into art and music. She bought herself a spinet and took to playing Dowland and Gibbons in the evening.

'For Christ's sake,' said William, exasperated by the tinny sound, 'you won't deduce their religious convictions from their key signatures.'

'More informative than ifs and ands, my dear,' she said, imperturbably, 'and at night so much more relaxing than pots and pans.'

Three years later, with well-received D. Phils, they moved on, inexorably in tandem, to college teaching fellowships. As the long shadow of fascism fell across Europe, they read, wrote, criticized and coached by quiet firesides in unchanging quadrangles.

'A rather dull Schools year for me,' said William, 'but I still managed five firsts from a field of eleven.'

'An even duller one for me,' said Philippa, 'but somehow I squeezed three firsts out of six, and you won't have to invoke the binomial theorem, William, to work out that it's an arithmetical victory for me.'

'The chairman of the examiners tells me,' said William, 'that a greater part of what your pupils say is no more than a recitation from memory.'

'He told me,' she retorted, 'that yours have to make it up as they go along.'

When they dined together in college the guest list was always quickly filled, and as soon as grace had been said, the sharpness of their dialogue would flash across the candelabra.

'I hear a rumour, Philippa, that the college doesn't feel able to renew your fellowship at the end of the year.'

'I fear you speak the truth, William,' she replied. 'They decided they couldn't renew mine at the same time as offering me yours.'

'Do you think they will ever make you a Fellow of the British Academy, William?'

'I must say, with some considerable disappointment, never.'

'I am sorry to hear that; why not?'

'Because when they did invite me, I informed the President that I would prefer to wait to be elected at the same time as my wife.'

Some non-university guests sitting in high table for the first time took their verbal battles seriously; others could only be envious of such love.

One Fellow uncharitably suggested they rehearsed their lines before coming to dinner for fear it might be thought they were getting on well together.

During their early years as young dons, they became acknowledged as the leaders in their respective fields. Like magnets, they attracted the brightest undergraduates while apparently remaining poles apart themselves.

'Dr Hatchard will be delivering half these lectures,' Philippa announced at the start of the Michaelmas Term of their joint lecture course on Arthurian legend. 'But I can assure you it will not be the better half. You would be wise always to check which Dr Hatchard is lecturing.'

When Philippa was invited to give a series of lectures at Yale, William took a sabbatical so that he could be with her.

On the ship crossing the Atlantic, Philippa said, 'Let's at least be thankful the journey is by sea, my dear, so we can't run out of petrol.'

'Rather let us thank God,' replied William, 'that the ship has an engine because you would even take the wind out of Cunard's sails.'

The only sadness in their lives was that Philippa could bear William no children, but if anything it drew the two closer together. Philippa lavished quasi-maternal affection on her tutorial pupils and allowed herself only the wry comment that she was spared the probability of producing a child with William's looks and William's brains.

At the outbreak of war William's expertise with handling words made a move into cipher-breaking inevitable. He was recruited by an anonymous gentleman who visited them at home with a briefcase chained to his wrist. Philippa listened shamelessly at the keyhole while they discussed the problems they had come up against and burst into the room and demanded to be recruited as well.

'Do you realize that I can complete *The Times* crossword puzzle in half the time my husband can?'

The anonymous man was only thankful that he wasn't chained to Philippa. He drafted them both to the Admiralty section to deal with enciphered wireless messages to and from German submarines.

The German signal manual was a four-letter code book and each message was reciphered, the substitution table changing daily. William taught Philippa how to evaluate letter frequencies and she applied her new knowledge to modern German texts, coming up with a frequency analysis that was soon used by every code-breaking department in the Commonwealth.

Even so, breaking the ciphers and building up the master signal book was a colossal task which took them the best part of two years.

'I never knew your ifs and ands could be so informative,' she said admiringly of her own work.

When the allies invaded Europe husband and wife could together often break ciphers with no more than half a dozen lines of encoded text to go on.

'They're an illiterate lot,' grumbled William. 'They don't encipher their umlauts. They deserve to be misunderstood.'

'How can you give an opinion when you never dot your i's, William?'

'Because I consider the dot is redundant and I hope to be responsible for removing it from the English language.'

'Is that to be your major contribution to scholarship, William? If so, I am bound to ask how anyone reading the work of most of our undergraduates' essays would be able to tell the difference between an l and an i.'

'A feeble argument, my dear, that if it had any conviction would demand that you put a dot on top of an n so as to be sure it wasn't mistaken for an h.'

'Keep working away at your theories, William, because I intend to spend my energy removing more than the dot and the l from Hitler.'

In May 1945 they dined privately with the Prime Minister and Mrs Churchill at Number Ten Downing Street.

'What did the Prime Minister mean when he said to me he could never understand what you were up to?' asked Philippa in the taxi to Paddington Station.

'The same as when he said to me he knew exactly what you were capable of, I suppose,' said William.

When the Merton Professor of English retired in the early nineteen-fifties the whole university waited to see which Doctor Hatchard would be appointed to the chair.

'If Council invite you to take the chair,' said William, putting his hand through his greying hair, 'it will be because they are going to make me Vice-Chancellor.'

'The only way you could ever be invited to hold a position so far beyond your ability would be nepotism, which would mean I was already Vice-Chancellor.'

The General Board, after several hours' discussion of the problem, offered two chairs and appointed William and Philippa full professors on the same day.

When the Vice-Chancellor was asked why precedent had been broken he replied: 'Simple; if I hadn't given them both a chair, one of them would have been after my job.'

That night, after a celebration dinner when they were walking home together along the banks of the Isis across Christ Church Meadows, in the midst of a particularly heated argument about the quality of the last volume of Proust's monumental works, a policeman, noticing the affray, ran over to them and asked:

'Is everything all right, madam?'

'No, it is not,' William interjected, 'this woman has been attacking me for over thirty years and to date the police have done deplorably little to protect me.'

In the late fifties Harold Macmillan invited Philippa to join the board of the IBA.

'I suppose you'll become what's known as a telly don,' said William, 'and as the average mental age of those who watch the box is seven you should feel quite at home.'

'Agreed,' said Philippa. 'Twenty years of living with you has made me fully qualified to deal with infants.'

The chairman of the BBC wrote to William a few weeks later inviting him to join the Board of Governors.

'Are you to replace "Hancock's Half Hour" or "Dick Barton, Special Agent"?' Philippa enquired.

'I am to give a series of twelve lectures.'

'On what subject, pray?'

'Genius.'

Philippa flicked through the *Radio Times*. 'I see that *Genius* is to be viewed at two o'clock on a Sunday morning, which is understandable, as it's when you are at your most brilliant.'

When William was awarded an honorary doctorate at Princeton, Philippa attended the ceremony and sat proudly in the front row.

'I tried to secure a place at the back,' she explained, 'but it was filled with sleeping students who had obviously never heard of you.'

'If that's the case, Philippa, I am only surprised you didn't mistake them for one of your tutorial lectures.'

As the years passed, many anecdotes, only some of which were apocryphal, passed into the Oxford fabric. Everyone in the English school knew the stories about the 'fighting Hatchards'. How they spent their first night together. How they jointly won the Charles Oldham. How Phil would complete *The Times* crossword before Bill had finished shaving. How they were both appointed to professorial chairs on the same day, and worked longer hours than any of their contemporaries as if they still had something to prove, if only to each other. It seemed almost required by the laws of symmetry that they should always be judged equals. Until it was announced in the New Year's Honours that Philippa had been made a Dame of the British Empire.

'At least our dear Queen has worked out which one of us is truly worthy of recognition,' she said over the college dessert.

'Our dear Queen,' said William, selecting the Madeira, 'knows only too well how little competition there is in the women's colleges: sometimes one must encourage weaker candidates in the hope that it might inspire some real talent lower down.'

After that, whenever they attended a public function together, Philippa would have the MC announce them as Professor William and Dame Philippa Hatchard. She looked forward to many happy years of starting every official occasion one up on her husband, but her triumph lasted for only six months as William received a knighthood in the Queen's Birthday Honours. Philippa feigned surprise at the dear Queen's uncharacteristic lapse of judgement and forthwith insisted on their being introduced in public as Sir William and Dame Philippa Hatchard.

'Understandable,' said William. 'The Queen had to make you a Dame first in order that no one should mistake you for a lady. When I married you, Philippa, you were a young fellow, and now I find I'm living with an old Dame.'

'It's no wonder,' said Philippa, 'that your poor pupils can't make up their minds whether you're homosexual or you simply have a mother fixation. Be thankful that I did not accept Girton's invitation: then you would have been married to a mistress.'

'I always have been, you silly woman.'

As the years passed, they never let up their pretended belief in the other's mental feebleness. Philippa's books, 'works of considerable distinction', she insisted, were published by Oxford University Press while William's 'works of monumental significance' he declared were printed at the presses of Cambridge University.

The tally of newly appointed professors of English they had taught as undergraduates soon reached double figures.

'If you will count polytechnics, I shall have to throw in Maguire's readership in Kenya,' said William.

'You did not teach the Professor of English at Nairobi,' said Philippa. 'I did. You taught the Head of State, which may well account for why the university is so highly thought of while the country is in such disarray.'

In the early sixties they conducted a battle of letters in the *TLS* on the works of Philip Sidney without ever discussing the subject in each other's presence. In the end the editor said the correspondence must stop and adjudicated a draw.

They both declared him an idiot.

If there was one act that annoyed William in old age about Philippa, it was her continued determination each morning to complete *The Times* crossword before he arrived at the breakfast table. For a time, William ordered two copies of the paper until Philippa filled them both in while explaining to him it was a waste of money.

One particular morning in June at the end of their final academic year before retirement, William came down to breakfast to find only one space in the crossword left for him to complete. He studied the clue: 'Skelton reported that this landed in the soup.' He immediately filled in the eight little boxes.

Philippa looked over his shoulder. 'There's no such word, you arrogant man,' she said firmly. 'You made it up to annoy me.' She placed in front of him a very hard-boiled egg.

'Of course there is, you silly woman; look whym-wham up in the dictionary.'

Philippa checked in the *Oxford Shorter* among the cookery books in the kitchen, and trumpeted her delight that it was nowhere to be found.

'My dear Dame Philippa,' said William, as if he were addressing a particularly stupid pupil, 'you surely cannot imagine because you are old and your hair has become very white that you are a sage. You must understand that the *Shorter Oxford Dictionary* was cobbled together for simpletons whose command of the English language stretches to no more than one hundred thousand words. When I go to college this morning I shall confirm the existence of the word in the *OED* on my desk. Need I remind you that the *OED* is a serious work which, with over five hundred thousand words, was designed for scholars like myself?'

'Rubbish,' said Philippa. 'When I am proved right, you will repeat this story word for word, including your offensive non-word, at Somerville's Gaudy Feast.'

'And you, my dear, will read the *Collected Works of John Skelton* and eat humble pie as your first course.'

'We'll ask old Onions along to adjudicate.'

'Agreed.'

'Agreed.'

With that, Sir William picked up his paper, kissed his wife on the cheek and said with an exaggerated sigh, 'It's at times like this that I wish I'd lost the Charles Oldham.'

'You did, my dear. It was in the days when it wasn't fashionable to admit a woman had won anything.'

'You won me.'

'Yes, you arrogant man, but I was led to believe you were one of those prizes one could return at the end of the year. And now I find I shall have to keep you, even in retirement.'

'Let us leave it to the *Oxford English Dictionary*, my dear, to decide the issue the Charles Oldham examiners were unable to determine,' and with that he departed for his college.

'There's no such word,' Philippa muttered as he closed the front door.

Heart attacks are known to be rarer among women than men. When Dame Philippa suffered hers in the kitchen that morning she collapsed on the floor calling hoarsely for William, but he was already out of earshot. It was the cleaning woman who found Dame Philippa on the kitchen floor and ran to fetch someone in authority. The Bursar's first reaction was that she was probably pretending that Sir William had hit her with a frying pan but nevertheless she hurried over to the Hatchards' house in Little Jericho just in case. The Bursar checked Dame Philippa's pulse and called for the college doctor and then the Principal. Both arrived within minutes.

The Principal and the Bursar stood waiting by the side of their illustrious academic colleague but they already knew what the doctor was going to say.

'She's dead,' he confirmed. 'It must have been very sudden and with the minimum of pain.' He checked his watch; the time was nine forty-seven. He covered his patient with a blanket and called for an ambulance. He had taken care of Dame Philippa for over thirty years and he had told her so often to slow down that he might as well have made a gramophone record of it for all the notice she took.

'Who will tell Sir William?' asked the Principal. The three of them looked at each other.

'I will,' said the doctor.

It's a short walk from Little Jericho to Radcliffe Square. It was a long walk from Little Jericho to Radcliffe Square for the doctor that day. He never relished telling anyone of the death of a spouse but this one was going to be the unhappiest of his career.

When he knocked on the professor's door, Sir William bade him enter. The great man was sitting at his

desk poring over the *Oxford Dictionary*, humming to himself.

'I told her, but she wouldn't listen, the silly woman,' he was saying to himself and then he turned and saw the doctor standing silently in the doorway. 'Doctor, you must be my guest at Somerville's Gaudy next Thursday week where Dame Philippa will be eating humble pie. It will be nothing less than game, set, match and championship for me. A vindication of thirty years' scholarship.'

The doctor did not smile, nor did he stir. Sir William walked over to him and gazed at his old friend

intently. No words were necessary. The doctor said only, 'I'm more sorry than I am able to express,' and he left Sir William to his private grief.

Sir William's colleagues all knew within the hour. College lunch that day was spent in a silence broken only by the Senior Tutor enquiring of the Master if some food should be taken up to the Merton professor.

'I think not,' said the Master. Nothing more was said.

Professors, Fellows and students alike crossed the front quadrangle in silence and when they gathered for dinner that evening still no one felt like conversation. At the end of the meal the Senior Tutor suggested once again that something should be taken up to Sir William. This time the Master nodded his agreement and a light meal was prepared by the college chef. The Master and the Senior Tutor climbed the worn stone steps to Sir William's room and while one held the tray the other gently knocked on the door. There was no reply, so the Master, used to William's ways, pushed the door ajar and looked in.

The old man lay motionless on the wooden floor in a pool of blood, a small pistol by his side. The two men walked in and stared down. In his right hand, William was holding the *Collected Works of John Skelton*. The book was open at 'The Tunnyng of Elynour Rummyng', and the word 'whym wham' was underlined.

a 1529, Skelton, *E. Rummyng* 75
After the Sarasyns gyse,
Woth a whym wham,
Knyt with a trym tram,
Upon her brayne pan.

Sir William, in his neat hand, had written a note in the margin: 'Forgive me, but I had to let her know.'

'Know what, I wonder?' said the Master softly to himself as he attempted to remove the book from Sir William's hand, but the fingers were already stiff and cold around it.

Legend has it that they were never apart for more than a few hours.

A Good Toss to Lose

MR GRUBER handed back the boys' essays before returning to his desk at the front of the class.

'Not a bad effort,' the young schoolmaster said, 'except for Jackson, who clearly doesn't believe Goethe is worthy of his attention. And as this is a voluntary class, I'm bound to ask, Jackson, why you bothered to enrol?'

'It was my father's idea,' admitted Jackson. 'He thought there might come a time when it would be useful to speak a little German.'

'How little did he have in mind?' asked the schoolmaster.

Jackson's friend Brooke, who was seated at the desk next to him, whispered loudly enough for everyone in the class to hear, 'Why don't you tell him the truth, Oliver?'

'The truth?' repeated Gruber.

'My father is convinced, sir, that it won't be too long before we are at war with Germany.'

'And why should he think that, may I ask? When Europe has never been at peace for such a long period of time.'

'I accept that, sir, but Pa works at the Foreign Office. Says the Kaiser is a warmonger, and given the slightest opportunity will invade Belgium.'

'But, remembering your treaty obligations,' said Gruber as he walked between the desks, 'that would also drag Britain and France into the conflict.' The schoolmaster paused for thought. 'So the real reason you want to learn German,' he continued, attempting to lighten the exchange, 'is so you can have a chat with the Kaiser when he comes marching down Whitehall.'

'No, I don't believe that's what Pa had in mind, sir. I think he felt that once the Kaiser had been sent packing, if I could speak a little German, I might be in line to be a regional governor.'

The whole class burst out laughing, and began to applaud.

'We must hope for the sake of your countrymen as well as mine, Jackson, that it's a very long line.'

'If Kaiser Bill were to wage war, sir,' said Brooke, sounding more serious, 'would you have to return to your country?'

'I pray that will never happen, Brooke,' said Gruber. 'I look upon England as my second home. Europe is at peace at the moment, so we must hope Jackson's father is wrong. Nothing would be gained from such a pointless act of folly other than to set the world

back a hundred years. Let us be thankful that King George V and Kaiser Wilhelm are cousins.'

'I've never cared much for my cousin,' said Jackson.

'Have you heard the news?' said Brooke, as he and Jackson strolled across to the refectory a few weeks later.

'What news?' said Jackson.

'Mr Gruber will be returning to Germany within a fortnight.'

'Why?' said Jackson.

'It seems the headmaster thought it wise given the circumstances.'

'I'm sorry to hear that,' said Jackson as they sat down on a wooden bench and waited to be served lunch.

'But I thought you didn't like having to study

German,' said Brooke, as he attempted to spear a soggy carrot with his fork.

'And I still don't. But that doesn't mean I don't like Mr Gruber. In fact he's always struck me as a thoroughly decent fellow. Not at all the sort of chap one would want to go to war with.'

'We might even be at war with him in a few months' time,' said Brooke, 'and if you're still thinking of making the army your career, you could find yourself on the front line.'

'I don't think you'll be exempt from that privilege, Rupert,' said Oliver, swamping his food with gravy, 'just because you're going up to Cambridge to swan around writing poetry.'

'Which reminds me,' said Brooke. 'My mother wondered if you'd like to join us in Grantchester for a couple of weeks this summer. And I can promise you some rather interesting gals will be joining us.'

'Can't think of anything better, old chap. That's assuming Kaiser Bill hasn't got other plans for us.'

Oliver Jackson did spend a couple of carefree weeks with his friend, Rupert Brooke, that summer, before they parted and went their separate ways. Brooke to read Classics at King's, while Jackson reported to the Royal Military Academy at Sandhurst, to accept the king's shilling and spend the next two years being trained as an officer in the British Army.

In October 1913, Second Lieutenant Jackson of the Lancashire Fusiliers reported to his regiment's depot in Chester, where he quickly discovered that talk of war with Germany was no longer confined to

the Foreign Office, but was now on everyone's lips. However, no one could be sure what would light the fuse.

When Kaiser Wilhelm's close friend and ally, the Archduke Franz Ferdinand of Austria, was assassinated in Sarajevo, the German emperor had at last found the excuse he needed for his troops to invade Belgium, giving him the chance to expand his empire.

The only good thing that had happened while Oliver was serving his tour of duty in Chester was that he fell in love with a Miss Rosemary Carter, the daughter of one of his father's colleagues at the Foreign Office. In the fathers' eyes, the marriage was no more than an *entente cordiale*, whereas both mothers quickly realized that this particular treaty had never required Foreign Office approval.

One of the many things Kaiser Bill did to irritate Oliver was to declare war while he and Rosemary were still on their honeymoon. Lieutenant Jackson received a telegram delivered to his Deauville hotel ordering him to report back to his regiment immediately.

A few weeks later the Lancashire Fusiliers were among the first to be shipped out to France, where Oliver quickly discovered that it was possible to live in far worse conditions and force down even more disgusting grub than he'd been made to endure at Rugby.

He settled down in a trench where rats were his constant companions, three inches of muddy water his pillow, and slowly learnt to sleep despite the sound of gunfire.

'It will be over by Christmas,' was the optimistic cry being passed down the line.

'But which Christmas?' asked a bus driver from Romford as he forked a billycan of corned beef and baked beans, while refilling his mug with rainwater.

In fact the only present the young subaltern got that Christmas was a third pip to be sewn next to the other two already on his shoulder, and then only after he replaced a brother officer who had not made it into 1915.

Captain Jackson had already been over the top three times by the winter of 1916, and didn't need reminding that the average survival period for a soldier on the front line was nineteen days; he was now in his third year. But at least they were allowing him to return home for a three-week furlough. What old soldiers referred to as a 'stay of execution'.

Jackson returned to the Marne after spending an idyllic carefree break with Rosemary in their country cottage at Crathorne. He was grateful to find that even his father was beginning to believe the war couldn't last much longer. Oliver prayed that he was right.

On arriving back at the front, Jackson immediately reported to his commanding officer.

'We are expecting to mount another attack on Jerry in a few days' time,' said Colonel Harding. 'So be sure your men are prepared.'

Prepared for what?, thought Oliver. Almost certain death, and not quick like the hangman's noose, but probably prolonged, in desperate agony. But he didn't voice his opinion.

Once he was back in the trenches, Oliver quickly tried to get to know the young impressionable men who'd just arrived at the front line, and hadn't yet heard a shot fired in anger. He couldn't think of them as soldiers, just keen young lads who had responded to a poster of a moustachioed old man pointing a finger at them and declaring YOUR COUNTRY NEEDS YOU.

'Once you go over the top, you need only remember one thing,' Oliver instructed them. 'If you don't kill them, as sure as hell they'll kill you. Think of it like a football match against your most bitter rivals. You've got to score every time you shoot.'

'But whose side is the ref on?' demanded a young, frightened voice.

Oliver didn't reply, because he no longer believed God was the referee and that therefore they must surely win.

The colonel joined them just before the kick-off and blew a whistle to show the match could begin. Captain Jackson was first over the top, leading his company, who followed closely behind. On, on, on, he charged as his men fell like fairground soldiers beside him, the lucky ones dying quickly.

He kept going, and was beginning to wonder if he was out there on his own, and then suddenly, without warning, he saw a lone figure running through the whirling smoke towards him. Like Oliver, the man had his bayonet fixed, ready for the kill. Oliver accepted that it would not be possible for both of them to survive, and probably neither would. He held his rifle steady, like a medieval jouster, determined to fell his opponent. He was prepared to thrust his bayonet, not this time into a horsehair bag while training, but into a petrified human being, but no more petrified than he was.

184

Don't strike until you see can the whites of his eyes, his training sergeant had drilled into him at Sandhurst. You can't be a moment too early, or a moment too late. Another oft-repeated maxim. But when he saw the whites of his eyes, he couldn't do it. He lowered his rifle, expecting to die, but to his surprise the German also dropped his rifle as they both came to a halt in the middle of no-man's-land.

For some time they just stared at each other in disbelief. But it was Oliver who burst out laughing, if only to release his pent-up tension.

'What are you doing here, Jackson?'

'I might ask you the same question, sir.'

'Carrying out someone else's orders,' said Gruber.

'Me too.'

'But you're a professional soldier.'

'Death doesn't discriminate in these matters,' said Oliver. 'I often recall your shrewd opinion of war, sir, and looking around the battlefield can only wonder how much talent has been squandered here.'

'On both sides,' said Gruber. 'But it gives me no pleasure to have been proved right.'

'So what shall we do now, sir? We can't just stand around philosophizing until peace is declared.'

'But equally, if we were to return meekly to our

own side, we would probably be arrested, court-martialled and shot at dawn.'

'Then one of us will have to take the other prisoner,' said Jackson, 'and return in triumph.'

'Not a bad idea. But how shall we decide?' asked Gruber.

'The toss of a coin?'

'How very British,' declared Gruber. 'Just a pity the whole war couldn't have been decided that way,' added the schoolmaster as he took a Goldmark out of his pocket. 'You call, Jackson,' he said. 'After all, you're the visiting team.'

Oliver watched as the coin spun high into the air and cried, 'Tails,' only because he couldn't bear the thought of the Kaiser's image staring up at him in triumph.

Gruber groaned as he bent down to look at the eagle. Oliver quickly took off his tie, bound the prisoner's wrists behind his back, and then began to march his old schoolmaster slowly back towards his own front line.

'What happened to Brooke?' asked Gruber as they squelched through the mud while stepping over the bodies of fallen men.

'He was attached to the Royal Naval Division when he last wrote to me.'

'I read his poem about Grantchester. Even attempted to translate it.'

' "The Old Vicarage",' said Jackson.

'That's the one. Ironic that he wrote it while he was on a visit to Berlin. Such a rare talent. Let's hope he survives this dreadful war,' Gruber said as the sun dipped below the horizon.

'Are you married, sir?' asked Oliver.

'Yes. Renate. And we have a son and two daughters. And you?'

'Rosemary. Just got married when the balloon went up.'

'Bad luck, old chap,' said Gruber, before taking his former pupil by surprise. 'I don't suppose you'd consider being a godfather to my youngest, Hans? You see, I consider it no more than my duty once the war is over to make sure this madness can never happen again.'

'I agree with you, Ernst, and I'd be honoured. And perhaps in time . . .'

'May I suggest, Oliver, for both our sakes,' said Gruber as the British front line came into sight, 'that when you hand me over, you don't make it too obvious we're old friends.'

'Good thinking, Ernst,' said Oliver, and grabbed his prisoner roughly by the elbow.

The next voice they heard demanded, 'Who goes there?'

'Captain Jackson, Lancashire Fusiliers, with a German prisoner.'

'Advance and be recognized.' Oliver pushed his old schoolmaster forward. 'Bloody good show,' said the

lookout sergeant. 'You can leave him to me, sir. And you can keep moving, you fucking Kraut.'

'Sergeant,' said Oliver sharply, 'try to remember he's an officer.'

The war was over by Christmas. Christmas 1918.

Captain Ernst Gruber spent two years in a prisoner-of-war camp on Anglesey. He passed the mornings teaching his fellow prisoners the local tongue as there might come a time when it would prove useful to speak a little English, he suggested, echoing Jackson's words.

Oliver sent Gruber the collected works of Rupert Brooke, which he translated in the evenings while he waited for the war to end.

Ernst Gruber was shipped back to Frankfurt in November 1919, and within days he wrote to Oliver to ask if he was still willing to be a godfather to his son Hans. It was several weeks before he received a reply from Oliver's wife Rosemary, to say that her husband had been killed on the Western Front only days before the Armistice was signed. They also had a son, Arthur Oliver, and on her husband's last furlough he'd told her that he hoped Ernst would agree to be one of Arthur's godparents.

With the assistance of Oliver's father, Herr Gruber was allowed to visit England to fulfil his role in the christening ceremony. As Ernst stood by the font alongside Oliver's family, he couldn't help wondering what would have happened if he had won the toss.

Postscript

19 September 1943

LIEUTENANT HANS OTTO GRUBER was blown up by a landmine while serving on the Western Front. He died three days later.

6 June 1944

CAPTAIN ARTHUR OLIVER JACKSON MC was killed while leading his platoon on the beaches of Normandy.

15 November 1944

PROFESSOR ERNST HELMUT GRUBER was executed by firing squad in Berlin for the role he played in the failed attempt to assassinate Adolf Hitler at Wolf's Lair.

May They Rest in Peace

One Man's Meat

COULD ANYONE be that beautiful?

I was driving round the Aldwych on my way to work when I first saw her. She was walking up the steps of the Aldwych Theatre. If I'd stared a moment longer I would have driven into the back of the car in front of me, but before I could confirm my fleeting impression she had disappeared into the throng of theatregoers.

I spotted a parking space on my left-hand side and swung into it at the last possible moment, without indicating, causing the vehicle behind me to let out several appreciative blasts. I leapt out of my car and ran back towards the theatre, realizing how unlikely it was that I'd be able to find her in such a mêlée, and that even if I did, she was probably meeting a boyfriend or husband who would turn out to be about six feet tall and closely to resemble Harrison Ford.

Once I reached the foyer I scanned the chattering crowd. I slowly turned 360 degrees, but could see no sign of her. Should I try to buy a ticket? I wondered. But she could be seated anywhere – the stalls, the dress circle, even the upper circle. Perhaps I should walk up and down the aisles until I spotted her. But I realized I wouldn't be allowed into any part of the theatre unless I could produce a ticket.

And then I saw her. She was standing in a queue in front of the window marked 'Tonight's Performance', and was just one away from being attended to. There were two other customers, a young woman and a middle-aged man, waiting in line behind her. I quickly joined the queue, by which time she had reached the front. I leant forward and tried to overhear what she was saying, but I could only catch the box office manager's reply: 'Not much chance with the curtain going up in a few minutes' time, madam,' he was saying. 'But if you leave it with me, I'll see what I can do.'

She thanked him and walked off in the direction of the stalls. My first impression was confirmed. It didn't matter if you looked from the ankles up or from the head down – she was perfection. I couldn't take my eyes off her, and I noticed that she was having exactly the same effect on several other men in the foyer. I wanted to tell them all not to bother. Didn't they realize she was with me? Or rather, that she would be by the end of the evening.

After she had disappeared from view, I craned my neck to look into the booth. Her ticket had been placed to one side. I sighed with relief as the young woman two places ahead of me presented her credit card and picked up four tickets for the dress circle.

I began to pray that the man in front of me wasn't looking for a single.

'Do you have one ticket for tonight's performance?' he asked hopefully, as the three-minute bell sounded. The man in the booth smiled.

I scowled. Should I knife him in the back, kick him in the groin, or simply scream abuse at him?

'Where would you prefer to sit, sir? The dress circle or the stalls?'

'Don't say stalls,' I willed. 'Say Circle . . . Circle . . . Circle . . .'

'Stalls,' he said.

'I have one on the aisle in row H,' said the man in the box, checking the computer screen in front of him. I uttered a silent cheer as I realized that the theatre would be trying to sell off its remaining tickets before it bothered with returns handed in by members of the public. But then, I thought, how would I get around that problem?

By the time the man in front of me had bought the ticket on the end of row H, I had my lines well rehearsed, and just hoped I wouldn't need a prompt.

'Thank goodness. I thought I wasn't going to make it,' I began, trying to sound out of breath. The man in the ticket booth looked up at me, but didn't seem all that impressed by my opening line. 'It was the traffic. And then I couldn't find a parking space. My girlfriend may have given up on me. Did she by any chance hand in my ticket for resale?'

He looked unconvinced. My dialogue obviously wasn't gripping him. 'Can you describe her?' he asked suspiciously.

'Short-cropped fair hair, hazel eyes, wearing a red silk dress that . . .'

'Ah, yes. I remember her,' he said, almost sighing. He picked up the ticket by his side and handed it to me.

'Thank you,' I said, trying not to show my relief that he had come in so neatly on cue with the closing line from my first scene. As I hurried off in the direction of the stalls, I grabbed an envelope from a pile on the ledge beside the booth.

I checked the price of the ticket: twenty pounds. I extracted two ten-pound notes from my wallet, put them in the envelope, licked the flap and stuck it down.

The girl at the entrance to the stalls checked my ticket. 'F-11. Six rows from the front, on the right-hand side.'

I walked slowly down the aisle until I spotted her. She was sitting next to an empty place in the middle of the row. As I made my way over the feet of those who were already seated, she turned and smiled, obviously pleased to see that someone had purchased her spare ticket.

I returned the smile, handed over the envelope containing my twenty pounds, and sat down beside her. 'The man in the box office asked me to give you this.'

'Thank you.' She slipped the envelope into her evening bag. I was about to try the first line of my second scene on her, when the house lights faded and the curtain rose for Act One of the real performance. I suddenly realized that I had no idea what play I was about to see. I glanced across at the programme on her lap and read the words '*An Inspector Calls*, by J. B. Priestley'.

I remembered that the critics had been full of praise for the production when it had originally opened at the National Theatre, and had particularly singled out the performance of Kenneth Cranham. I tried to concentrate on what was taking place on stage.

The eponymous inspector was staring into a house in which an Edwardian family were preparing for a dinner to celebrate their daughter's engagement. 'I was thinking of getting a new car,' the father was saying to his prospective son-in-law as he puffed away on his cigar.

At the mention of the word 'car', I suddenly remembered that I had abandoned mine outside the theatre. Was it on a double yellow line? Or worse? To hell with it. They could have it in part-exchange for the model sitting next to me. The audience laughed, so I joined in, if only to give the impression that I was following the plot. But what about my original plans

for the evening? By now everyone would be wondering why I hadn't turned up. I realized that I wouldn't be able to leave the theatre during the interval, either to check on my car or to make a phone call to explain my absence, as that would be my one chance of developing my own plot.

The play had the rest of the audience enthralled, but I had already begun rehearsing the lines from my own script, which would have to be performed during the interval between Acts One and Two. I was painfully aware that I would be restricted to fifteen minutes, and that there would be no second night.

By the time the curtain came down at the end of the first act, I was confident of my draft text. I waited for the applause to die down before I turned towards her.

'What an original production,' I began. 'Quite modernistic.' I vaguely remembered that one of the critics had followed that line. 'I was lucky to get a seat at the last moment.'

'I was just as lucky,' she replied. I felt encouraged. 'I mean, to find someone who was looking for a single ticket at such short notice.'

I nodded. 'My name's Michael Whitaker.'

'Anna Townsend,' she said, giving me a warm smile.

'Would you like a drink?' I asked.

'Thank you,' she replied, 'that would be nice.' I stood up and led her through the packed scrum that was heading towards the stalls bar, occasionally glancing back to make sure she was still following me. I was somehow expecting her no longer to be there, but each time I turned to look she greeted me with the same radiant smile.

'What would you like?' I asked, once I could make out the bar through the crowd.

'A dry martini, please.'

'Stay here, and I'll be back in a moment,' I promised, wondering just how many precious minutes would be wasted while I had to wait at the bar. I took out a five-pound note and held it up conspicuously, in the hope that the prospect of a large tip might influence the barman's sense of direction. He spotted the money, but I still had to wait for another four customers to be served before I managed to secure the dry martini and a Scotch on the rocks for myself. The barman didn't deserve the tip I left him, but I hadn't any more time to waste waiting for the change.

I carried the drinks back to the far corner of the foyer, where Anna stood studying her programme. She was silhouetted against a window, and in that stylish red silk dress, the light emphasized her slim, elegant figure.

I handed her the dry martini, aware that my limited time had almost run out.

'Thank you,' she said, giving me another disarming smile.

'How did you come to have a spare ticket?' I asked as she took a sip from her drink.

'My partner was held up on an emergency case at the last minute,' she explained. 'Just one of the problems of being a doctor.'

'Pity. They missed a quite remarkable production,' I prompted, hoping to tease out of her whether her partner was male or female.

'Yes,' said Anna. 'I tried to book seats when it was still at the National Theatre, but they were sold out for any performances I was able to make, so when a friend offered me two tickets at the last minute, I jumped at them. After all, it's coming off in a few weeks.' She took another sip from her martini. 'What about you?' she asked as the three-minute bell sounded.

There was no such line in my script.

'Me?'

'Yes, Michael,' she said, a hint of teasing in her voice. 'How did you come to be looking for a spare seat at the last moment?'

'Sharon Stone was tied up for the evening, and at the last second Princess Diana told me that she would have loved to have come, but she was trying to keep a low profile.' Anna laughed. 'Actually, I read some of the crits, and I dropped in on the off-chance of picking up a spare ticket.'

'And you picked up a spare woman as well,' said Anna, as the two-minute bell went. I wouldn't have dared to include such a bold line in her script – or was there a hint of mockery in those hazel eyes?

'I certainly did,' I replied lightly. 'So, are you a doctor as well?'

'As well as what?' asked Anna.

'As well as your partner,' I said, not sure if she was still teasing.

'Yes. I'm a GP in Fulham. There are three of us in the practice, but I was the only one who could escape tonight. And what do you do when you're not chatting up Sharon Stone or escorting Princess Diana to the theatre?'

'I'm in the restaurant business,' I told her.

'That must be one of the few jobs with worse hours and tougher working conditions than mine,' Anna said as the one-minute bell sounded.

I looked into those hazel eyes and wanted to say – Anna, let's forget the second act: I realize the play's superb, but all I want to do is spend the rest of the evening alone with you, not jammed into a crowded auditorium with eight hundred other people.

'Wouldn't you agree?'

I tried to recall what she had just said. 'I expect we get more customer complaints than you do,' was the best I could manage.

'I doubt it,' Anna said, quite sharply. 'If you're a woman in the medical profession and you don't cure your patients within a couple of days, they immediately want to know if you're fully qualified.'

I laughed, and finished my drink as a voice boomed over the Tannoy, 'Would the audience please take their seats for the second act. The curtain is about to rise.'

'We ought to be getting back,' Anna said, placing her empty glass on the nearest window ledge.

'I suppose so,' I said reluctantly, and led her in the opposite direction to the one in which I really wanted to take her.

'Thanks for the drink,' she said as we returned to our seats.

'Small recompense,' I replied. She glanced up at me questioningly. 'For such a good ticket,' I explained.

She smiled as we made our way along the row, stepping awkwardly over more toes. I was just about to risk a further remark when the house lights dimmed.

During the second act I turned to smile in Anna's direction whenever there was laughter, and was occasionally rewarded with a warm response. But my supreme moment of triumph came towards the end of the act, when the detective showed the daughter a photograph of the dead woman. She gave a piercing scream, and the stage lights were suddenly switched off.

Anna grabbed my hand, but quickly released it and apologized.

'Not at all,' I whispered. 'I only just stopped myself from doing the same thing.' In the darkened theatre, I couldn't tell how she responded.

A moment later the phone on the stage rang. Everyone in the audience knew it must be the detective on the other end of the line, even if they couldn't be sure what he was going to say. That final scene had the whole house gripped.

After the lights dimmed for the last time, the cast returned to the stage and deservedly received a long ovation, taking several curtain calls.

When the curtain was finally lowered, Anna turned to me and said, 'What a remarkable production. I'm so glad I didn't miss it. And I'm even more pleased that I didn't have to see it alone.'

'Me too,' I told her, ignoring the fact that I'd never planned to spend the evening at the theatre in the first place.

We made our way up the aisle together as the audience flowed out of the theatre like a slow-moving river. I wasted those few precious moments discussing the merits of the cast, the power of the director's interpretation, the originality of the macabre set and even the Edwardian costumes, before we reached the double doors that led back out into the real world.

'Goodbye, Michael,' Anna said. 'Thank you for adding to my enjoyment of the evening.' She shook me by the hand.

'Goodbye,' I said, gazing once again into those hazel eyes.

She turned to go, and I wondered if I would ever see her again.

'Anna,' I said.

She glanced back in my direction.

'If you're not doing anything in particular, would you care to join me for dinner . . .'

Author's Note

At this point in the story, the reader is offered the choice of four different endings.

You might decide to read all four of them, or simply select one, and consider that your own particular ending. If you do choose to read all four, they should be taken in the order in which they have been written:

1. *RARE*
2. *BURNT*
3. *OVERDONE*
4. *À POINT*

Rare

'Thank you, Michael. I'd like that.'

I smiled, unable to mask my delight. 'Good. I know a little restaurant just down the road that I think you might enjoy.'

'That sounds fun,' Anna said, linking her arm in mine. I guided her through the departing throng.

As we strolled together down the Aldwych, Anna continued to chat about the play, comparing it favourably with a production she had seen at the Haymarket some years before.

When we reached the Strand I pointed to a large grey double door on the other side of the road. 'That's it,' I said. We took advantage of a red light to weave our way through the temporarily stationary traffic, and after we'd reached the far pavement I pushed one of the grey doors open to allow Anna through. It

began to rain just as we stepped inside. I led her down a flight of stairs into a basement restaurant buzzing with the talk of people who had just come out of theatres, and waiters dashing, plates in both hands, from table to table.

'I'll be impressed if you can get a table here,' Anna said, eyeing a group of would-be customers who were clustered round the bar, impatiently waiting for someone to leave.

I strolled across to the reservations desk. The head waiter, who until that moment had been taking a customer's order, rushed over. 'Good evening, Mr Whitaker,' he said. 'How many are you?'

'Just the two of us.'

'Follow me, please, sir,' Mario said, leading us to my usual table in the far corner of the room.

'Another dry martini?' I asked her as we sat down.

'No, thank you,' she replied. 'I think I'll just have a glass of wine with the meal.'

I nodded my agreement, as Mario handed us our menus. Anna studied hers for a few moments before I asked if she had spotted anything she fancied.

'Yes,' she said, looking straight at me. 'But for now I think I'll settle for the fettucini, and a glass of red wine.'

'Good idea,' I said. 'I'll join you. But are you sure you won't have a starter?'

'No, thank you, Michael. I've reached that age when I can no longer order everything I'm tempted by.'

'Me too,' I confessed. 'I have to play squash three times a week to keep in shape,' I told her as Mario reappeared.

'Two fettucini,' I began, 'and a bottle of . . .'

'Half a bottle, please,' said Anna. 'I'll only have one glass. I've got an early start tomorrow morning, so I shouldn't overdo things.'

I nodded, and Mario scurried away.

I looked across the table and into Anna's eyes. 'I've always wondered about women doctors,' I said, immediately realizing that the line was a bit feeble.

'You mean, you wondered if we're normal?'

'Something like that, I suppose.'

'Yes, we're normal enough, except every day we have to see a lot of men in the nude. I can assure you, Michael, most of them are overweight and fairly unattractive.'

I suddenly wished I were half a stone lighter. 'But are there many men who are brave enough to consider a woman doctor in the first place?'

'Quite a few,' said Anna, 'though most of my patients are female. But there are just about enough intelligent, sensible, uninhibited males around who can accept that a woman doctor might be just as likely to cure them as a man.'

I smiled as two bowls of fettucini were placed in front of us. Mario then showed me the label on the half-bottle he had selected. I nodded my approval. He had chosen a vintage to match Anna's pedigree.

'And what about you?' asked Anna. 'What does being "in the restaurant business" actually mean?'

'I'm on the management side,' I

said, before sampling the wine. I nodded again, and Mario poured a glass for Anna and then topped up mine.

'Or at least, that's what I do nowadays. I started life as a waiter,' I said, as Anna began to sip her wine.

'What a magnificent wine,' she remarked. 'It's so good I may end up having a second glass.'

'I'm glad you like it,' I said. 'It's a Barolo.'

'You were saying, Michael? You started life as a waiter . . .'

'Yes, then I moved into the kitchens for about five years, and finally ended up on the management side. How's the fettucini?'

'It's delicious. Almost melts in your mouth.' She took another sip of her wine. 'So, if you're not cooking, and no longer a waiter, what do you do now?'

'Well, at the moment I'm running three restaurants in the West End, which means I never stop dashing from one to the other, depending on which is facing the biggest crisis on that particular day.'

'Sounds a bit like ward duty to me,' said Anna. 'So who turned out to have the biggest crisis today?'

'Today, thank heaven, was not typical,' I told her with feeling.

'That bad?' said Anna.

'Yes, I'm afraid so. We lost a chef this morning who cut off the top of his finger, and won't be back at work for at least a fortnight. My head waiter in our second restaurant is off, claiming he has 'flu, and I've just had to sack the barman in the third for fiddling the books. Barmen always fiddle the books, of course, but in this case even the customers began to notice what he was up to.' I paused. 'But I still wouldn't want to be in any other business.'

'In the circumstances, I'm amazed you were able to take the evening off.'

'I shouldn't have, really, and I wouldn't have, except . . .' I trailed off as I leaned over and topped up Anna's glass.

'Except what?' she said.

'Do you want to hear the truth?' I asked as I poured the remains of the wine into my own glass.

'I'll try that for starters,' she said.

I placed the empty bottle on the side of the table, and hesitated, but only for a moment. 'I was driving to one of my restaurants earlier this evening, when I spotted you going into the theatre. I stared at you for so long that I nearly crashed into the back of the car in front of me. Then I swerved across the road into the nearest parking space, and the car behind almost crashed into me. I leapt out, ran all the way to the theatre, and searched everywhere until I saw you standing in the queue for the box office. I joined the line and watched you hand over your spare ticket. Once you were safely out of sight, I told the box office manager that you hadn't expected me to make it in time, and that you might have put my ticket up for resale. After I'd described you, which I was able to do in great detail, he handed it over without so much as a murmur.'

Anna put down her glass of wine and stared across at me with a look of incredulity. 'I'm glad he fell for your story,' she said. 'But should I?'

'Yes, you should. Because then I put two ten-pound notes into a theatre envelope and took the place next to you. The rest you already know.' I waited to see how she would react.

She didn't speak for some time. 'I'm flattered,' she eventually said, and touched my hand. 'I didn't realize there were any old-fashioned romantics left in the world.' She squeezed my fingers and looked me in the eyes. 'Am I allowed to ask what you have planned for the rest of the evening?'

'Nothing has been planned so far,' I admitted. 'Which is why it's all been so refreshing.'

'You make me sound like an After Eight mint,' said Anna with a laugh.

'I can think of at least three replies to that,' I told her as Mario reappeared, looking a little disappointed at the sight of the half-empty plates.

'Was everything all right, sir?' he asked, sounding anxious.

'Couldn't have been better,' said Anna, who hadn't stopped looking at me.

'Would you like some coffee?' I asked.

'Yes,' said Anna. 'But perhaps we could have it somewhere a little less crowded.'

I was so taken by surprise that it was several moments before I recovered. I was beginning to feel that I was no longer in control. Anna rose from her place and said, 'Shall we go?' I nodded to Mario, who just smiled.

Once we were back out on the street, she linked her arm with mine as we retraced our steps along the Aldwych and past the theatre.

'It's been a wonderful evening,' she was saying as we reached the spot where I had left my car. 'Until you arrived on the scene it had been a rather dull day, but you've changed all that.'

'It hasn't actually been the best of days for me either,' I admitted. 'But I've rarely enjoyed an evening more. Where would you like to have coffee? Annabels? Or why don't we try the new Dorchester Club?'

'If you don't have a wife, your place. If you do . . .'

'I don't,' I told her simply.

'Then that's settled,' she said as I opened the door of my BMW for her. Once she was safely in I walked round to take my seat behind the wheel, and discovered that I had left my sidelights on and the keys in the ignition.

I turned the key, and the engine immediately purred into life. 'This has to be my day,' I said to myself.

'Sorry?' Anna said, turning in my direction.

'We were lucky to miss the rain,' I replied, as a few drops landed on the windscreen. I flicked on the wipers.

On our way to Pimlico, Anna told me about her childhood in the south of France, where her father had taught English at a boys' school. Her account of being the only girl among a couple of hundred teenage French boys made me laugh again and again. I found myself becoming more and more enchanted with her company.

'Whatever made you come back to England?' I asked.

'An English mother who divorced my French father, and the chance to study medicine at St Thomas's.'

'But don't you miss the south of France, especially on nights like this?' I asked as a clap of thunder crackled above us.

'Oh, I don't know,' she said. I was about to respond when she added, 'In any case, now the English have learnt how to cook, the place has become almost civilised.' I smiled to myself, wondering if she was teasing me again.

I found out immediately. 'By the way,' she said, 'I assume that was one of your restaurants we had dinner at.'

'Yes, it was,' I said sheepishly.

'That explains how you got a table so easily when it was packed out, why the waiter knew it was a Barolo you wanted without your having to ask, and how you could leave without paying the bill.'

I was beginning to wonder if I would always be a yard behind her.

'Was it the missing waiter, the four-and-a-half-fingered chef, or the crooked bartender?'

'The crooked bartender,' I replied, laughing. 'But I sacked him this afternoon, and I'm afraid his deputy didn't look as if he was coping all that well,' I explained as I turned right off Millbank, and began to search for a parking space.

'And I thought you only had eyes for me,' sighed Anna, 'when all the time you were looking over my shoulder and checking on what the deputy barman was up to.'

'Not all the time,' I said as I manoeuvred the car into the only space left in the mews where I lived. I got out of the car and walked round to Anna's side, opened the door and guided her to the house.

As I closed the door behind us, Anna put her arms

around my neck and looked up into my eyes. I leaned down and kissed her for the first time. When she broke away, all she said was, 'Don't let's bother with coffee, Michael.' I slipped off my jacket, and led her upstairs and into my bedroom, praying that it hadn't been the housekeeper's day off. When I opened the door I was relieved to find that the bed had been made and the room was tidy.

'I'll just be a moment,' I said, and disappeared into the bathroom. As I cleaned my teeth, I began to wonder if it was all a dream. When I returned to the bedroom, would I discover she didn't exist? I dropped the toothbrush into its mug and went back to the bedroom. Where was she? My eyes followed a trail of discarded clothes that led all the way to the bed. Her head was propped up on the pillow. Only a sheet covered her body.

I quickly took off my clothes, dropping them where they fell, and switched off the main lights, so that only the one by the bed remained aglow. I slid under the sheets to join her. I looked at her for sev-

eral seconds before I took her in my arms. I slowly explored every part of her body, as she began to kiss me again. I couldn't believe that anyone could be that exciting, and at the same time so tender. When we finally made love, I knew I never wanted this woman to leave me.

She lay in my arms for some time before either of us spoke. Then I began talking about anything that came into my head. I confided my hopes, my dreams, even my worst anxieties, with a freedom I had never experienced with anyone before. I wanted to share everything with her.

And then she leaned across and began kissing me once again, first on the lips, then the neck and chest, and as she slowly continued down my body I thought I would explode. The last thing I remember was turning off the light by my bed as the clock on the hall table chimed one.

When I woke the following morning, the first rays of sunlight were already shining through the lace curtains, and the glorious memory of the night before

was instantly revived. I turned lazily to take her in my arms, but she was no longer there.

'Anna?' I cried out, sitting bolt upright. There was no reply. I flicked on the light by the side of the bed, and glanced across at the bedside clock. It was 7.29. I was about to jump out of bed and go in search of her when I noticed a scribbled note wedged under a corner of the clock.

I picked it up, read it slowly, and smiled.

'So will I,' I said, and lay back on the pillow, thinking about what I should do next. I decided to send her a dozen roses later that morning, eleven white and one red. Then I would have a red one delivered to her on the hour, every hour, until I saw her again.

After I had showered and dressed, I roamed aimlessly around the house. I wondered how quickly I could persuade Anna to move in, and what changes she would want to make. Heaven knows, I thought as I walked through to the kitchen, clutching her note, the place could do with a woman's touch.

As I ate breakfast I looked up her number in the telephone directory, instead of reading the morning paper. There it was, just as she had said. Dr Townsend, listing a surgery number in Parsons Green Lane where she could be contacted between nine and six. There was a second number, but deep black lettering requested that it should only be used in case of emergencies.

Although I considered my state of health to be an emergency, I dialled the first number, and waited impatiently. All I wanted to say was, 'Good morning, darling. I got your note, and can we make last night the first of many?'

A matronly voice answered the phone. 'Dr Townsend's surgery.'

'Dr Townsend, please,' I said.

'Which one?' she asked. 'There are three Dr Townsends in the practice – Dr Jonathan, Dr Anna and Dr Elizabeth.'

'Dr Anna,' I replied.

'Oh, Mrs Townsend,' she said. 'I'm sorry, but she's not available at the moment. She's just taken the children off to school, and after that she has to go to the airport to pick up her husband, Dr Jonathan, who's returning this morning from a medical conference in Minneapolis. I'm not expecting her back for at least a couple of hours. Would you like to leave a message?'

There was a long silence before the matronly voice asked, 'Are you still there?' I placed the receiver back on the hook without replying, and looked sadly down at the hand-written note by the side of the phone.

Dear Michael,
I will remember tonight for the rest of my life.
Thank you.
Anna

Burnt

'Thank you, Michael. I'd like that.'

I smiled, unable to mask my delight.

'Hi, Anna. I thought I might have missed you.'

I turned and stared at a tall man with a mop of fair hair, who seemed unaffected by the steady flow of people trying to pass him on either side.

Anna gave him a smile that I hadn't seen until that moment.

'Hello, darling,' she said. 'This is Michael Whitaker. You're lucky – he bought your ticket, and if you hadn't turned up I was just about to accept his kind invitation to dinner. Michael, this is my husband, Jonathan – the one who was held up at the hospital. As you can see, he's now escaped.'

I couldn't think of a suitable reply.

Jonathan shook me warmly by the hand. 'Thank you for keeping my wife company,' he said. 'Won't you join us for dinner?'

'That's very kind of you,' I replied, 'but I've just remembered that I'm meant to be somewhere else right now. I'd better run.'

'That's a pity,' said Anna. 'I was rather looking forward to finding out all about the restaurant business. Perhaps we'll meet again sometime, whenever my husband next leaves me in the lurch. Goodbye, Michael.'

'Goodbye, Anna.'

I watched them climb into the back of a taxi together, and wished Jonathan would drop dead in front of me. He didn't, so I began to retrace my steps back to the spot where I had abandoned my car. 'You're a lucky man, Jonathan Townsend,' was the only observation I made. But no one was listening.

The next word that came to my lips was 'Damn!' I repeated it several times, as there was a distressingly large space where I was certain I'd left my car.

I walked up and down the street in case I'd forgotten where I'd parked it, cursed again, then marched off in search of a phone box, unsure if my car had been stolen or towed away. There was a pay phone just around the corner in Kingsway. I picked up the handset and jabbed three nines into it.

'Which service do you require? Fire, Police or Ambulance,' a voice asked.

'Police,' I said, and was immediately put through to another voice.

'Charing Cross Police Station. What is the nature of your enquiry?'

'I think my car has been stolen.'

'Can you tell me the make, colour and registration number please, sir.'

'It's a blue Ford Fiesta, registration H107 SHV.'

There was a long pause, during which I could hear other voices talking in the background.

'No, it hasn't been stolen, sir,' said the officer when he came back on the line. 'The car was illegally parked on a double yellow line. It's been removed and taken to the Vauxhall Bridge Pound.'

'Can I pick it up now?' I asked sulkily.

'Certainly, sir. How will you be getting there?'

'I'll take a taxi.'

'Then just ask the driver for the Vauxhall Bridge Pound. Once you get there, you'll need some form of identification, and a cheque for £105 with a banker's card – that is if you don't have the full amount in cash.'

'£105?' I repeated in disbelief.

'That's correct, sir.'

I slammed the phone down just as it started to rain. I scurried back to the corner of the Aldwych in search of a taxi, only to find that they were all being commandeered by the hordes of people still hanging around outside the theatre.

I put my collar up and nipped across the road, dodging between the slow-moving traffic. Once I had reached the far side, I continued running until I found an overhanging ledge broad enough to shield me from the blustery rain.

I shivered, and sneezed several times before an empty cab eventually came to my rescue.

'Vauxhall Bridge Pound,' I told the driver as I jumped in.

'Bad luck, mate,' said the cabbie. 'You're my second this evening.'

I frowned.

As the taxi manoeuvred its way slowly through the rainswept post-theatre traffic and across Waterloo Bridge, the driver began chattering away. I just about managed monosyllabic replies to his opinions on the weather, John Major, the England cricket team and foreign tourists. With each new topic, his forecast became ever more gloomy.

When we reached the car pound I passed him a ten-pound note and waited in the rain for my change. Then I dashed off in the direction of a little Portakabin, where I was faced by my second queue that evening. This one was considerably longer than the first, and I knew that when I eventually reached the front of it and paid for my ticket, I wouldn't be rewarded with any memorable entertainment. When my turn finally came, a burly policeman pointed to a form sellotaped to the counter.

I followed its instructions to the letter, first producing my driving licence, then writing out a cheque

for £105, payable to the Metropolitan Police. I handed them both over, with my cheque card, to the policeman, who towered over me. The man's sheer bulk was the only reason I didn't suggest that perhaps he ought to have more important things to do with his time, like catching drug dealers. Or even car thieves.

'Your vehicle is in the far corner,' said the officer, pointing into the distance, over row upon row of cars.

'Of course it is,' I replied. I stepped out of the Portakabin and back into the rain, dodging puddles as I ran between the lines of cars. I didn't stop until I reached the farthest corner of the pound. It still took me several more minutes to locate my blue Ford Fiesta – one disadvantage, I thought, of owning the most popular car in Britain.

I unlocked the door, squelched down onto the front seat, and sneezed again. I turned the key in the ignition, but the engine barely turned over, letting

out only the occasional splutter before giving up altogether. Then I remembered I hadn't switched the sidelights off when I made my unscheduled dash for the theatre. I uttered a string of expletives that only partly expressed my true feelings.

I watched as another figure came running across the pound towards a Range Rover parked in the row in front of me. I quickly wound down my window, but he had driven off before I could shout the magic words 'jump leads'. I got out and retrieved my jump leads from the boot, walked to the front of the car, raised the bonnet, and attached the leads to the battery. I began to shiver once again as I settled down for another wait.

I couldn't get Anna out of my mind, but accepted that the only thing I'd succeeded in picking up that evening was the 'flu.

In the following forty rain-drenched minutes, three people passed by before a young black man asked, 'So what's the trouble, man?' Once I had explained my problem he manoeuvred his old van alongside my car, then raised his bonnet and attached the jump leads to his battery. When he switched on his ignition, my engine began to turn over.

'Thanks,' I shouted, rather inadequately, once I'd revved the engine several times.

'My pleasure, man,' he replied, and disappeared into the night.

As I drove out of the car pound I switched on my radio, to hear Big Ben striking twelve. It reminded me that I hadn't turned up for work that night. The first thing I needed to do, if I wanted to keep my job, was to come up with a good excuse. I sneezed again, and decided on the 'flu. Although they'd probably taken the last orders by now, Gerald wouldn't have closed the kitchens yet.

I peered through the rain, searching the pavements for a pay phone, and eventually spotted a row of three outside a post office. I stopped the car and jumped out, but a cursory inspection revealed that they'd all been vandalised. I climbed back into the car and continued my search. After dashing in and out of the rain several times, I finally spotted a single phone box on the corner of Warwick Way that looked as if it might just be in working order.

I dialled the restaurant, and waited a long time for someone to answer.

'Laguna 50,' said an Italian-sounding young girl.

'Janice, is that you? It's Mike.'

'Yes, it's me, Mike,' she whispered, reverting to her Lambeth accent. 'I'd better warn you that every time your name's been mentioned this evening, Gerald picks up the nearest meat-axe.'

'Why?' I asked. 'You've still got Nick in the kitchen to see you through.'

'Nick chopped the top off one of his fingers earlier this evening, and Gerald had to take him to hospital. I was left in charge. He's not best pleased.'

'Oh, hell,' I said. 'But I've got . . .'

'The sack,' said another voice, and this one wasn't whispering.

'Gerald, I can explain . . .'

'Why you didn't turn up for work this evening?'

I sneezed, then held my nose. 'I've got the 'flu. If I'd come in tonight I would have given it to half the customers.'

'Would you?' said Gerald. 'Well, I suppose that might have been marginally worse than giving it to the girl who was sitting next to you in the theatre.'

'What do you mean?' I asked, letting go of my nose.

'Exactly what I said, Mike. You see, unfortunately

for you, a couple of our regulars were two rows behind you at the Aldwych. They enjoyed the show almost as much as you seemed to, and one of them added, for good measure, that he thought your date was "absolutely stunning".'

'He must have mistaken me for someone else,' I said, trying not to sound desperate.

'He may have done, Mike, but I haven't. You're sacked, and don't even think about coming in to collect your pay packet, because there isn't one for a head waiter who'd rather take some bimbo to the theatre than do a night's work.' The line went dead.

I hung up the phone and started muttering obscenities under my breath as I walked slowly back towards my car. I was only a dozen paces away from it when a young lad jumped into the front seat, switched on the ignition, and lurched hesitatingly into the centre of the road in what sounded horribly like third gear. I chased after the retreating car, but once the youth began to accelerate, I knew I had no hope of catching him.

I ran all the way back to the phone box, and dialled 999 once again.

'Fire, Police or Ambulance?' I was asked for a second time that night.

'Police,' I said, and a moment later I was put through to another voice.

'Belgravia Police Station. What is the nature of your enquiry?'

'I've just had my car stolen!' I shouted.

'Make, model and registration number please, sir.'

'It's a blue Ford Fiesta, registration H107 SHV.'

I waited impatiently.

'It hasn't been stolen, sir. It was illegally parked on a double . . .'

'No it wasn't!' I shouted even more loudly. 'I paid £105 to get the damn thing out of the Vauxhall Bridge Pound less than half an hour ago, and I've just seen it being driven off by a joyrider while I was making a phone call.'

'Where are you, sir?'

'In a phone box on the corner of Vauxhall Bridge Road and Warwick Way.'

'And in which direction was the car travelling when you last saw it?' asked the voice.

'North up Vauxhall Bridge Road.'

'And what is your home telephone number, sir?'

'081 290 4820.'

'And at work?'

'Like the car, I don't have a job any longer.'

'Right, I'll get straight onto it, sir. We'll be in touch with you the moment we have any news.'

I put the phone down and thought about what I should do next. I hadn't been left with a great deal of choice. I hailed a taxi and asked to be taken to Victoria, and was relieved to find that this driver showed no desire to offer any opinions on anything during the short journey to the station. When he dropped me I passed him my last note, and patiently waited while he handed over every last penny of my change. He also muttered an expletive or two. I bought a ticket for Bromley with my few remaining coins, and went in search of the platform.

'You've just about made it, mate,' the ticket collector told me. 'The last train's due in at any minute.' But I still had to wait for another twenty minutes on the cold, empty platform before the last train eventually pulled into the station. By then I had memorised every advertisement in sight, from Guinness to Mates, while continuing to sneeze at regular intervals.

When the train came to a halt and the doors squelched open I took a seat in a carriage near the front. It was another ten minutes before the engine lurched into action, and another forty before it finally pulled into Bromley station.

I emerged into the Kent night a few minutes before one o'clock, and set off in the direction of my little terraced house.

Twenty-five minutes later, I staggered up the short path to my front door. I began to search for my keys, then remembered that I'd left them in the car ignition. I didn't have the energy even to swear, and began to grovel around in the dark for the spare front-door key that was always hidden under a particular stone. But which one? At last I found it, put it in the lock, turned it and pushed the door open. No sooner had I stepped inside than the phone on the hall table began to ring.

I grabbed the receiver.

'Mr Whitaker?'

'Speaking.'

'This is the Belgravia police. We've located your car, sir, and . . .'

'Thank God for that,' I said, before the officer had a chance to finish the sentence. 'Where is it?'

'At this precise moment, sir, it's on the back of a pick-up lorry somewhere in Chelsea. It seems the lad who nicked it only managed to travel a mile or so before he hit the kerb at seventy, and bounced straight into a wall. I'm sorry to have to inform you, sir, that your car's a total write-off.'

'A total write-off?' I said in disbelief.

'Yes, sir. The garage who towed it away has been given your number, and they'll be in touch with you first thing in the morning.'

I couldn't think of any comment worth making.

'The good news is we've caught the lad who nicked it,' continued the police officer. 'The bad news is that he's only fifteen, doesn't have a driver's licence, and, of course, he isn't insured.'

'That's not a problem,' I said. 'I'm fully insured myself.'

'As a matter of interest, sir, did you leave your keys in the ignition?'

'Yes, I did. I was just making a quick phone call, and thought I'd only be away from the car for a couple of minutes.'

'Then I think it's unlikely you'll be covered by your insurance, sir.'

'Not covered by my insurance? What are you talking about?'

'It's standard policy nowadays not to pay out if you leave your keys in the ignition. You'd better check, sir,' were the officer's final words before ringing off.

I put the phone down and wondered what else could possibly go wrong. I slipped off my jacket and began to climb the stairs, but came to a sudden halt when I saw my wife waiting for me on the landing.

'Maureen . . .' I began.

'You can tell me later why the car is a total write-off,' she said, 'but not until you've explained why you didn't turn up for this evening, and just who this "classy tart" is that Gerald said you were seen with at the theatre.'

Overdone

'No, I'm not doing anything in particular,' said Anna.

I smiled, unable to mask my delight.

'Good. I know a little restaurant just down the road that I think you might enjoy.'

'That sounds just fine,' said Anna as she made her way through the dense theatre crowd. I quickly followed, having to hurry just to keep up with her.

'Which way?' she asked. I pointed towards the Strand. She began walking at a brisk pace, and we continued to talk about the play.

When we reached the Strand I pointed to a large grey double door on the other side of the road. 'That's it,' I said. I would have taken her hand as she began to cross, but she stepped off the pavement ahead of me, dodged between the stationary traffic, and waited for me on the far side.

She pushed the grey doors open, and once again I followed in her wake. We descended a flight of steps

into a basement restaurant buzzing with the talk of people who had just come out of theatres, and waiters dashing, plates in both hands, from table to table.

'I don't expect you'll be able to get a table here if you haven't booked,' said Anna, eyeing a group of would-be customers who were clustered round the bar, impatiently waiting for someone to leave.

'Don't worry about that,' I said with bravado, and strode across to the reservations desk. I waved a hand imperiously at the head waiter, who was taking a customer's order. I only hoped he would recognize me.

I turned round to smile at Anna, but she didn't look too impressed.

After the waiter had taken the order, he walked slowly over to me. 'How may I help you, sir?' he asked.

'Can you manage a table for two, Victor?'

'Victor's off tonight, sir. Have you booked?'

'No, I haven't, but . . .'

The head waiter checked the list of reservations and then looked at his watch. 'I might be able to fit you in around 11.15–11:30 at the latest,' he said, not sounding too hopeful.

'No sooner?' I pleaded. 'I don't think we can wait that long.' Anna nodded her agreement.

'I'm afraid not, sir,' said the head waiter. 'We are fully booked until then.'

'As I expected,' said Anna, turning to leave.

Once again I had to hurry to keep up with her. As we stepped out onto the pavement I said, 'There's a little Italian restaurant I know not far from here, where I can always get a table. Shall we risk it?'

'Can't see that we've got a lot of choice,' replied Anna. 'Which direction this time?'

'Just up the road to the right,' I said as a clap of thunder heralded an imminent downpour.

'Damn,' said Anna, placing her handbag over her head for protection.

'I'm sorry,' I said, looking up at the black clouds. 'It's my fault. I should have . . .'

'Stop apologising all the time, Michael. It isn't your fault if it starts to rain.'

I took a deep breath and tried again. 'We'd better make a dash for it,' I said desperately. 'I don't expect we'll be able to pick up a taxi in this weather.'

This at least secured her ringing endorsement. I began running up the road, and Anna followed closely behind. The rain was getting heavier and heavier, and although we couldn't have had more than seventy yards to cover, we were both soaked by the time we reached the restaurant.

I sighed with relief when I opened the door and found the dining room was half-empty, although I suppose I should have been annoyed. I turned and smiled hopefully at Anna, but she was still frowning.

'Everything all right?' I asked.

'Fine. It's just that my father had a theory about restaurants that were half-empty at this time of night.'

I looked quizzically at my guest, but decided not to make any comment about her eye make-up, which was beginning to run, or her hair, which had come loose at the edges.

'I'd better carry out some repair work. I'll only be a couple of minutes,' she said, heading for a door marked 'Signorinas'.

I waved at Mario, who was serving no one in particular. He hurried over to me.

'There was a call for you earlier, Mr Whitaker,' Mario said as he guided me across the restaurant to my usual table. 'If you came in, I was to ask you to phone Gerald urgently. He sounded pretty desperate.'

'I'm sure it can wait. But if he rings again, let me know immediately.' At that moment Anna walked over to join us. The make-up had been restored, but the hair could have done with further attention.

I rose to greet her.

'You don't have to do that,' she said, taking her seat.

'Would you like a drink?' I asked, once we were both settled.

'No, I don't think so. I have an early start tomorrow morning, so I shouldn't overdo things. I'll just have a glass of wine with my meal.'

Another waiter appeared by her side. 'And what would madam care for this evening?' he asked politely.

'I haven't had time to look at the menu yet,' Anna replied, not even bothering to look up at him.

'I can recommend the fettucini, madam,' the waiter said, pointing to a dish halfway down the list of entrées. 'It's our speciality of the day.'

'Then I suppose I might as well have that,' said Anna, handing him the menu.

I nodded, indicating 'Me too,' and asked for a half-bottle of the house red. The waiter scooped up my menu and left us.

'Do you . . . ?'

'Can I . . . ?'

'You first,' I said, attempting a smile.

'Do you always order half a bottle of the house wine on a first date?' she asked.

'I think you'll find it's pretty good,' I said, rather plaintively.

'I was only teasing, Michael. Don't take yourself so seriously.'

I took a closer look at my companion, and began to wonder if I'd made a terrible mistake. Despite her efforts in the washroom, Anna wasn't quite the same girl I'd first seen – admittedly at a distance – when I'd nearly crashed my car earlier in the evening.

Oh my God, the car. I suddenly remembered where I'd left it, and stole a glance at my watch.

'Am I boring you already, Michael?' Anna asked. 'Or is this table on a time share?'

'Yes. I mean no. I'm sorry, I've just remembered something I should have checked on before we came to dinner. Sorry,' I repeated.

Anna frowned, which stopped me saying sorry yet again.

'Is it too late?' she asked.

'Too late for what?'

'To do something about whatever it is you should have checked on before we came to dinner?'

I looked out of the window, and wasn't pleased to see that it had stopped raining. Now my only hope was that the late-night traffic wardens might not be too vigilant.

'No, I'm sure it will be all right,' I said, trying to sound relaxed.

'Well, that's a relief,' said Anna, in a tone that bordered on the sarcastic.

'So. What's it like being a doctor?' I asked, trying to change the subject.

'Michael, it's my evening off. I'd rather not talk about my work, if you don't mind.'

For the next few moments neither of us spoke. I tried again. 'Do you have many male patients in your practice?' I asked, as the waiter reappeared with our fettucini.

'I can hardly believe I'm hearing this,' Anna said, unable to disguise the weariness in her voice. 'When are people like you going to accept that one or two of us are capable of a little more than spending our lives waiting hand and foot on the male sex.'

The waiter poured some wine into my glass.

'Yes. Of course. Absolutely. No. I didn't mean it to sound like that . . .' I sipped the wine and nodded to the waiter, who filled Anna's glass.

'Then what did you mean it to sound like?' demanded Anna as she stuck her fork firmly into the fettucini.

'Well, isn't it unusual for a man to go to a woman doctor?' I said, realizing the moment I had uttered the words that I was only getting myself into even deeper water.

'Good heavens, no, Michael. We live in an enlightened age. I've probably seen more naked men than you have – and it's not an attractive sight, I can assure you.' I laughed, in the hope that it would ease the tension. 'In any case,' she added, 'quite a few men are confident enough to accept the existence of women doctors, you know.'

'I'm sure that's true,' I said. 'I just thought . . .'

'You didn't think, Michael. That's the problem with so many men like you. I bet you've never even considered consulting a woman doctor.'

'No, but . . . Yes, but . . .'

' "No but, yes but" – Let's change the subject before I get really angry,' Anna said, putting her fork down. 'What do you do for a living, Michael? It doesn't sound as if you're in a profession where women are treated as equals.'

'I'm in the restaurant business,' I told her, wishing the fettucini was a little lighter.

'Ah, yes, you told me in the interval,' she said. 'But what does being "in the restaurant business" actually mean?'

'I'm on the management side. Or at least, that's what I do nowadays. I started life as a waiter, then I moved into the kitchens for about five years, and finally . . .'

'. . . found you weren't very good at either, so you took up managing everyone else.'

'Something like that,' I said, trying to make light of it. But Anna's words only reminded me that one of my other restaurants was without a chef that night, and that that was where I'd been heading before I'd allowed myself to become infatuated by Anna.

'I've lost you again,' Anna said, beginning to sound

exasperated. 'You were going to tell me all about restaurant management.'

'Yes, I was, wasn't I? By the way, how's your fettucini?'

'Not bad, considering.'

'Considering?'

'Considering this place was your second choice.'

I was silenced once again.

'It's not that bad,' she said, taking another reluctant forkful.

'Perhaps you'd like something else instead? I can always . . .'

'No, thank you, Michael. After all, this was the one dish the waiter felt confident enough to recommend.'

I couldn't think of a suitable response, so I remained silent.

'Come on, Michael, you still haven't explained what restaurant management actually involves,' said Anna.

'Well, at the moment I'm running three restaurants in the West End, which means I never stop dashing from one to the other, depending on which is facing the biggest crisis on that particular day.'

'Sounds a bit like ward duty to me,' said Anna. 'So who turned out to have the biggest crisis today?'

'Today, thank heaven, was not typical,' I told her with feeling.

'That bad?' said Anna.

'Yes, I'm afraid so. We lost a chef this morning who cut off the top of his finger, and won't be back at work for at least a fortnight. My head waiter in our second restaurant is off, claiming he has 'flu, and I've just had to sack the barman in the third for fiddling the books. Barmen always fiddle the books, of course, but in this case even the customers began to notice what he was up to.' I paused, wondering if I should risk another mouthful of fettucini. 'But I still wouldn't want to be in any other business.'

'In the circumstances, I'm frankly amazed you were able to take the evening off.'

'I shouldn't have, really, and wouldn't have, except . . .' I trailed off as I leaned over and topped up Anna's wine glass.

'Except what?' she said.

'Do you want to hear the truth?' I asked as I poured the remains of the wine into my own glass.

'I'll try that for starters,' she said.

I placed the empty bottle on the side of the table, and hesitated, but only for a moment. 'I was driving to one of my restaurants earlier this evening, when I spotted you going into the theatre. I stared at you for so long that I nearly crashed into the back of the car in front of me. Then I swerved across the road into the nearest parking space, and the car behind almost crashed into me. I leapt out, ran all the way to the theatre, and searched everywhere until I saw you standing in the queue for the box office. I joined the line and watched you hand over your spare ticket. Once you were safely out of sight, I told the box office manager that you hadn't expected me to make it in time, and that you might have put my ticket up for resale. Once I'd described you, which I was able to do in great detail, he handed it over without so much as a murmur.'

'More fool him,' said Anna, putting down her glass and staring at me as if I'd just been released from a lunatic asylum.

'Then I put two ten-pound notes into a theatre envelope and took the place next to you,' I continued. 'The rest you already know.' I waited, with some trepidation, to see how she would react.

'I suppose I ought to be flattered,' Anna said after a moment's consideration. 'But I don't know whether to laugh or cry. One thing's for certain; the woman

I've been living with for the past ten years will think it's highly amusing, especially as you paid for her ticket.'

The waiter returned to remove the half-finished plates. 'Was everything all right, sir?' he asked, sounding anxious.

'Fine, just fine,' I said unconvincingly. Anna grimaced, but made no comment.

'Would you care for coffee, madam?'

'No, I don't think I'll risk it,' she said, looking at her watch. 'In any case, I ought to be getting back. Elizabeth will be wondering where I've got to.'

She stood up and walked towards the door. I followed a yard behind. She was just about to step onto the pavement when she turned to me and asked, 'Don't you think you ought to settle the bill?'

'That won't be necessary.'

'Why?' she asked, laughing. 'Do you own the place?'

'No. But it is one of the three restaurants I manage.'

Anna turned scarlet. 'I'm so sorry, Michael,' she said. 'That was tactless of me.' She paused for a moment before adding, 'But I'm sure you'll agree that the food wasn't exactly memorable.'

'Would you like me to drive you home?' I asked, trying not to sound too enthusiastic.

Anna looked up at the black clouds. 'That would be useful,' she replied, 'if it's not miles out of your way. Where's your car?' she said before I had a chance to ask where she lived.

'I left it just up the road.'

'Oh, yes, I remember,' said Anna. 'When you jumped out of it because you couldn't take your eyes off me. I'm afraid you picked the wrong girl this time.'

At last we had found something on which we could agree, but I made no comment as we walked towards the spot where I had abandoned my car. Anna limited her conversation to whether it was

about to rain again, and how good she had thought the wine was. I was relieved to find my Volvo parked exactly where I had left it.

I was searching for my keys when I spotted a large sticker glued to the windscreen. I looked down at the front offside wheel, and saw the yellow clamp.

'It just isn't your night, is it?' said Anna. 'But don't worry about me, I'll just grab a cab.'

She raised her hand and a taxi skidded to a halt. She turned back to face me. 'Thanks for dinner,' she managed, not altogether convincingly, and added, even less convincingly, 'Perhaps we'll meet again.' Before I could respond, she had slammed the taxi door closed.

As I watched her being driven away, it started to rain.

I took one more look at my immovable car, and decided I would deal with the problem in the morning.

I was about to rush for the nearest shelter when another taxi came around the corner, its yellow light indicating that it was for hire. I waved frantically and it drew up beside my clamped car.

'Bad luck, mate,' said the cabbie, looking down at my front wheel. 'My third tonight.'

I attempted a smile.

'So, where to, guv?'

I gave him my address in Lambeth and climbed into the back.

As the taxi manoeuvred its way slowly through the rainswept post-theatre traffic and across Waterloo Bridge, the driver began chattering away. I just about managed monosyllabic replies to his opinions on the weather, John Major, the England cricket team and foreign tourists. With each new topic, his forecast became ever more gloomy.

He only stopped offering his opinions when he came to a halt outside my house in Fentiman Road. I paid him, and smiled ruefully at the thought that this

213

would be the first time in weeks that I'd managed to get home before midnight. I walked slowly up the short path to the front door.

I turned the key in the lock and opened the door quietly, so as not to wake my wife. Once inside I went through my nightly ritual of slipping off my jacket and shoes before creeping quietly up the stairs.

Before I had reached the bedroom I began to get undressed. After years of coming in at one or two in the morning, I was able to take off all my clothes, fold and stack them, and slide under the sheets next to Judy without waking her. But just as I pulled back the cover she said drowsily, 'I didn't think you'd be home so early, with all the problems you were facing tonight.' I wondered if she was talking in her sleep. 'How much damage did the fire do?'

'The fire?' I said, standing in the nude.

'In Davies Street. Gerald phoned a few moments after you'd left to say a fire had started in the kitchen and had spread to the restaurant. He was just checking to make certain you were on your way. He'd cancelled all the bookings for the next two weeks, but he didn't think they'd be able to open again for at least a month. I told him that as you'd left just after six you'd be with him at any minute. So, just how bad is the damage?'

I was already dressed by the time Judy was awake enough to ask why I had never turned up at the restaurant. I shot down the stairs and out onto the street in search of another cab. It had started raining again.

A taxi swung round and came to a halt in front of me.

'Where to this time, guv?'

À Point

'Thank you, Michael. I'd like that,'

I smiled, unable to mask my delight.

'Hi, Pipsqueak. I thought I might have missed you.'

I turned and stared at a tall man with a mop of fair hair, who seemed unaffected by the steady flow of people trying to pass him on either side.

Anna gave him a smile that I hadn't seen until that moment.

'Hello, Jonathan,' she said. 'This is Michael Whitaker. You're lucky – he bought your ticket, and if you hadn't turned up I was just about to accept his kind invitation to dinner. Michael, this is my brother, Jonathan – the one who was held up at the hospital. As you can see, he's now escaped.'

I couldn't think of a suitable reply.

Jonathan shook me warmly by the hand. 'Thank you for keeping my sister company,' he said. 'Won't you join us for dinner?'

'That's kind of you,' I replied, 'but I've just remembered that I'm meant to be somewhere else right now. I'd better . . .'

'You're not meant to be anywhere else right now,' interrupted Anna, giving me the same smile. 'Don't be so feeble.' She linked her arm in mine. 'In any case, we'd both like you to join us.'

'Thank you,' I said.

'There's a restaurant just down the road that I've been told is rather good,' said Jonathan, as the three of us began walking off in the direction of the Strand.

'Great. I'm famished,' said Anna.

'So, tell me all about the play,' Jonathan said as Anna linked her other arm in his.

'Every bit as good as the critics promised,' said Anna.

'You were unlucky to miss it,' I said.

'But I'm rather glad you did,' said Anna as we reached the corner of the Strand.

'I think that's the place I'm looking for,' said Jonathan, pointing to a large grey double door on the far side of the road. The three of us weaved our way through the temporarily stationary traffic.

Once we reached the other side of the road Jonathan pushed open one of the grey doors to allow us through. It started to rain just as we stepped inside. He led Anna and me down a flight of stairs into a basement restaurant buzzing with the talk of people who had just come out of theatres, and waiters dashing, plates in both hands, from table to table.

'I'll be impressed if you can get a table here,' Anna said to her brother, eyeing a group of would-be customers who were clustered round the bar, impatiently waiting for someone to leave. 'You should have booked,' she added as he began waving at the head waiter, who was fully occupied taking a customer's order.

I remained a yard or two behind them, and as Mario came across, I put a finger to my lips and nodded to him.

'I don't suppose you have a table for three?' asked Jonathan.

'Yes, of course, sir. Please follow me,' said Mario, leading us to a quiet table in the corner of the room.

'That was a bit of luck,' said Jonathan.

'It certainly was,' Anna agreed. Jonathan suggested that I take the far chair, so his sister could sit between us.

Once we had settled, Jonathan asked what I would like to drink.

'How about you?' I said, turning to Anna. 'Another dry martini?'

Jonathan looked surprised. 'You haven't had a dry martini since . . .'

Anna scowled at him and said quickly, 'I'll just have a glass of wine with the meal.'

Since when? I wondered, but only said, 'I'll have the same.'

Mario reappeared, and handed us our menus. Jona-than and Anna studied theirs in silence for some time before Jonathan asked, 'Any ideas?'

'It all looks so tempting,' Anna said. 'But I think I'll settle for the fettucini and a glass of red wine.'

'What about a starter?' asked Jonathan.

'No. I'm on first call tomorrow, if you remember – unless of course you're volunteering to take my place.'

'Not after what I've been through this evening, Pipsqueak. I'd rather go without a starter too,' he said. 'How about you, Michael? Don't let our domestic problems get in your way.'

'Fettucini and a glass of red wine would suit me just fine.'

'Three fettucini and a bottle of your best Chianti,' said Jonathan when Mario returned.

Anna leaned over to me and whispered conspiratorially, 'It's the only Italian wine he can pronounce correctly.'

'What would have happened if we'd chosen fish?' I asked her.

'He's also heard of Frascati, but he's never quite sure what he's meant to do when someone orders duck.'

'What are you two whispering about?' asked Jonathan as he handed his menu back to Mario.

'I was asking your sister about the third partner in the practice.'

'Not bad, Michael,' Anna said. 'You should have gone into politics.'

'My wife, Elizabeth, is the third partner,' Jonathan said, unaware of what Anna had been getting at. 'She, poor darling, is on call tonight.'

'You note, two women and one man,' said Anna as the wine waiter appeared by Jonathan's side.

'Yes. There used to be four of us,' said Jonathan, without explanation. He studied the label on the bottle before nodding sagely.

'You're not fooling anyone, Jonathan. Michael has already worked out that you're no sommelier,' said

Anna, sounding as if she was trying to change the subject. The waiter extracted the cork and poured a little wine into Jonathan's glass for him to taste.

'So, what do you do, Michael?' asked Jonathan after he had given a second nod to the wine waiter. 'Don't tell me you're a doctor, because I'm not looking for another man to join the practice.'

'No, he's in the restaurant business,' said Anna, as three bowls of fettucini were placed in front of us.

'I see. You two obviously swapped life histories during the interval,' said Jonathan. 'But what does being "in the restaurant business" actually mean?'

'I'm on the management side,' I explained. 'Or at least, that's what I do nowadays. I started life as a waiter, then I moved into the kitchens for about five years, and finally ended up in management.'

'But what does a restaurant manager actually do?' asked Anna.

'Obviously the interval wasn't long enough for you to go into any great detail,' said Jonathan as he jabbed his fork into some fettucini.

'Well, at the moment I'm running three restaurants in the West End, which means I never stop dashing from one to the other, depending on which is facing the biggest crisis on that particular day.'

'Sounds a bit like ward duty to me,' said Anna. 'So who turned out to have the biggest crisis today?'

'Today, thank heaven, was not typical,' I said with feeling.

'That bad?' said Jonathan.

'Yes, I'm afraid so. We lost a chef this morning who cut off the top of his finger, and won't be back at work for at least a fortnight. My head waiter in our second restaurant is off, claiming he has 'flu, and I've just had to sack the barman in the third for fiddling the books. Barmen always fiddle the books, of course, but in this case even the customers began to notice what he was up to.' I paused. 'But I still wouldn't want to be in any other . . .'

A shrill ring interrupted me. I couldn't tell where the sound was coming from until Jonathan removed a tiny cellular phone from his jacket pocket.

'Sorry about this,' he said. 'Hazard of the job.' He pressed a button and put the phone to his ear. He listened for a few seconds, and a frown appeared on his face. 'Yes, I suppose so. I'll be there as quickly as I can.' He flicked the phone closed and put it back into his pocket.

'Sorry,' he repeated. 'One of my patients has chosen this particular moment to have a relapse. I'm afraid I'm going to have to leave you.' He stood up and turned to his sister. 'How will you get home, Pipsqueak?'

'I'm a big girl now,' said Anna, 'so I'll just look around for one of those black objects on four wheels with a sign on the top that reads T-A-X-I, and then I'll wave at it.'

'Don't worry, Jonathan,' I said. 'I'll drive her home.'

'That's very kind of you,' said Jonathan, 'because if it's still pouring by the time you leave, she may not be able to find one of those black objects to wave at.'

'In any case, it's the least I can do, after I ended up getting your ticket, your dinner and your sister.'

'Fair exchange,' said Jonathan as Mario came rushing up.

'Is everything all right, sir?' he asked.

'No, it isn't. I'm on call, and have to go.' He handed over an American Express card. 'If you'd be kind enough to put this through your machine, I'll sign for it and you can fill in the amount later. And please add fifteen per cent.'

'Thank you, sir,' said Mario, and rushed away.

'Hope to see you again,' said Jonathan. I rose to shake him by the hand.

'I hope so too,' I said.

Jonathan left us, headed for the bar and signed a slip of paper. Mario handed him back his American Express card.

As Anna waved to her brother, I looked towards the bar and shook my head slightly. Mario tore up the little slip of paper and dropped the pieces into a waste-paper basket.

'It hasn't been a wonderful day for Jonathan, either,' said Anna, turning back to face me. 'And what with your problems, I'm amazed you were able to take the evening off.'

'I shouldn't have, really, and wouldn't have, except . . .' I trailed off as I leaned over and topped up Anna's glass.

'Except what?' she asked.

'Do you want to hear the truth?' I asked as I poured the remains of the wine into my own glass.

'I'll try that for starters,' she said.

I placed the empty bottle on the side of the table, and hesitated, but only for a moment. 'I was driving to one of my restaurants earlier this evening, when I spotted you going into the theatre. I stared at you for so long that I nearly crashed into the back of the car in front of me. Then I swerved across the road into the nearest parking space, and the car behind almost crashed into me. I leapt out, ran all the way to the theatre, and searched everywhere until I saw you standing in the queue for the box office. I joined the line and watched you hand over your spare ticket. Once you were safely out of sight, I told the box office manager that you hadn't expected me to make it in time, and that you might have put my ticket up for resale. After I'd described you, which I was able to do in great detail, he handed it over without so much as a murmur.'

Anna put down her glass of wine and stared across at me with a look of incredulity. 'I'm glad he fell for your story,' she said. 'But should I?'

'Yes, you should. Because then I put two ten-pound notes into a theatre envelope and took the place next to you,' I continued. 'The rest you already know.' I

waited to see how she would react. She didn't speak for some time.

'I'm flattered,' she said eventually. 'I didn't realize there were any old-fashioned romantics left in the world.' She lowered her head slightly. 'Am I allowed to ask what you have planned for the rest of the evening?'

'Nothing has been planned so far,' I admitted. 'Which is why it's all been so refreshing.'

'You make me sound like an After Eight mint,' said Anna with a laugh.

'I can think of at least three replies to that,' I told her as Mario reappeared, looking a little disappointed at the sight of the half-empty plates.

'Is everything all right, sir?' he asked, sounding anxious.

'Couldn't have been better,' said Anna, who hadn't stopped looking at me.

'Would you like a coffee, madam?' Mario asked her.

'No, thank you,' said Anna firmly. 'We have to go in search of a marooned car.'

'Heaven knows if it will still be there after all this time,' I said as she rose from her place.

I took Anna's hand, led her towards the entrance, back up the stairs and out onto the street. Then I began to retrace my steps to the spot where I'd abandoned my car. As we strolled up the Aldwych and chatted away, I felt as if I was with an old friend.

'You don't have to give me a lift, Michael,' Anna was saying. 'It's probably miles out of your way, and in any case it's stopped raining, so I'll just hail a taxi.'

'I want to give you a lift,' I told her. 'That way I'll have your company for a little longer.' She smiled as we reached a distressingly large space where I had left the car.

'Damn,' I said. I quickly checked up and down the road, and returned to find Anna laughing.

'Is this another of your schemes to have more of

my company?' she teased. She opened her bag and took out a mobile phone, dialled 999, and passed it over to me.

'Which service do you require? Fire, Police or Ambulance?' a voice asked.

'Police,' I said, and was immediately put through to another voice.

'Charing Cross Police Station. What is the nature of your enquiry?'

'I think my car has been stolen.'

'Can you tell me the make, colour and registration number please, sir.'

'It's a blue Rover 600, registration K857 SHV.'

There was a long pause, during which I could hear other voices talking in the background.

'No, it hasn't been stolen, sir,' said the officer who had been dealing with me when he came back on the line. 'The vehicle was illegally parked on a double yellow line. It's been removed and taken to the Vauxhall Bridge Pound.'

'Can I pick it up now?' I asked.

'Certainly, sir. How will you be getting there?'

'I'll take a taxi.'

'Then just ask the driver for the Vauxhall Bridge Pound. Once you get there, you'll need some form of identification, and a cheque for £105 with a banker's card – that is if you don't have the full amount in cash.'

'£105?' I said quietly.

'That's correct, sir.'

Anna frowned for the first time that evening.

'Worth every penny.'

'I beg your pardon, sir?'

'Nothing, officer. Goodnight.'

I handed the phone back to Anna, and said, 'The next thing I'm going to do is find you a taxi.'

'You certainly are not, Michael, because I'm staying with you. In any case, you promised my brother you'd take me home.'

I took her hand and hailed a taxi, which swung across the road and came to a halt beside us.

'Vauxhall Bridge Pound, please.'

'Bad luck, mate,' said the cabbie. 'You're my fourth this evening.'

I gave him a broad grin.

'I expect the other three also chased you into the theatre, but luckily they were behind me in the queue,' I said to Anna as I joined her on the back seat.

As the taxi manoeuvred its way slowly through the rainswept post-theatre traffic and across Waterloo Bridge, Anna said, 'Don't you think I should have been given the chance to choose between the four of you? After all, one of them might have been driving a Rolls-Royce.'

'Not possible.'

'And why not, pray?' asked Anna.

'Because you couldn't have parked a Rolls-Royce in that space.'

'But if he'd had a chauffeur, that would have solved all my problems.'

'In that case, I would simply have run him over.'

The taxi had travelled some distance before either of us spoke again.

'Can I ask you a personal question?' Anna eventually said.

'If it's what I think it is, I was about to ask you the same thing.'

'Then you go first.'

'No – I'm not married,' I said. 'Nearly, once, but she escaped.' Anna laughed. 'And you?'

'I was married,' she said quietly. 'He was the fourth doctor in the practice. He died three years ago. I spent nine months nursing him, but in the end I failed.'

'I'm so sorry,' I said, feeling a little ashamed. 'That was tactless of me. I shouldn't have raised the subject.'

'I raised it, Michael, not you. It's me who should apologize.'

Neither of us spoke again for several minutes, until Anna said, 'For the past three years, since Andrew's death, I've immersed myself in work, and I seem to spend most of my spare time boring Jonathan and Elizabeth to distraction. They couldn't have been more understanding, but they must be heartily sick

of it by now. I wouldn't be surprised if Jonathan hadn't arranged an emergency for tonight, so someone else could take me to the theatre for a change. It might even give me the confidence to go out again. Heaven knows,' she added as we drove into the car pound, 'enough people have been kind enough to ask me.'

I passed the cabbie a ten-pound note and we dashed through the rain in the direction of a little Portakabin.

I walked up to the counter and read the form sellotaped to it. I took out my wallet, extracted my driving licence, and began counting.

I only had eighty pounds in cash, and I never carry a chequebook.

Anna grinned, and took the envelope I'd presented to her earlier in the evening from her bag. She tore it open and extracted the two ten-pound notes, added a five-pound note of her own, and handed them over to me.

'Thank you,' I said, once again feeling embarrassed.

'Worth every penny,' she replied with a grin.

The policeman counted the notes slowly, placed them in a tin box, and gave me a receipt.

'It's right there, in the front row,' he said, pointing out of the window. 'And if I may say so, sir, it was perhaps unwise of you to leave your keys in the ignition. If the vehicle had been stolen, your insurance company would not have been liable to cover the claim.' He passed me my keys.

'It was my fault, officer,' said Anna. 'I should have sent him back for them, but I didn't realize what he was up to. I'll make sure he doesn't do it again.'

The officer looked up at me. I shrugged my shoulders and led Anna out of the cabin and across to my car. I opened the door to let her in, then nipped round to the driver's side as she leant over and pushed my door open. I took my place behind the wheel and turned to face her. 'I'm sorry,' I said. 'The rain has ruined your dress.' A drop of water fell off the end of her nose. 'But, you know, you're just as beautiful wet or dry.'

'Thank you, Michael,' she smiled. 'But if you don't have any objection, on balance I'd prefer to be dry.'

I laughed. 'So, where shall I take you?' I asked, suddenly aware that I didn't know where she lived.

'Fulham, please. Forty-nine Parsons Green Lane. It's not too far.'

I pushed the key into the ignition, not caring how far it was. I turned the key and took a deep breath. The engine spluttered, but refused to start. Then I realized I had left the sidelights on.

'Don't do this to me,' I begged, as Anna began

laughing again. I turned the key a second time, and the motor caught. I let out a sigh of relief.

'That was a close one,' Anna said. 'If it hadn't started, we might have ended up spending the rest of the night together. Or was that all part of your dastardly plan?'

'Nothing's gone to plan so far,' I admitted as I drove out of the pound. I paused before adding, 'Still, I suppose things might have turned out differently.'

'You mean if I hadn't been the sort of girl you were looking for?'

'Something like that.'

'I wonder what those other three men would have thought of me,' said Anna wistfully.

'Who cares? They're not going to have the chance to find out.'

'You sound very sure of yourself, Mr Whitaker.'

'If you only knew,' I said. 'But I would like to see you again, Anna. If you're willing to risk it.'

She seemed to take an eternity to reply. 'Yes, I'd like that,' she said eventually. 'But only on condition that you pick me up at my place, so I can be certain you park your car legally, and remember to switch your lights off.'

'I accept your terms,' I told her. 'And I won't even add any conditions of my own if we can begin the agreement tomorrow evening.'

Once again Anna didn't reply immediately. 'I'm not sure I know what I'm doing tomorrow evening.'

'Neither do I,' I said. 'But I'll cancel it, whatever it is.'

'Then so will I,' said Anna as I drove into Parsons Green Lane, and began searching for number forty-nine.

'It's about a hundred yards down, on the left,' she said.

I drew up and parked outside her front door.

'Don't let's bother with the theatre this time,' said Anna. 'Come round at about eight, and I'll cook you some supper.' She leant over and kissed me on the cheek before turning back to open the car door. I jumped out and walked quickly round to her side of the car as she stepped onto the pavement.

'So, I'll see you around eight tomorrow evening,' she said.

'I'll look forward to that.' I hesitated, and then took her in my arms. 'Goodnight, Anna.'

'Goodnight, Michael,' she said as I released her. 'And thank you for buying my ticket, not to mention dinner. I'm glad my other three would-be suitors only made it as far as the car pound.'

I smiled as she pushed the key into the lock of her front door.

She turned back. 'By the way, Michael, was that the restaurant with the missing waiter, the four-and-a-half-fingered chef, or the crooked bartender?'

'The crooked bartender,' I replied with a smile.

She closed the door behind her as the clock on a nearby church struck one.

Endgame

CORNELIUS BARRINGTON hesitated before he made his next move. He continued to study the board with great interest. The game had been going on for over two hours, and Cornelius was confident that he was only seven moves away from checkmate. He suspected that his opponent was also aware of the fact.

Cornelius looked up and smiled across at Frank Vintcent, who was not only his oldest friend but had over the years, as the family solicitor, proved to be his wisest adviser. The two men had many things in common: their age, both over sixty; their background, both middle-class sons of professionals; they had been educated at the same school and at the same university. But there the similarities ended. For Cornelius was by nature an entrepreneur, a risk-taker, who had made his fortune mining in South Africa and Brazil. Frank was a solicitor by profession, cautious, slow to decision, fascinated by detail.

Cornelius and Frank also differed in their physical appearance. Cornelius was tall, heavily built, with a head of silver hair many men half his age would have envied. Frank was slight, of medium stature, and apart from a semicircle of grey tufts, was almost completely bald.

Cornelius had been widowed after four decades of happy married life. Frank was a confirmed bachelor.

Among the things that had kept them close friends was their enduring love of chess. Frank joined Cornelius at The Willows for a game every Thursday evening, and the result usually remained in the balance, often ending in stalemate.

The evening always began with a light supper, but only one glass of wine each would be poured – the two men took their chess seriously – and after the game was over they would return to the drawing room to enjoy a glass of brandy and a cigar; but tonight Cornelius was about to shatter that routine.

'Congratulations,' said Frank, looking up from the board. 'I think you've got me beaten this time. I'm fairly sure there's no escape.' He smiled, placed the red king flat on the board, rose from his place and shook hands with his closest friend.

'Let's go through to the drawing room and have a brandy and a cigar,' suggested Cornelius, as if it were a novel idea.

'Thank you,' said Frank as they left the study and strolled towards the drawing room. As Cornelius passed the portrait of his son Daniel, his heart missed a beat – something that hadn't changed for the past twenty-three years. If his only child had lived, he would never have sold the company.

As they entered the spacious drawing room the two men were greeted by a cheerful fire blazing in the grate, which had been laid by Cornelius's housekeeper Pauline only moments after she had finished clearing up their supper. Pauline also believed in the virtues of routine, but her life too was about to be shattered.

'I should have trapped you several moves earlier,' said Cornelius, 'but I was taken by surprise when you captured my queen's knight. I should have seen that coming,' he added, as he strolled over to the sideboard. Two large cognacs and two Monte Cristo cigars had been laid out on a silver tray. Cornelius picked up the cigar-clipper and passed it across to his friend, then struck a match, leaned over and watched Frank puff away until he was convinced his cigar was alight. He then completed the same routine himself before sinking into his favourite seat by the fire.

Frank raised his glass. 'Well played, Cornelius,' he said, offering a slight bow, although his host would have been the first to acknowledge that over the years his guest was probably just ahead on points.

Cornelius allowed Frank to take a few more puffs before shattering his evening. Why hurry? After all, he had been preparing for this moment for several weeks, and was unwilling to share the secret with his oldest friend until everything was in place.

They both remained silent for some time, relaxed in each other's company. Finally Cornelius placed his brandy on a side table and said, 'Frank, we have been friends for over fifty years. Equally importantly, as my legal adviser you have proved to be a shrewd advocate. In fact, since the untimely death of Millicent there has been no one I rely on more.'

Frank continued to puff away at his cigar without interrupting his friend. From the expression on his face, he was aware that the compliment was nothing more than an opening gambit. He suspected he would have to wait some time before Cornelius revealed his next move.

'When I first set up the company some thirty years ago, it was you who was responsible for executing the original deeds; and I don't believe I've signed a legal document since that day which has not crossed your desk – something that was unquestionably a major factor in my success.'

'It's generous of you to say so,' said Frank, before taking another sip of brandy, 'but the truth is that it was always your originality and enterprise that made it possible for the company to go from strength to strength – gifts that the gods decided not to bestow on me, leaving me with little choice but to be a mere functionary.'

'You have always underestimated your contribution to the company's success, Frank, but I am in no doubt of the role you played over the years.'

'Where is this all leading?' asked Frank with a smile.

'Patience, my friend,' said Cornelius. 'I still have a few moves to make before I reveal the stratagem I have in mind.' He leaned back and took another long puff of his cigar. 'As you know, when I sold the company some four years ago, it had been my intention to slow down for the first time in years. I had promised to take Millie on an extended holiday to India and the Far East – ' he paused ' – but that was not to be.'

Frank nodded his head in understanding.

'Her death served to remind me that I am also mortal, and may myself not have much longer to live.'

'No, no, my friend,' protested Frank. 'You still have a good many years to go yet.'

'You may be right,' said Cornelius, 'although funnily enough it was you who made me start to think seriously about the future . . .'

'Me?' said Frank, looking puzzled.

'Yes. Don't you remember some weeks ago, sitting in that chair and advising me that the time had come for me to consider rewriting my will?'

'Yes, I do,' said Frank, 'but that was only because in your present will virtually everything is left to Millie.'

'I'm aware of that,' said Cornelius, 'but it nevertheless served to concentrate the mind. You see, I still rise at six o'clock every morning, but as I no longer have an office to go to, I spend many self-indulgent hours considering how to distribute my wealth now that Millie can no longer be the main beneficiary.'

Cornelius took another long puff of his cigar before continuing. 'For the past month I have been considering those around me – my relatives, friends, acquaintances and employees – and I began to think about the way they have always treated me, which caused me to wonder which of them would show the same amount of devotion, attention and loyalty if I were not worth millions, but was in fact a penniless old man.'

'I have a feeling I'm in check,' said Frank, with a laugh.

'No, no, my dear friend,' said Cornelius. '*You* are absolved from any such doubts. Otherwise I would not be sharing these confidences with you.'

'But are such thoughts not a little unfair on your immediate family, not to mention . . .'

'You may be right, but I don't wish to leave that to chance. I have therefore decided to find out the truth for myself, as I consider mere speculation to be unsatisfactory.' Once again, Cornelius paused to take a puff of his cigar before continuing. 'So indulge me for a moment while I tell you what I have in mind, for I confess that without your cooperation it will be impossible for me to carry out my little subterfuge. But first allow me to refill your glass.' Cornelius rose from his chair, picked up his friend's empty goblet and walked to the sideboard.

'As I was saying,' continued Cornelius, passing the refilled glass back to Frank, 'I have recently been wondering how those around me would behave if I were penniless, and I have come to the conclusion that there is only one way to find out.'

Frank took a long gulp before enquiring, 'What do you have in mind? A fake suicide perhaps?'

'Not quite as dramatic as that,' replied Cornelius. 'But almost, because – ' he paused again ' – I intend to declare myself bankrupt.' He stared through the haze of smoke, hoping to observe his friend's immediate reaction. But, as so often in the past, the old solicitor remained inscrutable, not least because, although his friend had just made a bold move, he knew the game was far from over.

He pushed a pawn tentatively forward. 'How do you intend to go about that?' he asked.

'Tomorrow morning,' replied Cornelius, 'I want you to write to the five people who have the greatest claim on my estate: my brother Hugh, his wife Elizabeth, their son Timothy, my sister Margaret, and finally my housekeeper Pauline.'

'And what will be the import of this letter?' asked Frank, trying not to sound too incredulous.

'You will explain to all of them that, due to an unwise investment I made soon after my wife's death, I now find myself in debt. In fact, without their help I may well be facing bankruptcy.'

'But . . .' protested Frank.

Cornelius raised a hand. 'Hear me out,' he pleaded, 'because your role in this real-life game could prove crucial. Once you have convinced them that they can no longer expect anything from me, I intend to put the second phase of my plan into operation, which should prove conclusively whether they really care for me, or simply for the prospect of my wealth.'

'I can't wait to learn what you have in mind,' said Frank.

Cornelius swirled the brandy round in his glass while he collected his thoughts.

'As you are well aware, each of the five people I have named has at some time in the past asked me

for a loan. I have never required anything in writing, as I have always considered the repayment of these debts to be a matter of trust. These loans range from £100,000 to my brother Hugh to purchase the lease for his shop – which I understand is doing quite well – to my housekeeper Pauline, who borrowed £500 for a deposit on a secondhand car. Even young Timothy needed £1,000 to pay off his university loan, and as he seems to be progressing well in his chosen profession, it should not be too much to ask him – like all of the others – to repay his debt.'

'And the second test?' enquired Frank.

'Since Millie's death, each of them has performed some little service for me, which they have always insisted they enjoyed carrying out, rather than it being a chore. I'm about to find out if they are willing to do the same for a penniless old man.'

'But how will you know . . .' began Frank.

'I think that will become obvious as the weeks go by. And in any case, there is a third test, which I believe will settle the matter.'

Frank stared across at his friend. 'Is there any point in trying to talk you out of this crazy idea?' he asked.

'No, there is not,' replied Cornelius without hesitation. 'I am resolved in this matter, although I accept that I cannot make the first move, let alone bring it to a conclusion, without your cooperation.'

'If it is truly what you want me to do, Cornelius, then I shall carry out your instructions to the letter, as I have always done in the past. But on this occasion there must be one proviso.'

'And what might that be?' asked Cornelius.

'I shall not charge a fee for this commission, so that I will be able to attest to anyone who should ask that I have not benefited from your shenanigans.'

'But . . .'

'No "buts", old friend. I made a handsome profit from my original shareholding when you sold the company. You must consider this a small attempt to say thank you.'

Cornelius smiled. 'It is I who should be grateful, and indeed I am, as always, conscious of your valued assistance over the years. You are truly a good friend, and I swear I would leave my entire estate to you if you weren't a bachelor, and if I didn't know it wouldn't change your way of life one iota.'

'No, thank you,' said Frank with a chuckle. 'If you did that, I would only have to carry out exactly the same test with a different set of characters.' He paused. 'So, what is your first move?'

Cornelius rose from his chair. 'Tomorrow you will send out five letters informing those concerned that a bankruptcy notice has been served on me, and that I require any outstanding loans to be repaid in full, and as quickly as possible.'

Frank had already begun making notes on a little pad he always carried with him. Twenty minutes later, when he had written down Cornelius's final instruction, he placed the pad back in an inside pocket, drained his glass and stubbed out his cigar.

When Cornelius rose to accompany him to the front door, Frank asked, 'But what is to be the third of your tests, the one you're convinced will prove so conclusive?'

The old solicitor listened carefully as Cornelius outlined an idea of such ingenuity that he departed feeling all the victims would be left with little choice but to reveal their true colours.

The first person to call Cornelius on Saturday morning was his brother Hugh. It must have been only moments after he had opened Frank's letter. Cornelius had the distinct feeling that someone else was listening in on the conversation.

'I've just received a letter from your solicitor,' said Hugh, 'and I simply can't believe it. Please tell me there's been some dreadful mistake.'

'I'm afraid there has been no mistake,' Cornelius replied. 'I only wish I could tell you otherwise.'

'But how could you, who are normally so shrewd, have allowed such a thing to happen?'

'Put it down to old age,' Cornelius replied. 'A few weeks after Millie died I was talked into investing a large sum of money in a company that specialized in supplying mining equipment to the Russians. All of us have read about the endless supply of oil there, if only one could get at it, so I was confident my investment would show a handsome return. Last Friday I was informed by the company secretary that they had filed a 217 order, as they were no longer solvent.'

'But surely you didn't invest everything you had in the one company?' said Hugh, sounding even more incredulous.

'Not originally, of course,' said Cornelius, 'but I fear I got sucked in whenever they needed a further injection of cash. Towards the end I had to go on investing more, as it seemed to me the only way I would have any chance of getting back my original investment.'

'But doesn't the company have any assets you can lay your hands on? What about all the mining equipment?'

'It's all rusting away somewhere in central Russia, and so far we haven't seen a thimbleful of oil.'

'Why didn't you get out when your losses were still manageable?' asked Hugh.

'Pride, I suppose. Unwilling to admit I'd backed a loser, always believing my money would be safe in the long run.'

'But they must be offering some recompense,' said Hugh desperately.

'Not a penny,' replied Cornelius. 'I can't even afford to fly over and spend a few days in Russia to find out what the true position is.'

'How much time have they given you?'

'A bankruptcy notice has already been served on

me, so my very survival depends on how much I can raise in the short term.' Cornelius paused. 'I'm sorry to remind you of this, Hugh, but you will recall that some time ago I loaned you £100,000. So I was rather hoping . . .'

'But you know that every penny of that money has been sunk into the shop, and with High Street sales at an all-time low, I don't think I could lay my hands on more than a few thousand at the moment.'

Cornelius thought he heard someone whispering the words 'And no more' in the background.

'Yes, I can see the predicament you're in,' said Cornelius. 'But anything you can do to help would be appreciated. When you've settled on a sum – ' he paused again ' – and naturally you'll have to discuss with Elizabeth just how much you can spare – perhaps you could send a cheque direct to Frank Vintcent's office. He's handling the whole messy business.'

'The lawyers always seem to end up getting their cut, whether you win or lose.'

'To be fair,' said Cornelius, 'Frank has waived his fee on this occasion. And while you're on the phone, Hugh, the people you're sending to refit the kitchen were due to start later this week. It's even more important now that they complete the job as quickly as possible, because I'm putting the house on the market and a new

kitchen will help me get a better price. I'm sure you understand.'

'I'll see what I can do to help,' said Hugh, 'but I may have to move that particular team onto another assignment. We've got a bit of a backlog at the moment.'

'Oh? I thought you said money was a little tight right now,' Cornelius said, stifling a chuckle.

'It is,' said Hugh, a little too quickly. 'What I meant

to say was that we're all having to work overtime just to keep our heads above water.'

'I think I understand,' said Cornelius. 'Still, I'm sure you'll do everything you can to help, now you're fully aware of my situation.' He put the phone down and smiled.

The next victim to contact him didn't bother to phone, but arrived at the front door a few minutes later, and wouldn't take her finger off the buzzer until the door had been opened.

'Where's Pauline?' was Margaret's first question when her brother opened the door. Cornelius stared down at his sister, who had put on a little too much make-up that morning.

'I'm afraid she's had to go,' said Cornelius as he bent down to kiss his sister on the cheek. 'The petitioner in bankruptcy takes a rather dim view of people who can't afford to pay their creditors, but still manage to retain a personal entourage. It was considerate of you to pop round so quickly in my hour of need, Margaret, but if you were hoping for a cup of tea, I'm afraid you'll have to make it yourself.'

'I didn't come round for a cup of tea, as I suspect you know only too well, Cornelius. What I want to know is how you managed to fritter away your entire fortune.' Before her brother could deliver some well-rehearsed lines from his script, she added, 'You'll have to sell the house, of course. I've always said that since Millie's death it's far too large for you. You can always take a bachelor flat in the village.'

'Such decisions are no longer in my hands,' said Cornelius, trying to sound helpless.

'What are you talking about?' demanded Margaret, rounding on him.

'Just that the house and its contents have already been seized by the petitioners in bankruptcy. If I'm to avoid going bankrupt, we must hope that the house sells for a far higher price than the estate agents are predicting.'

'Are you telling me there's absolutely nothing left?'

'Less than nothing would be more accurate,' said Cornelius, sighing. 'And once they've evicted me from The Willows, I'll have nowhere to go.' He tried to sound plaintive. 'So I was rather hoping that you would allow me to take up the kind offer you made at Millie's funeral and come and live with you.'

His sister turned away, so that Cornelius was unable to see the expression on her face.

'That wouldn't be convenient at the present time,' she said without explanation. 'And in any case, Hugh and Elizabeth have far more spare rooms in their house than I do.'

'Quite so,' said Cornelius. He coughed. 'And the small loan I advanced you last year, Margaret – I'm sorry to raise the subject, but . . .'

'What little money I have is carefully invested, and my brokers tell me that this is not a time to sell.'

'But the allowance I've provided every month for the past twenty years – surely you have a little salted away?'

'I'm afraid not,' Margaret replied. 'You must understand that being your sister has meant I am expected to maintain a certain standard of living, and now that I can no longer rely on my monthly allowance, I shall have to be even more careful with my meagre income.'

'Of course you will, my dear,' said Cornelius. 'But any little contribution would help, if you felt able . . .'

'I must be off,' said Margaret, looking at her watch. 'You've already made me late for the hairdresser.'

'Just one more little request before you go, my dear,' said Cornelius. 'In the past you've always been kind enough to give me a lift into town whenever . . .'

'I've always said, Cornelius, that you should have learned to drive years ago. If you had, you wouldn't expect everyone to be at your beck and call night and day. I'll see what I can do,' she added as he opened the door for her.

'Funny, I don't recall you ever saying that. But then, perhaps my memory is going as well,' he said as he followed his sister out onto the drive. He smiled. 'New car, Margaret?' he enquired innocently.

'Yes,' his sister replied tartly as he opened the door for her. Cornelius thought he detected a slight colouring in her cheeks. He chuckled to himself as she drove off. He was learning more about his family by the minute.

Cornelius strolled back into the house, and returned to his study. He closed the door, picked up the phone on his desk and dialled Frank's office.

'Vintcent, Ellwood and Halfon,' said a prim voice.

'I'd like to speak to Mr Vintcent.'

'Who shall I say is calling?'

'Cornelius Barrington.'

'I'll have to see if he's free, Mr Barrington.'

Very good, thought Cornelius. Frank must have convinced even his receptionist that the rumours were true, because in the past her response had always been, 'I'll put you straight through, sir.'

'Good morning, Cornelius,' said Frank. 'I've just put the phone down on your brother Hugh. That's the second time he's called this morning.'

'What did he want?' asked Cornelius.

'To have the full implications explained to him, and also his immediate obligations.'

'Good,' said Cornelius. 'So can I hope to receive a cheque for £100,000 in the near future?'

'I doubt it,' said Frank. 'From the tone of his voice I don't think that's what he had in mind, but I'll let you know just as soon as I've heard back from him.'

'I shall look forward to that, Frank.'

'I do believe you're enjoying yourself, Cornelius.'

'You bet I am,' he replied. 'I only wish Millie was here to share the fun with me.'

'You know what she would have said, don't you?'

'No, but I have a feeling you're about to tell me.'

'You're a wicked old man.'

'And, as always, she would have been right,' Cornelius confessed with a laugh. 'Goodbye, Frank.' As he replaced the receiver there was a knock at the door.

'Come in,' said Cornelius, puzzled as to who it could possibly be. The door opened and his housekeeper entered, carrying a tray with a cup of tea and a plate of shortbread biscuits. She was, as always, neat and trim, not a hair out of place, and showed no sign of embarrassment. She can't have received Frank's letter yet, was Cornelius's first thought.

'Pauline,' he said as she placed the tray on his desk, 'did you receive a letter from my solicitor this morning?'

'Yes, I did, sir,' Pauline replied, 'and of course I shall sell the car immediately, and repay your £500.' She paused before looking straight at him. 'But I was just wondering, sir . . .'

'Yes, Pauline?'

'Would it be possible for me to work it off in lieu? You see, I need a car to pick up my girls from school.'

For the first time since he had embarked on the enterprise, Cornelius felt guilty. But he knew that if he agreed to Pauline's request, someone would find out, and the whole enterprise would be endangered.

'I'm so sorry, Pauline, but I've been left with no choice.'

'That's exactly what the solicitor explained in his letter,' Pauline said, fiddling with a piece of paper in the pocket of her pinafore. 'Mind you, I never did go much on lawyers.'

This statement made Cornelius feel even more guilty, because he didn't know a more trustworthy person than Frank Vintcent.

'I'd better leave you now, sir, but I'll pop back this evening just to make sure things don't get too untidy. Would it be possible, sir . . . ?'

'Possible . . . ?' said Cornelius.

'Could you give me a reference? I mean, you see, it's not that easy for someone of my age to find a job.'

'I'll give you a reference that would get you a position at Buckingham Palace,' said Cornelius. He immediately sat down at his desk and wrote a glowing homily on the service Pauline Croft had given for over two decades. He read it through, then handed it across to her. 'Thank you, Pauline,' he said, 'for all you have done in the past for Daniel, Millie and, most of all, myself.'

'My pleasure, sir,' said Pauline.

Once she had closed the door behind her, Cornelius could only wonder if water wasn't sometimes thicker than blood.

He sat back down at his desk and began writing some notes to remind him what had taken place that morning. When he had finished he went through to the kitchen to make himself some lunch, and found a salad had been laid out for him.

After lunch, Cornelius took a bus into town – a novel experience. It was some time before he located a bus stop, and then he discovered that the conductor didn't have change for a twenty-pound note. His first call after he had been dropped off in the town centre was to the local estate agent, who didn't seem that surprised to see him. Cornelius was delighted to find how quickly the rumour of his financial demise must be spreading.

'I'll have someone call round to The Willows in the morning, Mr Barrington,' said the young man, rising from behind his desk, 'so we can measure up and take some photographs. May we also have your permission to place a sign in the garden?'

'Please do,' said Cornelius without hesitation, and barely stopped himself from adding, the bigger the better.

After he'd left the estate agent, Cornelius walked a few yards down the street and called into the local removal firm. He asked another young man if he could make an appointment for them to take away the entire contents of the house.

'Where's it all to go, sir?'

'To Botts' Storeroom in the High Street,' Cornelius informed him.

'That will be no problem, sir,' said the young assistant, picking up a pad from his desk. Once Cornelius had completed the forms in triplicate, the assistant said, 'Sign there, sir,' pointing to the bottom of the form. Then, looking a little nervous, he added, 'We'll need a deposit of £100.'

'Of course,' said Cornelius, taking out his chequebook.

'I'm afraid it will have to be cash, sir,' the young man said in a confidential tone.

Cornelius smiled. No one had refused a cheque from him for over thirty years. 'I'll call back tomorrow,' he said.

On the way back to the bus stop Cornelius stared through the window of his brother's hardware store, and noted that the staff didn't seem all that busy. On arriving back at The Willows, he returned to his study and made some more notes on what had taken place that afternoon.

As he climbed the stairs to go to bed that night, he reflected that it must have been the first afternoon in years that no one had called him to ask how he was. He slept soundly that night.

When Cornelius came downstairs the following morning, he picked up his post from the mat and made his way to the kitchen. Over a bowl of cornflakes he checked through the letters. He had once been told that if it was known you were likely to go bankrupt, a stream of brown envelopes would begin to drop through the letterbox, as shopkeepers and small businessmen tried to get in before anyone else could be declared a preferred creditor.

There were no brown envelopes in the post that morning, because Cornelius had made certain every bill had been covered before he began his journey down this particular road.

Other than circulars and free offers, there was just one white envelope with a London postmark. It turned out to be a handwritten letter from his nephew Timothy, saying how sorry he was to learn of his uncle's problems, and that although he didn't get back to Chudley much nowadays, he would make every effort to travel up to Shropshire at the weekend and call in to see him.

Although the message was brief, Cornelius silently noted that Timothy was the first member of the family to show any sympathy for his predicament.

When he heard the doorbell ring, he placed the letter on the kitchen table and walked out into the hall. He opened the front door to be greeted by Elizabeth, his brother's wife. Her face was white, lined and drained, and Cornelius doubted if she had slept a great deal the previous night.

The moment Elizabeth had stepped into the house she began to pace around from room to room, almost as though she were checking to see that everything was still in place, as if she couldn't accept the words she had read in the solicitor's letter.

Any lingering doubts must have been dispelled when, a few minutes later, the local estate agent appeared on the doorstep, tape measure in hand, with a photographer by his side.

'If Hugh was able to return even part of the hundred thousand I loaned him, that would be most helpful,' Cornelius remarked to his sister-in-law as he followed her through the house.

It was some time before she spoke, despite the fact that she had had all night to consider her response.

'It's not quite that easy,' she eventually replied. 'You see, the loan was made to the company, and the shares are distributed among several people.'

Cornelius knew all three of the several people. 'Then perhaps the time has come for you and Hugh to sell off some of your shares.'

'And allow some stranger to take over the company, after all the work we've put into it over the years? No, we can't afford to let that happen. In any case, Hugh asked Mr Vintcent what the legal position was, and he confirmed that there was no obligation on our part to sell any of our shares.'

'Have you considered that perhaps you have a moral obligation?' asked Cornelius, turning to face his sister-in-law.

'Cornelius,' she said, avoiding his stare, 'it has been your irresponsibility, not ours, that has been the cause of your downfall. Surely you wouldn't expect your brother to sacrifice everything he's worked for over the years, simply to place my family in the same perilous position in which you now find yourself?'

Cornelius realized why Elizabeth hadn't slept the previous night. She was not only acting as spokeswoman for Hugh, but was obviously making the decisions as well. Cornelius had always considered her to be the stronger-willed of the two, and he doubted if he would come face to face with his brother before an agreement had been reached.

'But if there's any other way we might help . . .' Elizabeth added in a more gentle tone, as her hand rested on an ornate gold-leafed table in the drawing room.

'Well, now you mention it,' replied Cornelius, 'I'm putting the house on the market in a couple of weeks' time, and will be looking for . . .'

'That soon?' said Elizabeth. 'And what's going to happen to all the furniture?'

'It will all have to be sold to help cover the debts. But, as I said . . .'

'Hugh has always liked this table.'

'Louis XIV,' said Cornelius casually.

'I wonder what it's worth,' Elizabeth mused, trying to make it sound as if it were of little consequence.

'I have no idea,' said Cornelius. 'If I remember correctly, I paid around £60,000 for it – but that was over ten years ago.'

'And the chess set?' Elizabeth asked, picking up one of the pieces.

'It's a worthless copy,' Cornelius replied. 'You could pick up a set just like it in any Arab bazaar for a couple of hundred pounds.'

'Oh, I always thought . . .' Elizabeth hesitated before replacing the piece on the wrong square. 'Well, I must be off,' she said, sounding as if her task had been completed. 'We must try not to forget that I still have a business to run.'

Cornelius accompanied her as she began striding back down the long corridor in the direction of the front door. She walked straight by the portrait of her nephew Daniel. In the past she had always stopped to remark on how much she missed him.

'I was wondering . . .' began Cornelius as they walked out into the hall.

'Yes?' said Elizabeth.

'Well, as I have to be out of here in a couple of weeks, I hoped it might be possible to move in with you. That is, until I find somewhere I can afford.'

'If only you'd asked a week ago,' said

Elizabeth, without missing a beat. 'But unfortunately we've just agreed to take in my mother, and the only other room is Timothy's, and he comes home most weekends.'

'Is that so?' said Cornelius.

'And the grandfather clock?' asked Elizabeth, who still appeared to be on a shopping expedition.

'Victorian – I purchased it from the Earl of Bute's estate.'

'No, I meant how much is it worth?'

'Whatever someone is willing to pay for it,' Cornelius replied as they reached the front door.

'Don't forget to let me know, Cornelius, if there's anything I can do to help.'

'How kind of you, Elizabeth,' he said, opening the door to find the estate agent hammering a stake into the ground with a sign on it declaring FOR SALE. Cornelius smiled, because it was the only thing that morning that had stopped Elizabeth in her tracks.

•

Frank Vintcent arrived on the Thursday evening, carrying a bottle of cognac and two pizzas.

'If I'd realized that losing Pauline was to be part of the deal, I would never have agreed to go along with your plan in the first place,' Frank said as he nibbled at his microwaved pizza. 'How do you manage without her?'

'Rather badly,' Cornelius admitted, 'although she still drops in for an hour or two every evening. Otherwise this place would look like a pigsty. Come to think of it, how do *you* cope?'

'As a bachelor,' Frank replied, 'you learn the art of survival from an early age. Now, let's stop this small-talk and get on with the game.'

'Which game?' enquired Cornelius with a chuckle.

'Chess,' replied Frank. 'I've had enough of the other game for one week.'

'Then we'd better go through to the library.'

Frank was surprised by Cornelius's opening moves, as he had never known his old friend to be so daring. Neither of them spoke again for over an hour, most of which Frank spent trying to defend his queen.

'This might well be the last game we play with this set,' said Cornelius wistfully.

'No, don't worry yourself about that,' said Frank. 'They always allow you to keep a few personal items.'

'Not when they're worth a quarter of a million pounds,' replied Cornelius.

'I had no idea,' said Frank, looking up.

'Because you're not the sort of man who has ever been interested in worldly goods. It's a sixteenth-century Persian masterpiece, and it's bound to cause considerable interest when it comes under the hammer.'

'But surely you've found out all you need to know by now,' said Frank. 'Why carry on with the exercise when you could lose so much that's dear to you?'

'Because I still have to discover the truth.'

Frank sighed, stared down at the board and moved his queen's knight. 'Checkmate,' he said. 'It serves you right for not concentrating.'

Cornelius spent most of Friday morning in a private meeting with the managing director of Botts and Company, the local fine art and furniture auctioneers.

Mr Botts had already agreed that the sale could take place in a fortnight's time. He had often repeated that he would have preferred a longer period to prepare the catalogue and send out an extensive mailing for such a fine collection, but at least he showed some sympathy for the position Mr Barrington found himself in. Over the years, Lloyd's of London, death duties and impending bankruptcy had proved the auctioneer's best friends.

'We will need to have everything in our storeroom as soon as possible,' said Mr Botts, 'so there's enough time to prepare a catalogue, while still allowing the customers to view on three consecutive days before the sale takes place.'

Cornelius nodded his agreement.

The auctioneer also recommended that a full page be taken in the *Chudley Advertiser* the following Wednesday, giving details of what was coming under the hammer, so they could reach those people they failed to contact by post.

Cornelius left Mr Botts a few minutes before midday, and on his way back to the bus stop dropped into the removal company. He handed over £100 in fives and tens, leaving the impression that it had taken him a few days to raise the cash.

While waiting for the bus, he couldn't help noticing how few people bothered to say good morning, or even acknowledge him. Certainly no one crossed the road to pass the time of day.

Twenty men in three vans spent the next day loading and unloading as they travelled back and forth between The Willows and the auctioneers' storeroom in the High Street. It was not until the early evening that the last stick of furniture had been removed from the house.

As he walked through the empty rooms, Cornelius was surprised to find himself thinking that, with one or two exceptions, he wasn't going to miss many of his worldly possessions. He retired to the bedroom – the only room in the house that was still furnished – and continued to read the novel Elizabeth had recommended before his downfall.

The following morning he only had one call, from his nephew Timothy, to say he was up for the weekend, and wondered if Uncle Cornelius could find time to see him.

'Time is the one thing I still have plenty of,' replied Cornelius.

'Then why don't I drop round this afternoon?' said Timothy. 'Shall we say four o'clock?'

'I'm sorry I can't offer you a cup of tea,' said Cornelius, 'but I finished the last packet this morning, and as I'm probably leaving the house next week . . .'

'It's not important,' said Timothy, who was unable to mask his distress at finding the house stripped of his uncle's possessions.

'Let's go up to the bedroom. It's the only room that still has any furniture in it – and most of that will be gone by next week.'

'I had no idea they'd taken everything away. Even the picture of Daniel,' Timothy said as he passed an oblong patch of a lighter shade of cream than the rest of the wall.

'And my chess set,' sighed Cornelius. 'But I can't complain. I've had a good life.' He began to climb the stairs to the bedroom.

Cornelius sat in the only chair while Timothy perched on the end of the bed. The old man studied his nephew more closely. He had grown into a fine young man. An open face, with clear brown eyes that served to reveal, to anyone who didn't already know, that he had been adopted. He must have been twenty-seven or twenty-eight – about the same age Daniel would have been if he were still alive. Cornelius had always had a soft spot for his nephew, and had imagined that his affection was reciprocated. He wondered if he was about to be disillusioned once again.

Timothy appeared nervous, shuffling uneasily from foot to foot as he perched on the end of the bed. 'Uncle Cornelius,' he began, his head slightly bowed, 'as you know, I have received a letter from Mr Vintcent, so I thought I ought to come to see you and explain that I simply don't have £1,000 to my name, and therefore I'm unable to repay my debt at present.'

Cornelius was disappointed. He had hoped that just one of the family . . .

'However,' the young man continued, removing a long, thin envelope from an inside pocket of his jacket, 'on my twenty-first birthday my father presented me with shares of 1 per cent of the company, which I think must be worth at least £1,000, so I wondered if you would consider taking them in exchange for my debt – that is, until I can afford to buy them back.'

Cornelius felt guilty for having doubted his nephew even for a moment. He wanted to apologize, but knew he couldn't if the house of cards was to remain in place for a few more days. He took the widow's mite and thanked Timothy.

'I am aware just how much of a sacrifice this must be for you,' said Cornelius, 'remembering how many times you have told me in the past of your ambition to take over the company when your father eventually retires, and your dreams of expanding into areas he has refused even to contemplate.'

'I don't think he'll ever retire,' said Timothy, with a sigh. 'But I was hoping that after all the experience I've gained working in London he might take me seriously as a candidate for manager when Mr Leonard retires at the end of the year.'

'I fear your chances won't be advanced when he learns that you've handed over 1 per cent of the company to your bankrupt uncle.'

'My problems can hardly be compared with the ones you are facing, Uncle. I'm only sorry I can't hand over the cash right now. Before I leave, is there anything else I can do for you?'

'Yes, there is, Timothy,' said Cornelius, returning to the script. 'Your mother recommended a novel, which I've been enjoying, but my old eyes seem to tire earlier and earlier, and I wondered if you'd be kind enough to read a few pages to me. I've marked the place I've reached.'

'I can remember you reading to me when I was a child,' said Timothy. '*Just William* and *Swallows and Amazons*,' he added as he took the proffered book.

Timothy must have read about twenty pages when he suddenly stopped and looked up.

'There's a bus ticket at page 450. Shall I leave it there, Uncle?'

'Yes, please do,' said Cornelius. 'I put it there to remind me of something.' He paused. 'Forgive me, but I'm feeling a little tired.'

Timothy rose and said, 'I'll come back soon and finish off the last few pages.'

'No need to bother yourself, I'll be able to manage that.'

'Oh, I think I'd better, Uncle, otherwise I'll never find out which one of them becomes Prime Minister.'

The second batch of letters, which Frank Vintcent sent out on the following Friday, caused another flurry of phone calls.

'I'm not sure I fully understand what it means,' said Margaret, in her first communication with her brother since calling round to see him a fortnight before.

'It means exactly what it says, my dear,' said Cornelius calmly. 'All my worldly goods are to come under the hammer, but I am allowing those I consider near and dear to me to select one item that, for sentimental or personal reasons, they would like to see remain in the family. They will then be able to bid for them at the auction next Friday.'

'But we could all be outbid and end up with nothing,' said Margaret.

'No, my dear,' said Cornelius, trying not to sound exasperated. 'The *public* auction will be held in the afternoon. The selected pieces will be auctioned separately in the morning, with only the family and close friends present. The instructions couldn't be clearer.'

'And are we able to see the pieces before the auction takes place?'

'Yes, Margaret,' said her brother, as if addressing a backward child. 'As Mr Vintcent stated clearly in his letter, "Viewing Tuesday, Wednesday, Thursday, 10 a.m. to 4 p.m., before the sale on Friday at eleven o'clock".'

'But we can only select one piece?'

'Yes,' repeated Cornelius, 'that is all the petitioner in bankruptcy would allow. But you'll be pleased to know that the portrait of Daniel, which you have commented on so many times in the past, will be among the lots available for your consideration.'

'Yes, I do like it,' said Margaret. She hesitated for a moment. 'But will the Turner also be up for sale?'

'It certainly will,' said Cornelius. 'I'm being forced to sell everything.'

'Have you any idea what Hugh and Elizabeth are after?'

'No, I haven't, but if you want to find out, why don't you ask them?' he replied mischievously, aware that they scarcely exchanged a word from one year's end to the next.

The second call came only moments after he had put the phone down on his sister.

'At last,' said a peremptory voice, as if it were somehow Cornelius's fault that others might also wish to speak to him.

'Good morning, Elizabeth,' said Cornelius, immediately recognizing the voice. 'How nice to hear from you.'

'It's about the letter I received this morning.'

'Yes, I thought it might be,' said Cornelius.

'It's just, well, I wanted to confirm the value of the table – the Louis XIV piece – and, while I'm on the line, the grandfather clock that used to belong to the Earl of Bute.'

'If you go to the auction house, Elizabeth, they will give you a catalogue, which tells you the high and low estimate for every item in the sale.'

'I see,' said Elizabeth. She remained silent for some time. 'I don't suppose you know if Margaret will be bidding for either of those pieces?'

'I have no idea,' replied Cornelius. 'But it was Margaret who was blocking the line when you were trying to get through, and she asked me a similar question, so I suggest you give her a call.' Another long silence. 'By the way, Elizabeth, you do realize that you can only bid for one item?'

'Yes, it says as much in the letter,' replied his sister-in-law tartly.

'I only ask because I always thought Hugh was interested in the chess set.'

'Oh no, I don't think so,' said Elizabeth. Cornelius wasn't in any doubt who would be doing the bidding on behalf of that family on Friday morning.

'Well, good luck,' said Cornelius. 'And don't forget the 15 per cent commission,' he added as he put the phone down.

Timothy wrote the following day to say he was hoping to attend the auction, as he wanted to pick up a little memento of The Willows and his uncle and aunt.

Pauline, however, told Cornelius as she tidied up the bedroom that she had no intention of going to the auction.

'Why not?' he asked.

'Because I'd be sure to make a fool of myself and bid for something I couldn't afford.'

'Very wise,' said Cornelius. 'I've fallen into that trap once or twice myself. But did you have your eye on anything in particular?'

'Yes, I did, but my savings would never stretch to it.'

'Oh, you can never be sure with auctions,' said Cornelius. 'If no one else joins in the bidding, sometimes you can make a killing.'

'Well, I'll think about it, now I've got a new job.'

'I'm so pleased to hear that,' said Cornelius, who was genuinely disappointed to learn her news.

Neither Cornelius nor Frank was able to concentrate on their weekly chess match that Thursday evening, and after half an hour they abandoned the game and settled on a draw.

'I must confess that I can't wait for things to return to normal,' said Frank as his host poured him a glass of cooking sherry.

'Oh, I don't know. I find the situation has its compensations.'

'Like what, for example?' said Frank, who frowned after his first sip.

'Well, for a start, I'm looking forward to tomorrow's auction.'

'But that could still go badly wrong,' said Frank.

'What can possibly go wrong?' asked Cornelius.

'Well, for a start, have you considered . . . ?' But he didn't bother to complete the sentence, because his friend wasn't listening.

Cornelius was the first to arrive at the auction house the following morning. The room was laid out with 120 chairs in neat rows of twelve, ready for the anticipated packed house that afternoon, but Cornelius thought the real drama would unfold in the morning, when only six people would be in attendance.

The next person to appear, fifteen minutes before the auction was due to begin, was Cornelius's solicitor Frank Vintcent. Observing his client deep in conversation with Mr Botts, who would be conducting the auction, he took a seat towards the back of the room on the right-hand side.

Cornelius's sister Margaret was the next to make an appearance, and she was not as considerate. She charged straight up to Mr Botts and asked in a shrill voice, 'Can I sit anywhere I like?'

'Yes, madam, you most certainly can,' said Mr Botts. Margaret immediately commandeered the centre seat in the front row, directly below the auctioneer's podium.

Cornelius gave his sister a nod before walking down the aisle and taking a chair three rows in front of Frank.

Hugh and Elizabeth were the next to arrive. They stood at the back for some time while they considered the layout of the room. Eventually they strolled up the aisle and occupied two seats in the eighth row, which afforded them a perfect sightline to the podium, while at the same time being able to keep an eye on Margaret. Opening move to Elizabeth, thought Cornelius, who was quietly enjoying himself.

As the hour hand of the clock on the wall behind the auctioneer's rostrum ticked inexorably towards eleven, Cornelius was disappointed that neither Pauline nor Timothy made an appearance.

Just as the auctioneer began to climb the steps to the podium, the door at the back of the room eased open and Pauline's head peered round. The rest of her body remained hidden behind the door until her eyes settled on Cornelius, who smiled encouragingly. She stepped inside and closed the door, but showed no interest in taking a seat, retreating into a corner instead.

The auctioneer beamed down at the handpicked invitees as the clock struck eleven.

'Ladies and gentlemen,' he began, 'I've been in the business for over thirty years, but this is the first time I've conducted a private sale, so this is a most unusual auction even for me. I'd better go over the ground rules, so that no one can be in any doubt should a dispute arise later.

'All of you present have some special association, whether as family or friends, with Mr Cornelius Barrington, whose personal effects are coming under the hammer. Each of you has been invited to select one item from the inventory, for which you will be allowed to bid. Should you be successful you may not bid for any other lot, but if you fail on the item of your first choice, you may join in the bidding for any other lot. I hope that is clear,' he said, as the door was flung open and Timothy rushed in.

'So sorry,' he said a little breathlessly, 'but my train was held up.' He quickly took a seat in the back row. Cornelius smiled – every one of his pawns was now in place.

'As there are only five of you eligible to bid,' continued Mr Botts as if there had been no interruption, 'only five items will come under the hammer. But the law states that if anyone has previously left a written bid, that bid must be recognized as part of the auction. I shall make things as easy to follow as possible by saying if I have a bid at the table, from which you should assume it is a bid left at our office by a member of the public. I think it would be only fair to point out,' he added, 'that I have outside bids on four of the five items.

'Having explained the ground rules, I will with your permission begin the auction.' He glanced towards the back of the room at Cornelius, who nodded his assent.

'The first lot I am able to offer is a long-case clock, dated 1892, which was purchased by Mr Barrington from the estate of the late Earl of Bute.

'I shall open the bidding for this lot at £3,000. Do I see £3,500?' Mr Botts asked, raising an eyebrow. Elizabeth looked a little shocked, as three thousand was just below the low estimate and the figure she and Hugh had agreed on that morning.

'Is anyone interested in this lot?' asked Mr Botts, looking directly at Elizabeth, but she remained apparently mesmerized. 'I shall ask once again if anyone wishes to bid £3,500 for this magnificent long-case clock. Fair warning. I see no bids, so I shall have to withdraw this item and place it in the afternoon sale.'

Elizabeth still seemed to be in a state of shock. She immediately turned to her husband and began a whispered conversation with him. Mr Botts looked a little disappointed, but moved quickly on to the second lot.

'The next lot is a charming watercolour of the Thames by William Turner of Oxford. Can I open the bidding at £2,000?'

Margaret waved her catalogue furiously.

'Thank you, madam,' said the auctioneer, beaming down at her. 'I have an outside bid of £3,000. Will anyone offer me £4,000?'

'Yes!' shouted Margaret, as if the room were so crowded that she needed to make herself heard above the din.

'I have a bid of five thousand at the table – will you bid six, madam?' he asked, returning his attention to the lady in the front row.

'I will,' said Margaret equally firmly.

'Are there any other bids?' demanded the auctioneer, glancing around the room – a sure sign that the bids at the table had dried up. 'Then I'm going to let this picture go for £6,000 to the lady in the front row.'

'Seven,' said a voice behind her. Margaret looked round to see that her sister-in-law had joined in the bidding.

'Eight thousand!' shouted Margaret.

'Nine,' said Elizabeth without hesitation.

'Ten thousand!' bellowed Margaret.

Suddenly there was silence. Cornelius glanced across the room to see a smile of satisfaction cross Elizabeth's face, having left her sister-in-law with a bill for £10,000.

Cornelius wanted to burst out laughing. The auction was turning out to be even more entertaining than he could have hoped.

'There being no more bids, this delightful watercolour is sold to Miss Barrington for £10,000,' said Mr Botts as he brought the hammer down with a thump. He smiled down at Margaret, as if she had made a wise investment.

'The next lot,' he continued, 'is a portrait simply entitled *Daniel*, by an unknown artist. It is a well-executed work, and I was hoping to open the bidding at £100. Do I see a bid of one hundred?'

To Cornelius's disappointment, no one in the room seemed to be showing any interest in this lot.

'I am willing to consider a bid of £50 to get things started,' said Mr Botts, 'but I am unable to go any lower. Will anyone bid me £50?'

Cornelius glanced around the room, trying to work out from the expressions on their faces who had selected this item, and why they no longer wished to bid when the price was so reasonable.

'Then I fear I will have to withdraw this lot as well.'

'Does that mean I've got it?' asked a voice from the back. Everyone looked round.

'If you are willing to bid £50, madam,' said Mr Botts, adjusting his spectacles, 'the picture is yours.'

'Yes please,' said Pauline. Mr Botts smiled in her direction as he brought down the hammer. 'Sold to the lady at the back of the room,' he declared, 'for £50.'

'Now I move on to lot number four, a chess set of unknown provenance. What shall I say for this item? Can I start someone off with £100? Thank you, sir.'

Cornelius looked round to see who was bidding. 'I have two hundred at the table. Can I say three hundred?'

Timothy nodded.

'I have a bid at the table of three fifty. Can I say four hundred?'

This time Timothy looked crestfallen, and Cornelius assumed the sum was beyond his limit. 'Then I am going to have to withdraw this piece also and place it in this afternoon's sale.' The auctioneer stared at Timothy, but he didn't even blink. 'The item is withdrawn.'

'And finally I turn to lot number five. A magnificent Louis XIV table, circa 1712, in almost mint condition. Its provenance can be traced back to its original owner, and it has been in the possession of Mr Barrington for the past eleven years. The full details are in your catalogue. I must warn you that there has been a lot of interest in this item, and I shall open the bidding at £50,000.'

Elizabeth immediately raised her catalogue above her head.

'Thank you, madam. I have a bid at the table of sixty thousand. Do I see seventy?' he asked, his eyes fixed on Elizabeth.

Her catalogue shot up again.

'Thank you, madam. I have a bid at the table of eighty thousand. Do I see ninety?' This time Elizabeth seemed to hesitate before raising her catalogue slowly.

'I have a bid at the table of one hundred thousand. Do I see a hundred and ten?'

Everyone in the room was now looking towards Elizabeth, except Hugh, who, head down, was staring at the floor. He obviously wasn't going to have any influence on the bidding. 'If there are no further bids, I shall have to withdraw this lot and place it in the afternoon sale. Fair warning,' declared Mr Botts. As he raised his hammer, Elizabeth's catalogue suddenly shot up.

'One hundred and ten thousand. Thank you, madam. Are there any more bids? Then I shall let this fine piece go for £110,000.' He brought down his hammer and smiled at Elizabeth. 'Congratulations, madam, it is indeed a magnificent example of the period.' She smiled weakly back, a look of uncertainty on her face.

Cornelius turned round and winked at Frank, who remained impassively in his seat. He then rose from his place and made his way to the podium to thank Mr Botts for a job well done. As he turned to leave, he smiled at Margaret and Elizabeth, but neither acknowledged him, as they both seemed to be preoccupied. Hugh, head in hands, continued to stare down at the floor.

As Cornelius walked towards the back of the hall, he could see no sign of Timothy, and assumed that his nephew must have had to return to London. Cornelius was disappointed, as he had hoped the lad might join him for a pub lunch. After such a successful morning he felt a little celebrating was in order.

He had already decided that he wasn't going to attend the afternoon sale, as he had no desire to witness his worldly goods coming under the hammer, even though he wouldn't have room for most of them once he moved into a smaller house. Mr Botts had promised to call him the moment the sale was over and report how much the auction had raised.

Having enjoyed the best meal since Pauline had left him, Cornelius began his journey back from the pub to The Willows. He knew exactly what time the bus would appear to take him home, and arrived at the bus stop with a couple of minutes to spare. He now took it for granted that people would avoid his company.

Cornelius unlocked the front door as the clock on the nearby church struck three. He was looking forward to the inevitable fall-out when it sank in to Margaret and Elizabeth how much they had really bid. He grinned as he headed towards his study and glanced at his watch, wondering when he might expect a call from Mr Botts. The phone began to ring just as he entered the room. He chuckled to himself. It was too early for Mr Botts, so it had to be Elizabeth or Margaret, who would need to see him urgently. He picked up the phone to hear Frank's voice on the other end of the line.

'Did you remember to withdraw the chess set from the afternoon sale?' Frank asked, without bothering with any formalities.

'What are you talking about?' said Cornelius.

'Your beloved chess set. Have you forgotten that as it failed to sell this morning, it will automatically come up in the afternoon sale? Unless of course you've already given orders to withdraw it, or tipped off Mr Botts about its true value.'

'Oh my God,' said Cornelius. He dropped the phone and ran back out of the door, so he didn't hear Frank say, 'I'm sure a telephone call to Mr Botts's assistant is all that will be needed.'

Cornelius checked his watch as he ran down the path. It was ten past three, so the auction would have only just begun. Running towards the bus stop, he tried to recall what lot number the chess set was. All he could remember was that there were 153 lots in the sale.

Standing at the bus stop, hopping impatiently from foot to foot, he scanned the road in the hope of hailing a passing taxi, when to his relief he saw a bus heading towards him. Although his eyes never left the driver, that didn't make him go any faster.

When it eventually drew up beside him and the doors opened, Cornelius leapt on and took his place on the front seat. He wanted to tell the driver to take him straight to Botts and Co. in the High Street, and to hell with the fare, but he doubted if the other passengers would have fallen in with his plan.

He stared at his watch – 3.17 p.m. – and tried to remember how long it had taken Mr Botts that morning to dispose of each lot. About a minute, a minute and a half perhaps, he concluded. The bus came to a halt at every stop on its short journey into town, and Cornelius spent as much time following the progress of the minute hand on his watch as he did the journey. The driver finally reached the High Street at 3.31 p.m.

Even the door seemed to open slowly. Cornelius leapt out onto the pavement, and despite not having run for years, sprinted for the second time that day. He covered the two hundred yards to the auction house in less than record pace, but still arrived exhausted. He charged into the auction room as Mr Botts declared, 'Lot number 32, a long-case clock originally purchased from the estate of s. . .'

Cornelius's eyes swept the room, coming to rest on an auctioneer's clerk who was standing in the corner with her catalogue open, entering the hammer price after each lot had been sold. He walked over to her just as a woman he thought he recognized slipped quickly past him and out of the door.

'Has the chess set come up yet?' asked a still-out-of-breath Cornelius.

'Let me just check, sir,' the clerk replied, flicking back through her catalogue. 'Yes, here it is, lot 27.'

'How much did it fetch?' asked Cornelius.

'£450, sir,' she replied.

Mr Botts called Cornelius later that evening to inform him that the afternoon sale had raised £902,800 – far more than he had estimated.

'Do you by any chance know who bought the chess set?' was Cornelius's only question.

'No,' replied Mr Botts. 'All I can tell you is that it was purchased on behalf of a client. The buyer paid in cash and took the item away.'

As he climbed the stairs to go to bed, Cornelius had to admit that everything had gone to plan except for the disastrous loss of the chess set, for which he realized he had only himself to blame. What made it worse was that he knew Frank would never refer to the incident again.

Cornelius was in the bathroom when the phone rang at 7.30 the following morning. Obviously someone had been lying awake wondering what was the earliest moment they could possibly disturb him.

'Is that you, Cornelius?'

'Yes,' he replied, yawning noisily. 'Who's this?' he added, knowing only too well.

'It's Elizabeth. I'm sorry to call you so early, but I need to see you urgently.'

'Of course, my dear,' Cornelius replied, 'why don't you join me for tea this afternoon?'

'Oh no, it can't wait until then. I have to see you this morning. Could I come round at nine?'

'I'm sorry, Elizabeth, but I already have an appointment at nine.' He paused. 'But I could fit you in at ten for half an hour, then I won't be late for my meeting with Mr Botts at eleven.'

'I could give you a lift into town if that would help,' suggested Elizabeth.

'That's extremely kind of you, my dear,' said Cornelius, 'but I've got used to taking the bus, and in any case I wouldn't want to impose on you. Look forward to seeing you at ten.' He put the phone down.

Cornelius was still in the bath when the phone rang a second time. He wallowed in the warm water until the ringing had ceased. He knew it was Margaret, and he was sure she would call back within minutes.

He hadn't finished drying himself before the phone rang again. He walked slowly to the bedroom, picked up the receiver by his bed and said, 'Good morning, Margaret.'

'Good morning, Cornelius,' she said, sounding surprised. Recovering quickly, she added, 'I need to see you urgently.'

'Oh? What's the problem?' asked Cornelius, well aware exactly what the problem was.

'I can't possibly discuss such a delicate matter over the phone, but I could be with you by ten.'

'I'm afraid I've already agreed to see Elizabeth at ten. It seems that she also has an urgent matter she needs to discuss with me. Why don't you come round at eleven?'

'Perhaps it would be better if I came over immediately,' said Margaret, sounding flustered.

'No, I'm afraid eleven is the earliest I can fit you in, my dear. So it's eleven or afternoon tea. Which would suit you best?'

'Eleven,' said Margaret without hesitation.

'I thought it might,' said Cornelius. 'I'll look forward to seeing you then,' he added before replacing the receiver.

When Cornelius had finished dressing, he went down to the kitchen for breakfast. A bowl of cornflakes, a copy of the local paper and an unstamped envelope were awaiting him, although there was no sign of Pauline.

He poured himself a cup of tea, tore open the envelope and extracted a cheque made out to him for £500. He sighed. Pauline must have sold her car.

He began to turn the pages of the Saturday supplement, stopping when he reached 'Houses for Sale'. When the phone rang for the third time that morning, he had no idea who it might be.

'Good morning, Mr Barrington,' said a cheerful voice. 'It's Bruce from the estate agents. I thought I'd give you a call to let you know we've had an offer for The Willows that is in excess of the asking price.'

'Well done,' said Cornelius.

'Thank you, sir,' said the agent, with more respect in his voice than Cornelius had heard from anyone for weeks, 'but I think we should hold on for a little longer. I'm confident I can squeeze some more out of them. If I do, my advice would be to accept the offer and ask for a 10 per cent deposit.'

'That sounds like good advice to me,' said Cornelius. 'And once they've signed the contract, I'll need you to find me a new house.'

'What sort of thing are you looking for, Mr Barrington?'

'I want something about half the size of The Willows, with perhaps a couple of acres, and I'd like to remain in the immediate area.'

'That shouldn't be too hard, sir. We have one or two excellent houses on our books at the moment, so I'm sure we'll be able to accommodate you.'

'Thank you,' said Cornelius, delighted to have spoken to someone who had begun the day well.

He was chuckling over an item on the front page of the local paper when the doorbell rang. He checked his watch. It was still a few minutes to ten, so it couldn't be Elizabeth. When he opened the front door he was greeted by a man in a green uniform, holding a clipboard in one hand and a parcel in the other.

'Sign here,' was all the courier said, handing over a biro.

Cornelius scrawled his signature across the bottom of the form. He would have asked who had sent the parcel if he had not been distracted by a car coming up the drive.

'Thank you,' he said. He left the package in the hall and walked down the steps to welcome Elizabeth.

When the car drew up outside the front door, Cornelius was surprised to find Hugh seated in the passenger seat.

'It was kind of you to see us at such short notice,' said Elizabeth, who looked as if she had spent another sleepless night.

'Good morning, Hugh,' said Cornelius, who suspected his brother had been kept awake all night. 'Please come through to the kitchen – I'm afraid it's the only room in the house that's warm.'

As he led them down the long corridor, Elizabeth stopped in front of the portrait of Daniel. 'I'm so glad to see it back in its rightful place,' she said. Hugh nodded his agreement.

Cornelius stared at the portrait, which he hadn't seen since the auction. 'Yes, back in its rightful place,' he said, before taking them through to the kitchen. 'Now, what brings you both to The Willows on a Saturday morning?' he asked as he filled the kettle.

'It's about the Louis XIV table,' said Elizabeth diffidently.

'Yes, I shall miss it,' said Cornelius. 'But it was a fine gesture on your part, Hugh,' he added.

'A fine gesture . . .' repeated Hugh.

'Yes. I assumed it was your way of returning my hundred thousand,' said Cornelius. Turning to Elizabeth, he said, 'How I misjudged you, Elizabeth. I suspect it was your idea all along.'

Elizabeth and Hugh just stared at each other, then both began speaking at once.

'But we didn't . . .' said Hugh.

'We were rather hoping . . .' said Elizabeth. Then they both fell silent.

'Tell him the truth,' said Hugh firmly.

'Oh?' said Cornelius. 'Have I misunderstood what took place at the auction yesterday morning?'

'Yes, I'm afraid you have,' said Elizabeth, any remaining colour draining from her cheeks. 'You see, the truth of the matter is that the whole thing got out of control, and I carried on bidding for longer than I should have done.' She paused. 'I'd never been to an auction before, and when I failed to get the grandfather clock, and then saw Margaret pick up the Turner so cheaply, I'm afraid I made a bit of a fool of myself.'

'Well, you can always put it back up for sale,' said Cornelius with mock sadness. 'It's a fine piece, and sure to retain its value.'

'We've already looked into that,' said Elizabeth. 'But Mr Botts says there won't be another furniture auction for at least three months, and the terms of the sale were clearly printed in the catalogue: settlement within seven days.'

'But I'm sure that if you were to leave the piece with him . . .'

'Yes, he suggested that,' said Hugh. 'But we didn't realize that the auctioneers add 15 per cent to the sale price, so the real bill is for £126,500. And what's worse, if we put it up for sale again they also retain 15 per cent of the price that's bid, so we would end up losing over thirty thousand.'

'Yes, that's the way auctioneers make their money,' said Cornelius with a sigh.

'But we don't have thirty thousand, let alone 126,500,' cried Elizabeth.

Cornelius slowly poured himself another cup of tea, pretending to be deep in thought. 'Umm,' he finally offered. 'What puzzles me is how you think I could help, bearing in mind my current financial predicament.'

'We thought that as the auction had raised nearly a million pounds . . .' began Elizabeth.

'Far higher than was estimated,' chipped in Hugh.

'We hoped you might tell Mr Botts you'd decided to keep the piece; and of course we would confirm that that was acceptable to us.'

'I'm sure you would,' said Cornelius, 'but that still doesn't solve the problem of owing the auctioneer £16,500, and a possible further loss if it fails to reach £110,000 in three months' time.'

Neither Elizabeth nor Hugh spoke.

'Do you have anything you could sell to help raise the money?' Cornelius eventually asked.

'Only our house, and that already has a large mortgage on it,' said Elizabeth.

'But what about your shares in the company? If you sold them, I'm sure they would more than cover the cost.'

'But who would want to buy them,' asked Hugh, 'when we're only just breaking even?'

'I would,' said Cornelius.

Both of them looked surprised. 'And in exchange for your shares,' Cornelius continued, 'I would release you from your debt to me, and also settle any embarrassment with Mr Botts.'

Elizabeth began to protest, but Hugh asked, 'Is there any alternative?'

'Not that I can think of,' said Cornelius.

'Then I don't see that we're left with much choice,' said Hugh, turning to his wife.

'But what about all those years we've put into the company?' wailed Elizabeth.

'The shop hasn't been showing a worthwhile profit for some time, Elizabeth, and you know it. If we don't accept Cornelius's offer, we could be paying off the debt for the rest of our lives.'

Elizabeth remained unusually silent.

'Well, that seems to be settled,' said Cornelius. 'Why don't you just pop round and have a word with my solicitor? He'll see that everything is in order.'

'And will you sort out Mr Botts?' asked Elizabeth.

'The moment you've signed over the shares, I'll deal with the problem of Mr Botts. I'm confident we can have everything settled by the end of the week.'

Hugh bowed his head.

'And I think it might be wise,' continued Cornelius – they both looked up and stared apprehensively at him – 'if Hugh were to remain on the board of the company as Chairman, with the appropriate remuneration.'

'Thank you,' said Hugh, shaking hands with his brother. 'That's generous of you in the circumstances.' As they returned down the corridor Cornelius stared at the portrait of his son once again.

'Have you managed to find somewhere to live?' asked Elizabeth.

'It looks as if that won't be a problem after all, thank you, Elizabeth. I've had an offer for The Willows far in excess of the price I'd anticipated, and what with the windfall from the auction, I'll be able to pay off all my creditors, leaving me with a comfortable sum over.'

'Then why do you need our shares?' asked Elizabeth, swinging back to face him.

'For the same reason you wanted my Louis XIV table, my dear,' said Cornelius as he opened the front door to show them out. 'Goodbye Hugh,' he added as Elizabeth got into the car.

Cornelius would have returned to the house, but he spotted Margaret coming up the drive in her new car, so he stood and waited for her. When she brought the little Audi to a halt, Cornelius opened the car door to allow her to step out.

'Good morning, Margaret,' he said as he accompanied her up the steps and into the house. 'How nice to see you back at The Willows. I can't remember when you were last here.'

'I've made a dreadful mistake,' his sister admitted, long before they had reached the kitchen.

Cornelius refilled the kettle and waited for her to tell him something he already knew.

'I won't beat about the bush, Cornelius. You see, I had no idea there were two Turners.'

'Oh, yes,' said Cornelius matter-of-factly. 'Joseph Mallord William Turner, arguably the finest painter ever to hail from these shores, and William Turner of Oxford, no relation, and although painting at roughly the same period, certainly not in the same league as the master.'

'But I didn't realize that . . .' Margaret repeated. 'So I ended up paying far too much for the wrong Turner – not helped by my sister-in-law's antics,' she added.

'Yes, I was fascinated to read in the morning paper that you've got yourself into the *Guinness Book of Records* for having paid a record price for the artist.'

'A record I could have done without,' said Margaret. 'I was rather hoping you might feel able to have a word with Mr Botts, and . . .'

'And what . . . ?' asked Cornelius innocently, as he poured his sister a cup of tea.

'Explain to him that it was all a terrible mistake.'

'I'm afraid that won't be possible, my dear. You see, once the hammer has come down, the sale is completed. That's the law of the land.'

'Perhaps you could help me out by paying for the picture,' Margaret suggested. 'After all, the papers are saying you made nearly a million pounds from the auction alone.'

'But I have so many other commitments to consider,' said Cornelius with a sigh. 'Don't forget that once The Willows is sold, I will have to find somewhere else to live.'

'But you could always come and stay with me . . .'

'That's the second such offer I've had this morning,' said Cornelius, 'and as I explained to Elizabeth, after being turned down by both of you earlier, I have had to make alternative arrangements.'

'Then I'm ruined,' said Margaret dramatically, 'because I don't have £10,000, not to mention the 15 per cent. Something else I didn't know about. You see, I'd hoped to make a small profit by putting the painting back up for sale at Christie's.'

The truth at last, thought Cornelius. Or perhaps half the truth.

'Cornelius, you've always been the clever one in the family,' Margaret said, with tears welling up in her eyes. 'Surely you can think of a way out of this dilemma.'

Cornelius paced around the kitchen as if in deep thought, his sister watching his every step. Eventually he came to a halt in front of her. 'I do believe I may have a solution.'

'What is it?' cried Margaret. 'I'll agree to anything.'

'Anything?'

'Anything,' she repeated.

'Good, then I'll tell you what I'll do,' said Cornelius. 'I'll pay for the picture in exchange for your new car.'

Margaret remained speechless for some time. 'But the car cost me £12,000,' she said finally.

'Possibly, but you wouldn't get more than eight thousand for it second-hand.'

'But then how would I get around?'

'Try the bus,' said Cornelius. 'I can recommend it. Once you've mastered the timetable it changes your whole life.' He glanced at his watch. 'In fact, you could start right now; there's one due in about ten minutes.'

'But . . .' said Margaret as Cornelius stretched out his open hand. Then, letting out a long sigh, she opened her handbag and passed the car keys over to her brother.

'Thank you,' said Cornelius. 'Now I mustn't hold you up any longer, or you'll miss the bus, and there won't be another one along for thirty minutes.' He led his sister out of the kitchen and down the corridor. He smiled as he opened the door for her.

'And don't forget to pick up the picture from Mr Botts, my dear,' he said. 'It will look wonderful over the fireplace in your drawing room, and will bring back so many happy memories of our times together.'

Margaret didn't comment as she turned to walk off down the long drive.

Cornelius closed the door and was about to go to his study and call Frank to brief him on what had taken place that morning when he thought he heard a noise coming from the kitchen. He changed direction and headed back down the corridor. He walked into the kitchen, went over to the sink, bent down and kissed Pauline on the cheek.

'Good morning, Pauline,' he said.

'What's that for?' she asked, her hands immersed in soapy water.

'For bringing my son back home.'

'It's only on loan. If you don't behave yourself, it goes straight back to my place.'

Cornelius smiled. 'That reminds me – I'd like to take you up on your original offer.'

'What are you talking about, Mr Barrington?'

'You told me that you'd rather work off the debt than have to sell your car.' He removed her cheque from an inside pocket. 'I know just how many hours you've worked here over the past month,' he said, tearing the cheque in half, 'so let's call it quits.'

'That's very kind of you, Mr Barrington, but I only wish you'd told me that before I sold the car.'

'That's not a problem, Pauline, because I find myself the proud owner of a new car.'

'But how?' asked Pauline as she began to dry her hands.

'It was an unexpected gift from my sister,' Cornelius said, without further explanation.

'But you don't drive, Mr Barrington.'

'I know. So I'll tell you what I'll do,' said Cornelius. 'I'll swap it for the picture of Daniel.'

'But that's not a fair exchange, Mr Barrington. I only paid £50 for the picture, and the car must be worth far more.'

'Then you'll also have to agree to drive me into town from time to time.'

'Does that mean I've got my old job back?'

'Yes – if you're willing to give up your new one.'

'I don't have a new one,' said Pauline with a sigh. 'They found someone a lot younger than me the day before I was due to begin.'

Cornelius threw his arms around her.

'And we'll have less of that for a start, Mr Barrington.'

Cornelius took a pace back. 'Of course you can have your old job back, and with a rise in salary.'

'Whatever you consider is appropriate, Mr Barrington. After all, the labourer is worthy of his hire.'

Cornelius somehow stopped himself from laughing.

'Does this mean all the furniture will be coming back to The Willows?'

'No, Pauline. This house has been far too large for me since Millie's death. I should have realized that some time ago. I'm going to move out and look for something smaller.'

'I could have told you to do that years ago,' Pauline said. She hesitated. 'But will that nice Mr Vintcent still be coming to supper on Thursday evenings?'

'Until one of us dies, that's for sure,' said Cornelius with a chuckle.

'Well, I can't stand around all day chattering, Mr Barrington. After all, a woman's work is never done.'

'Quite so,' said Cornelius, and quickly left the kitchen. He walked back through the hall, picked up the package, and took it through to his study.

He had removed only the outer layer of wrapping paper when the phone rang. He put the package to one side and picked up the receiver to hear Timothy's voice.

'It was good of you to come to the auction, Timothy. I appreciated that.'

'I'm only sorry that my funds didn't stretch to buying you the chess set, Uncle Cornelius.'

'If only your mother and aunt had shown the same restraint . . .'

'I'm not sure I understand, Uncle.'

'It's not important,' said Cornelius. 'So, what can I do for you, young man?'

'You've obviously forgotten that I said I'd come over and read the rest of that story to you – unless of course you've already finished it.'

'No, I'd quite forgotten about it, what with the drama of the last few days. Why don't you come round tomorrow evening, then we can have supper as well. And before you groan, the good news is that Pauline is back.'

Then he recalled the face of the woman who had slipped past him at the auction house. Of course, it had been his brother's secretary. The second time he had misjudged someone.

'What an irony,' he said out loud. 'If Hugh had put the set up for sale at Sotheby's, he could have held on to the Louis XIV table and had the same amount left over. Still, as Pauline would have said, it's the thought that counts.'

He was writing a thank-you note to his brother when the phone rang again. It was Frank, reliable as ever, reporting in on his meeting with Hugh.

'Your brother has signed all the necessary documents, and the shares have been transferred as requested.'

'That was quick work,' said Cornelius.

'The moment you gave me instructions last week, I had all the legal papers drawn up. You're still the most impatient client I have. Shall I bring the share certificates round on Thursday evening?'

'No,' said Cornelius. 'I'll drop in this afternoon and pick them up. That is, assuming Pauline is free to drive me into town.'

'Am I missing something?' asked Frank, sounding a little bewildered.

'Don't worry, Frank. I'll bring you up to date when I see you on Thursday evening.'

'That's excellent news, Uncle Cornelius. I'll see you around eight tomorrow.'

'I look forward to it,' said Cornelius. He replaced the receiver and returned to the half-opened package. Even before he had removed the final layer of paper, he knew exactly what was inside. His heart began beating faster. He finally raised the lid of the heavy wooden box and stared down at the thirty-two exquisite ivory pieces. There was a note inside: 'A small appreciation for all your kindness over the years. Hugh.'

Timothy arrived at The Willows a few minutes after eight the following evening. Pauline immediately put him to work peeling potatoes.

'How are your mother and father?' asked Cornelius, probing to discover how much the boy knew.

'They seem fine, thank you Uncle. By the way, my father's offered me the job of shop manager. I begin on the first of next month.'

'Congratulations,' said Cornelius. 'I'm delighted. When did he make the offer?'

'Some time last week,' replied Timothy.

'Which day?'

'Is it important?' asked Timothy.

'I think it might be,' replied Cornelius, without explanation.

The young man remained silent for some time, before he finally said, 'Yes, it was Saturday evening, after I'd seen you.' He paused. 'I'm not sure Mum's all that happy about it. I meant to write and let you know, but as I was coming back for the auction, I thought I'd tell you in person. But then I didn't get a chance to speak to you.'

'So he offered you the job before the auction took place?'

'Oh yes,' said Timothy. 'Nearly a week before.' Once again, the young man looked quizzically at his uncle, but still no explanation was forthcoming.

Pauline placed a plate of roast beef in front of each of them as Timothy began to reveal his plans for the company's future.

'Mind you, although Dad will remain as Chairman,' he said, 'he's promised not to interfere too much. I was wondering, Uncle Cornelius, now that you own 1 per cent of the company, whether you would be willing to join the board?'

Cornelius looked first surprised, then delighted, then doubtful.

'I could do with your experience,' added Timothy, 'if I'm to go ahead with my expansion plans.'

'I'm not sure your father would consider it a good idea to have me on the board,' said Cornelius, with a wry smile.

'I can't think why not,' said Timothy. 'After all, it was his idea in the first place.'

Cornelius remained silent for some time. He hadn't expected to go on learning more about the players after the game was officially over.

'I think the time has come for us to go upstairs and find out if it's Simon Kerslake or Raymond Gould who becomes Prime Minister,' he eventually said.

Timothy waited until his uncle had poured himself a large brandy and lit a cigar – his first for a month – before he started to read.

He became so engrossed in the story that he didn't look up again until he had turned the last page, where he found an envelope sellotaped to the inside of the book's cover. It was addressed to 'Mr Timothy Barrington'.

'What's this?' he asked.

Cornelius would have told him, but he had fallen asleep.

The doorbell rang at eight, as it did every Thursday evening. When Pauline opened the door, Frank handed her a large bunch of flowers.

'Oh, Mr Barrington will appreciate those,' she said. 'I'll put them in the library.'

'They're not for Mr Barrington,' said Frank, with a wink.

'I'm sure I don't know what's come over you two gentlemen,' Pauline said, scurrying away to the kitchen.

As Frank dug into a second bowl of Irish stew, Cornelius warned him that it could be their last meal together at The Willows.

'Does that mean you've sold the house?' Frank asked, looking up.

'Yes. We exchanged contracts this afternoon, but on the condition that I move out immediately. After such a generous offer, I'm in no position to argue.'

'And how's the search for a new place coming along?'

'I think I've found the ideal house, and once the surveyors have given the all clear, I'll be putting an offer in. I'll need you to push the paperwork through as quickly as possible so that I'm not homeless for too long.'

'I certainly will,' said Frank, 'but in the meantime, you'd better come and camp out with me. I'm all too aware what the alternatives are.'

'The local pub, Elizabeth or Margaret,' said Cornelius, with a grin. He raised his glass. 'Thank you for the offer. I accept.'

'But there's one condition,' said Frank.

'And what might that be?' asked Cornelius.

'That Pauline comes as part of the package, because I have no intention of spending all my spare time tidying up after you.'

'What do you think about that, Pauline?' asked Cornelius as she began to clear away the plates.

'I'm willing to keep house for both of you gentlemen, but only for one month. Otherwise you'd never move out, Mr Barrington.'

'I'll make sure there are no hold-ups with the legal work, I promise,' said Frank.

Cornelius leant across to him conspiratorially. 'She hates lawyers, you know, but I do think she's got a soft spot for you.'

'That may well be the case, Mr Barrington, but it won't stop me leaving after a month, if you haven't moved into your new house.'

'I think you'd better put down that deposit fairly quickly,' said Frank. 'Good houses come on the market all the time, good housekeepers rarely.'

'Isn't it time you two gentlemen got on with your game?'

'Agreed,' said Cornelius. 'But first, a toast.'

'Who to?' asked Frank.

'Young Timothy,' said Cornelius, raising his glass, 'who will start as Managing Director of Barrington's, Chudley, on the first of the month.'

'To Timothy,' said Frank, raising his glass.

'You know he's asked me to join the board,' said Cornelius.

'You'll enjoy that, and he'll benefit from your experience. But it still doesn't explain why you gave him all your shares in the company, despite him failing to secure the chess set for you.'

'That's precisely why I was willing to let him take control of the company. Timothy, unlike his mother and father, didn't allow his heart to rule his head.'

Frank nodded his approval as Cornelius drained the last drop of wine from the one glass they allowed themselves before a game.

'Now, I feel I ought to warn you,' said Cornelius as he rose from his place, 'that the only reason you have won the last three encounters in a row is simply because I have had other things on my mind. Now that those matters have been resolved, your run of luck is about to come to an end.'

'We shall see,' said Frank, as they marched down the long corridor together. The two men stopped for a moment to admire the portrait of Daniel.

'How did you get that back?' asked Frank.

'I had to strike a mean bargain with Pauline, but we both ended up with what we wanted.'

'But how . . . ?' began Frank.

'It's a long story,' Cornelius replied, 'and I'll tell you the details over a brandy after I've won the game.'

Cornelius opened the library door and allowed his friend to enter ahead of him, so that he could observe his reaction. When the inscrutable lawyer saw the chess set laid out before him, he made no comment, but simply walked across to the far side of the table, took his usual place and said, 'Your move first, if I remember correctly.'

'You're right,' said Cornelius, trying to hide his irritation. He pushed his queen's pawn to Q4.

'Back to an orthodox opening gambit. I see I shall have to concentrate tonight.'

They had been playing for about an hour, no word having passed between them, when Cornelius could bear it no longer. 'Are you not in the least bit curious to discover how I came back into possession of the chess set?' he asked.

'No,' said Frank, his eyes remaining fixed on the board. 'Not in the least bit.'

'But why not, you old dullard?'

'Because I already know,' Frank said as he moved his queen's bishop across the board.

'How can you possibly know?' demanded Cornelius, who responded by moving a knight back to defend his king.

Frank smiled. 'You forget that Hugh is also my client,' he said, moving his king's rook two squares to the right.

Cornelius smiled. 'And to think he need never have sacrificed his shares, if he had only known the true value of the chess set.' He returned his queen to its home square.

'But he did know its true value,' said Frank, as he considered his opponent's last move.

'How could he possibly have found out, when you and I were the only people who knew?'

'Because I told him,' said Frank matter-of-factly.

'But why would you do that?' asked Cornelius, staring across at his oldest friend.

'Because it was the only way I could find out if Hugh and Elizabeth were working together.'

'So why didn't he bid for the set in the morning auction?'

'Precisely because he didn't want Elizabeth to know what he was up to. Once he discovered that Timothy was also hoping to purchase the set in order to give it back to you, he remained silent.'

'But he could have kept bidding once Timothy had fallen out.'

'No, he couldn't. He had agreed to bid for the Louis XIV table, if you recall, and that was the last item to come under the hammer.'

'But Elizabeth failed to get the long-case clock, so she could have bid for it.'

'Elizabeth is not my client,' said Frank, as he moved his queen across the board. 'So she never discovered the chess set's true value. She believed what you had told her – that at best it was worth a few hundred pounds – which is why Hugh instructed his secretary to bid for the set in the afternoon.'

'Sometimes you can miss the most obvious things, even when they are staring you right in the face,' said Cornelius, pushing his rook five squares forward.

'I concur with that judgement,' said Frank, moving his queen across to take Cornelius's rook. He looked up at his opponent and said, 'I think you'll find that's checkmate.'

Confession

1

Saint Rochelle, June 1941

NOTHING WOULD HAVE stopped them playing poker on a Friday evening. Even the outbreak of war.

The four of them had been friends – well, at least colleagues – for the past thirty years. Max Lascelles, a huge man who was used to throwing his weight about, sat at the top of the old wooden table, which he considered no more than his right. After all, he was a lawyer and mayor of Saint Rochelle, while the other three were only town councillors.

Claude Tessier, the chairman of Tessiers Private Bank, sat opposite him. He'd inherited the position, rather than earned it. A sharp, wily, cynical man, who was in no doubt that charity began at home.

To his right sat André Parmentier, the headmaster of Saint Rochelle College. Tall, thin, with a bushy red moustache that indicated what the colour of his hair must have been before he went bald. Respected and admired by the local community.

And finally, Dr Philippe Doucet, who was the senior physician at Saint Rochelle Hospital, sat on the mayor's right. A shy, good-looking man, whose head of thick black hair and warm open smile made several nurses dream about becoming Madame Doucet. But they were all to be disappointed.

All four men placed ten francs in the middle of the table before Tessier began to deal. Philippe Doucet smiled when he saw his hand, which the other three players noticed. The doctor was a man who couldn't hide his feelings, which was why he'd lost the most money over the years. Like so many gamblers, he tried not to think about his long-term losses, only rejoice in his short-term gains. He discarded one card, and asked for another, which the banker quickly replaced. The smile remained in place. He wasn't bluffing. Doctors don't bluff.

'Two,' said Max Lascelles, who was seated on the doctor's left. The mayor showed no emotion as he studied his new hand.

'Three,' said André, who always stroked his bushy moustache whenever he felt he was in with a chance. The banker dealt the headmaster three new cards, and once he'd checked them, he placed his cards face down on the table. When your hand is that bad, there's no point in bluffing.

'I'll also take three,' said Claude Tessier, but like the mayor, once the banker had considered his hand, he gave nothing away.

'Your call, Mr Mayor,' said Tessier, glancing across the table.

Lascelles tossed another ten francs into the pot, to indicate he was still in the game.

'How about you, Philippe?' asked Tessier.

The doctor continued to study his cards for some time before saying confidently, 'I'll match your ten and raise you a further ten.' He placed his last two grubby notes on top of the mounting pile.

'Too rich for me,' Parmentier said with a shake of the head.

'Me too,' said the banker, also placing his cards face down on the table.

'Then it's just the two of us, Philippe,' said the mayor, wondering if the doctor could be tempted to part with any more money.

Philippe's eyes remained fixed on his cards, as he waited to see what the mayor would do.

'I'll see you,' Lascelles said, nonchalantly tossing another twenty francs into the centre of the table.

The doctor smiled and turned his cards over to reveal a pair of aces, a pair of queens and a ten, the smile remaining firmly in place.

The mayor began to turn his cards over one by one, prolonging the agony. A nine, a seven, a nine, a seven. Philippe's smile was still in place until the mayor revealed his final card, another nine.

'A full house,' said Tessier. 'The mayor wins.' The doctor frowned as the mayor gathered up his winnings without revealing the slightest emotion.

'You're a lucky bastard, Max,' said Philippe.

The mayor would like to have explained to Philippe that luck had very little to do with it, when it came to playing poker. Nine times out of ten, statistical probability and the ability to bluff would decide the final outcome.

The headmaster began to shuffle the pack, and was about to start dealing another hand when they all heard the key turning in the lock. The mayor checked his gold pocket watch: a few minutes past midnight.

'Who could possibly consider disturbing us at this time of night?' he said.

They all looked towards the door, annoyed to have their game interrupted.

The four of them immediately stood up when the door was pushed open and the prison commandant marched in. Colonel Müller came to a halt in the middle of the cell, and placed his hands on his hips. Captain Hoffman and his ADC, Lieutenant Dieter, followed in his wake. Another full house. They were all wearing the black uniform of the SS. Their shoes were the only thing that shone.

'Heil Hitler!' said the commandant, but none of the prisoners responded as they waited anxiously to discover the reason for the visit. They feared the worst.

'Please be seated, Mr Mayor, gentlemen,' said the commandant as Captain Hoffman put a bottle of wine on the centre of the table, while his ADC, like a well-trained sommelier, placed a glass in front of each of them.

Once again, the doctor was unable to hide his surprise, while his colleagues remained poker-faced.

'As you know,' continued the commandant, 'the four of you are due to be released at six o'clock tomorrow morning, having served your sentences.' Eight suspicious eyes never left the commandant. 'Captain Hoffman will accompany you to the railway station where you will take a train back to Saint Rochelle. Once you're home, you will resume your former duties as members of the town council, and as long as you keep your heads down, I feel sure no stray bullets will hit you.'

The two junior officers dutifully laughed, while the four prisoners remained silent.

'However, it is my duty to remind you, gentlemen,' continued the commandant, 'that martial law is still in force, and applies to everyone, whatever their rank or position. Do I make myself clear?'

'Yes, Colonel,' said the mayor, speaking on behalf of his colleagues.

'Excellent,' said the commandant. 'Then I will leave you to your game, and see you again in the morning.' Without another word, the colonel turned on his heel and departed, with Captain Hoffman and Lieutenant Dieter following closely behind.

All four of the prisoners remained standing until the heavy door was slammed shut, and they heard the key turning in the lock.

'Did you notice,' said the mayor once he'd lowered his heavy frame back down onto his chair, 'that the commandant addressed us as gentlemen for the first time?'

'And you as Mr Mayor, but why the sudden change of heart,' said the headmaster, as he nervously touched his moustache.

'The town's affairs can't have been running quite as smoothly without us, would be my bet,' said the mayor. 'And I suspect the colonel will be only too happy to see us back in Saint Rochelle. He clearly hasn't got enough staff to administer the town's affairs.'

'You may well be right,' said Tessier. 'But that doesn't mean we have to fall in line.'

'I agree,' said the mayor, 'especially if the colonel is no longer holding all the aces.'

'What makes you think that?' asked Dr Doucet.

'The bottle of wine, for a start,' said the mayor, as he studied the label and smiled for the first time that day. 'Not vintage, but quite acceptable.' He poured himself a glass before passing the bottle across to Tessier.

'Not to mention his demeanour,' added the banker. 'Not the usual bombastic rhetoric suggesting that it can only be a matter of time before the master race has conquered the whole of Europe.'

'I agree with Claude,' said Parmentier. 'I can always tell when one of my boys knows he's about to be punished but still hopes to get off lightly.'

'Once France is free again, I have no intention of letting anybody off lightly,' said the mayor. 'The moment the Hun retreat back to the Fatherland where they belong, I shall round up all the quislings and collaborators, and impose my own form of martial law.'

'What do you have in mind, Mr Mayor?' asked the headmaster.

'The whores who made themselves available to anyone in uniform will have their heads shorn in public, while those who assisted the enemy will be hanged in the market square.'

'I would have thought as a lawyer, Max, you would have wanted to conduct a fair and open trial before passing judgement,' suggested the doctor. 'After all, we can't begin to know what pressures some of our countrymen must have been under. I can tell you as a doctor that sometimes there's a fine line between compliance and rape.'

'I can't agree, Philippe, but then you've always been willing to give everyone the benefit of the doubt,' said the mayor. 'An indulgence I cannot afford. I shall punish anyone and everyone I consider to be a traitor, while honouring our brave resistance fighters who, like us, have stood up to the enemy whatever the consequences.'

Philippe bowed his head.

'I can't pretend I've always stood up to them,' said the headmaster, 'and am well aware that as town councillors we have often received preferential treatment.'

'Only because it was our duty to ensure the town's affairs are run smoothly in the interest of those who elected us.'

'Let's not forget that some of our fellow councillors felt it more honourable to resign than collaborate with the enemy.'

'I am not a collaborator, Philippe, and never have

been,' said the mayor, thumping his fist on the table. 'On the contrary, I have always tried to be a thorn in their flesh, and feel I can safely say I've drawn blood on several occasions, and I'll continue to do so given the slightest opportunity.'

'Not that easy while the swastika still flies above the town hall,' suggested Tessier.

'And you can be assured, Claude,' continued the mayor, 'I will personally burn that evil symbol the moment the Germans depart.'

'Which might not be for some time,' murmured the headmaster.

'Possibly, but that's no reason to forget we are Frenchmen,' said the mayor, raising his glass, 'Vive la France!'

'Vive la France!' the four men cried in unison, as they all raised their glasses.

'What's the first thing you'll do when you get home, André?' asked the doctor, trying to lighten the mood.

'Have a bath,' said the headmaster. They all laughed. 'Then I shall return to my classroom and attempt to teach the next generation that war serves little or no purpose, either for victor or the vanquished. How about you, Philippe?'

'Report back to the hospital, where I expect to find the wards full of young men returning from the front, scarred in more ways than we can imagine. And then there will be the sick and elderly, who had hoped to enjoy the fruits of retirement, only to find themselves overrun by a foreign power.'

'All very commendable,' said Tessier. 'But that won't stop me going straight home and jumping into bed with my wife. And I certainly won't be bothering to have a bath.'

They all burst out laughing.

'Amen to that,' said the headmaster with a chuckle, 'and I'd do the same if my wife was twenty years younger than me.'

'But then, unlike Claude,' said the mayor, 'André hasn't deflowered half the virgins in Saint Rochelle, with promises of an overdraft.'

'Well, at least it's girls I'm interested in,' said Tessier, once the mayor had stopped laughing.

'And can I assume, Tessier,' said the mayor, his tone changing, 'you will then return to the bank, and make sure all our affairs are in order? I can remember exactly how much was in my account the day we were arrested.'

'And every last franc will still be there,' said Tessier, looking directly at the mayor.

'Plus six months' interest?'

'And what about you, Max,' responded the banker, equally sharply. 'What will you do after you've hanged half the population of Saint Rochelle, and shorn the hair off the other half?'

'I shall continue my practice as a lawyer,' said the mayor, ignoring his friend's barb, 'as I suspect there will be a long queue waiting outside my office in need of my services,' he added, as he refilled everyone's glass.

'Including me,' said Philippe. 'I'll want someone to defend me when I can't afford to pay my gambling debts,' he added without a hint of self-pity.

'Perhaps we should call a truce,' suggested the headmaster. 'Forget the past six months, and wipe the slate clean.'

'Certainly not,' said the mayor. 'We all agreed to abide by the same rules that applied while we were on the outside. A gentleman always honours his gambling debts, if I recall your exact words, André.'

'But that would clean me out,' said Philippe, as he checked the bottom line in the banker's little black book. He didn't add that while they'd been incarcerated, every night had become a Friday night, and Dr Doucet had come to realize for the first time just how much the mayor must have pocketed over the years.

'The time has come to consider the future, not the past,' said the mayor, wanting to change the subject. 'I intend to convene a council meeting as soon as we get back to Saint Rochelle and expect you all to be present.'

'And what will the first item on the agenda be, Mr Mayor?' asked Tessier.

'We must pass a resolution denouncing Marshal Pétain and the Vichy regime, and make it clear that we consider them nothing more than a bunch of quislings, and in future will be supporting General de Gaulle as the next president of France.'

'I don't recall you expressing those views at any of our recent council meetings,' said Tessier, not attempting to hide his sarcasm.

'No one knows better than you, Claude, the pressures I've been under, attempting to keep the show on the road,' said the mayor. 'Which resulted in me being arrested and thrown in jail for collaboration.'

'Along with the rest of us, who did no more than attend the private meeting you'd called without notice,' said Tessier. 'Just in case you'd forgotten.'

'I offered to serve all your sentences,' said the mayor, 'but the commandant wouldn't hear of it.'

'As you never stop reminding us,' said the doctor.

'I do not regret my decision,' said the mayor haughtily. 'And once I'm released, I shall continue to harass the enemy whenever possible.'

'Which wasn't all that often in the past, if I recall,' said Tessier.

'Children, children,' said the headmaster, aware that six months locked up together hadn't improved their relationship. 'Let us not forget we're all meant to be on the same side.'

'Not all the Germans have treated us badly,' the doctor said. 'I confess I've even come to like one or two of them, including Captain Hoffman.'

'More fool you, Philippe,' said the mayor. 'Hoffman would string us all up without a second thought if he believed it would benefit the Fatherland. Never forget the Hun are either on their knees or at your throats.'

'And they certainly don't believe in an eye for an eye when it comes to our brave resistance fighters,' said Tessier. 'You kill one of them, and they'll happily hang two of us in revenge.'

'True,' said the mayor. 'And if any of them should fail to make it back across the border after the war is over, I'll be the first to sharpen the guillotine, so help me God.'

The mention of the Almighty stopped everyone in their tracks, and both the headmaster and the doctor crossed themselves.

'Well, at least we won't have a lot to confess after spending six months in this hellhole,' said the headmaster, interrupting the eerie silence.

'Although I feel sure Father Pierre would not approve of us gambling,' said Philippe. 'I'm reminded that Our Lord threw the moneylenders out of the temple.'

'I won't tell him, if you don't,' said the mayor as he refilled his glass with what was left in the bottle.

'That's even assuming Father Pierre will still be around when we get back,' said Philippe. 'When I last saw him at the hospital, he was putting in hours that would have broken a normal man. I begged him to slow down, but he simply ignored me.'

A clock in the distance chimed once.

'Time for one more hand before we turn in?' suggested Tessier, handing the cards to the mayor.

'Count me out,' said Philippe, 'before I'm declared bankrupt.'

'Perhaps it's your turn to win,' said the mayor as he began to shuffle the pack, 'and you'll get everything back on the next hand?'

'That's just not going to happen, and you know it, Max, so I think I'll call it a day. Not that I expect to get much sleep. I feel like a schoolboy on his last day of term who can't wait to go home.'

'I hope my school isn't this bad,' said the headmaster, as he began to deal another hand.

Philippe rose from his place and made his way slowly across to his bed on the far side of the cell, before climbing up onto the top bunk. He was just about to lie down, when he saw him standing there, in the centre of the room. The doctor stared at him for a few moments, before he said, 'Good evening, Father. I didn't hear you come in.'

'God bless you, my son,' replied Father Pierre, giving the sign of the cross.

The headmaster immediately stopped dealing when he heard the familiar voice. They all swung round and stared at the priest.

Father Pierre was bathed in a shard of light shining from the skylight above. He was wearing his familiar long black cassock, white collar and silk bands. A simple silver cross hung around his neck, as it had done since the day of his consecration.

The four men continued to stare at the priest, but said nothing. Tessier tried to hide the cards under the table, like a child who'd been caught with his hand in the biscuit tin.

'Bless you, my children, I hope you are all well,' the priest said, once again making the sign of the cross, 'although I fear I am sadly the bearer of bad tidings.' The four of them froze like rabbits caught in the headlights, all of them assuming they were no longer going to be released in the morning.

'Earlier this evening,' continued the priest, 'a train travelling to Saint Rochelle was blown up by local resistance fighters. Three German officers were killed, along with three of our own countrymen.' He hesitated a few moments before adding, 'It will not come as a surprise to you, gentlemen, that the German High Command are demanding reprisals.'

'But three Frenchmen were killed,' said Tessier, 'isn't that enough?'

'I fear not,' said the priest. 'As in the past, the Germans are demanding that two Frenchmen are to be executed for every German killed.'

'But what has this to do with us?' demanded the mayor. 'We were locked up in here at the time of the bombing, so how could we possibly have been involved?'

'I did point that out to the commandant, but he

remains adamant that if three of the town's leading citizens were to be made an example of, it would send a clear message to anyone who might consider taking similar action in the future. And let me assure you, no amount of pleading on your behalf would move him. Colonel Müller has decreed that three of you will be hanged in the town square at six o'clock tomorrow morning.'

The four men all began speaking at once, and only stopped when the mayor raised a hand. 'All we wish to know, Father, is how the three will be chosen?' he asked, a bead of sweat appearing on his forehead, although the cell was freezing.

'Colonel Müller has come up with three suggestions, but has decided to leave the final choice to you.'

'How considerate of him,' said Tessier. 'I can't wait to hear what he has in mind.'

'He felt the simplest solution would be to draw straws.'

'I don't believe in chance,' said the mayor. 'What are the alternatives?'

'A final round of poker, when the stakes could not be higher, if I recall the colonel's exact words.'

'I would be happy to go along with that,' said the mayor.

'I bet you would, Max,' said Claude. 'After all, the odds would be stacked in your favour. What's the final choice?'

'I hesitate to mention this,' said the priest, 'as it is the one that least appeals to me.'

'Do enlighten us, Father,' said the mayor, no longer able to mask his feelings.

'You will all agree to make a final confession before you face your maker, and I will be left with the unenviable task of deciding which one of you should be spared.'

'That would certainly be my choice,' said the headmaster, without hesitation.

'However, should you decide to go down that par-ticular path,' continued the priest, 'there is a caveat which I insisted on.'

'And what was that?' demanded the mayor.

'Each one of you will be expected to confess to the worst sin you have committed. And you would do well to remember that I have heard all your confessions over the years, so there isn't much I don't know about you. And possibly more important, I have also been privy to the confessions of over a thousand of my parishioners, some of whom have considered it their sacred duty to share with me their innermost secrets. Not all of which reflect well on you. One of them, an unimpeachable source, says one of you is a collaborator. Therefore, I must warn you gentlemen, should you lie, I would not hesitate to strike your name from the list. So I'll ask you once again, which of the three options would you prefer?'

'I'm quite happy to draw straws,' said Tessier.

'I'll opt for one final game of poker,' said the mayor, 'and leave God to deal the cards.'

'I'm willing to confess to the worst sin I've ever committed,' said the headmaster, 'and face the consequences.'

They all turned to Philippe, who was still considering his options.

'If you agree to play one final game of poker,' said the mayor, 'I'd be willing to wipe the slate clean.'

'Don't listen to him, Philippe,' said Tessier. 'Take my advice and draw straws. At least that way you'd still be in with a chance.'

'Possibly, but with my luck, Claude, I don't suppose drawing straws would make any difference. No, I'll join my friend André and admit to the worst sin I've ever committed, and leave you, Father, to make the final judgement.'

'Then that's settled,' said Tessier, shifting uneasily in his chair. 'So what happens next?'

'Now all you have to decide,' said Father Pierre, 'is which one of you will go first?'

'Shall we leave the cards to decide?' said the mayor, who dealt four cards, face up. When he looked down at the queen of hearts he said, 'Lowest goes first.'

The headmaster left the group to join Father Pierre.

André Parmentier, the Headmaster

The priest blessed the headmaster as he knelt before him.

'Blessed are the merciful, for they shall receive mercy. May God, the Father of all mercies, assist you as you make your final confession.' Father Pierre smiled at a man whom he'd admired for so many years. He had followed André's career with considerable pleasure and satisfaction. Textbook, you might have described it. Young Parmentier had begun his life as a student at Saint Rochelle College for Boys, where he would end his days as headmaster, with breaks only to graduate from the Sorbonne in Paris and to spend a sabbatical year as a supply teacher in Algiers.

On his return to Saint Rochelle, André had taken up the position of junior history teacher, and, as the cliché has it, the rest was history. He had progressed rapidly through the ranks, and no one was surprised when the Board of Governors invited him to be head-master, a position he'd held for the past decade.

Many of his colleagues were surprised that André hadn't deserted Saint Rochelle for plusher pastures, as it was well known that several other more renowned schools had approached him over the years. But he had always turned them down, however tempting the offer. Some suggested it was because of family problems, while others accepted his explanation that he had found his vocation and was happy to remain in Saint Rochelle.

By the time war broke out, Saint Rochelle College was among the most respected schools in France, attracting young and ambitious teachers from all over the country. Recently the Board of Governors had begun to consider the problem of who would replace their respected headmaster when he retired in a couple of years' time.

When the Germans marched into Saint Rochelle, André had faced new challenges and tackled them with the same resolution as he had always done in the past. He considered occupation by a foreign power was an inconvenience, not an excuse to lower one's standards.

André Parmentier had never married. He treated all his charges as if they were his first-born. He wasn't surprised to find that many of them who hadn't excelled in the classroom, shone on the battlefield. After all, this wasn't the first time he'd had to come to terms with a brutal and pointless war.

Sadly, many of his charges were destined to die in the heat of battle and, like a grieving father, he wept for them. Somehow André kept his spirits up, never doubting that in time this barbaric war, like the last, must surely come to an end. And when it did, he would be given the opportunity to teach the next generation not to repeat the mistakes of their fathers and forefathers. But that was before a German decree had ordered that three of them must be hanged at six in the morning. And he didn't need to be a maths teacher to know the odds were against him.

'Forgive me, Father,' said André, 'for I have sinned and beg your forgiveness. My last confession was just before I was arrested and sent to prison.'

Father Pierre found it hard to believe that André had ever done anything reprehensible in his life.

'I accept your remorse, my son, aware of the good work you have done in the community for many years,' said the priest. 'But as this could be your final confession, you must reveal the greatest transgression you have committed so that I can judge whether you should be spared, or be one of the three who the com-mandant has condemned to death.'

'When you have heard my confession, Father, you will not be able to absolve me, as my sin is cardinal, and I have long since given up any hope of entering the kingdom of Heaven.'

'I cannot believe, my son,' said Father Pierre, 'that you are the collaborator.'

'Far worse, Father. I must admit,' continued André, 'I have considered sharing my secret with you many times in the past, but like a coward on the battlefield, I've always retreated at the first sound of gunfire. But now I welcome this final chance of redemption before I meet my maker. Be assured that death for me, to quote the gospel, will have no sting, and the grave no victory.' The headmaster bowed his head and wept uncontrollably.

The priest couldn't believe the words he was hearing, but made no attempt to interrupt him.

'As you know, Father,' the headmaster continued, 'I have a younger brother.'

'Guillaume,' said the priest, 'whom you have loyally supported over the years, despite a tragic lapse in his youth, for which he paid dearly.'

'It wasn't his lapse, Father, but mine, and it is I who should have paid dearly.'

'What are you saying, my son? Everyone knows that your younger brother was rightly sent to prison for the grievous offence he committed.'

'It was I who committed the grievous offence, Father, and should have been sent to prison.'

'I don't understand.'

'How could you,' said André, 'when you only saw what was in front of you, and didn't need to look any further.'

'But you weren't even with your brother when he killed that young girl.'

'Yes, I was,' said André. 'Allow me to explain. My brother and I had been out earlier that evening celebrating his twenty-first birthday, and both of us had a little too much to drink. When we were finally thrown out of the last bar, Guillaume passed out, so I had to drive him home.'

'But the police found him behind the wheel.'

'Only because I'd careered onto a pavement and hit a girl, a girl I taught, who later died. Would she still be alive today if I hadn't run away but stopped and called for an ambulance? But I didn't. Instead I panicked and drove quickly away, purposely crashing

the car into a tree not too far from Guillaume's home. When the police eventually arrived, they found my brother behind the wheel and no one else in the car.'

'But that was exactly what the police did find,' said Father Pierre.

'The police found what I wanted them to find,' said André. 'But then they had no way of knowing. I had climbed out of the car, pulled my brother across to the driver's seat, and then abandoned him with his head resting on the steering wheel, the horn blaring out for all to hear.'

The priest crossed him-
self.

'I made my way quickly back to my own flat on the other side of town, slipping in and out of the shadows, to make sure no one saw me, although there weren't many people around at that time in the morning. When I eventually got home, I let myself in through the back door, crept upstairs and went to bed. But I didn't sleep. Truth is, I haven't had a good night's sleep since.'

The headmaster put his head in his hands and remained silent for some time, before he continued.

'I waited for the police to knock on my door in the middle of the night, arrest me and lock me up, but they didn't, so I knew I'd got away with it. After all, it was Guillaume they discovered behind the wheel, only a hundred metres from his home. The following day, several witnesses confirmed they'd seen him the night before, and he was in no fit state to drive.'

'But the police must eventually have interviewed you?'

'Yes, they visited the school the following morn-ing,' admitted André.

'When you could have told them it was you who was driving the car, and not your brother.'

'I told them I'd had a little too much to drink so walked home, and that was the last time I'd seen him.'

'And they believed you?'

'And so did you, Father.'

The priest bowed his head.

'The local paper had a field day. Photos of a pretty young girl with her whole life ahead of her. A head-line that remains etched in my memory to this day. A crashed car, and a young man being dragged out of the front seat at two in the morning. The only mention I got was as the poor unfortu-nate brother, whom they described as a popular and respected young teacher from the local college. I even attended the girl's funeral, only exacerbating my crime. By the time it came to the trial, the verdict had been decided long before the judge passed sentence.'

'But the trial was several months later, so you still could have told the jury the truth.'

'I told them what they'd read in the papers,' said André, his head bowed.

'And your brother was sentenced to six years?'

'He was sentenced to life, Father, because the only job he could get after he came out of prison was as a janitor in the school, where I was able to pull a few strings. Few remember that Guillaume was training to be an architect at the time, and had a promising career ahead of him, which I cut short. But now I've been granted one last chance to put the record straight,' said André, looking up at the priest for the first time. 'I want you to promise me, Father, that after they hang me tomorrow, you will tell everyone who attends my funeral what actually happened that night, so that my brother can at least spend the rest of his days in peace and not continue to take the blame for a crime he didn't commit.'

'Perhaps Our Lord will decide to spare you, my son,' said the priest, 'so you can tell the world the truth and begin to understand what your brother must have suffered for all these years.'

'I would rather die.'

'Perhaps we should leave that decision to the Almighty?' the priest said, as he bent down and helped the headmaster back onto his feet. André turned and walked slowly away, his head still bowed.

'What can he possibly have told Father Pierre that we didn't already know about?' said the mayor when he saw André collapse onto his bunk and turn his face to the wall, like a badly wounded soldier who knows nothing can save him.

The priest turned his attention to those still seated at the table.

'Which one of you will be next?' he asked.

The mayor dealt three cards.

Claude Tessier, the Banker

'Forgive me, Father, for I have sinned,' said Claude. 'I wish to seek God's understanding and forgiveness.'

'Blessed are the poor in spirit, for theirs is the kingdom of Heaven.' Father Pierre couldn't recall when Tessier had last attended church, let alone confession, although there wasn't much he didn't know about the man. However, there remained one mystery that still needed to be explained,  and he hoped that the thought of eternal damnation might prompt the banker to finally admit to the truth.

Claude Tessier had become chairman of the family bank when his father died in 1940, only days before the Germans marched down the Champs-Elysées. Lucien Tessier had been both respected and admired by the local community. Tessiers might not have been the largest bank in town, but Lucien was trusted, and his customers never doubted that their savings were in safe hands. The same could not always be said of his son.

The old man had admitted to his wife that he wasn't sure Claude was the right person to follow him as chairman. 'Feckless and foolhardy' were the words he murmured on his deathbed, and then whispered to the priest that he feared for the widow's mite when he was no longer there to oversee every transaction.

Lucien Tessier's problems were compounded by having a daughter who was not only brighter than Claude, but also honest to the degree of embarrassment. However, the old man realized that Saint Rochelle was not yet ready to accept a woman as chairman of the bank.

Claude's only other banking rival in the town was Bouchards, a well-run establishment that the old man admired. Its chairman, Jacques Bouchard, also had a son, Thomas, who had already proved himself well worthy of succeeding him.

Claude Tessier and Thomas Bouchard had advanced through life together, admittedly at a different pace on their predestined course. School, national service, and later university, before returning to Saint Rochelle to begin their banking careers.

It was Bouchard's father's idea, and one he quickly regretted, that the two boys should serve their apprenticeships at rival banks. Claude's father happily agreed to the arrangement, and got the better deal. After two years, Bouchard never wanted to set eyes on young Claude again, while Lucien wished Thomas would join him on the board of Tessiers. Nothing much changed as both boys progressed towards becoming chairman of their banks; that is until the Germans parked their tanks in the town square.

'May God, the Father of all mercies, help you when you make your final confession,' said the priest as he blessed Tessier.

'I was rather hoping, Father, that it wouldn't be my final confession,' admitted Claude.

'For your sake, let us hope you are right, my son. However, this might be your last chance to admit to the most grievous transgression you have committed.'

'Which believe me, Father, I intend to do.'

'I'm glad to hear that, my son,' said the priest. He leant back, folded his arms and waited.

'I readily admit, Father,' began Claude, 'that I failed to stand by my oldest friend when he most needed me, and I beg the Lord's forgiveness for this lapse, which I hope you will feel is out of character.'

'Should I assume you are referring to the fate that has befallen your closest friend and banking rival, Thomas Bouchard?' enquired the priest.

'Yes, Father. Thomas and I have been friends for so long, I can't ever remember when I didn't know him. We were at school together, served as young lieutenants in the army, and even attended the same university. I was also his best man when he married Esther, and am godfather to their first child, Albert, but when he most needed the support of a friend, like Saint Peter I denied him.'

'But how could that be possible after such a long friendship?'

'To understand that, Father,' said Claude, 'I have to take you back to our university days when we both fell in love with the same girl. Esther was not only beautiful, but brighter than both of us. To be fair, she never showed the slightest interest in me, but I still lived in hope. So I was devastated when Thomas told me that he'd proposed to her and she'd agreed to be his wife.'

'But despite the sin of envy, you still agreed to be his best man?'

'I did. And they were married in a local town hall on the outskirts of Paris, just days after we graduated. They then returned to Saint Rochelle as man and wife.'

'I well remember,' said the priest. 'And confess that at the time, I was disappointed not to have been invited to conduct the wedding ceremony. However, I only recently discovered why that would not have been possible, and admire you for keeping your friend's secret.' Father Pierre fell silent as he realized Claude had reached a crossroads, but was still unsure which path he would take.

'And be assured, Father, I have continued to do so, and was horrified when the Germans discovered Esther was Jewish and the daughter of a distinguished academic who had denounced the Nazis.'

'I was equally horrified,' said the priest, 'but did you keep your side of the bargain, and remain silent about Esther's heritage?'

'I did better than that, Father. I warned Thomas that the Germans had found out that Esther was Professor Cohen's daughter, and he shouldn't delay in taking his wife and children to America, and only return when the war was over.'

'Are you sure it wasn't the other way round?' said the priest quietly.

'What are you suggesting?' said Tessier, his voice rising with every word, causing his colleagues to look across in his direction.

'That it was in fact Thomas who confided in you that he was planning to escape before the Germans found out the truth about his wife, and then you betrayed him.'

'Who would consider accusing me of such treachery? I even offered to manage Thomas's affairs while he was away, and hand back the bank the moment he and Esther returned.'

'But if you were the only person in Saint Rochelle who knew Esther was Jewish, how could the Germans have possibly found out, if it wasn't you who told them?'

'It was covered by the national press that Professor Cohen had been arrested and disappeared overnight, which would explain how the Germans found out.'

'I don't think the professor would have informed the Nazis that he had a daughter and a grandson living in Saint Rochelle.'

'I swear on all that is sacred, Father, that I would never have told the Germans his secret. Thomas was my dearest friend.'

'That's not what Captain Hoffman told me,' said the priest.

Claude looked up, his face drained and chalk white, his whole body trembling. 'But he's a German, Father, who cannot be trusted. Surely you wouldn't take his word against mine?'

'No, I wouldn't in normal circumstances. But I would take his word in the presence of Our Lord after he'd sworn an oath on the Bible.'

'I don't understand,' said Claude.

'What you couldn't know is that Karl Hoffman is a devout Roman Catholic, as are millions of Germans.'

'But he's first and foremost a Nazi.'

'The man who attends my church privately every Thursday to take Mass before making his confession is no Nazi, of that I can assure you. In fact, it was Hoffman who first warned me that the commandant was planning to arrest Esther and have her sent to a concentration camp in Poland.'

'He's lying, Father, so help me God. I did everything I could to help my friend escape.'

'But Hoffman warned me a week before Esther

was arrested,' said the priest, 'giving the partisans more than enough time to organize a safe passage for the family to America. Esther's bags were packed and ready when the Gestapo turned up in the middle of the night, arrested her, took her to the station, and threw her on a train that didn't require a ticket.'

Tessier slumped down, burying his head in his hands.

'And something else you could not have known. Your friend Thomas also attempted to board that train so he could be with his wife, and only the butt of a German rifle prevented him from doing so.'

'But—'

'And because you betrayed your friend, he will spend the rest of his life only being able to imagine the abject horror and degradation his wife must be going through.'

'But you have to understand, Father, the Germans were putting pressure on me,' pleaded Tessier. 'They were making my life hell.'

'Nothing compared to the hell Thomas is now experiencing while you sit and watch his whole life crumble in front of him. Even some of his customers have begun to cross the road and transfer their accounts to Tessiers, for fear of reprisals from the Germans.'

'That wasn't what I intended, Father, and if you'll give me a chance, I swear I'll make it up to him.'

'I think it's a little late for that,' said the priest.

'No, no. If I get out of here alive, I'll merge the two banks and make Thomas the senior partner. And what's more, I'll donate a hundred thousand francs to the church.'

'Would you be willing to make a will confirming this, whatever my decision?'

'Yes,' said Claude, 'you have my word on it.'

'And the Almighty's,' said the priest.

'And the Almighty's,' repeated Claude.

'That's most generous of you, my son,' said the priest. 'If you do keep your word, I feel sure Our Lord will be merciful.'

'Thank you, Father,' said Claude. 'And perhaps you might mention my offer to the commandant,' he added, as he raised his head and looked directly at the priest.

'You have given your word to Our Lord,' said Father Pierre, 'which should surely be more than enough.'

Claude got off his knees and, not looking totally convinced, bowed to the priest and returned to join the mayor and the doctor.

'How did it go?' asked Max.

'I simply told him the truth,' said the banker, his poker face back in place, 'and am content to await the Almighty's decision.'

'I have a feeling it won't be the Almighty who makes that decision,' said the mayor, as he dealt two more cards.

The doctor stared down at the five and said, 'My turn, it seems.'

'Be warned, Philippe,' said Tessier. 'If you bluff, he'll catch you out.'

'I think we're all agreed that I'm not much good at bluffing.'

But then Philippe knew exactly what he was going to tell Father Pierre.

PHILIPPE DOUCET, THE DOCTOR

When Philippe Doucet knelt in front of the priest, Father Pierre had never seen him looking more at peace with himself. The priest had often witnessed that same contentment when the old finally accept they are going to die, and almost welcome it.

Father Pierre gave the sign of the cross, touched the doctor's forehead and pronounced, 'Blessed are they that mourn, for they shall be comforted. May the God of all mercies assist you when you make your final confession.'

There was little the priest didn't know about Philippe Doucet. After all, he was a regular church-goer, and made his confession at least once a month. His idea of sin rarely demanded more than half a dozen Hail Marys.

Philippe was an open book, and the only chapter that the priest hadn't read was the first one. No one could explain how he'd ever ended up in a backwater like Saint Rochelle. Unlike the mayor, the banker and the headmaster, he hadn't been born in the town, or attended its only college, although everyone now accepted him as a local.

It was common knowledge that he'd been educated at Paris Sud Medical School, and graduated with honours, as the several certificates and diplomas hanging from the walls of his surgery confirmed. However, it remained a mystery why a man who was surely destined to become the senior partner of a large medical practice had ended up as a hospital doctor in Saint Rochelle.

Was Philippe Doucet about to turn the first page?

'Forgive me, Father, for I have sinned. My last confession was on the Friday before I was arrested.'

'I am not expecting this to take too long, my son, because as long as I've known you, your life has been an open book.'

'But there is one chapter you don't know about, Father, that was written before I came to Saint Rochelle.'

'I feel sure that Our Lord will forgive some youthful indiscretion,' said the priest. 'That could hardly compare with being a collaborator.'

'What I have done is far worse than being a collaborator, Father.' Doucet was clearly distraught. 'I have broken the sixth commandment, for which I must suffer eternal damnation.'

'You, a murderer, my son?' The priest was stunned. 'I don't believe it. Every doctor makes mistakes . . .'

'But this was not a mistake, Father, as I will now explain. After leaving university,' Doucet continued, 'I began my medical career as a junior doctor in a large and prestigious practice in my home town of Lyon. As over sixty other graduates had applied for the post, I considered myself fortunate to be chosen. When I wasn't working, I was reading the latest medical journal, so I would always be one step ahead of my contemporaries. Within a year, I was promoted, and already preparing to take my next step on the medical ladder.'

'Which surely can't have been as a junior doctor at Saint Rochelle Hospital,' suggested the priest.

'No, it was not, Father,' admitted Philippe, 'but Saint Rochelle was the only hospital that offered me a job at the time.'

'Why was that?' asked the priest. 'When you'd already proved to be a shining light among your contemporaries?'

'It was a Thursday in November 1921 when I fell off the ladder,' said Philippe. 'I had been working at the practice for just over a year when one of my colleagues, Victor Bonnard, a doctor not much older than myself, asked me if I would visit one of his patients. He explained that she was an elderly lady who suffered from the illnesses of the rich, and once a week liked to while away an hour or two with her doctor. Victor explained that an emergency had arisen at Saint Joseph's that he considered far more pressing.

'I readily agreed, not least because Victor always seemed to have time for the practice's latest recruit. I grabbed my bag and headed for the Boulevard des Belges, an arrondissement usually only visited by senior doctors. When I arrived outside a magnificent Palladian mansion, I stopped to catch my breath. An experience that was to be repeated moments later when the front door was opened by a beautiful young woman whom I assumed must be an actress or a model. She had long blonde hair and deep blue eyes accompanied by a captivating smile that made you feel you were an old friend.

'"Hello, I'm Celeste Picard," she told me, offering her hand.

'"Philippe Doucet," I replied. "I'm sorry that Dr Bonnard can't make it, but he was held up at the hospital," I explained. Although in truth I wasn't at all sorry.

'"It's not important," Celeste assured me as she led me upstairs to the first floor. "No one pretends Great-aunt Manon is ill, but she does enjoy a weekly visit from the doctor. Especially the younger ones," she said with a grin.

'When she opened the bedroom door, I found an old lady sitting up in bed waiting for me. It didn't take a very thorough examination to realize there wasn't much wrong with Great-aunt Manon that holding her hand and listening to her endless stories wouldn't have taken care of. I realized that it was no wonder the practice was so successful with patients like this.'

The priest smiled but didn't interrupt.

'When I left the house an hour later, Celeste rewarded me with the same disarming smile, and if I hadn't been so shy, I might have attempted to strike up a conversation, whereas I only managed "Goodbye", as she closed the front door.

'It was about a week later that Victor told me the old lady had asked to see me again.

'"You're clearly in favour," he teased. But my only thought was that I might see Celeste again. After I'd examined the old lady a second time, her niece invited me to join her for tea, and when I left an hour later, she said, "I hope you'll come again next week, Dr Doucet."

'I floated back to the surgery, unable to believe such a goddess would even give me a second look. But to my surprise, tea was followed by a walk in Parc de la Tête d'or, an evening at l'Opéra de Lyon, and dinner at Le Café du Peintre, that I couldn't afford, after which we became lovers. I couldn't have been happier, because I knew I'd found the woman I wanted to spend the rest of my life with.

'I waited for almost a year before I proposed, and was heartbroken when she turned me down. But Celeste explained it wasn't because she didn't want to marry me, but as she was the sole beneficiary of her great-aunt's will, she couldn't consider leaving the old lady until she died. I was shattered. Great-aunt Manon may have been eighty-two, but I couldn't see why she wouldn't live to a hundred.

'I tried to assure Celeste that I earned more than enough for us to live on, even though I knew it wasn't true. She did, however, agree to become engaged, but refused to wear a ring for fear her great-aunt would see it and dismiss me, and possibly even her.'

'And you went along with the deception?' said the priest.

'Yes, but it wasn't until Celeste said, "Don't worry, darling, she won't live forever," that the idea first crossed my mind, and I considered using my skills not to prolong life, but to shorten it. I didn't share those thoughts with Celeste.'

'How did the thought become the deed?' asked the priest.

'It must have been a few weeks after we'd become engaged that Great-aunt Manon complained about not being able to sleep at night. I recommended a course of sleeping pills, which seemed to do the trick. But whenever she complained about not having a good night's sleep, I found myself increasing the dosage, until finally she didn't wake up.'

Philippe bowed his head, but the priest said nothing as he knew there was more to come.

'When I filled in the death certificate, I wrote that she had died of natural causes. No one questioned my judgement; after all, she was eighty-four.

'I assumed that after a suitable period of mourning, Celeste and I would be married. However, when I attended the old lady's funeral, she turned her back on me. I tried to convince myself this was only sensible, as she wouldn't want to attract any unnecessary gossip.

'Some weeks later I was working at my desk when I heard laughter and raised voices coming from the corridor outside. I poked my head around the door to see Victor surrounded by doctors and nurses, who were warmly congratulating him.

'"What's the cause of the celebration?" I asked the receptionist.

'"Dr Bonnard has just got engaged."

'"Anyone I know?"

'"Celeste Picard," said the receptionist, without realizing how painful her words were. "You must have come across her, doctor, when you looked after her great-aunt."

'What a naive fool I'd turned out to be, Father, as it slowly dawned on me what role the two lovers had chosen for me to play. I started to drink, often arriving late for work, and began to make small mistakes at first, but then bigger ones that are unforgivable for someone in my profession. So when I came to the end of my trial period, it was hardly a surprise that my contract wasn't renewed.

'On the day of Victor and Celeste's wedding, I even considered committing suicide, and only my faith prevented me from doing so. However, I knew that I had to get as far away from Celeste as possible if I hoped to lead a normal life.'

'Which is how you ended up in Saint Rochelle?'

'Yes, Father. When the vacancy for a junior doctor was advertised in the medical journal, I immediately applied for the post. The hospital's supervisor admitted he was surprised that such a highly qualified doctor had even considered the position, and he didn't hesitate to offer me the job, even though the references from my former employer weren't exactly overwhelming.

'I have practised my profession in this town for over twenty years,' continued Philippe, 'and not a day goes by when I don't fall to my knees and beg the Almighty to forgive me for cutting short the life of an innocent old lady.'

'But your record during your time at the hospital has been exemplary, my son. Don't you think by now Our Lord may feel you have served your sentence?'

'The truth is, Father, I should have been struck off the medical register, and sent to prison.'

'Jesus told a sinner on one of the other crosses at Calvary that he would that night sit on his right hand in Heaven.'

'I can only hope Our Lord will show me the same mercy.'

'Have you considered, my son, while the war continues unabated, Saint Rochelle will need the skills God gave you as never before?'

'No more than the headmaster,' said Philippe, 'who will be responsible for teaching future generations that war can never be the answer.'

'Bless you, my son,' said the priest, as he gave him the sign of the cross. 'I absolve you of your sins and pray you will enter the kingdom of Heaven.'

Philippe Doucet rose from his place, a look of serenity on his face, no longer fearful of facing his maker. He bowed and left the priest without another word and rejoined his colleagues.

'You look very pleased with yourself, Philippe,' said the mayor. 'Did Father Pierre promise you anything?'

'Nothing,' said Philippe. 'But I could not have asked for more.'

The mayor placed the cards back down on the table and looking at the banker said, 'Shuffle the cards, Claude. This shouldn't take too long, so there should still be time for another hand.' He sauntered across to the priest, trying to recall when he'd made his last confession.

Father Pierre was well prepared for the mayor, and suspected he would not display the same humility as his colleagues. But Our Lord would not have expected him to make a judgement before the lawyer had been allowed to admit to what he considered his worst sin. Where would he begin, wondered the priest.

Max Lascelles, the Mayor

'Blessed are the meek, for they shall inherit the earth,' said the priest, giving the sign of the cross. 'Are you prepared to make your final confession, my son?'

'No, Father, I am not,' responded the mayor. 'Not least because it is not going to be my final confession.'

'How can you be so sure it will be you that the Almighty spares?'

'Because it is not going to be the Almighty who makes that decision, but the commandant,' said the mayor, 'and I can assure you, Father, Colonel Müller is not on his knees at this moment seeking guidance from above because he's already decided that I am the chosen one.'

'But you were the one arrested for sedition. You even admitted that you'd arranged the meeting, and that your three colleagues were innocent of any charge.'

'True, but then it was the commandant who suggested I should set up the meeting in the first place, and during that conversation we also agreed on a six-month sentence and regular reports that I was being treated badly.'

'But that still doesn't explain why Colonel Müller would consider your life more important than that of a headmaster, a doctor or even a banker,' said Father Pierre.

'Because he knows none of them, even Tessier, would be willing to fall in with his long-term plans.'

The priest paused. 'So you are the collaborator.'

'I consider myself a realist, which is why my three colleagues will be hanged in the morning, and not me. However, you can be assured, Father, that as the town's leading citizen, I shall attend all three of their funerals and deliver glowing eulogies emphasizing their service to the community and how much they will be missed.'

'But if the Germans were to lose the war, the partisans wouldn't hesitate to string you up from the nearest lamp post,' said the priest, trying not to lose his temper.

'That's a risk I'm willing to take. But then I always try to make sure the odds are in my favour, and if I have to back the Germans or the British to win this war, I still consider it a one-horse race.'

'Mr Churchill may have something to say about that.'

'Churchill's nothing more than a fog-horn on a sinking ship, and once he's been replaced, Hitler will quickly take control of the rest of Europe. By which time I will no longer be mayor of Saint Rochelle, but the governor of one of his new provinces.'

'You seem to have forgotten one thing, my son.'

'And what might that be, Father?' said the mayor, raising an eyebrow.

'The intervention of the Almighty.'

'That's another risk I'm willing to take,' said Lascelles, 'as he's certainly taken his time over the Second Coming.'

'May God have mercy on your immortal soul.'

'I'm not interested in mortality, only in which one of us will be on the train back to Saint Rochelle in the morning, which I can assure you, Father, will be me.'

'Unless the partisans were to find out the truth,' said the priest.

'I don't have to remind you, Father, that if you utter one word of my confession to anyone, it will be you who will be condemned to spend an eternity in hell.'

'You're an evil man,' said the priest.

'At last we've found something we can agree on, Father,' said the mayor as the priest fell to his knees and began to pray.

The mayor gave the sign of the cross, before saying in a loud voice, 'God bless you, Father.' He smiled and returned to his seat at the top of the table.

The Short, the Long and the Tall

'That didn't take too long,' said Claude.

'No, but then I've led a fairly blameless life, and had little to confess other than my desire to continue serving my maker.'

'That's noble of you,' said Doucet, looking down at the priest. 'He was clearly moved by your testimony.'

'Possibly, but then I did make it clear to the good father,' continued the mayor, 'that I was content to let the Almighty decide which one of us should be spared, stressing that all three of you were far more worthy of his beneficence than I was.'

Tessier raised his eyes to Heaven in disbelief.

'Do you think Father Pierre has made his decision?' asked Philippe.

'I've no idea,' said Lascelles, as he turned to face the priest, who was still on his knees praying.

The mayor raised his glass and said, 'May the Lord guide you in your deliberations, Father.'

The other three raised their glasses and said in unison, 'May the Lord guide you—' but before they could finish, the mayor's face drained of all colour and he began to tremble. He dropped his glass and it shattered on the table as he continued to stare in front of him.

His three colleagues turned to look in the same direction, but the priest was no longer there.

2

They all counted the chimes as they rang out: one, two, three, four. Two more hours before they would discover their fate.

'What are you doing, Claude?' asked the mayor as he sat back down in his seat.

'Writing my will.'

'Would you like me to draw it up for you? After all, you wouldn't want there to be any disputes or misunderstandings after your death.'

'Good idea,' said Tessier. 'Then I'll be able to say it was drafted by a lawyer, should I live.'

'Touché,' said the mayor.

Claude tore half a dozen pages out of his little black book, and handed them across to the lawyer.

The mayor spent some time studying the banker's efforts at making a will before he settled down to write.

'You've been extremely generous to your sister and your friend Thomas Bouchard,' he said, after he'd turned the second page.

'As I had always intended,' said Tessier.

'And your young wife?' said the mayor, raising an eyebrow. 'Is she to get nothing?'

'She's young enough to find another husband.'

The lawyer turned another page.

'And I see you've left a large donation to the church. Was that also something you'd always intended?'

'No more than I promised Father Pierre years ago,' Tessier replied defensively.

'I also made promises to the good father that I intend to keep,' said the mayor, before adding, 'should I live.'

The lawyer continued to write for some time before he presented the testament to his client.

Once Claude had read the document a second time, he asked, 'Where do I sign?'

The mayor placed a forefinger on the dotted line. 'You'll need two witnesses who are conveniently on hand at no extra charge.'

Tessier looked across at the doctor, who could have been in another world. 'Philippe,' he said, interrupting his friend's thoughts. 'I need you to witness my will.'

The doctor blinked, picked up the pen and, turning to the last page, added his signature.

'Are you still awake, André?' asked the mayor, looking across at the headmaster's back.

'I haven't slept a wink,' came the weary reply.

'I need a second witness to Claude's will, and wondered if you'd do the honours.'

André heaved himself slowly up off the bottom bunk and placed his feet on the cold stone floor before making his way across to the table.

'Do I need to read the document before I sign it?' he asked.

'No, that won't be necessary,' said the mayor. 'You're simply witnessing Claude's signature.' He watched as André Parmentier scribbled his name below that of Philippe Doucet. The lawyer placed the will in his battered briefcase.

Tessier jumped up from the table and began pacing around the cell as he thought about the document he'd just signed. If he was to die, it made sense for Thomas Bouchard to merge the two banks and allow his sister to play her part. He didn't doubt that, between them, they'd make a far better fist of it than he'd managed. He only wished he'd taken his father's advice and put Louise on the board years ago.

The mayor was taken by surprise when André didn't return to his bunk, but said, 'I would also like to make a will, Max.'

'I'd be delighted to assist you,' said the lawyer, ripping some more pages out of Claude's little black book before picking up a pen. 'Who will be the main beneficiaries?'

'I want to leave everything to my brother Guillaume.'

'Don't you think you've done more than enough for him already?'

'Not nearly enough, I'm afraid,' the headmaster replied. He extracted a sheet of paper from the pile and began writing a letter to his brother.

Dear Guillaume…

The mayor didn't have time to argue with his client, so set about preparing the headmaster's will. A simple exercise that only took him a few minutes, and once he'd double-checked each paragraph, he handed the single sheet of paper across to the headmaster.

'Thank you,' said André, who read it slowly, before signing on the bottom of the page and handing it to Tessier and Doucet for their signatures. 'I'd also like this letter to be attached to my will,' he added, giving a folded sheet of paper to the lawyer before returning to his bunk.

Once again André closed his eyes, although he knew he wouldn't sleep. If he were among the three picked, at least Guillaume and his family would live in comparative comfort for the rest of their lives. And he hoped the letter would finally make it clear that his brother had not been responsible for killing the young girl – especially since Guillaume believed he was still the guilty party. When five chimes interrupted his reverie, André wasn't troubled by the thought of only having one more hour to live.

Once the mayor had placed the headmaster's will and his letter to Guillaume in his battered attaché case, he smiled at Philippe and said, 'What about you, my friend, have you thought about making a will?'

'What's the point,' said the doctor, 'when I'd have to leave everything to you just to clear my gambling debts, and that there still wouldn't be enough to pay your fee.'

'Prison visits are pro bono,' said the mayor with a chuckle.

Philippe leant on the table and placed his head in his hands as the lawyer began writing a third will. The doctor's thoughts drifted back to Celeste as they so often did when he was alone. She'd be middle-aged by now, and he wondered if she was still married to Victor Bonnard. Did they have any children? Had they migrated to their home in the country after the Germans had marched down the Champs-Elysées? Had the Palladian mansion been requisitioned by the German High Command? Not a day went by when Celeste didn't creep into his thoughts.

Once the mayor had completed a document of which he was the only beneficiary – not strictly legal, but who would know – he swivelled it round for Philippe to sign. Claude and André added their signatures without comment.

'Will you be making a will, Max?' asked Claude.

'That won't be necessary,' replied the mayor without explanation.

A strange and eerie silence descended on the cell. Four men lost in their thoughts as the seconds ticked by and they waited to learn their fate.

The mayor occasionally checked his watch, only to find time was something he couldn't influence as it progressed on its predetermined course, like a runner on his final lap. No one spoke when the first chime rang out, echoing around the cell. Long before the sixth bell had struck, they all heard the key turning in the lock.

'You can rely on the Germans to be on time,' said the mayor.

'Especially for a hanging,' added the banker as he stopped pacing and stared at the door. The mayor placed the deck of cards neatly back on the table. The headmaster sat bolt upright in his bunk, while Philippe continued to think about Celeste. Was he finally going to be released from her spell?

They all watched apprehensively as the massive door swung open and Captain Hoffman marched into the cell, a large smile on his face.

'Good morning, gentlemen,' he said. 'I hope you all had a good night's sleep.'

No one responded as they waited to find out which one of them would be reprieved.

'I have your tickets,' said Hoffman, before handing each of them a small green *billet*. 'We'd better get a move on, as the only train to Saint Rochelle today leaves in about half an hour.'

The four of them still didn't move, wondering if they were taking part in some elaborate Teutonic version of gallows humour.

'Can I ask,' said the doctor, the only one willing to voice what he knew was on all their minds. 'How many people were injured in last night's train crash?'

'What train crash?' Hoffman asked.

'The one that took place yesterday evening. We heard three German officers and three Frenchmen were killed by a bomb that had been planted on the track.'

'I've no idea what you're talking about,' said Hoffman. 'There hasn't been a bombing on the Saint Rochelle line for several months. A fact that the commandant is particularly proud of. I think you must have had a bad dream, doctor. Let's get moving, we can't expect the train to wait for us.'

Hoffman turned to leave, and the four men reluctantly followed him out of the cell.

André wondered if he was about to wake up.

Hoffman led his little band down a long dark corridor, up a steep flight of worn stone steps and out into a sharp morning light that the four of them hadn't experienced for the past six months. As they walked across the courtyard, their eyes focused on the gallows.

Colonel Müller and his ADC marched into the station and came to a halt in the centre of the platform. When the locals saw them, they immediately scattered to the far ends of the platform, as if the colonel was Moses, parting the Red Sea.

'I've allowed the mayor and the three councillors to travel back to Saint Rochelle first-class,' said the commandant. 'The occasional concession does no harm if we hope to keep things running smoothly.'

'Is the mayor still onside?' asked Dieter.

'For the moment, yes,' responded the commandant.

'But that man would switch sides without a second thought if it suited his purpose.'

Dieter nodded. 'And I fear I'm going to have to leave you to deal with the damn man, sir, because I've just received orders from Berlin instructing me to join my regiment in East Prussia. It looks as if the Führer has called off an invasion of England, and has decided to attack Russia.'

'I'm sorry to hear that, Dieter,' said the colonel. 'And I suspect it won't be too long before I'll have to join you, and leave the mayor in charge of Saint Rochelle.'

'Perish the thought,' said Dieter.

'I'd rather the mayor perished,' the colonel replied as Captain Hoffman marched onto the platform, his four charges in his wake.

Captain Hoffman walked across to join his colleagues beside the first-class carriage in the centre of the train, while the mayor and the three councillors kept their distance. Hoffman clicked his heels and gave the commandant a Nazi salute. 'The paperwork has been completed, sir, and as instructed, they've been issued with first-class tickets.'

'Don't acknowledge them,' said the colonel as he turned his back on the mayor. 'No need to give the partisans any reason to suspect we have someone on the inside.'

'Frankly, I wish I could send the mayor to the Eastern Front,' said Hoffman.

'Amen to that,' said Dieter as the three German officers boarded the first compartment in the first-class carriage.

'Say nothing,' whispered the mayor to his three colleagues, 'until we're on board, when no one else can overhear us.'

The four Frenchmen waited until everyone else had got into the second-class carriages before they climbed into the last compartment in first-class, leaving an empty compartment between themselves and the three Germans.

The mayor placed his briefcase on the rack above him, and settled down in a corner seat.

'Max, I've been thinking about my will,' said Tessier, who sat down opposite him, 'and I've decided I'd like to make a few changes.'

'Why?' demanded the mayor, staring innocently across the carriage at the banker.

'Circumstances have changed.'

'But you gave your word to Father Pierre—' The mayor stopped in mid-sentence, aware that he'd raised the one subject none of them wanted to discuss.

3

The two resistance fighters picked up the bomb the moment the sun disappeared behind a solitary cloud. They crept out of the forest, moved stealthily down the grassy slope and planted it in the middle of the track.

The older man began to walk backwards, unwinding a wheel of fuse wire, until they were once again safely out of sight. Once the correct length of wire had been cut and attached to the detonator they both slithered back down the slope and spent the next twenty minutes covering the exposed wire with bracken, stones and tufts of grass.

'Just in case an observant driver spots the wire glinting in the sun,' Marcel explained to his latest recruit.

Once the job was done to the older man's satisfaction, they clambered back up the hill to their hiding place and waited.

'How old are you, Albert?' asked the resistance commander as he lit a cigarette.

'Sixteen,' the boy replied.

'Shouldn't you be at school?' he teased.

'Not until I've seen the last German leave France in a wooden box.'

'Why made you so keen to join our cause?'

'The Germans came in the middle of the night and arrested my mother. Father says we'll never see her again.'

'What was her crime?'

'Being Jewish.'

'Then it's your lucky day, Albert, because my contact in Saint Rochelle has assured me that three German officers, including the prison commandant, will be on the train this morning.'

'How will we know which carriage to blow up?'

'That's easy. German officers always travel first-class, so we are only interested in the carriage in the centre of the train.'

'Won't some of our own people be injured, even killed by the blast?' asked Albert.

'Unlikely. Once it's known there are German officers on a train, the two second-class carriages on either side of first-class will be deserted.'

Albert stared at the plunger, his hands trembling.

'Patience, my boy,' said Marcel as the train rounded the bend and came into sight, billowing clouds of smoke into a clear blue sky. 'It won't be long now.'

Albert placed both hands on the plunger.

'Not yet,' said Marcel. 'I'll tell you when.'

The young recruit could feel the sweat pouring down his face as the train came closer and closer.

'Any moment now,' said the older man as the engine clattered over the bomb. 'Get ready.' It was only a few seconds, but it felt like a lifetime to Albert, before Marcel gave the order, 'Now!'

Albert Bouchard pressed firmly down on the plunger, and watched as the bomb exploded in front of his eyes. As the blast tore through the carriage, a ball of purple and blue flames shot into the air, mixed with shards of glass and debris. The carriage was blown unceremoniously off the track, landing with a thud on the far bank, a mass of twisted, molten metal embedded in the grass. Albert sat there, mesmerized by the scene. His only thought was that no one could possibly have survived. He stared at the other two carriages lying like abandoned children by its side, doors flapping and windows smashed.

'Let's go, Albert!' shouted the older man, who was already on his feet. But the boy couldn't take his eyes off the carnage.

Marcel grabbed his new recruit by his collar and yanked him up. He quickly disappeared into the forest with young Bouchard following in his footsteps. No longer a schoolboy.

The guard who had been stationed in the rear carriage was among the first on the scene. When he came across the bodies of three German officers, including Colonel Müller, he crossed himself. He moved on and was surprised to find the bodies of three of his countrymen lying nearby. They must have been travelling first-class. But why, he wondered. Everyone had been briefed about the latest directive from the commander of the resistance.

Next on the scene was the driver, who'd been furthest from the blast.

'How many dead?' he asked.

'Six,' replied the guard. 'Three Germans and sadly three of our own.'

'And I passed several passengers lying by the side of the track,' said the driver. 'But none of them were badly injured. They got lucky, because there was a local doctor on the train, and he's looking after them.'